PRAISE FOR THE M[...] JUSTICE NOVELS

"The Montgomery Justice series satisfies on all levels, with plots that dovetail into one another and characters that aren't always what they seem."

—*RT Book Reviews* on *Behind the Lies*

"Robin Perini is synonymous with stellar romantic suspense."

—*USA Today*'s Happy Ever After blog on *Behind the Lies*

"Perini refreshes romantic suspense."

—*Publishers Weekly* on *In Her Sights*

"This riveting book will keep readers on the edge of their seats and surprise them at the end. The tightly woven plot, quick pace, and complex characters make for a remarkable read."

—*RT Book Reviews* on *In Her Sights*

"Robin Perini will keep you perched on the edge of your seat. Danger, excitement, and romance . . . everything a reader craves!"

—Brenda Novak, *New York Times* bestselling author, on *In Her Sights*

"Robin Perini delivers the goods—*Game of Fear* is an intelligent, fast-paced romantic thriller that kept my heart racing and the pages flying."

—Karen Rose, *New York Times* bestselling author

"Robin Perini crafts the perfect blend of hot romance and chilling suspense that leaves you breathless!"

—Allison Brennan, *New York Times* bestselling author, on *Game of Fear*

"The world of computer hacking is taken to extreme levels in this exceptional action adventure . . . The story moves quickly and captivates readers with every page."

—*RT Book Reviews* on *Game of Fear*

PRAISE FOR THE SINGING RIVER NOVELS

"Romantic suspense favorite Robin Perini blends mystery, drama, thriller, and love story into *Forgotten Secrets*, an intense, sophisticated novel crafted with an extra portion of poignant . . . A breathtaking read."

—Kathy Altman, *USA Today*'s Happy Ever After blog

"As always, Robin Perini never disappoints when it comes to romantic suspense. Her latest book, *Forgotten Secrets*, takes the reader through a web of secrets about missing children, broken families, and a grandmother with Alzheimer's witness to her own granddaughter's abduction with no way to tell what she saw. Throw in an FBI agent and an ex-Navy SEAL with a little history of their own, unaware they are on diverging paths to solving mysteries old and new, and you have a superb tale unfolding before your eyes."

—Sharon Sala, *New York Times* bestselling author

FORGOTTEN LEGACY

ALSO BY ROBIN PERINI

Carder Texas Connections

Finding Her Son

Cowboy in the Crossfire

Christmas Conspiracy

Undercover Texas

The Cradle Conspiracy

Secret Obsession

Christmas Justice

San Antonio Secret

Cowboy's Secret Son

Last Stand in Texas

The Montgomery Justice Novels

In Her Sights (Luke's story)

Behind the Lies (Zach's story)

Game of Fear (Gabe's story)

Singing River Novels

Forgotten Secrets

FORGOTTEN LEGACY

ROBIN PERINI

Montlake
Romance

Published by Montlake Romance, Seattle

www.apub.com

ISBN-13: 9781503903449
ISBN-10: 1503903443

Cover design by David Drummond

Printed in the United States of America

This book is dedicated to the long-term caregivers whose unselfish actions make the unbearable survivable. Their knowledge, empathy, loyalty, dedication, devotion, and commitment cannot be overestimated or overappreciated. They are a beacon of light guiding families through a terrifying journey. From my heart to yours, thank you for all that you do and all that you are: angels on earth.

Faith is the strength by which a shattered world
shall emerge into the light.

—Helen Keller (1937)

PROLOGUE

For seven years they'd been safe. Longer than she'd expected, far shorter than she'd hoped.

Kim Jordan cut the engine to her family's rusted pickup. Her headlights automatically blinked off, and the inky black of nothing enveloped her, suffocating her with the maliciousness of the nightmare she'd prayed she and her daughter had left behind long ago.

Unable to move, she clutched the steering wheel until her fingers ached. She didn't know how, but someone had discovered their secret. The alternative explanation froze her insides.

She glanced at the small diamond ring on her left hand. She dreaded walking through the front door. How could she tell Aaron they'd been found? Her husband had kept her secrets from everyone all these years. Including her daughter.

Oh, Chloe. She buried her face in her hands. So many lies, so much deceit, for so many years.

She'd had no choice. She'd vowed to protect her little girl from the danger they'd escaped. Kim refused to give in now.

A wicked gust of Wyoming wind buffeted the truck, and she braced herself for the next assault. With all her strength she shoved open the door. A blast of air whipped through her homemade coat, and she hunched down, stiffening against the unusually vicious September weather.

The sun had set halfway through the drive home from selling her produce at the farmers' market. She'd run out of options. Again. Unable to stop the grip of foreboding squeezing her heart, she seized her coat's natural wool with numb fingers and wrapped it close around her.

Besides her husband, only one other person knew the truth. The man she'd left behind. The man who'd vowed to break her. The man who'd been inches away from killing her.

A loud metal clatter pierced the night. Startled, she ducked, the sound triggering old patterns she'd believed she'd vanquished. The terror she'd lived under never left, though. Not really.

She squinted through the darkness. Her gaze tore right, then left, but nothing appeared out of the ordinary. Still, she couldn't shake the sense of doom choking her. Why hadn't Aaron turned on the porch light? She needed the strength beaming from that beacon of hope.

Her husband must have forgotten. Tonight of all nights.

She slammed the door of the decades-old truck and shuddered. Frost-laden wind needled her skin, and a low groan echoed from her family's haven at the base of the Wind River Range.

She'd whispered a fervent prayer every day since she'd set foot on the outskirts of Singing River seven years ago that she'd outrun her past for good.

She'd needed her old life dead. Deader than her garden after a late Wyoming frost.

Unfortunately, seven had never been Kim's lucky number.

A blast of nature's fury shoved her forward. She stumbled, struggling to reach the comforting wooden door of the house that had safeguarded their family. She didn't want to say goodbye to their home, but leaving was the only surefire way to stay ahead of the past. Unless Aaron could come up with another plan.

They'd done everything in their power to protect their small family. They'd chosen a home in the middle of nowhere, self-sufficient, away from the nearest town's prying eyes. Living as close to off the grid as they could in this world.

Where had they gone wrong?

The dead of night gnawed apprehension beneath her skin. Taking a breath, praying for courage, Kim shouldered her way through the front door. She closed it behind her and flipped the dead bolt.

"Aaron, honey, are you here?" She forced her tone to the pretense that today was like any other.

Only silence greeted her.

She slipped off her gloves. Strange. He should be home by now.

A dim light shone from the kitchen.

"Aaron?"

Her tentative voice echoed through the silent living room. She slipped out of her coat and hung it on the rack before noticing Chloe's parka was missing from its hook. Aaron and Chloe were probably in the barn, bedding down the animals. Kim couldn't have married a better man. Aaron loved her and had found it in his heart to love her daughter as his own. He'd rescued her from a life of fear and suspicions. He'd taught her that love could be gentle and kind.

She had no doubt he would forgive her for their having to disappear again, but to soften the blow, she'd fix his favorite meal. Chloe, on the other hand . . . Kim didn't want to think about what this would do to her daughter. At twelve Chloe still had nightmares, even if she'd blocked out most of their life before Singing River.

Instinctively, her daughter knew monsters existed; she just didn't know how close to home they could prey. More than anything, Kim hated the possibility that she'd have to destroy her daughter's innocence.

She dug into her purse and eyed the blank envelope that had been taped to their post office box. She didn't want to touch it. Her hands trembled at the thought. They'd grown complacent over the years, living in this small, sheltered town, keeping to themselves, not inviting attention or raising too many questions.

The years had passed, and she'd felt safe.

She'd been a fool. She'd ignored the warning signs the last few months. An item out of place here or there in the house. That tingle at the base of her neck of someone watching, waiting.

She disregarded her gut, and her instincts.

With a sigh she straightened her shoulders. They'd face the future as one, the way they always had. Together, their family would start over once again.

At first she hadn't known where to turn. Their small family couldn't afford to bring anyone into their confidence, but she hadn't had a choice. Even now she couldn't shake the feeling she'd made a mistake, but she trusted only one person outside of her family. She'd already called the number she'd been given, hoping she hadn't just made the biggest mistake of her life. Kim snapped on the lamp beside the sofa and walked into the kitchen. She froze in horror.

Aaron sat in his chair, bound with rope, his mouth duct-taped, his eyes wide with terror. Kim stiffened. She could feel a presence behind her. She whirled around and gasped. "What are you doing here?"

He pointed a gun at her chest and smiled. "We've been waiting for you, *Kim*. Or should I use your real name?"

She gaped at him.

"Should I reveal every lie you've told, every way you've betrayed your vows?"

Kim swallowed, the gulp echoing through the silence.

"Your marriage is a fraud, a fabrication, a betrayal." He smiled, his eyes dead and cold and terrifying. "Don't bother to apologize or beg for forgiveness. All you can do now is accept your punishment."

◆ ◆ ◆

"Your bed will be your tomb." The words were calm, with an oddly cheerful tone.

Kim had no idea how much time had passed, but the midmorning sun bathed her face in warmth, piercing the crack between the drapes. She forced open her eyes to the nightmare she and Aaron shared.

Their bedroom, once a haven from the outside world, had become a prison. They had been covered with the quilt she'd sewn for their fifth wedding anniversary, as if their murderer were tucking them in for a good night's sleep.

She knew better. Her legs were leaden and her arms refused to move. She couldn't plead for mercy. Whatever had been injected into her and Aaron had thickened her tongue, and even her desperation had grown silent.

She no longer cared about herself. They were dead. She knew that.

With the last of her strength, Kim turned her head on the pillow. Aaron stared at her. Sorrow filled his eyes.

No anger, no condemnation. Simply unconditional love shone from his face. He was such a good man. He loved her. She loved him. They both loved Chloe.

That her daughter hadn't been captured remained their only solace. Kim had to believe her daughter had hidden in a safe place. Chloe was smart and braver than she knew. She would survive.

Kim understood Aaron well enough to know he would gladly die now as long as their daughter escaped this hell.

"That's right. Catch one last look at each other." Their tormenter flicked a lighter, anger ripping off him as he lit the end of one of Aaron's cigarettes and simply touched the burning embers to the edge of the quilt.

Kim could only watch in horror.

With a light push, he knocked over an oil lamp. A whoosh surged from the floor.

Black smoke billowed and flames shot up the side of the bed. Inside Kim screamed, the echo pounding against her head.

Smoke burned her lungs with each breath.

Without so much as a word, he strode out of the room and, with a final, satisfied smirk, closed the door behind him, trapping them inside the inferno.

No! You can't do this! Come back.

Sparks arced over the bed. Kim blinked through the swirls of black and brown and white poisonous clouds. Fingers of heat scorched closer and closer, ripping at her flesh, peeling it away.

Chloe! God help you. Don't come home, baby! Please stay safe.

One final, agonizing scream reverberated silently through her head, and the world went black.

CHAPTER ONE

Rusted cars and twisted metal stretched out for hundreds of feet behind the chained and padlocked gate of the bankrupt salvage yard. An iron cemetery of sorts. FBI special agent Riley Lambert gripped the fence. On days like today, she couldn't help but despise her ability to place herself firmly into the mind of the worst kind of killer.

Three days ago, Riley had left Singing River, Wyoming, for Washington, DC, to review the meager evidence in a series of kidnappings that had terrorized Baltimore and the surrounding counties. All women about the same age, same build, all commuting late at night, all vanished along with their vehicles. No signs of struggle, no clues, no bodies except the unrecognizable, mangled remains of Tiffany Hoyt, and even then, the evidence was scant to nothing.

Forty-eight hours later, after little sleep, she'd lucked out and narrowed the suspect pool based on the social media video of a truck towing the latest victim's vehicle.

This morning, she'd identified the prime suspect.

Now, bumping up on noon, she could only pray Sarah Ann Conway was still alive. Somewhere in this maze of metal carcasses.

Riley peered through the torrent of steel skeletons. The view would give anyone nightmares, and some of these vehicles could very well double as coffins.

If she was right.

She tensed her fist. The fence's metal sliced into her hand, but she didn't feel a thing. She could only gaze through the chain-link. The forensics team had identified the rust and three types of automotive paint from the victim's home, which suggested the kidnapper frequented somewhere with a lot of old cars. Add that to the evidence of industrial oil used in railroad cars embedded in their suspect's shoes, and this was the only location that fit the profile within the triangle of his abduction zone.

The victims were here. They had to be.

She peered at the seemingly endless rows of empty chassis, acres of them, stacked ten feet high, at least. The pulsing throb of a headache hadn't receded. Footsteps padded up behind her. Riley recognized the rhythm. Her back stiffened.

"You sure this is the place?" her boss asked when he stopped at her side. "It'll take days to search, and tonight's my thirtieth anniversary. If this turns into a snipe hunt, I'll be paying for it on the home front for at least a decade."

She ignored the skepticism in Supervisory Special Agent Tom Hickok's voice. She recognized the tone. Her old boss didn't doubt her theory. He doubted her hope.

Riley fought to stay calm. She knew this case was a test. One she needed to pass. "Sarah Ann Conway was kidnapped a week ago. The others were taken every seven days. We only found the first victim's body, and Harrison likes collections so I think he kept them alive. Until he needed a replacement." Riley dug her thumbnail into her palm. "Since he hasn't had time to come back and kill her, she still has a chance."

"Your theory hinges on your positive identification of Joseph Clyde Harrison," Tom said. "And since he jumped off that bridge so we couldn't arrest him, much less interrogate him, this case is all on you, Riley."

"Thanks for the vote of confidence."

He gave her that can't-you-play-by-the-rules-once look, and she dug her nails into her hand.

"Everything about him fits my profile," she countered, pretending she wasn't trying to convince herself more than her boss. Her assumptions about the disappearances in Baltimore and the surrounding counties *had* to be true. "Highly educated, yet he settled on a banal job. He separated himself from his family. Ostracized himself from any relationships except those his mind conjured. He was delusional, yet functioning. You saw his apartment." She chewed on her lower lip and cast a sidelong glance at Tom. "Harrison smiled directly at me before he jumped off that bridge. I think he knew she was still alive. I think he was taunting us, daring us to find her before it's too late. I won't let him win another one. Not this time. Sarah *has* to be here."

Tom's phone beeped. "Search warrant's here for the salvage yard and the surrounding area. We got lucky with the judge."

Riley spun on her heel. "Let's find her."

Tom's hand gripped Riley's shoulder. His knowing eyes gazed into hers, and he shook his head. "Hold on. I recognize that look. You're living off wasabi nuts and coffee and haven't slept in three days. You're emotionally involved again. Maybe not like before, but—"

"It's how I work. You knew that when you called me last week." She glanced over at him. "It's why you contacted me in the first place."

And why she'd said yes.

She could still remember the jolt that had run through her at his words. Unit 6 had been trying their best to save the latest victim of an unknown serial kidnapper, but they were failing. Their only chance was if Riley, the best and brightest of her boss's analysts, came back.

"It's also why I forced you to take a break, Riley. This is a test run, and I need to see you're in control or I'll red-flag your file permanently. No matter how uncanny you are at tracking these perps." He leaned toward her. "I want you to think hard if you want this life, and if you can live with my rules."

He strode over to the rest of the team. Riley slammed her hand against the fence. Why had she ever agreed to come here?

For most people, getting a call from your former boss begging you to return to work would've been a dream come true. For Riley it was a two-pronged fork in a road she desperately longed to see as straight and unwavering. Though his request validated all the years she'd spent training as a behavioral analyst, it put a choice in her life she wasn't sure she wanted.

What she hadn't expected was her gut reaction to the call: complete joy. For more reasons than Riley cared to admit. Even to herself.

All she'd wanted to know—in that gut-deep knowledge that could never be erased—was that she was truly needed.

It didn't matter that her emotions still hovered dangerously close to the surface after rescuing her sister from the madman who'd kidnapped her when they were children. It didn't matter that her relationship with her fiancé was on uncertain ground as they attempted to meld their very different lives into a future together in Singing River.

She loved the town. She loved her fiancé, Thayne.

But Sarah *needed* her.

Riley rubbed hard at the base of her neck. The moment she'd arrived in DC, pressure had settled in the knot. It hadn't left since then. The dull throb had worked its way forward on her skull and now pulsed at her forehead, a gnawing, painful, and all-too-familiar ache.

She wasn't about to share those facts with her boss. For the dozenth time that day, she wished Thayne were here with her. He understood more than most what lowering herself into the dark recesses of seriously disturbed minds did to Riley. The truth was, more often than not, she lost herself in their delusions.

Thayne knew just how to help center her, to keep her focused. But the Blackwood family needed him at home.

Riley had to save Sarah.

She zipped her fleece-lined jacket and made her way to the main gate of the salvage yard. She stepped back for a broader view, peering north, toward the city, then off to the south.

Old railroad tracks sliced through the landscape. Her heart stumbled. A slight shiver skirted up her spine.

Yes. *This* was the place, all right.

She looked up at the ten-foot-high fencing.

"Let's do this thing." Tom unholstered his standard-issue Glock and nodded. A local cop snapped through the lock's chain with a heavy-duty bolt cutter.

Riley's throat tightened.

She tried to shut down the hope quivering beneath her skin, but she couldn't completely quell the wish that they'd find Sarah and the others alive. Maybe not well, but . . .

The local law enforcement officers pushed open the huge gates.

Tom lifted his bullhorn. "Everyone has a list of the victims' license plates. Find them."

Riley thrust her hand through her hair and turned in a full circle. A section of fence caught her gaze. "Over there. Near the fence closest to the train tracks."

"He could've dumped the cars into the river," her boss countered.

"He's a collector." Riley picked her way through the mountains of junk. "Did you notice the miniature trains, the baseball cards, the marbles at his home? He needs to be close to his treasures." She skidded to a halt. "Look at that."

Through the fence, a dilapidated train wheelhouse stood with six locomotives positioned, one on each spoke of track.

"Another collection." Tom let out a low curse.

"She's nearby," Riley said, frantically searching the pile of cars that had blocked the view. "She has to be."

Tom headed to an adjoining stack.

"Sarah," Riley called out. "Can you hear me? We're here to help."

She stopped to listen. Voices shouting echoed from all over the yard. Thousands of cars.

Think, Riley.

Her mind reverted to Harrison's apartment, to all his collections, perfectly organized, put away. Each in their own specific cubbyhole along the walls. All except one.

In the center of the room, on a round coffee table, he'd organized six trains. A work in progress.

Her gaze snapped to the wheelhouse. In exactly the same pattern.

"Tom. The trains."

Without a thought, Riley rushed out of the salvage yard and veered toward the abandoned roundabout. She climbed onto the first locomotive and pushed up into the cab.

The stench of death overtook her senses.

"Oh, Sarah."

The back of a blonde's head showed just above a seat, her body slumped down.

Riley eased toward her. The body had keeled over to the right side, badly decomposed and still dressed, but not in Sarah's clothes. Riley perused the antique earrings hanging off the victim's ears. She recognized them from another case. This wasn't Sarah.

With a grunt, she jumped down. "Check the other trains," she called out to Tom. "They're here. They're *all* here."

Her legs pumping, Riley raced to the next train and peered inside. The odor didn't knock her over this time, and the victim's hair was dark. Decomposition had set in even longer ago. Dead, and not Sarah.

The local LEOs streamed toward the trains. Riley hurried to the next locomotive. With a rusted red paint job, this one appeared eerily similar to one of the trains on Harrison's coffee table.

She pulled herself into the cab and faced the seat's back. A head of blonde hair leaned back against the vinyl. Riley's breath caught. "Sarah? Sarah Ann Conway?"

No movement. Riley rushed over.

"Sarah!"

Chains pinned her against the chair. Her head lolled to one side. Riley touched her cheek. Still warm.

"Here, she's here!" Riley shouted through the window. "I need those bolt cutters and an ambulance."

Within moments a couple of local LEOs snapped apart the metal rings and carried Sarah outside to the ground. She hadn't moved.

Riley plopped to her knees. "Sarah. Can you hear me?" She laid her fingers over the carotid.

No pulse. Riley yanked open Sarah's shirt and lined up the heel of her hand at the center of the woman's chest. Compressions had to be one hundred beats per minute to do any good. She leaned over her body and pressed fast and hard to the beat of "Stayin' Alive."

Time slowed; the world around Riley fell silent. All she could do was battle to bring Sarah back from the dead.

Pulse after pulse.

The sound of a siren reverberated through the locomotive.

Hands gripped her shoulders. "Let them in, Riley."

Tom dragged her away, and the paramedics pushed past them.

Breath after breath. Compression after compression. A shock to the heart. An IV. Another shock.

The world spun around. Riley couldn't look away. A hand cupped her elbow, but she refused to remove her gaze from Sarah's face.

Live. Please, Sarah.

Riley didn't know how long she stood there, watching, praying.

Suddenly Sarah sputtered and sucked in a deep breath. Riley's knees buckled.

"She's back," one of the paramedics shouted. "Let's move."

Riley nearly collapsed to the ground, but Tom held her up. He smiled at her. "Congratulations, Riley. You did it. You saved her."

Her mind whirled in disbelief. How long had it been since she'd saved anyone on the job?

Far too long.

Minutes later, the ambulance screeched away and the train yard went quiet, except for some muttering from the cops as they cordoned off the area until the forensics team arrived.

"Nothing more we can do here," her boss said. "They'll process the scene. The locals can wrap up the case. That's our deal with them, but at least the other families will get closure."

Riley's mind had gone blank. The throbbing in her head threatened to turn into a full-blown migraine. She missed her fiancé's magic hands. He knew just how to beat back the headaches and quell the vibrating thoughts that whirled through her mind.

Sarah Ann Conway was alive. Alive, alive, alive. Thayne wasn't here, though.

"You freaking out on me, Riley?"

She squeezed her eyes shut and sucked in several deep breaths. Finally, she looked up into Tom's worried face. "I can't believe we actually found her alive."

"She wouldn't have been alive much longer. She owes you her life." Her boss cocked his head at her. "You held it together better than I thought you would. This may not be the best time, but we could use you full-time in the unit. If you think you can handle it."

"You're the one who said I couldn't cut it."

"Damn it, Riley." He scowled. "You've always been the best behavioral analyst I've ever seen, but now that you've found your sister in Wyoming, you've changed. You're more restrained. I think it's time to consider coming back to DC. You didn't lose yourself during this search the way you used to. I can't believe I'm saying this, but you're even better. We need you in Unit 6."

Words Riley had been waiting to hear all her life.

Except her world had changed. After fifteen years she'd finally found her sister, Madison. Alive. Madison's kidnapping out of their bedroom when Riley was ten and Madison was twelve was the reason Riley had become obsessed with profiling criminals. She'd spent her entire life searching for what had happened to her older sister.

Riley'd never expected to actually rescue Madison, not after so many years. She'd certainly never expected to fall in love with the man who'd been instrumental in helping her find her sister. But without Thayne Blackwood's strength and faith, Riley had no idea what would've happened in those Wyoming mountains.

Riley owed Thayne everything, and she loved him.

"Come on, Riley," Tom said. "You're tempted. I can tell."

She met his gaze. "You can't promise me a job. I know what the deputy director thinks of what I do."

"I'll talk to him."

Her lips twisted. "Can you convince them to give me room to work my way? My own board, my own methods? No more trying to make me fit into the FBI's box?"

"As long as you follow the rules, I can make that happen." He held out his hand. "Can I welcome you back?"

Riley hesitated. He was saying everything she had always longed to hear, but . . . "I have others to consider besides me. Can I have a few days to think about it?"

Her boss scowled. "What does Wyoming have for you, Riley? Come on. You belong in the FBI, using your talents, saving lives. Solving crimes no one else can solve. It's who you are. We both know that."

He was right, but what about the family she'd found in Singing River? She'd never been more content.

"I'll call you, Tom." Riley shook his hand and turned her back on the crime scene and her old boss.

Head spinning, she made her way to her rental car and slid inside. She leaned forward against the steering wheel and stared through the windshield at the frenetic activity. She glanced down at her phone. A voice mail notice flashed at her. From yesterday? Was it Thayne? Her heart skipped a bit, then sagged. She didn't recognize the number, though it had a Wyoming area code.

She'd check on it later. Riley had a choice to make and needed to disconnect from both worlds. She had no idea how she'd ever decide.

◆ ◆ ◆

Sheriff Thayne Blackwood threw his brand-new official hat on his father's—no, make that *his*—desk and plopped into the chair. The Singing River Sheriff's Office was quiet. Too quiet. Just like it'd been every day for the last two weeks. Since the moment he'd accepted the job to replace his father.

He peered into the small room. The three deputies who made up the office were on patrol. His dispatcher, Alicia, sat by the radio, waiting for the rare call.

Not what he'd imagined when he'd filed his separation paperwork from the Navy. His SEAL team was deployed somewhere classified, and he didn't have their six. Not to mention Riley had gone back to DC to assist her old FBI unit with a case. She'd agreed to his proposal but left without his ring on her finger and without setting a wedding date. A small niggle in his brain made him wonder if she'd come back at all.

And here he was sitting in his office. Alone. In a town he could traverse within five minutes.

A sharp knock sounded on the door. "Hey there, son. You busy?"

Thayne let out a sigh as he stood. His father. Carson Blackwood visited every day without fail at eleven in the morning. Forced to retire because of a heart condition, he hadn't been able to give up the law enforcement bug. Thayne had no idea what to do about it.

Especially since he couldn't exactly say he was overly busy.

"Hey, Dad. How're Pops and Gram?"

"I just dropped them off at the diner for an ice-cream soda." His father smiled. "Your grandmother's having a good day. She wanted a treat. She also said she wants to come by. She has a message for Riley. Can't remember it of course, but she's adamant."

"And Pops?"

Worry lines creased his father's forehead. "I'm concerned. Caring for her is becoming tougher. She doesn't recognize him more and more often now."

Gram's Alzheimer's had changed their family and was one of the reasons Thayne had decided to take the job. Especially with his father's illness, the family needed him. He refused to regret the decision he'd made. He'd just have to get used to the changes.

His dad sat in the chair across from Thayne. "So when's Riley coming back?"

"Honestly, I don't know if she is." Thayne sat behind his desk and took a sip of coffee, grimacing at the cold, bitter taste. "I thought I'd have heard from her by now."

"What are you talking about? That girl loves you."

"I thought so, but you should've seen how fast she caught a flight out of here when her old boss called. They needed her and she went running."

"Just like she did when you asked for her help to find Cheyenne after she was kidnapped. She brought your sister home safe. She's got a gift."

Thayne scowled at his father. "When you put it like that—"

"You miss her."

"It's more than that." Thayne hadn't voiced his concerns aloud. Not to anyone. Not even to Riley. "She's special. I don't know if Singing River's going to ever be enough for her."

Before his father could respond, the outer door of the sheriff's office slammed, and Thayne shot to his feet.

"I wanna see the sheriff right now. You hear me, young lady?"

Thayne gazed beyond his open office door at a gray-headed, unkempt man shouting at his dispatcher, his face red with fury. "Isn't that Old Man Peterson?" He strode out of the door. "Sir? No need to take it out on Alicia. I'm here. What can I do for you?"

The man frowned at him. "Where's the real sheriff? You're just that young rabble-rousing son of his."

Thayne didn't respond, but inside he sighed. One more reason he wasn't certain this whole sheriff gig was going to work out. Too many people remembered him as the troublemaking Blackwood.

"Dan?" Thayne's father walked up behind him.

A smile calmed Dan Peterson's features. "It's about time, Carson. What kind of place you running here?"

"I ask myself that all the time." He guided the older man to the door. "Why don't you come into the office?"

Thayne followed his father and pulled out a chair. "Would you sit down?"

"I'm here, ain't I?" Dan muttered. He stared at his boots, then sighed. "I don't like coming to the law, but my daughter says I got to. Olivia's stubborn that way. She's furious at her stepmother."

Thayne's dad hitched his hip on the side of his old desk. "What's going on?"

"My wife's trying to kill me."

The words pierced Thayne with shock. He shut the office door and met his father's gaze with a question in his eyes. "What makes you say that, sir?"

Dan ignored Thayne and looked straight at the man he considered sheriff. "This."

He slipped off his shirt, and just below his collarbone, a dark, mottled bruise stood out against his pale skin. "Damned woman hit me with a pipe."

"A pipe?" Thayne narrowed his gaze.

"You're saying little ol' Kate did this?" his father asked, his tone incredulous.

"Well, who else coulda done it?" Dan frowned. "That woman is acting strange. She's ordering me around, spending money on strange things. Just the other day, some fella came over and told me he'd been promised a thousand dollars to dig up the trees around the house. Now who in their right mind would pay that much to dig up a few trees?" He leaned forward. "I think she might be stepping out on me with the tree guy."

Thayne recognized the expression on his father's face as he moved through one scenario after another.

Finally, he stroked his chin. "Don't you worry. I'll take care of this, Dan. I'll talk to Kate."

Dan shook his head. "Time for talk is done. She ain't listening to me. I want her put in jail. That's where my girl says she belongs." He glared at his old friend.

Thayne crossed the office and opened the door. "Mr. Peterson, could you wait outside with Alicia for a moment? We need to take your statement in writing."

"In writing. I like that," he said and stalked out of the office.

As soon as he'd gone, Thayne turned on his father. "What do you think you're doing?"

"Well, I'm going to take my friend home to Kate and get them to talk it out, that's what. That's part of the job."

Thayne crossed one booted leg and cocked his head. "Who exactly is sheriff in this town?"

His father winced. "Sorry, Thayne. Of course you are, but he's my friend. He and Kate both are. They've been married for over ten years, ever since his first wife passed from cancer." His dad pulled at his eyebrow. "Look, part of the job is knowing folks' backstory. You'll learn the ropes soon enough. Besides, Kate had a bit of trouble drinking back in the day. I want to check it out. Make sure she's still on the wagon."

Oh no. This wasn't happening. Thayne had promised his sister. "First off, I'm driving Dan to the clinic so Cheyenne can check out that bruise and see if there are any more injuries. Then I'll follow Dan home, and I'll evaluate the situation."

"I'm coming with you." His father planted his feet and placed his hands on his hips in challenge.

"I'm the sheriff, Dad. Not you. This isn't your job anymore."

His dad stilled, and inside Thayne grimaced. He hadn't meant to sound so harsh, but his father could get worked up. It wasn't good for his heart. Besides, Cheyenne wasn't just his sister; she was the only doctor in town. She'd forced a promise from Thayne and their brothers to keep Dad calm. Not let him do too much.

"Wait here," Thayne said to his father.

"Don't treat me like I should be out in the pasture or up on a rock on those mountains just waiting to die. I may not be one hundred percent anymore, but I'm not on my last mile, either."

The start of a headache pushed at Thayne's temples. They had to find his father a purpose. And soon. His dad was right. He was barely sixty; unfortunately, a virus had given him the heart of a seventy-five-year-old. He had to take it easy.

Thayne closed the door to his office and walked over to Dan. "Mr. Peterson. I'd like to take you to—"

The radio on Alicia's desk squawked to life.

"We've got a fire at the Jordans' place. No one noticed anything until . . ." The voice broke with emotion. "We need all the volunteers for the fire truck and everybody else we can spare. It's bad."

CHAPTER TWO

Riley couldn't deny she'd missed Singing River. The hills on the outskirts of the small town rolled like an ocean of grass until they bumped against the Wind River Mountains. The first time she'd visited, she'd been on the hunt for her sister's kidnapper. The second time, she'd come because Thayne had asked.

This time, she wasn't quite sure. She wanted to say she was coming home. She'd fallen in love with Wyoming—the expanse of sky, the fresh air, but also, more important than all that, the people.

One person in particular.

But life wasn't simple. Her boss had given her a lot to think about yesterday.

Normally, Riley would've headed straight to the sheriff's office to see Thayne, to walk into his arms, but his SUV hadn't been parked outside.

She'd tried to call, but he hadn't picked up. Besides, unlike during the first year of their relationship, the phone wasn't enough anymore. She needed to be with him.

The thought made her pause. She'd never allowed herself to be vulnerable to anyone until Thayne. She'd learned early that love was conditional, not to be trusted.

He'd convinced her to have faith in more than herself. To have faith in him.

She'd needed a distraction. And she'd found one. The moment she'd listened to that unidentified message—Kim Jordan's message—on her trip, her Spidey sense had gone haywire. A mystery, a question, and a hint of danger. Her pulse raced in anticipation. An addiction she'd fed in DC.

Was that her problem? Was she obsessed with investigations?

She shoved the thought aside. The trees spiked high in the sky as she curved around the bend. The house shouldn't be far. The scent of burning wood filtered in from the outside. The memory of a warm, cozy fire reminded her of Thayne and countless nights spent in front of his fireplace. A flash of heat warmed her cheeks. Maybe she should have tried to find him first.

Hopefully Kim Jordan or her husband would be home. Riley had no idea why the woman had left her such an odd and cryptic message. They'd never met before.

One last turn, and at the sight in front of her, Riley hit the brakes. All four sheriff's vehicles and the lone fire engine from Singing River were parked off to the side. Tongues of smoke rose from the smoldering remains of the house and barn. Burned timbers lay strewn in a pile of rubble.

Riley jumped out of her vehicle and raced over to where Thayne stood, his mouth covered with a mask.

"What happened?" she asked.

"Riley?" Thayne's eyes widened. "Get out of here. You need protective gear."

He dragged her away from the fire, ripped his mask off, and hugged her close. Riley clutched him and let out a long, slow breath, taking in his warmth. "I missed you," she said against his jacket. "More than you'll ever know."

"I missed you, too."

His arms held her so tight she didn't know if she could move. She loved this feeling. He was home to her.

"What are you doing here?" he asked.

"Kim Jordan left me a message while I was in DC. She didn't say much, just that she'd been given my name, was in trouble, and needed my help as soon as possible."

Thayne pulled away from her. "Did you know her?"

Riley shook her head. "We'd never met. I don't even know how she got my number, but she sounded . . . anxious." Riley scanned what was left of the Jordan home. "I guess she had reason to be. What happened?"

"The fire investigator from Riverton stopped by. Said it was a tragic accident. Cigarette started the fire in the bedroom. Aaron and Kim were in bed. Didn't make it out. It's been so dry the sparks made their way to the barn, too."

"From the evidence, I guess it seems open and shut," Riley said. "If it weren't for that phone call . . ."

Thayne stared at her. He could see through her thoughts. It was one of the things that drove her crazy. She couldn't hide much of anything from him.

"I recognize that look on your face," he said. "You say Kim sounded worried?"

Riley nodded. "Do you mind if I take a look?"

He gave her some gear. Once she'd donned the boots, suit, and mask, she wandered through the house.

The place hadn't turned completely to ash. She could make out the bedroom. She knelt next to the bed. "The fire started here."

"Cigarette and a kerosene lamp. They didn't have a prayer. Their bedding was burned into their bodies," he said.

Deputy Michael Ironcloud strode over to them. "No sign of their daughter. No tracks around the house. She wasn't in her bedroom."

"Maybe she's with a friend." Thayne frowned, his brow furrowed. "She could come home later. School just let out."

"Chloe was homeschooled," Ironcloud said. "The Jordans hardly ever came to town. Aaron worked on ranches around the county doing whatever work he could get. Kim sold fresh produce and homemade jams. They've lived here for six or seven years and never had much to do with anyone else."

Thayne glanced up at the sky. "It'll be dark in three hours, and the temperature's getting close to freezing at night. Organize several search parties. Even a homeschooled kid has friends. Go to the houses of kids about her age and find out if anyone's seen her. If that doesn't work, we'll fan out from here."

Deputy Ironcloud nodded and took off in his vehicle down the dirt road.

"How old is Chloe?" Riley asked, hating the sick feeling in her gut.

"Twelve."

"The same age as Maddy when she was kidnapped." Riley swallowed. She'd spent fifteen years searching for her sister, and even though they'd found Madison last month, Riley still blamed herself for not stopping the kidnapping in the first place.

She wouldn't let that happen to Chloe.

As if he could read her mind, Thayne slipped his fingers into her hand. "I won't ask you to get some rest, even though I can tell you haven't slept for days. You're going to help with the search?"

"Of course." Riley ignored the grit behind her eyes. How could she sleep when a young girl was missing? "Can I look around here first? Something here might lead us to Chloe."

Thayne kissed her cheek. "Thank you. Pendergrass has already taken photos. We were finishing up so the fire department can turn the ashes and confirm the fire danger has passed."

She picked her way through the rubble of what was left of the Jordans' bedroom, where the smell of burned flesh hung heavy in the air. "Aaron Jordan smoked?" she asked with a tilt of her head. "And his body was on *this* side of the bed?"

"You've got it backwards."

Riley circumnavigated the ash heap. Inch by inch she surveyed the entire area where the Jordans had died. "You're sure?"

Thayne stilled, and she could see she'd piqued his interest with her question. She'd meant to.

"That's what I was told," he said.

Riley squatted and glanced at what was left of a lighter. "It's all wrong, then." She stood and faced Thayne. "This wasn't an accident. I'm almost certain they were murdered."

◆ ◆ ◆

The stench of burned, wet wood with an aftermath of charred flesh stuck in Thayne's throat. "Murdered?"

Hip deep in a crime scene wasn't how he'd planned to welcome her home. He'd dreamed for days of what he would say, what he would do. Assuming she did come back. Now, instead of greeting Riley with a good meal, a night alone, and a reminder of how much he loved her, they were standing in the middle of a death scene. Definitely not part of his playbook.

Already he could see her focus lasering in on the secret she believed she'd uncovered in what remained of the Jordans' house. He couldn't discount her gut. He'd witnessed her gift firsthand.

She squatted next to where the fire had started. "This should be his side of the bed. And what was in his drawer? A metal tube of lipstick. On the other side, I can make out the remains of a revolver. Looks like an old Colt. There's even what appears to be a lighter." She sent Thayne a long, slow gaze. "Who do *you* think slept where?"

Thayne studied the evidence for a moment. "The investigator didn't notice those details." He didn't want her to be right; having a murderer in their midst would cause a panic, but damn it, Riley was very good at her job.

She gripped his arm. "What if the person who set the fire took Chloe? You've got to warn Deputy Ironcloud."

Thayne pulled her to her feet. "Hold on. You're making a lot of assumptions. There weren't any tire tracks or prints leading to or from the house. How can you be so sure this wasn't an accident? Maybe Kim was worried about Chloe. Maybe her parents switched sides of the bed. Maybe Chloe's spending the night with a friend."

"That's a lot of maybes, Thayne."

"Do you think I don't know that?" He shifted his shoulders, trying to unknot the tension her suspicions had caused. Hell, Riley was probably right. She usually was.

"I'm not seeing a crime where there isn't one. You know that as well as I do. Something's wrong here. Whatever happened, we have to find Chloe."

Thayne hated the haunted look in Riley's eyes. When her sister had been taken, Riley's parents had spiraled into dysfunction. Riley had practically raised herself. It was a wonder she'd turned out halfway normal, much less the extraordinary person she was.

"I'll call Ironcloud, have him ask around town for any strangers, though it's hard to tell these days with all the natural-gas workers that come through heading toward the fields outside Boulder."

He made his way around the ashes and contacted his deputy. He wanted Riley to be wrong, but he'd witnessed that look more than once when she'd been searching for his sister. Riley's gut was gold. Which meant there was a murderer out there.

A rumbling engine exploded in backfire, and Thayne spun around. Dust kicked up from an old pickup. The truck skidded to a halt on the dirt road and tapped Thayne's SUV on the bumper.

Dan Peterson scowled from behind the wheel, yanked his vehicle into reverse, and backed up a few feet.

"Unbelievable," Thayne said under his breath, glancing over at Riley. "I'll be right back."

At his words, her brow wrinkled in concern, but she nodded before her focus returned to the crime scene.

Thayne stalked over to Dan. The older man shoved open his door. "Sheriff," he said with a frown, "your father has been a pain in my backside. Invited himself to dinner, hung out at our place all night long. Won't stop bugging me to get checked out. Do I look like I need a doctor?"

Thayne couldn't argue that his father had inserted himself into the situation. He obviously hadn't been able to get anywhere. "Dan, what are you doing here? I'm a little busy right now. I've assigned my father to your case."

"I got no case." Dan wrinkled his nose. "Heard about this place. Heard his daughter was nowhere to be found. Thought you might not look everywhere you should. You interested in my information or not?" He muttered something about young folks and respect and turned on his heel.

Thayne paused and touched Dan's sleeve. "You know the Jordans?"

The older man removed his hat and twisted it in his hands before slowly facing Thayne. "Did some work for him over the years. His wife made the best blackberry jam in the state, but he could be a pain in the butt on the job."

Thayne reached into his pocket for his notebook. "You two get along okay?"

Dan shrugged. "Well enough, I suppose. He wasn't exactly a friendly fellow. Had a lot of secrets, for sure. Didn't want no one knowing his business. Made me promise never to tell anyone about the last project."

"Really?" Thayne glanced over his shoulder. As if Riley had read his mind, she'd already picked her way through the ashes and paused beside him. "You remember Special Agent Lambert?" he asked.

"Seen her around town." Dan doffed his hat. "Ma'am."

Now this was the Dan that Thayne remembered. "What kind of secrets did Aaron Jordan have, Dan?"

Riley raised a brow.

"Didn't want anyone to know his business, that's for sure. Lived off the grid as much as possible. Didn't trust the law—or anyone else for that matter. Most didn't want to work for him because he didn't deal in money. Liked to trade. And I loved to slather my biscuits in Mrs. Jordan's—"

"Blackberry jam," Thayne finished.

Dan's eyes lit up. "Cobbler, too. My wife's cobbler is pretty much like sawdust."

"Sir," Riley said, "did you notice any changes in their behavior recently?"

"Oh, I hadn't seen them in a while." Dan curled his hat. "He'd finished up his big jobs. Repaired the barn, put in that solar electricity. Finished that crazy doomsday cellar. Big waste of time, if you asked me."

"Wait a minute. Are you saying there's a cellar in this house?"

"Yeah."

Thayne clasped Dan's arm. "Show us where."

Dan led them into what was left of the living room and pointed to an area near the center. Riley stomped her foot, then moved over a couple of feet and stomped again.

"Metal." Thayne knelt in the center of the floor and shoved aside the ash. A round metal handle lay flush with the floor. With a grunt, he lifted up, and a metal covering hinged open. Below, steps aimed downward, the walls charred with smoke. At the bottom of the stairs, a metal door blocked the way.

Carefully Thayne navigated the metal stairs. They creaked under his weight but held. "It got hotter than hell down here."

"A panic room?" Riley asked from above.

"That's what Aaron called it," Dan said.

"So the Jordans were survivalists." Thayne reached the door barricading the way. He touched the discolored steel. "Smoke filled up the stairwell."

He shoved the handle down. It didn't budge.

"Pendergrass, I need a crowbar and an ax," he called to one of his other deputies.

Dan hovered nearby, and after a few moments, Riley passed Thayne the tools. He slipped the crowbar's edge into the sealed jamb and used all his strength.

The door popped open. A whiff of smoke assaulted his senses. Bracing himself, Thayne peered inside. A young girl lay on the floor just inside the door.

He knelt and turned her over. "Chloe?"

Riley knelt on the girl's other side. "Is she . . . ?"

He bent over and felt a small pull of breath from her mouth. "She's alive." Thayne jumped to his feet. "Pendergrass. We need that ambulance back. Now! We have a survivor."

◆ ◆ ◆

The Singing River Hospital could house only a dozen patients, but Riley had always been impressed at the care provided. She paced the floor near Chloe Jordan's room. Smoke still lingered in her nose. The smell had permeated Chloe's sweater and jeans, yet somehow there'd been enough oxygen in the panic room for the girl to breathe. And survive.

Thayne strode in from taking Dan Peterson's statement, Stetson in his hand. "How is she doing?"

"Still unconscious," Riley said with a sigh. "Your sister's with her."

"If Dan hadn't come by, we may not have found her in time. Thank God for nosy small-town neighbors." Thayne stroked the stubble on his jaw. "She's lucky to be alive. The fire inspector thinks she was hiding in the stairwell until the smoke got to be too much. The panic room was airtight, but the vent was blocked off when the house collapsed. She wouldn't have lasted another twenty-four hours. I told Dad to buy him and Kate dinner on me as a thank-you."

Riley couldn't imagine how terrified Chloe had been. But waking up wouldn't be easy. Not with both her parents gone.

Riley couldn't shake the guilt, though. If she'd only checked her messages sooner. Talked to Kim Jordan. Maybe Riley could've stopped this from happening.

Thayne pulled her into his arms. "Don't do that," he said, rubbing her back. "This wasn't your fault."

"Her mother called me. She needed help, and I wasn't here. I've been here for weeks, and the one time someone needed me . . ."

Before Thayne could respond, his sister, Dr. Cheyenne Blackwood-Riverton, walked into the hallway and closed the door quietly behind her. She held a tablet that connected her to all her patient records and wore a stethoscope around her neck. She looked exactly like a competent doctor should. She'd impressed Riley from the moment they'd met.

"Is she awake?" Thayne asked, standing toe to toe with his sister. "I need to talk to her. I need to know if someone set the fire."

"They did," Riley said.

Cheyenne glanced back and forth between them but didn't say a word. Instead she reviewed the chart in her hand and frowned. "She won't be able to answer you for a while. She's unconscious with some serious smoke inhalation. I had to put her on a ventilator."

Riley lifted a hand to her throat. "But she'll be okay?"

"I don't know." Cheyenne's eyes darkened with emotion. "If she makes it through the next forty-eight hours, she has a good chance.

Smoke inhalation is a tricky thing. She breathed in hydrocarbons. Her bronchial tubes are compromised. The tissue in her nose and throat is swollen." Cheyenne studied her brother. "You could help me out, though. We don't have any information on her. Not even her date of birth. She's never been to my clinic. Does she have any other family around here? I need to identify someone who can make medical decisions for her."

Thayne shook his head. "Anything they had went up in flames. And as far as I can tell, no one knows anything about them. Michael Ironcloud is contacting possible friends, but so far he's had no luck."

Thayne's phone rang. "Blackwood." He stepped down the hall.

Cheyenne sent Riley a twisted smile. "I'm glad you're back. Thayne was a bear while you were gone, snapping at everyone. Like you weren't coming back or something."

Riley shifted back and forth, unwilling to meet Cheyenne's gaze. She admired Thayne's sister so much. She connected with people, empathized with them, but after being held against her will last month, she'd also shown more guts than most of the FBI agents Riley worked with.

Her sister-in-law-to-be clasped Riley's arm. "You were coming back, weren't you?"

After a quick glance over her shoulder at Thayne, Riley bit her lip. "Of course."

"You don't look certain." Cheyenne tilted her head to study Riley.

What was it about the Blackwoods that gave them special powers to see right into a person's soul? "Don't do that voodoo on me and read my mind."

"You're too easy," Cheyenne said with a wink. "Look, I get it. Singing River's not exactly the center of the FBI universe. It's not the center of medical research, either."

"You wanted to go into research?" Riley studied Cheyenne's face. "I had no idea."

"One of my professors offered me a position on his team. I was tempted to change paths. Especially once Gram started showing early symptoms of Alzheimer's."

"Then why'd you come back to Singing River? From what Thayne told me, you could have gone anywhere."

"Not exactly. I agreed to set up practice for five years in a rural area in exchange for my med school tuition. But the truth is, I never wanted to be anywhere else. These are my people, you know."

Riley didn't know. She'd never really belonged anywhere once her sister had been kidnapped.

"What if the job you'd trained for your entire life wasn't needed here?" Riley twisted her fingers. "I love this town, and I love Thayne, but my career isn't here." She met Cheyenne's sympathetic gaze. "Do I give up everything I've ever worked for, every skill I've developed over the years to help others?"

"What happened while you were gone?" Cheyenne asked.

"I did my job, and I saved a woman's life."

"You were part of saving Chloe's life today," Cheyenne reminded her.

"It's not the same—" Riley caught a movement in the corner of her eye.

Thayne strode toward them and pocketed his phone. "Seems we have a bit of a mystery on our hands. Ironcloud ran the number Kim used to call you on your cell phone, Riley. Kim said someone gave her your name. Well, according to the logs, the previous call on her phone was to the Blackwood Ranch. She called someone at our ranch." He turned to Cheyenne. "Is Chloe stable?"

"For the moment," Cheyenne said. "Nurse Crawley is keeping an eye on her."

"Good. Make sure she knows to call me the minute Chloe wakes up." Thayne held out his hand to Riley. "You up for a ride out to the Blackwood Ranch? We've got more than a few questions that need answering."

"Absolutely." She couldn't imagine who had given Kim Jordan her name. It didn't make sense. Everyone knew she was on leave from the FBI. She had no official capacity these days.

She followed him out to the SUV. He opened the door for her, rounded the car, and slid in beside her. He let out a sigh. "You going to tell me what's going on and what you and my sister were talking about?"

"Not bad detective work for a former SEAL who's only been sheriff for a couple of weeks," Riley teased.

"I won't let you evade the issue forever." Thayne set the car into gear and pulled out on the highway toward his family's ranch. "How about we start with something easy. How was DC?"

"I found the guy and one of his victims. She's going to make a full recovery."

"Congratulations." Thayne squeezed her hand. "I know how much that means to you."

Riley's throat closed up, and she struggled to keep her emotions tamped down. Normally she prided herself on her control, but these days, that part of her couldn't seem to keep it together.

"Thanks." She cleared her throat. "Tom asked me to come back to the unit full-time."

The words rushed out fast and furious.

"I see." Thayne's grip tightened on her before he deliberately placed his hands on the steering wheel. "What did you tell him?"

"I didn't give him an answer." She chanced a glance at Thayne. His jaw had tightened, that way it did when he tried to hold his own emotions in check. "Not yet."

"You want to do it." His words weren't a question; they were a statement. "I understand."

"Do you? Really?"

Thayne met her gaze straight on. "Hell yeah. You think I don't miss my old life? That I don't watch the news and wonder if my team isn't eyebrow deep in holding the line on the latest insurgency?"

When had she last heard that kind of passion in Thayne's voice? Maybe he did understand.

"Look, I've known since Madison left that you've been restless. You miss her. You miss your job. And this town, it's not what you need. Is it?"

She twisted in her seat. "I need you."

He swallowed deeply, and Riley's throat tightened in response. "I love you, Riley, and I don't want to make this easier, but I won't hold you back, either. Not if working for the FBI makes you happy."

"I'm not sure *happy* is the right word."

"*Needed*, then? *Valued?*"

He *did* understand.

Thayne drove under the large iron arch and entered his family's land. After crossing the cattle guard, he parked in front of the main house and turned in his seat. He stroked her cheek with his thumb. "You're exhausted. You look like you could use about a week's worth of sleep. How about we check out the phone call, and then I take you back to Fannie's Bed and Breakfast? I'll even swipe one of her famous cinnamon rolls from the kitchen."

She smiled and kissed his lips. "You've got yourself a deal."

◆ ◆ ◆

The smell of antiseptic burned his nose. He peeked through the door of the unused hospital room and watched the doc greet a deputy stationed just outside where they were keeping the girl. The doc disappeared inside.

The deputy glanced his way, and he quickly stepped back so he wouldn't be seen.

He'd made a mistake. How had he missed Chloe's being in the house? She wasn't even supposed to be there. Had she seen him? Had she seen everything?

Back and forth, back and forth, he paced, waiting. One thing was clear. He didn't want to kill her, but he couldn't take the chance. It was he or she, and he believed in self-preservation . . . at all costs.

It wouldn't be easy. The damn hospital was too small for him to go unnoticed. He'd have to keep to the shadows. Once in, if Chloe was weak, it wouldn't take much to keep her from breathing. A pillow over her face, a few seconds, and it would be done.

"Dr. Riverton," the deputy said, "how is she? The sheriff asked for regular updates."

He couldn't resist. He cracked open the door. His luck held. The deputy's back faced him.

"She's not showing any signs of improvement yet," the doctor said with a frown. "I'm concerned. If I can't get her off the ventilator in the next couple of days, her prognosis is grim."

Well, well. Maybe he wouldn't have to take any action after all. He'd wait and see. It'd be much better if she died on her own.

"Thayne really wants to talk to her." The deputy lowered his voice to a whisper. "Special Agent Lambert thinks it was murder. They hope the girl might have seen something."

What the hell? He closed the door softly.

Pacing, thinking. Back and forth, back and forth, back and forth. This wouldn't do. No, this wouldn't do at all. One mistake couldn't ruin his punishment. He'd been so careful. Had planned it so perfectly. He wouldn't let anyone take away a perfect win. Not even Chloe.

◆ ◆ ◆

The moment Thayne opened the front door of the Blackwood ranch house, the scent of Thayne's grandmother's apple pull-apart cake filled the air. He'd know that smell anywhere.

Thayne led Riley into the kitchen. His grandmother and grandfather sat at the table, with the dessert between them. He breathed in deeply. "How'd you two know I was starving?" he asked.

He walked over to his grandmother slowly, and from the front, so as not to startle her. Gram's peripheral vision seemed to have deteriorated the last few months.

Pops watched his wife with sad eyes, the cake on his plate untouched. Gram's plate was crumb-free. She picked at the Bundt-shaped cake and twisted out a small piece before popping it into her mouth and chewing enthusiastically.

"Mmmm. Tastes so good. Who made this?" she asked with a grin. "I love apples and cinnamon."

Thayne sent his grandfather a quizzical look.

"Hudson figured it out," Pops said with a smile. "Though your brother's first two tries ended up in the garbage."

"A heaping cup and a smidge aren't forms of measure," Thayne's older brother groused as he made his way from behind the long kitchen island.

He slowly made his way to Gram and knelt in front of her. "Do you like it, Gram?"

She nodded and shoved another piece into her mouth even though she hadn't finished the last. He kissed her forehead, and she frowned at him. "I'm not that kind of girl."

"Of course not. I would never presume. I know Pops is your one true love." Hudson walked over to the coffeepot. "Want a cup, Riley?"

"I could use it."

Riley sidestepped Thayne and practically raced over to her drug of choice.

Thayne frowned at his brother. "You didn't ask me?"

"You've been mooching since Riley's been gone," Hudson said. "Get it yourself."

"You boys shouldn't fight." Gram frowned. Her eyes narrowed when they landed on Thayne. "Lincoln, I don't like it when you fight with Cal Riverton. I told you I don't want to marry him. I want to marry you."

Thayne winced. He hadn't realized he looked so much like his grandfather. More often than not these days, she addressed him with Pops's name.

Pops reached out tentatively and patted his wife's hand. "Helen? Riley's back. You said you wanted to talk to her."

Gram used her left hand to pop another piece of cake in her mouth. She'd made an odd-shaped dent in the dessert. Her silverware went untouched more often than not these days.

The new behavior had just started. They'd all searched Gram's cookbook for finger food to avoid eating chicken strips and fries every night.

Riley took a sip of coffee and sat at the table next to Gram. Her patience with his grandmother was one of the things Thayne loved about her.

"Helen."

Gram blinked once, and her eyes cleared a bit. "Riley. You left and that grandson of mine didn't smile once." She clasped Riley's hand. "It's not good for him when you leave."

Riley's eyes widened. "I missed him, too."

"Good. I pined over Lincoln so much when he went off to war. And then when . . ." Her voice trailed off. "We thought he was dead."

She rose to her feet, her entire body fidgeting. Pops stood and let her walk into his arms. She clung to him. "Don't leave me, Lincoln. Something's wrong."

"We're going for a drive, Helen. Maybe down to the pond?" Pops gave them all a tired look.

"Our place." She grinned. "Can we play our song?"

He kissed her forehead. "Don't we always?"

"I need my jacket." She rubbed her hands up and down her arms.

"I'll get it, Gram." Hudson left the room and quickly returned with her favorite sweater. She wrapped it around her shoulders and started pacing around the room. Every time she passed the table, she nibbled once again at the cake.

"Sundowning," Pops mouthed and turned to Helen. "Let's go, my darling."

She linked her hand with his, and they headed out of the room. She paused and turned to Riley. "Someone needs your help. I gave her your number. Can't go to the sheriff, though. That wouldn't be good. Keep her secret, dear. It's important."

Riley placed her hand on Gram's arm. "Was it Kim Jordan, Helen? Is that who called you?"

"I don't know anyone by that name, dear." She glanced over at Thayne. "Take your girl dancing," she said. "Dancing makes all the troubles go away."

She began to hum "Could I Have This Dance" under her breath and put her head on Pops's shoulder. "Right, Lincoln?"

"Always, my love."

Pops led her out the door with one last pointed look at Thayne.

"He'll try to find out what she remembers," Thayne said, "but at least we know who Kim spoke with."

"Why would your grandmother give her my number?" Riley asked. "It doesn't make sense. How did she even get my number?"

"Gram doesn't live in our world these days," Hudson said with a sigh. "But your number's on the fridge." He pointed to the emergency list stuck to the refrigerator.

"Hudson's right." Thayne's gaze rested on the door his grandparents had just exited. "There's no way to know what she's thinking. Since none of us were in the room, we may never know exactly what happened."

"I understand she can't tell us," Riley said. "But what about the family? Do any of you recall Helen mentioning the Jordans? Did she know them?"

"Pops would've mentioned it, and if he doesn't know, I doubt it. They're joined at the hip. Always have been." Hudson grabbed a small bite of cake. "Not as good as Gram's. Maybe more apple." He covered the cake and stowed it on the bar. "I'm heading to the barn to check on Timber. He favored his left front leg after our ride this morning." He sent Riley a genuine smile. "Glad you're back. Do something with him, won't you?"

The door closed behind Hudson. Thayne studied Riley's rueful expression. "I think they like you more than me."

"That's not true and you know it."

Thayne poured himself a cup of coffee and sat down at the table, scooping up the crumbs his grandmother had left behind.

"Want something to eat?" he asked. "We have chicken strips, or maybe a sandwich?"

Riley shook her head. "Let's suppose for a moment Kim called Helen."

Thayne could see her mind working through the problem.

She leaned forward in her chair. "Why would Kim call your grandmother? If she was in trouble, why wouldn't she call the sheriff? You?"

They both knew the answer, but Thayne liked the idea of working the problem aloud. And together. "Living off the grid doesn't jibe with trust of law enforcement. In fact, they may very well be mutually exclusive."

"Exactly. And yet she calls the sheriff's grandmother for help." Riley gnawed her lower lip. "The logic doesn't follow."

"Desperation causes people to act irrationally. They take risks they wouldn't normally take."

"Kim Jordan was worried enough to try to get help from someone she doesn't even know." Riley rubbed her eyes. "If only she could tell us."

"I'm not sure Gram even knows. Sometimes she'll say something out of the blue like she knows it, and if you ask her a question thirty seconds later, it's gone. Like it's buried down in her memory and she can't find it. We can't count on her recollection. Half the time I don't know where her mind is or what era she's reliving." He shoved his hands through his hair. "We're supposed to try to be in *her* reality, not ours, because she can't be here. That can be frustrating sometimes."

Riley squeezed his hand. "I'm sorry. I know her illness breaks your heart. It breaks mine, too. For you, for everyone."

"She's getting worse," he said.

Riley placed her hand on his cheek. "I know. I'm only just getting to know her, but even I noticed in the last month she's stopped drawing in her book."

"Did you know Gram's the one who taught me to fly a crop duster? Pops sold the plane, but damn, I loved the freedom of flying that old girl." He met Riley's gaze. "I wish you'd known her then." He paused for a moment. "You handle Gram well. I know it can be uncomfortable. Not everyone can deal with someone who has dementia."

"I love your family. All of them."

"It will only get worse and tougher to cope with her illness." His shoulders tensed. "I can't guarantee lots of good times ahead."

"I don't expect perfection, Thayne. I never have." She refilled her coffee mug. She sipped and closed her eyes. "We have to move forward in the investigation as if Gram can't help. You know that."

"Play the voice mail again," Thayne said, his voice huskier than he'd have liked. "Maybe there's something we missed."

Riley tapped the phone to play the message.

"Umm," Kim's hesitant voice said through the speaker. "This message is for Riley Lambert. I got your name from . . . a good friend. I need to talk to you. You may be the only one who can help me."

"She's nervous. She paused at the end of each sentence. I halfway expected her to hang up before she finished," Thayne said.

"She needed my help, and I didn't get back to her soon enough." She shoved her fingers through her hair.

"You couldn't have known what would happen." Thayne frowned at her. "This isn't your fault."

"Every instinct is screaming that she and her husband should never have died. That I should've been more aware, taken a call from Singing River as seriously as I take calls from DC."

"We can't change the past. You know that better than anyone." Thayne took both her hands in his and stroked her palm. "But we can go forward from here. We can find out who killed the Jordans. You have more experience than I do evaluating murder suspects, but every course I've taken over the last several months says to look at home first."

He could see Riley grabbing on to the facts. His fiancée had a misplaced sense of accountability. Thayne understood. He used to feel that way, but his grandmother's illness had taught him that some things couldn't be fixed. Some things never worked out. Riley had to internalize her limitations. She could do only so much.

"National statistics indicate around eighty percent of murderers know their victim. Spouses, jilted lovers, coworkers, neighbors. A stranger being the murderer is much less common." Riley ticked off the facts.

"The Jordans hardly knew anyone in town, at least not very well. Ironcloud lives out there and would've called me if he'd found any reports of strange activity."

"They kept to themselves," Riley mused, the frown line between her eyes deepening. "That must have been hard for their daughter. She's at that age where kids rebel against their parents."

Thayne studied Riley's disturbed expression. "What are you thinking?"

Riley let out a long sigh. "I'm not suggesting anything yet, but Chloe is the sole survivor, and the closest relative to the victims. We have to consider whether she set the fire."

CHAPTER THREE

Twelve-year-old Chloe a murderer? Thayne had pulled her out of the panic room. She'd been so vulnerable. He didn't want to believe it, but he'd seen more than his share of depravity during his tours. He'd witnessed children brainwashed and willing to strap a bomb to their chest without considering who might be hurt or killed.

Mercy on a mission had resulted more than once in unacceptable death and destruction. Man could be the most uncivilized of animals.

The Blackwood living room went silent, save for the thrumming call of the sage grouse that inhabited the land around the ranch house.

Riley's gaze captured his, her jaw hard and her stance tense. She was waiting for his response. "Go ahead and say it. I know you want to. I'm overreacting. Overreaching in my assumptions."

He couldn't lie. He wanted to deny her observations, yet he couldn't.

"I don't want you to be right on this one," he said finally, "but I know you might be." He stood and made his way to the sliding glass door, searching the tall grass for the grouse as a distraction. His teeth ground together to fight back the frustration. "Why do you always think I'm going to disagree with you? How am I supposed to convince you to trust me?" he said, his voice soft. He loved her, damn it. He'd done everything in his power to show her that his love encompassed everything about her, including her abilities to uncover what criminals tried to hide. Was it too much to ask for her to have a little faith in him?

"I do—"

He faced her. "You don't. I can see it in your eyes. You believe I'll fight you on your conclusions, that I won't believe you."

Her shoulders tensed, and she lifted her chin. "I get that reaction all the time at work. I saw the look you gave me. You don't want to consider I'm right."

"This isn't about not believing you." Thayne shoved his hand through his hair. "I respect what you do, Riley. I've witnessed you do the impossible, but that doesn't mean I don't wish the young girl we've found is innocent. I don't want a murderer loose in Singing River putting the town, my family, and you in danger." He shoved his hands in his pockets. "I spent over a decade expecting every person I encountered who wasn't on my team to shoot me down or slit my throat. Do you know how difficult it is for me to trust people? But with you, it wasn't hard at all. I don't just love you—I trust you. The two go hand in hand. Maybe this isn't about me not trusting you. Maybe it's about you not trusting me."

Before she could respond, the door to the Blackwood house flew open. The echo of heavy footsteps pounded toward the kitchen.

Thayne's father entered the room and crossed his arms over his chest. "I've spent the last hour arguing with Dan. Again. He still refuses to visit the clinic, but I did have an early dinner with him and Kate last night. He refused to talk about the bruises in front of her, and she seemed like the caring—and sober—woman I've always known. I don't know what happened between them. We have to keep an eye on him, though."

Carson stalked past his son toward the long hallway leading to the bedroom. Being under the eye of the former sheriff—who was also his dad—meant no matter what Thayne did, he'd be measured.

Thayne rubbed his temple. "Great, just great."

Riley placed her hand on his arm. "Thayne—"

"Don't, Riley." He didn't want to push her away, but he couldn't trust himself not to say something he'd regret. All he wanted was to go home, grab a beer, and not think for the next twelve hours. "How about we don't talk any more tonight. I'll drive you to your car, and we can figure this out tomorrow. Maybe by then Pendergrass will come up with some forensic evidence from the fire that we can use."

Thayne didn't wait for an answer but walked toward the door. His heart hurt. He'd imagined when Riley had finally admitted she loved him that everything would work out fine. He'd been wrong.

Falling in love hadn't been easy. *Staying* in love was turning out to be a lot tougher than he'd expected.

The ringtone from his phone pierced the uncomfortable silence. He tapped the screen. "Sheriff Blackwood."

"This is dispatch. We've got a fight at Clive's Dance Hall and Saloon." Alicia sounded shaken. "It's those oil workers again. Clive said they're tearing the place up."

"On my way," Thayne said. "Have Deputy Ironcloud meet me there if he can."

He ended the call and snatched his keys before heading out the door. So much for a quiet evening.

"I'm coming with you." Riley had already zipped up her coat. "You'll need someone to watch your six."

She wasn't wrong. Plus, she was a damn good shot and a hell of a fighter. Just another thing he loved about her.

"Let's go."

They jumped into his official vehicle, and he sped down the road. The saloon was about five miles outside the city limits, a leftover from the Prohibition days. Unfortunately, the Blackwood Ranch was a solid fifteen minutes in the opposite direction.

He flipped on the siren and picked up the phone and tapped his father's number.

"What happened?" Carson said.

"Bar fight. I'll be back later." Thayne let him know where Pops and Gram were. "Dad, I'm sorry about today."

His father sighed. "It's my fault. That damn virus forced me to retire too soon, and I don't like it. You shouldn't have had to leave your career in the SEALs for me."

"I separated for a lot of reasons, Dad."

"You did it a lot sooner than you planned. Just like me."

Thayne couldn't deny the words. He shot Riley a quick glance. If his father hadn't been ill, would he and Riley have ever taken a chance on their relationship? He would've liked to think so, but right now he wasn't sure. Maybe they'd still be talking on the phone every week. Truth was, he missed their Friday-night phone dates.

The past didn't matter now. Only the present. And the future. "How about we work something out? Maybe make you a consultant?"

"You don't have the budget," Carson said with a huff. "I ought to know."

"I figured you'd work for free."

Riley turned to him and lifted an eyebrow.

"You buy me lunch every day and I'll think about it."

"Deal. Dan Peterson is your first case. He helped us find Chloe Jordan today. I owe him. Convince him to get that bruise checked out at Cheyenne's clinic, and see if you can't figure out what's bugging him."

"I'm telling you it's all right between Dan and Kate, but if that's what it takes, I'll do it."

Thayne ended the call and set down the phone.

"Well played." Riley opened her bag and checked her Glock. "Everyone needs to feel needed."

"I should've thought of it the day after he retired," Thayne muttered with a frown.

"Probably."

He chuckled. "You don't give an inch, do you?"

"Neither do you." Riley twisted in her seat. "If you haven't noticed, being in a relationship is new territory for me."

"I get that. I really do." Thayne turned down the highway. "Do you sometimes feel like you've gone down the rabbit hole into a place you never thought you'd be?"

"Oh yeah. Be patient with me, Thayne. I'll figure it out."

Thayne smiled at her. "How about we figure it out together?"

"That sounds perfect."

He pulled into the saloon parking lot. Along with the slew of pickups he recognized, several oil company vehicles lined the rustic building. "Used to be I'd know everyone in the place. Those oil workers bring in a lot of money, but they've changed the town. Pinedale's got it worse, of course. We get the spillover."

Riley slid the gun into her shoulder holster and slipped on her jacket.

A crash sounded from inside Clive's.

"Damn it." Thayne grabbed a shotgun from the back seat, rushed inside, and skidded to a halt. The country band had hunkered down in the corner. A few folks stood at the bar, but it was a free-for-all.

Thayne let out an ear-piercing whistle that splintered the shouts.

Everyone looked up, except one idiot, who'd slammed a wooden chair across Clive's back.

◆ ◆ ◆

Riley's ears rang at the high-pitched whistle, and the entire bar gasped. Thayne definitely knew how to make an entrance. His jaw had tightened, and Riley recognized the cold fury on his face. She wouldn't want to be one of the brawlers.

"That's it," he snapped. "Fun's over. Everyone stand up and keep still. If you move, I'll pepper you with salt," he said, patting his gun, his voice firm and inscrutable. "I don't miss, and it'll hurt like hell."

They took him at his word, because not a soul tried to make a run for it. Thayne glanced at Riley and nodded away from the crowd. She positioned herself near the bar, where she had a good view.

Thayne strode down the middle of the dance floor, the heels of his boots crunching on the peanut shells. He turned to his left. "Move toward the wall and place your hands where I can see them."

The sea of bodies followed his orders until the center of the room was empty. A few women sniffed, but they followed instructions.

Thayne hurried over to the crumpled heap in the middle of the floor. He grabbed Clive's arm. "You okay?"

With help, the older man rose to his feet and groaned. "I've been better."

"Who can I send home?" Thayne asked.

"The band, the women. Those oil workers started the whole thing." Clive pointed out the troublemakers.

In short order and with a stern warning, Thayne emptied the saloon until he faced four of the newcomers and a couple of ranch hands from Brett Riverton's place. His brother-in-law wouldn't be happy.

"Keep an eye on them," Thayne ordered Riley, "while I find transportation. The jail's gonna be full tonight."

He placed the cell phone to his ear and spoke softly while Riley stared down the group, their cut faces, swollen jaws, and torn clothes clear enough evidence of what had happened.

A rustling sound came from behind the bar. Apparently, someone was trying to dodge a night in jail. Riley didn't like the feeling of her back being at risk of an attack.

"Don't move," she warned the men. "The sheriff's nicer than I am. I don't have salt in my Glock. I use real bullets."

Not shifting her focus from the rough-looking group, she backed toward the bar and peered behind it. Carol Wallace crouched low, her hand gripping a bottle of tequila. Her bloodshot eyes looked too familiar.

All the tension melted away. "Oh, Carol."

Riley couldn't help but feel sorry for the woman. She hadn't caught a break in decades. A bad relationship. A volatile addiction to alcohol and a daughter who had gone missing only to be found years later and sent to jail for murder.

The men shifted, a couple eyeing the door.

Riley shifted her jacket back to reveal her holster. "Don't even think about running."

"What the hell is going on here?" A tall man burst in the room. "Sheriff, what have you done to my men?"

"Nothing, Mr. Decker. Your employees decided they'd do a little reorganizing of Clive's place, and he's pressing charges."

The man frowned at the men, who immediately looked away. "I see." He smiled at Thayne, one of those smarmy smiles when a man believes he's got the upper hand. He didn't know Thayne very well.

"Now, Sheriff. Maybe we can come to some sort of agreement." Decker opened up his wallet and pulled out a stack of bills. "I'm sure this will take care of the damages, and then we can call it even."

Thayne crossed his arms. "I don't take bribes."

Clive tapped Thayne's shoulder and leaned forward. Riley couldn't make out what he was whispering in Thayne's ear.

Thayne frowned but gave Clive a quick nod. "Seems like Clive's willing to do you a favor for cash. Your men spend one night in jail to sleep it off, you pay Clive damages, and we'll call it lessons learned. No insurance involved."

Decker's grin widened. "Now you're talking sensible. It's a deal."

He stuck out his hand, but Thayne ignored the gesture.

Riley hid a smile. Thayne had his own set of rules, rules he didn't compromise.

"I'm not finished. I don't want to see any of your men in Clive's place again. You understand me, Decker? I won't be so forgiving next time."

A familiar law enforcement siren sounded toward the building. The men grew restless, and one of them shifted back and forth. "I'm not spending the night in jail," he whispered, though not very quietly. He bolted toward the exit.

What a drunken idiot. She sidestepped him and, with a quick move, twisted his arm. His momentum landed him on his back. He whimpered, complaining she'd busted his arm, and when he tried to get up, she planted her foot on his chest and quirked a smile at Thayne. "I thought Wyoming men were tough."

Thayne grinned at her. During moments like this, she could almost read his mind.

Decker let out an exasperated sigh and kneaded the back of his neck. "Earnhardt, you're an idiot. You just won a week without pay. Now stop your whining, get up, and do your time, or I'll find someone to replace you."

Riley studied the boss. He'd surprised her. It was refreshing to see someone hold people accountable for their actions.

Thayne folded his arms across his chest. "You're not offering a little more green to sweeten the pot?"

Decker shook his head. "I don't make the same mistake twice, Sheriff. I've got a quota, and if these guys end up in jail for more than a night, I could lose my job, but there's only so far I'll go. Earnhardt crosses too many lines for my taste. He could use a little extra rehabilitation from where I'm sitting."

"At least he'll dry out," Thayne said.

Earnhardt groaned and stumbled to his feet just as Deputy Ironcloud walked into the room.

"You brought the van?" Thayne asked.

Ironcloud nodded, and within minutes the three of them had fastened zip ties around the men's wrists.

Thayne paused. "Decker, you want to ride with your men?"

"Hell no. But I do appreciate your understanding." He stuck out his hand once more. This time Thayne took it. "I'll be by in the morning—hopefully to pick up a crew who are a little more sober and a whole lot wiser."

Decker sauntered out the door, and Ironcloud watched their prisoners.

Thayne crossed to Riley. He stood so close she could feel the heat emanating from him. "I'll go with Ironcloud. Can you take my car and meet me at the sheriff's office?"

She placed her hand on his chest and nodded, but her glance rested on the pitiable woman behind the bar. "I might be a few minutes. Carol's here and she's not looking good. I need to make certain she gets home."

"You sure you want to take her on?" Thayne sighed and met her gaze. "She's not your responsibility. She couldn't stay sober even before she discovered how broken her daughter became," he said quietly.

"I know, but I could have *been* her if I'd let the guilt of not protecting my sister take me over. When I see her like this . . ." She didn't mention how the years she'd spent obsessed with Madison's case had been her own type of addiction. They both knew.

"Okay. I'll see you soon." Thayne dropped the keys in her hand and bent to kiss her. His lips lingered on hers until he finally raised his head, his gaze dark and full of promise.

Riley shivered, her body tingling with response. Thayne made her feel things she'd thought she'd never feel. She kept waiting for the first flush to dissipate, but it didn't. His eyes glinted with a secret laughter as if he knew what she was thinking. With one last heated gaze, he joined Ironcloud.

After the van headed to Singing River, Riley returned inside. While Clive swept the floor, she hunkered down behind the bar next to Carol.

The woman hadn't moved, but the tequila bottle had drained several inches.

Riley didn't speak for a moment, but when it became clear Carol wasn't interested in a conversation, Riley shifted to face her. "It wasn't your fault, Carol. It took me a long time to accept that I wasn't to blame. And neither are you."

"We both know you're lying." Carol tilted the bottle and took a long, slow swallow. "I twisted my daughter up so bad she'll never get out of jail. What kind of mother does that make me?"

"We both know the man who kidnapped her was responsible. He took her from your house in the middle of the night. *He* messed her up."

Carol lifted her bleary gaze to Riley's. "Why don't you blame me for what my girl did?"

With a sigh, Riley set the bottle aside and took Carol's hands in hers. "Because I spent fifteen years blaming myself for not alerting my parents when my sister was taken."

"You still do, though," Carol said, "don't you?"

Riley couldn't tell many people the truth. She squeezed Carol's hands. "Deep inside, every time I solve a case, I hope I evened the score just a little."

"You're stronger than I am." Carol stared, almost mesmerized by the nearly empty tequila bottle. "Whatever fight I had died out years ago. I can't even bear to visit my daughter in jail." She lifted the bottle and tilted her head back to take another drink. "No use trying to win this one, Agent Lambert. I'm a lost cause."

Riley hated that Carol's words might be true—some people couldn't be saved. "Clive's closing down. Can I take you home?"

The woman blinked, eyes unfocused, her face sallow and unhealthy. She chuckled, the kind of hollow laugh that reeked of despair. "I *am* home. Clive lets me stay in the room above the bar. Even that drunk Ed kicked me out of our house. After twenty years together. Can you believe the drunk SOB did that?"

"I'm sorry." Riley couldn't stop the wave of regret twisting her heart. When Riley's sister had been kidnapped, it had destroyed her life, and her family. Riley could picture her father or her, or even her mother, drowning their sorrows so easily.

Honestly, she wasn't quite sure how they'd avoided it.

Heavy footsteps shuffled behind them, and Riley turned to see Clive pressing an ice pack against the back of his neck.

"I'll take care of Carol," he said. "I've gotten used to it."

Clive clasped Carol's arm, and Riley stood. Carol sagged against Clive and closed her eyes.

Riley bit her lip in concern. "Is there anything I can do?"

The saloon owner shook his head. "Until she wants to change, no one can help, I'm sorry to say."

"Me too."

Clive helped Carol to the stairs, and Riley closed the door to the bar. Bright pinpoints of starlight covered the black canvas of sky. Whenever Riley saw Carol, the truth roared through her ears: The past never lets go. It can't be vanquished. No matter how hard you fight.

She traveled the five minutes back to Singing River, lingering memories—and nightmares—coalescing in the recesses of her mind.

The streets of Singing River were deserted, not providing her with a distraction, either. Something else she missed about DC. The noise and bustle of a city could clog up the mind and make it easier to push away unwanted thoughts and feelings.

She pulled Thayne's car in front of the sheriff's office. Every instinct screamed at her to dive into the Jordan case. Until Chloe woke up, Riley would have to dig into their lives to pull together a list of suspects.

She found herself ticking through a list of tasks: Review the fire marshal's report and the forensic evidence. Walk the crime scene again. Go through any papers in the Jordans' panic room, not that she'd seen anything.

She had yet to investigate a perfect murder. Everyone made mistakes. Her job would be to find this killer's vulnerability.

Riley gripped the steering wheel, stopping herself. This wasn't her job. She wasn't Special Agent Riley Lambert anymore. She had no authority. Not here. Or anywhere. Even if Thayne requested her help, her boss would have to reinstate her to assign her the job, and it really wasn't an FBI case.

So here she was, face-to-face with the same dilemma that had driven her back to DC in the first place. She'd never be happy with the crumbs Thayne could hand her. Tonight had been a rush. A much-needed one, but how often could he call on her to help? She knew the answer to that without having to do an extensive analysis. Singing River barely needed a sheriff—let alone a deputized civilian. Her uncertainty overwhelmed her. Being with Thayne had temporarily driven the reality away. No longer.

Debating whether to go inside, she tapped the steering wheel with indecision. She could walk back to her car and just go to her room. Except Thayne would follow her.

As if he could read her mind, Thayne walked out the front door, removed his Stetson, and slid into the passenger side. "You planning to sleep out here?"

"Everyone okay?" she asked.

"Complaining but settled." He drummed his fingers on the rim. "It's odd. Until the last year or so, Dad rarely locked up anyone he didn't know. Pops experienced the same when he was sheriff. I'm third generation, and tonight I arrested eight people. Only two live here. I'm not convinced this change is good for Singing River. I spoke with the Pinedale sheriff last week. He said their population has doubled.

There might be a few additional shops and more money circulating, but houses are twice as much, crime's up, and too many strangers are passing through."

"You expected Singing River to stay stagnant?" Riley didn't put the SUV into gear.

"It didn't change the first eighteen years I lived here. Of course, I never expected to come back so soon, either." He turned in the seat to face her and grimaced. "I'd planned something completely different for the night you came home."

"Me too." She bowed her head. "Look, I don't know what to say—"

"How about we don't talk at all?" Thayne cupped her neck and pulled her into his arms. His lips pressed against hers, insistent, passionate, a reminder of what she'd missed from the day she'd left.

Her heart thudded against her chest, and her legs quivered as he explored her mouth in a kiss that held so much promise. When he lifted his head, his own body trembled. "Welcome home."

She touched his cheek. He made her feel things she'd never believed possible. Why was this so hard?

"Are you going to see Chloe in the morning?"

He pulled back from her, and his expression grew thoughtful. "If I were the kind of man who wanted to delude myself, I'd say you'd be happy to spend the next seventy-two hours with me, alone, but after three nights apart, you seem more interested in burying yourself in the Jordan investigation than in spending the night with me."

"I love you—"

"Damn, I hate that you started your sentence with those three words," he muttered. "You want to go back to DC."

"Yes." She twisted her hands in her lap. She'd finally admitted it to herself. And to him. But it wasn't the end of everything. Thayne could come with her. Being a sheriff had never been his dream. He'd already admitted that.

"It's not what I wanted to hear," he said quietly, "but I figured. When are you leaving?"

Hearing him say it aloud hurt.

"Part of me would give anything to stay here with you, but I can't. I don't fit." She clutched at his arm. "Why can't this be a movie or a book where love conquers all obstacles?"

Thayne snapped on his seat belt. "Because real life is messy. And complicated." He glanced down Main Street, frowning. "Your car's at the hospital."

He sat rigidly beside her, not looking her way. She needed to know what he was thinking, but she didn't dare ask. They rode in silence the short distance to the hospital. Her car sat with three others in the parking lot. "I think I'll check on Chloe while we're here," she said before she opened the driver's side door.

"As a witness or a suspect?" he asked, stopping her from leaving.

"Neither. I'm not on this case. We both know that." Riley snapped the words. The fatigue had to be getting to her. She was taking her own misery out on Thayne, and he didn't deserve it.

She got out, and as she closed her door, Thayne met her on her side. "The hell you aren't."

Her gaze shot up to his. A sudden sadness radiated from her core, heating her skin. "Don't make this harder, Thayne. You know I can't stay."

"Life's messy, complicated, and it's *hard*. You're the one who identified this case as a murder investigation. You're damn well going to see it through. I'm not holding water on your theory by myself. Not when the fire marshal starts justifying his report to keep his job."

He was trying to find a reason for her to remain in Singing River. "It won't work. I don't have an official capacity here."

"DC drove you to a bad place. We both know that," he challenged and let out a low curse. "You can't leave yet. We still have a lot to talk about. Call yourself a consultant, and my office will hire you."

She paused for a moment and looked up at him, thunderstruck. "You're serious?"

"It's a line item in the budget I added this fiscal year."

"A consultant." She chewed it over. She didn't want to leave, not like this. He was right. There was too much left unsaid between them. Too much to still do. Her mouth tilted up. "I like it, but you know it won't solve the long-term problem."

"It'll give us time." Thayne opened his door and headed toward the hospital entrance. "Do we have an agreement?"

"Deal." Riley grabbed her bag and walked into the hospital beside him.

"Hi, Sheriff, Agent Lambert," the attendant seated at the emergency room desk greeted them both. "You here to see that poor girl? She's not awake yet, but Dr. Blackwood-Riverton is down the hall."

Thayne smiled at the woman and bent down to whisper something that made her chuckle, before heading toward Chloe's room.

"She's got a crush on you," Riley said. "All the women in town do."

"Too bad my charm doesn't hypnotize you." He glanced down the deserted hallway and lowered his voice. "After you left for DC, I missed you."

She started to speak, but he held up his hand. "No, let me finish." He shifted from one foot to the other. "While you were gone, I started wondering about living here permanently. I never pictured myself as the Singing River sheriff. Part of me thought I might retire here after another ten in the Navy, after I commanded a SEAL team."

His words, so very like her own feelings, stunned her. "But you didn't hesitate to quit. I assumed you were sure. That you had no doubts."

"I didn't. I was committed to making our relationship work, and my family needs me. They still do."

"You do have doubts, though," she insisted.

"Yeah. Then today, Dan Peterson, my father's longtime friend, came to me for help. Then Aaron and Kim Jordan were killed, and now Chloe's down the hall, in danger. I realized something, Riley. Somewhere in the last few months they became *my* people. *My* responsibility."

Riley's stomach fell as she realized what his words meant. "What exactly are you saying?"

"This might not be the most exciting job ever, but my heart's taken root in this town."

Riley stilled at the unspoken truth behind his words.

He turned to her and clasped her hands in his. "I believe you love me, but you were born to see what others don't in a crime scene. You proved that in DC. You proved it today. Your past formed you into someone the FBI—and those victims—can't live without. But today I realized that while you may not belong in Singing River . . ." He sucked in a deep breath. "I do."

CHAPTER FOUR

Thayne belonged here.

Parked in front of Fannie's Bed and Breakfast, Riley watched the taillights from his SUV disappear in the distance. A wave of loneliness urged her to go after him, but he hadn't asked to stay the night, and she hadn't invited him.

Her mind still couldn't process Thayne's words. She didn't know what she'd expected after she'd admitted her desire to go back to DC, but down deep, she'd thought he'd go with her. She felt as if the earth had tilted on its axis.

She glanced at the welcoming light on the front porch of Fannie's B&B. It had been Riley's home from the time she'd arrived in Singing River a month ago. Fannie had even held the room while she'd traveled to DC. The woman's Southern hospitality, not to mention her famous cinnamon rolls and to-die-for coffee, had seduced Riley almost as easily as Thayne had. She'd known she couldn't afford to stay here much longer, not without a job, but she'd resisted moving out to the Blackwood Ranch. She loved Thayne's family, but sometimes she simply needed an escape.

She definitely needed one tonight.

The thing she'd always found disconcerting about her relationship with Thayne was his innate ability to understand her, and not on a superficial level—he *got* her, from deep within. She'd been broken when she arrived in Singing River, inches away from burning out. Thayne and this place had healed her.

It had given her the strength to return to the job she loved. Did he really believe she belonged here?

Trouble was, everything Thayne had said to her tonight had been simmering in the back of her mind. Damn him.

She rounded the car, opened the back door, and stilled. She stiffened her back and studied the position of her suitcase and computer bag. Had they been moved? She shook her head. This was ridiculous. She'd thrown them into the back seat right after the plane had landed at the Singing River Municipal Airport. They would've landed cockeyed.

"You've lost it, Riley. You need a cinnamon roll, some of Fannie's coffee, and sleep—and in that order."

Bags in hand, she trudged up the steps to the Victorian-style home and slipped her key into the lock. She entered the foyer. A low light shone from the dining table. A tray of cinnamon rolls and coffee waited for her.

Thank goodness one thing had remained the same while she'd been gone. Riley snagged the huge, ooey-gooey roll and filled a small carafe from the coffeepot. Before she even trudged up the stairs, she took in a whiff of whatever crazy blend Fannie ground. When she left, she'd have to find a way for Fannie to send her some.

Leave. The idea hurt Riley's heart, and she shoved it aside. She wasn't going anywhere until she figured out what had happened to Kim and Aaron Jordan. She'd made a commitment.

Balancing her bags in one hand, with the carafe tucked under her arm and the cinnamon roll in the other hand, she wasn't exactly graceful, but Riley managed to climb the stairs to her room. She set down her bags and fumbled for the room key.

She pushed inside and then froze. Her gaze swept the room. The rumpled bedspread was her first clue something was very wrong. Fannie would never allow a bed to look like that. A partially eaten roll waited on the small table. This was her room. Fannie wouldn't have offered it to someone else. All her things were still tucked into the nooks and crannies.

Careful not to make any noise, Riley unloaded everything in her arms and in a practiced move pulled her Glock from its holster. There was nowhere to hide in the small room, save two places. Gun in hand, she searched beneath the bed. Empty and creepily clean and free of dust bunnies.

One place left to look.

She eased to the bathroom and glanced under the door. A light peeked through the crack. Ever so slowly she gripped the handle. With a deep breath, she threw open the door.

A loud shriek echoed through the room. At her sister's shout, Riley's heart beat again. She lowered her weapon. "Maddy, what are you doing here?"

Her sister clutched her chest and fell back against the vanity. "Oh my God, Riley, you scared me."

"*I* scared *you*? You nearly gave me a heart attack."

"Is everything okay up there?" Fannie's voice carried into the room. "Madison?"

Riley stuck her head out the door. "I was just surprised to see my sister. Sorry."

"Welcome back, dear." Her seventy-five-year-old landlady frowned, wrapping the flowing dressing gown tighter around her body. "I assumed you knew she was coming."

"It's fine. Sorry to bother you."

"I want to hear all about your trip at breakfast in the morning," Fannie said with a smile. "Right now, I have to finish up my skin routine."

Riley shook her head in bemusement as the former beauty queen disappeared into her quarters downstairs. She should probably get a few lessons from Fannie. Her landlady's skin could pass for early sixties most of the time.

She closed the door and locked it. Madison was on her knees, trying to rescue Riley's midnight snack and the coffee carafe.

"You're lucky Fannie likes spill-proof pitchers," Madison said.

"I can't believe you're here." Riley hugged her sister tight. "You don't know how glad I am to see you."

Madison gripped her so hard that Riley could barely breathe. After several moments, Riley pulled back and studied the woman who had been missing from her life since she was ten. Madison had been only twelve when she'd been kidnapped. Riley still couldn't quite comprehend that after all these years Madison was in front of her, alive and surprisingly well.

"Let me put this stuff away, and then you can spill the beans." Riley placed her computer on the desk and removed her jacket and holster before stowing her weapon in the bedside table.

She tilted her head and studied her sister carefully. Madison hadn't changed much since leaving Singing River. Her auburn hair had been styled, probably at their mother's salon. She looked good except for the faint lines of stress around her eyes.

"I didn't expect to see you back so soon."

"Me, either." Madison grimaced. She sat on the bed and crossed her legs. "Portland is too big, too noisy, just too much. I couldn't think, couldn't sleep. And . . ." Her sister studied her nails.

"Mom?" Riley asked sympathetically.

Madison slumped. "She's nuts, Riley. She really is. She thinks I'm still twelve years old. It's like time stopped the day I left. My bedroom is exactly like it was when I disappeared, including the posters on the wall, the books on the bookcases. I didn't know Destiny's Child wasn't still a group or that there were seven Harry Potter books. I read them all while I was home."

"I guess time did stop for Mom. Her world revolved around you, and where you might be."

"I understand. Really, I do. I feel sorry for her." Madison shook her head. "But seriously, how did you end up so . . . normal?"

Riley fell into her chair and laughed. "You're the only person on the planet that would think of me as normal, Maddy. Seriously, you were only gone two weeks."

Madison crawled across the bed and grabbed her half-eaten cinnamon roll from the table. She used her finger to swirl a glob of frosting and stuck it in her mouth. "Mmm. That's so good." She picked at the snack. "I know she wants me to stay, to move in, but everything was so awkward. I tried looking up a couple of friends. Some I couldn't find at all. The few I did find had moved away years ago and are now married. Some even have kids. Every conversation was so awkward. They didn't know what to say, and neither did I. It feels like everyone grew up without me. I finally quit trying. The past is gone, you know."

Riley joined her sister on the bed and hugged her. "I'm sorry going home wasn't what you'd hoped."

"Poor Mom. She's so clingy. She won't let me out of her sight. She checks on me half a dozen times in the middle of the night. Dad doesn't know what to do, either. They barely talk to each other. I'm not exactly sure how their relationship has lasted, but if I ever find someone to love, it's not going to be like that."

Riley didn't know what to say. Madison didn't need to hear the rehash of a decade and a half's worth of family drama. "Families handle trauma differently. Ours was—"

"Dysfunctional?"

Riley's jaw dropped open, and she let out a long laugh. "Oh yeah."

Her stress and uncertainty fell away as her sister regaled her with tales of discovering what had been going on in the world. She'd missed a lot while the man who had kidnapped her—along with so many others—held her in his compound. Freedom was complicated.

Madison popped the last bite of her cinnamon roll in her mouth. "This has been the best day I've had since you found me. Do you think we could stay in this room forever and forget about the outside world?"

"I wish we could." She touched her sister's hand. "Why did you really come back, Maddy?"

Her sister didn't speak for a moment. She stared at their hands. "You're the only person I can talk to, Ri. I was so alone. All those people in Portland, and I had no one."

Madison's eyes teared up. "I'm not allowed to contact the kids from the compound. Their parents don't want me to. They're trying to move on, and I get that. I'm almost thirty, and I've never had a boyfriend, never been in a relationship."

"What about Bobby Frost?"

Madison's jaw dropped. "You knew about him?"

"He was your first crush. When I started investigating you, I found out. He was my prime suspect, until I realized he wasn't the sharpest pencil in the pack."

Madison's eyes brightened. "You never stopped looking for me, did you?"

Riley shook her head. "It's why I came to Singing River in the first place. Your trail led here."

"So you found love with Thayne because I was abducted. There's something twisted about that."

"Yeah." Though she wanted to talk to her sister about Thayne, she felt vulnerable where he was concerned. Maddy had so much to deal with already. Adding to the pile felt wrong.

Riley's phone rang. She glanced at the screen. "It's Mom. Please tell me you didn't leave without saying goodbye."

"I left a note." Madison's cajoling voice caused Riley to shake her head.

"Not cool, Maddy." Riley tapped the speakerphone icon. "Hi, Mom. Madison's here with me and she's safe."

"Oh, thank God." Her mother breathed hard into the phone. "It was like before. She wasn't here, I . . ."

"I left a note," Madison repeated, but this time at least she had the grace to show some guilt.

"It could've been faked," their mother argued.

"I know. I'm sorry, Mom. It was all . . . too much."

"What are you talking about? This is your home."

Madison pinched the bridge of her nose and mouthed a desperate plea to Riley. *Please.*

"Mom, Madison's going to stay with me for a few days. The traffic, the people—she needs it to be quiet."

"Our house is quiet. She needs time with her family, not to be in some town in the middle of nowhere with a bunch of strangers."

Riley gripped the bedspread. "I'm her family, too, Mom."

"And I'm her mother. I'll send money for a plane ticket. Madison, you need to come home. You need care and treatment and—"

"Shut up, Adrienne." Their father's voice came through the speakerphone loud and clear. "You girls take care of each other. Call us every few days, though." He let out an audible sigh. "We miss you."

"Thanks, Daddy," Madison choked out. "I love you."

"Love you, too, sweetie."

Riley ended the call and met Madison's gaze. "That was really bad of you."

"I didn't think. I just needed to get out of there." She covered her face with her hands. "What's wrong with me? I can't seem to make the right choices. It's like I'm disconnected from everything."

"I know Mom's a lot to handle, but when you disappeared, it nearly killed her." Their mother's life had narrowed in an unhealthy way when Madison was taken, but that wasn't her sister's fault.

"Do you want me to go back? Because I'm not sure I can survive her right now," Madison said. "It's like she really is from another planet. I just can't relate. Not yet. It's too much."

"Stay with me." Riley hugged her sister and yawned. "How about I get into my pajamas and we have an old-fashioned slumber party. We could talk until dawn?"

"Slumber party." Madison's eyes flew open. "Oh my gosh, right before I was taken, you were supposed to come to my slumber party. I disinvited you." She grimaced. "I'm sorry, Ri. I was a real jerk when I was twelve."

"And I was a pest. The good news is we get a do-over. Tonight."

"Can I pilfer more cinnamon rolls?" Madison asked.

"Fannie would be insulted if you didn't."

◆ ◆ ◆

The house had burned to the ground, turning every lying memory into ashes. *Kim* hadn't deserved mercy. She'd done what most women do when the going gets tough: run out on their marriage.

He should have known better. He should've learned his lesson when his mother ran out on him and his father.

Women couldn't be trusted. They pretended to love you, and then they just walked away with your heart and turned your kids against you.

Payment for the crime of abandonment had been served.

He longed to walk through the remnants and take in the scents, the destruction. The ashes he'd made of their fake life.

He'd cleansed them of their sins. He took in a deep, long breath. Now he had to finish what he'd started.

The rumble of a motor sent him back into hiding, crouched behind a row of trees.

A beat-up truck stopped in front of the house.

He ground his teeth together until they ached. This was *his* time. He needed to say goodbye.

A familiar-looking gray-headed man opened the door, then closed it. One glance into the research notebook he always carried and he had the name: Dan. Handyman.

Dan walked into the old house and bent down in the middle of the former living room. He grunted and lifted a metal door and peered down.

So that's where they must have found Chloe, why she hadn't died along with her mother and the man pretending to be her father.

The nosy old man disappeared beneath the earth.

A flutter of fear settled across his shoulders. He stood and stared. Surely this man hadn't seen him. He'd been careful. So very careful.

There was only one rule he knew he had to follow. He couldn't get caught. No one could ever know what he'd done. At that moment the man poked his head from the underground room.

Their gazes met.

The old man's eyes widened.

In recognition?

He couldn't be certain, but it didn't matter. Another loose end to tie up.

Because of a woman's deceit, he'd have to kill again.

◆ ◆ ◆

The rays of early dawn crept through the slatted blinds of Thayne's office, where he sat in forlorn silence behind his desk. He'd been unable to sleep all night. He was an idiot, giving Riley every reason to turn her back on him and this town.

He was fairly confident he could try seducing her into staying. They created Fourth of July–level fireworks between the sheets. Despite popular opinion, passion *could* last a lifetime—he was a firsthand witness—but fire didn't see you through the hard times. Love, commitment, and trust did. His pops and gram had taught him that lesson, especially over the last couple of years.

Riley might stay, but if she grew to resent him, he couldn't live with that, so instead of rolling an uncertain future around in his mind, he'd escaped his lonely bed and retreated to a deserted sheriff's office.

The only other business open this early happened to be the hospital. Chloe hadn't awakened yet, which was starting to worry Cheyenne. He'd heard it in her voice. He'd have to contact the fire inspector and let him know he planned to investigate further. He trusted Riley's instincts. He always would.

The bell on the front door jingled. Only bad news arrived this early in the morning. His whole body tensed for what was to come.

Riley walked into the room. He shouldn't have been surprised. His heart thudded against his chest at the sight of her, his usual reaction, but today something else rushed through his blood. Nerves. Was she here to tell him goodbye after what he'd said yesterday?

She paused at his door and knocked. Not a good sign.

"Hi."

The awkward greeting caused Thayne's insides to knot.

"You ready to start your new job?" He rushed through the words. "There's no real office space, but you can use the conference room."

She stilled, and a slow smile lightened her eyes. "We make a good team," she said, cautiously. "But it doesn't change my methods or how I work."

He raised his hands. "Don't worry. I know you'll need to use the wall of your room at the B and B as a murder board. I won't interfere. Much."

She tilted her head and arched a brow.

Thayne met her gaze squarely. He refused to lie. "I'm not as certain as you are, but I trust your instincts. Besides, Kim, Aaron, and Chloe deserve the truth."

"No matter what seemingly crazy places it takes me?" she asked, pressing the issue.

"I'll accept whatever you can give me. We need to know what happened. I'm committed to justice for them."

Her entire body relaxed. "That's all I can ask."

"You look like you could use a hug." He stood, unsure but hopeful they might be able to work things out. "I wouldn't be opposed to giving one."

She flung herself into his arms, and he pressed her close. She felt so right in his arms, yet he hadn't been wrong yesterday. Riley had to decide what she wanted her future to be, and he couldn't turn his back on his family. If she couldn't stay in Singing River . . .

Damn, he didn't want to consider the future without Riley.

He forced his expression calm and collected and pulled back from her. "I suppose you want to start with photos of the crime scene for your wall?" He slipped a memory card into his laptop and turned it around so she could see the images.

"Yeah." She paused. "I should tell you Madison came back last night."

"Your parents went overboard?" Thayne had seen them in action. He understood how damaged they were.

"They drove her crazy."

"They would me. How long is she staying?"

"I didn't ask. As long as she needs to be here, I guess. Fannie's putting her up at the B and B in the room next to mine." Riley leaned forward in her chair. "She's a bit lost. She wants to be normal, and I don't know how to help her transition. Fifteen years is a lot to lose."

"Give her time. It's only been a month since she escaped. She can't just expect to start living again after being held virtually a prisoner for so long. Even if she wasn't chained up, she was still a captive." He paused. "Do you think she would speak with a professional to get some help?"

Riley wrinkled her nose in skepticism. "I don't know. Mom forced her to visit a therapist the day after she flew to Portland. It didn't go well."

"Her entire world was controlled for fifteen years. I'm no expert, but the psychological impact of confinement is real. The military has created a series of training exercises and treatments on dealing with captivity."

"I'd have to do a lot of convincing, but I agree with you. She needs someone who can help her with coping strategies. She's putting on a good front. I haven't seen her break, and I'm afraid she will."

Thayne had seen more than one soldier fight a psych battle and lose. It wasn't a conflict he'd want to fight alone. "Would she talk to Cheyenne? She knows a therapist in Jackson Hole."

The tension on Riley's face relaxed. "Cheyenne saved Madison's life. She's the one person my sister might actually listen to." Riley hugged him again. "Thank you. If I didn't have you, I don't know what I'd do."

And that was the big question: What would either of them do without the other?

◆ ◆ ◆

Riley hovered near the printer in the sheriff's office. The machine spewed out the final sheet of photos. Riley pulled out each image and scanned it for details with hungry eyes. She'd feel more centered when she tacked them all to the wall in her room and organized them according to patterns.

Deputy Quinn Pendergrass strode into the building with two file boxes. He nodded at her in greeting. She picked up the folder to meet him in the small conference room where Thayne waited.

He placed the boxes on the table. "Ironcloud's still interviewing anyone who might have come into contact with the Jordans. I have his notes so far, but it's nothing we didn't know. They were pretty much living off the grid. Most of the townsfolk thought they were standoffish and odd. Chloe didn't have any friends that we've found so far."

"A twelve-year-old girl and no one knew her?" Riley could barely fathom the reality of Chloe's life. Would the isolation have caused her to snap, to want to end her life? Or maybe escape from a type of captivity?

She didn't say anything, but Thayne's frown had deepened. Human beings weren't meant to function in a bubble.

Quinn flicked through some of his notes. "No one will admit to socializing with them. They moved here six years ago, paid cash for everything. Mostly worked under the table. They generated their own electricity. Had their own well. No internet, no cable."

Thayne leaned back in one of the chairs. "So, if I wanted to disappear, you've given me the perfect blueprint. Anything pop in the law enforcement databases?"

"Nothing. I ran their names, and there's no records prior to them moving here and buying the land. Once again, cash only."

Riley had heard of living off the grid, but she'd never actually had firsthand experience. Not like these people.

"Any evidence at the house?"

Quinn shoved the box at Thayne. "A big fat goose egg. We got nothing to go on, and when I say nothing, I mean nothing. If I had a vote, I'd call it an accident, because we're sure not making any kind of case in court. Not unless Chloe can give us something concrete."

Riley peered at the meager evidence. "Do you mind if I have a look?"

"Knock yourself out. I'm cross-eyed. I have samples, but I don't see the point in sending them out for testing."

"How long have you been up?" Thayne asked his deputy.

Quinn glanced at his watch. "Going on thirty-six hours."

"Get some rest. We'll take it from here and hope Chloe wakes up soon."

Quinn exited the room, and Riley leaned forward. "The Jordans might have been survivalists, but there's one other option as to why they were living this way. If someone in the family witnessed a crime, they could be living under the Federal Witness Protection Program."

"WITSEC." Thayne let out a soft whistle. "That would explain a lot."

A loud knock sounded on the glass. Riley jumped when Greg Decker entered the room. Uninvited.

CHAPTER FIVE

If discovering the truth about the Jordans and helping Dan Peterson gave Thayne a reason to stay sheriff, Greg Decker represented every justification for reupping into the Navy and rejoining his SEAL team.

At their first meeting, Decker had oozed smooth-talking company man ready to bail his boys out of trouble no matter what they'd done. If Clive hadn't revealed his money troubles, Thayne would've handled the entire situation in a very different way. However, when Decker hadn't backed Earnhardt and had let the boys go to jail for the night, the man had earned a portion of Thayne's respect.

Banging on the glass and barging in like he owned the place didn't earn Decker any prizes. For now, the jury teetered on Decker's worth, but Thayne rarely reversed himself about a man's character.

"You're early, Decker," Thayne said, his voice curt.

"Time is money. I was hoping I could get my boys out of jail."

"I'm in a conference right now. There's a chair at Deputy Ironcloud's desk. I suggest you wait there until we're finished."

Decker glanced at his watch. "They're already late for their shift. I'm out of time."

Thayne stood and closed the door in the man's face.

Riley smiled at him. "I like your style, Sheriff Blackwood."

"I thought he might be okay, but he reeks of big-city entitlement. The guy deserves to wait all day, but I don't want to leave him alone out there too long." He paused for a moment. "Now back to the WITSEC theory. You have any contacts at the marshal's office?"

"I have a friend in DC."

"Call them. I want to know what we're dealing with." He hitched his hip on the table. "What's your plan?"

"Check on Chloe again and, if she hasn't improved, return to the house and start my process. I need to look around some more with direct light. Take more photos."

"Sounds good. If you call Cheyenne for an update, I'll take care of Decker, and then we can head out."

Riley was already digging into the boxes Quinn had left as Thayne walked out the door. Decker had made himself at home all right, standing just outside the steel doorway leading to the jail cells. He peered inside.

Shoving past the visitor, Thayne grabbed the key and opened the door. "Sit down and I'll process these guys," he said.

One by one, he filled out the release paperwork, unlocked the appropriate cell, and handed the signed copy to Alicia for filing. To a man, each walked out muttering an apology and avoiding his gaze. They deserved to be embarrassed. Thayne had enjoyed his share of drinks when he was younger, but losing control—that was something entirely different.

When he picked up the final form, Thayne paused before signing it. Earnhardt.

He walked over to the cell and faced the man through the bars. The guy stood, arms crossed, stance challenging. He hadn't learned a damn thing. "You seriously giving me attitude after last night, Earnhardt? Did you learn nothing?"

"Oh, I learned that Singing River is full of a bunch of holier-than-thou know-it-alls."

Thayne leaned back and crossed one booted leg in front of the other and rattled the keys in front of him. "Exactly what's your IQ? You do realize I'm the one who can let you out or keep you here another day."

Earnhardt sucked up a ball of spit and let it fly at Thayne's feet. "My boss paid you off. You don't have a choice."

"And the fine just doubled. You want to try for triple?" Thayne asked with a smile.

Decker let out a loud curse behind Thayne. "Earnhardt, you trying to get fired?"

The worker grumbled under his breath but didn't directly challenge his boss. Because of one stupid act, Thayne could've kept Earnhardt another night, but Clive needed the money, and, personally, Thayne didn't need the headache. He opened the cell, handed Earnhardt his release paperwork, and turned to Decker. "This is the only free pass you get. Any of your crew show up at Clive's again and do so much as spit on the wrong side of the law, I'll parade them before Judge Gibson so fast they'll be shocked how quickly they earn a month in jail. He doesn't take kindly to lawbreakers, especially stupid, drunk ones."

Decker's jaw tightened when Earnhardt walked past him. "Go stand with the others." At that moment, his ringtone sounded. He glanced at the screen and flushed red. "You won't have any trouble from my men. That I'll guarantee."

He stalked over to his four employees. "I've avoided *my* boss's calls four times coming to pick up you yahoos. That makes me unhappy. I suggest the rest of this week go *very* well. You get my meaning?"

Decker whirled to the exit and led them out, but Earnhardt paused. He glared at Thayne, eyes full of hatred. Blaming him for his week without pay, no doubt, before he joined his crewmates outside.

The front door closed, and Alicia gave a noticeable shiver. "I don't like all the strangers in town these days."

Thayne sent her a sympathetic smile. "I doubt we'll have any more to do with Decker or his men. I'm pretty certain the word'll get out." He walked back to the holding area where the two Riverton ranch hands waited. "You boys ready to go home?"

Not saying a single word, they nodded, heads bowed.

He released them. "Now get out of here before I decide to call your boss—who also happens to be my brother-in-law. And next time go light on the booze."

The men practically fell over themselves running out of the sheriff's office. Their trucks were still at Clive's. He'd let them figure out how to collect them.

He pushed into the conference room to stacks of color-coded documents. Riley stood over the piles, her brow furrowed in concentration and the corners of her mouth turned down.

"You make any headway?" From her expression he knew the answer.

She plopped into a chair. "Quinn was right. There's nothing here. I copied the autopsy photos and a few others, but I have more questions than answers. There wasn't much left, except the matching plain bands on their left ring fingers. So sad." She leaned forward with a sigh. "There's a bit of good news. Chloe is breathing on her own now, but she's still unconscious. Cheyenne's worried, though. She'd expected her to wake up by now."

"We're starting from scratch then, aren't we?"

"We have no choice."

For a moment Thayne considered that in some ways the question had as much to do with their relationship as the investigation.

Riley repacked the boxes and filed away copies of the photos that had interested her, then grabbed her bag before they headed to his SUV.

Once he drove out of town, she pulled out a notebook. "I don't even have house plans. Aaron built the place himself and never filed anything with the county."

Thayne glanced over at her. "You ever had this little to go on?"

"Usually the victims are more defined. The more I know about them, the more I can intuit about the suspect."

Riley focused her attention on the papers in her lap.

"So you're in new territory?"

She nodded. "When Tom calls me in, it's because they're stuck on motive or they've come up against a brick wall on suspects, but the premise is the same. If we can figure out why Kim called me, I believe we'll have the killer in sight."

The vehicle wound through the rolling hills and grass. It had taken only a few days to shatter the peaceful illusion of Singing River. He wanted it back, not just for himself, but for the people he loved.

"They're really hidden out here," Riley said. "I'm surprised the fire was visible."

"It wasn't. At least not from town. Seeing it was a complete fluke. Their nearest neighbor is ten miles out of line of sight."

Thayne veered along the final bend leading to the Jordans' and parked his vehicle. The embers no longer smoked, and the charred remains made for a sad scene. Two lives' work undone in a few hours.

Riley scribbled a few notes in a red notebook, her expression thoughtful. "There's another possibility we haven't discussed. What if the Jordans did this on purpose? It doesn't explain the disconnect concerning which side of the bed they were discovered on, but it might explain Chloe. Perhaps they wanted her to survive. Or perhaps she was able to save herself."

"Hopefully she'll wake up soon and we can ask her."

"Until then, we need to know more about the Jordans."

They exited the vehicle. A gust fluttered the pages from Riley's notebook as well as her sketchbook. The crime scene tape flapped in the stiff wind.

"Where do you want to start?" Thayne asked.

"The main house." She passed him her books. "Could you hold these for me? I want to get a feel for the place."

Thayne stood back. Her work methods fascinated him. Photos, sketches, and scene walk-throughs. He'd watched her immerse herself so deeply her entire body shook in reaction. Was it wrong to hope this time would be different? He wanted answers, but not at her expense.

Slowly Riley stepped into the Jordans' bedroom. She breathed in and out and sank to her knees. Her eyes went glassy.

"Why cover themselves with a blanket if they did it to themselves? The quilt burned to their bodies. If you were trying to kill someone, the cotton quilt makes a perfect conduit for the fire. There's no sign of a struggle, of pushing the bedding aside. They weren't bound. It doesn't make sense."

Thayne didn't bother answering. When Riley was ready, they'd talk about her conjecture.

She wandered into the living area where they'd discovered the panic room. "They built this to hide. And survive, but Chloe didn't barricade herself before the fire started. Otherwise her clothes wouldn't have smelled of smoke."

Riley blinked and faced Thayne, addressing him for the first time. "I don't believe the fire was a suicide. It doesn't fit. As for it being an accident, I don't think so. If they'd fallen asleep, the fire would have wakened them, even if they couldn't make it out of the house. Why would they lie there burning to death without some effort to get away from the flames?"

He knew from her expression she was asking a question of him this time. "Smoke inhalation?"

"The fire started at the bedside. I don't buy it."

Thayne couldn't argue with her logic. "Not an accident. Not a suicide."

"All that's left is murder. But why?" Riley moved away from the house toward the charred outline of the barn. "Quinn didn't take as many photos of this building," she said.

"Because the fire leapt from building to building."

Riley cocked her head. "I care about the fire, but right now I care more about understanding our victims. If you're hiding, would you keep something from your past?"

"I probably shouldn't, but I'd want photos of Pops and Gram, of Mom and Dad."

"Me too. I'd take a picture of Madison, even if I had to hide it away." She glanced back at the house. "Quinn didn't find anything in the panic room except survival gear and MREs. If they'd kept something of their prior lives, it could've burned up."

Thayne entered the area where the barn door had been. "Aaron built a panic room. He didn't trust banks, but he obviously believed in hiding his valuables. Maybe he has a safe."

"Good thought." Riley's smile glinted in her eyes. "I'll search the panic room for a hidden safe."

"I'll take the barn." Thayne watched Riley head down the stairs to the metal room below the floor. He'd definitely learned one thing from her today. Focusing on the people, instead of focusing strictly on the crime, broadened the investigation.

His gaze swept the barn. The walls had collapsed. If anything had been hidden in the walls or loft, it had burned beyond recognition. He grabbed a stick. Starting in one corner, he tapped the floor, moving methodically through the destroyed building. Three-fourths of the way through, he'd found nothing when his gaze landed on a slight indentation in the dirt floor. He knelt down and snapped on a pair of gloves. He could feel that the ground surrounding the indentation was firm and packed. Someone had been digging recently. "Riley! I found something."

Within a few moments she'd raced over and crouched beside him. They studied the shifted dirt.

"Someone's disturbed this area recently," Thayne said.

"Good catch."

Thayne shrugged. "I spent a lot of years hunting in these woods, and a decade staying alive. You learn quick to read the ground."

Riley snapped several photos before Thayne brushed away the dirt. Less than six inches beneath the surface, he encountered something solid.

"Something's definitely here," he said and worked the earth back until he felt metal edges. He reached into the hole and pulled out a steel lockbox.

He looked at Riley. "Bingo."

She suddenly pressed a hard, excited kiss to his cheek. "God, I love you."

◆ ◆ ◆

After being caught once, he wasn't taking any chances. The mud and dirt in the ditch made for an unpleasant lookout. His pants and shoes were caked with mud, his jacket ruined. The camouflage net concealed his identity and binoculars. He wasn't worried. The sheriff and his lover hadn't glanced his way once. They were too involved with their find.

Damn it. His entire plan had unraveled. None of this should've happened. So he'd have to make up for a single oversight. Well, maybe three: Chloe's presence, Kim's phone call to the FBI woman, and the old man.

Chloe he could take care of easily enough. The doctor was worried. If she died, no one would question it.

The old man hadn't been any trouble. He'd die of exposure soon enough.

Former FBI special agent Riley Lambert was something else entirely. He'd done his homework on her. She was impressive. How could he have known she'd be holed up in a place like Singing River? He'd learned several details about her, but the most important was that she wouldn't be easy to dissuade. Damn her. He should've been home free by now. Taking his pound of flesh as payment for their sins should've been done, with no one being the wiser.

He took a few calming breaths. The agent was intelligent, and determined, but not as much as he. He'd find a way to stop her. He'd come too far. Failure was not an option.

◆ ◆ ◆

The SUV hit a pothole and Riley bounced, her head nearly hitting the roof of the vehicle. The distance between the Jordan property and the sheriff's office had never seemed so long. Still wearing gloves, she clutched the metal box in her lap. Unwilling to take a chance they'd missed any other evidence, they'd completed their search of the barn. If this box didn't give them some clue, Riley couldn't fathom where a break in the case would come from.

She chanced a look at Thayne. His back held too much tension; the muscle at the base of his jaw throbbed.

"What's wrong?" she asked softly. "We found our first real lead."

He shoved his fingers through his hair. "I know. It just occurred to me that our relationship seems to work best when we're in the midst of a murder investigation."

Ouch.

She touched his thigh, and the muscle beneath her fingers tensed. "Once this case is over, can't we talk this out? I don't want to lose you."

He placed his hand over hers. "I don't want to lose you, either, but I have to ask myself if what we feel is desire based on a heavy dose of adrenaline. I even considered if we should go back to the long-distance weekly phone calls. You're my best friend, and I don't want to screw that up." He glanced over at her. "Is that what you want?"

She sagged back against the seat. "You're saying what we feel for each other isn't real?"

"I'm saying I don't know anymore. I would never have thought you'd think about leaving, either. But you are."

"You're my best friend, too. I don't want to lose you."

"What about your fiancé? Your lover?" He moved her hand off his thigh and to the seat.

Riley looked away. She wanted to promise. She wanted to believe she could be happy here, but she had the terrifying belief that the restless urge inside her would return.

"I don't know what to think," she finally admitted. She glanced down at the metal box. "I'd burned myself out. I wanted—no, I needed—to quit, but now . . . I'm confused. I miss my job. I'm good at what I do, but more than that, I need to feel like there's somewhere I belong, where I can help people with a skill that most would never need." She let out a low chuckle. "Who in their right mind would want to spend most of their days digging into the minds of people who, for one reason or another, live to harm others? I must be crazy."

"You think I don't know how special you are, Riley? You have a gift, and you never give up. You give families hope. I'd never ask you to change, but for me—at least for now—my life has to be here in Singing River. Gram's getting worse. Dad's heart will weaken over time. Hudson has to keep the ranch running, Cheyenne has her practice, and Jackson's firefighting forces him to travel. I'm needed." He parked his SUV in front of the sheriff's office, turned off the engine, and faced her. "When you agreed to marry me, you'd already resigned from the FBI. You've changed your mind about that decision. We both know it."

She grabbed his hand. "I want to figure out how to make this work. I do love you."

He cupped her cheek and swept his thumb across her skin. A gentle smile tugged at his lips. "I don't doubt that, and I'm not going anywhere," he said.

She pressed her cheek harder into his palm, needing his touch to soothe the ache that pulsed through her.

He slowly withdrew his hand. "We can't keep doing this."

"Doing what?"

"Getting distracted. Besides, right now, we have a murder to solve."

Just like that he cut off discussion. She should be worried by the relief that washed through her, but she didn't want to think about losing him, of not having him in her life.

He opened the SUV's door for her.

With a deep breath, Riley carried the box inside the sheriff's office and over to Quinn's desk.

The deputy stopped what he was doing and frowned. "What's this?"

Riley gave him a rundown of their visit to the crime scene. As he pulled on a set of gloves, he let out a low whistle. "You're too spooky for words, Riley. Do you talk to dead people or something?"

"I just listen," she said with a grin. "But this time, it's not me communing with the spirit world. Thayne's the one who found the lockbox. Can you check this for prints? When you're done, we want to break it open."

"Will do," Quinn said and disappeared into the back room with the box.

The sheriff's office was mostly empty. Except for Alicia at dispatch. Within a few hours, dusk would fall. Riley made her way into the conference room, watching Thayne from a safe distance. He looked comfortable, from the way he kicked his feet up on the table to the way he stretched for a pen on the cabinet behind him. He knew every inch of the place without even looking. He belonged here. She just didn't know if she did. She opened her file and let her mind filter through the photos, desperate to notice the smallest detail that might help her fit the pieces of this maddening puzzle together.

She didn't know how long she'd been at it when Thayne brought the lockbox and a large bolt cutter into the conference room. He set them on the table, and Riley reached for a pair of gloves.

"Chloe's still unconscious," he said. "You hear anything from your WITSEC contact?"

She shook her head. "Not yet. I'll give him another couple hours, then try again."

"We're getting nowhere," he said. "I sent Ironcloud home for some sleep. If anyone knows anything about the Jordans, they're not talking. This could be our only shot if Chloe doesn't wake up."

"They hid the box for a reason," she said as she wiggled her hands into the last glove. "Let's find out why."

"Quinn pulled a set of fingerprints off of it. He's going to run a local search. If that doesn't work, we'll go nationwide." Thayne snipped the lock, and it fell to the table with a high-pitched thunk.

Holding her breath, Riley opened the six-by-eight-by-four-inch box. On the top lay a photo of a woman with long blonde hair, holding the hand of an approximately three-year-old girl. "Do you recognize either one of them?" she asked.

"Maybe. Where's that photograph of the Jordan family that Ironcloud found at the newspaper?"

Riley pulled out her portfolio and held up an original photo of the local farmers' market. "It's the only picture of them that exists as far as we know. Kim's selling jam, and her husband and daughter are behind the table with her."

Thayne studied the image closely. "Short brown hair, at least fifteen pounds heavier." He tilted the photo at an angle and held it up to the light. His eyes crinkled. "Well, I'll be damned."

He placed the image from the lockbox next to the farmers' market photo. "Look at the birthmark on the side of her neck and the small cleft in both of their chins."

"The blonde in the photo and Kim Jordan are the same person." Riley let out a low whistle. On a hunch she flipped the picture over.

KRISTIN AND ASHLEY (AGE 3).

"They changed their names." Riley pulled out her phone. "If she was in WITSEC, Chloe could still be in danger."

CHAPTER SIX

Thayne elbowed back into the conference room with two cups of coffee brewed from his stash of Fannie's special blend. From where he stood, they were going to need the shot of caffeine.

Riley held the phone to her ear. "You're sure?" She frowned as her US Marshal contact spoke. "I know you can't say anything, but unless you tell me to stop, we're distributing the photos wide." She motioned Thayne over and pressed the speakerphone button.

He set her coffee in front of her.

"You won't cause me any heartburn if you try to find a relative," a man's voice said, loudly and clearly. "Riley"—his voice had transformed into a whisper—"not everyone who needs to disappear is in WITSEC. There are specific requirements to enter the program, and this woman may not have met them. It doesn't mean she wasn't justified to disappear."

"I'm not sure we have a choice."

"I understand, but be aware—the situation might not end the way you hope."

A click sounded, and the phone went silent.

Thayne took a gulp of coffee. “Obviously the Jordans weren’t in WITSEC.”

“Without explicitly confirming, which he can’t do, the message was clear.” She warmed her hands on the coffee mug and sipped. Her eyes closed and she let out a low groan of pleasure. “Fannie’s elixir. You’re my hero.”

After pushing the two photos to the side, he removed the remaining items one by one from the box. “A homemade baby’s dress. No name, no label.” She placed it in an evidence bag. “A lock of blonde hair, but without any roots, so no DNA.” She passed it over to Thayne, who sealed the item and filled out the label.

One item after another, they filtered and cataloged everything in the small container. More photos with Kim and Chloe. She could study the backgrounds, but at first glance she didn’t recognize any location triggers.

“What’s this?” Thayne asked.

He’d retrieved a hand-drawn map, and she leaned just past his shoulder, pressing to his side.

“There are no labels or identifiable landmarks.” She dragged her gloved finger just above the paper. “That could be a river, maybe a path?”

“Whoever drew this definitely wasn’t an artist.” Thayne turned the paper ninety degrees, then one-eighty. “The square could be a building. The triangles might be trees. Or maybe mountains.” He slipped the map into a plastic sleeve. “It could be anywhere.”

Riley let out a long sigh. “Could Quinn take a pass at fingerprints?”

“Worth a try. I could request the state crime lab analyze the crime scene items for trace evidence, but that could take weeks. Or longer.”

“Which doesn’t solve our immediate problem.”

She set the map with their other finds.

“There’s always plan B,” Thayne said and kicked back in his chair. “Distribute the old and a more recent photo to the media in the surrounding states and see what falls out. If we get nothing, we expand nationally. How do you feel about Chloe being the murderer?"

A guarded expression laced Riley's gaze. "There's still a strong chance. But let's say she isn't. If we publicize those photos, we could place her in danger."

"Do we have a choice?"

"I wish I could say yes, but we're no closer to understanding why they were killed." Riley gripped the edge of the table, and her knuckles whitened. "We don't know anything. *I* don't know anything."

She leaned heavily over the table, sliding the images back and forth. Thayne recognized her frustration, even understood it. He'd observed her in awe as she worked her way through the puzzle of Cheyenne's kidnapping. Thayne and his father had been stymied until Riley had viewed the crime scene. There was one significant difference in the cases, however: the Jordan evidence had been decimated to ashes.

She glanced over at him, anguish etched on her face. "It's not just the limited information in the crime scene. Aaron, Kim, and Chloe are shadows to me. Ghostly shadows without substance. They're not flesh and blood. They're flat, with no present and no past. How am I supposed to understand the person who set this fire if everyone involved slips through my fingers like smoke?"

She touched the edge of Kim's photo, and her shoulders sagged. Thayne couldn't help, not unless he uncovered more information. Riley counted on employing her extraordinary skills in behavior analysis to piece together motive and MO to identify and catch the perpetrator. She'd succeeded time and time again, solving cases no one else could solve. Her ability to take obscure facts and paint a picture was her biggest strength, but without facts, she couldn't work her magic.

She gripped Thayne's arm, her nails driving into his flesh. "I don't know if I can give the Jordans justice."

Thayne unclawed her hand and wrapped it in his. "We both know someone who might be able to help."

"Chloe." Her mouth twisted. "Victim or suspect?"

"We won't know until she wakes up." Thayne squeezed her hand once hopefully, reminding her they were in this together. "I'll have Quinn deal with the forensics. We'll hit the hospital. If she's still not awake, we'll discuss plan B."

At least they had a strategy, albeit a weak one. While Riley photographed the evidence to use for her personal murder board, Thayne passed the originals off to Quinn. By the time he returned, she'd stuffed everything she needed into her massive evidence bag.

Thayne carried the satchel to his SUV and got inside.

"Dad was sheriff when the Jordans arrived in town." He fastened his seat belt with a snap. "I'd like to show him the contents of the box. Maybe he'll recognize something, or it'll jog his memory."

"Pulling your father into an investigation. That's a change. I like it."

Her tone needled at him, and he growled under his breath. "You want me to admit I should've listened to you before you left, don't you?"

"I like *you* knowing that *I* was right."

The satisfaction in her voice should've annoyed him, but it didn't. "Fine, I'll say it. You were right about using his expertise when I can."

He pulled onto the road, and she patted his arm. "You would've figured it out eventually. He's been a cop all his life. He cares about the people in this town. No way, even on doctor's orders, would he cut himself off cold turkey."

"That may be true, but he also needs to respect boundaries. For his own health and my sanity. I'm already dealing with Quinn's frustrations. I have enough conflict in the office."

"I didn't see any tension between the two of you."

"He holds it in most of the time, but he's not happy Dad convinced the county commission to name me sheriff." Thayne shrugged. His father's decision had bothered him from the beginning, but Carson could outstubborn almost anyone. Except maybe Riley. "I understand Quinn's reaction. He's been a deputy for years, and my dad's right hand for most of it. My bet is he'll run against me when the next election comes up."

"Why'd your dad push you to be sheriff so badly?"

"As a big fat carrot to get me to stay in Singing River. I have to admit it's working."

Before she could ask him any more questions that he didn't know the answers to, he parked near the front of the hospital, and they entered together.

Kyle Baker, Thayne's newest deputy, sat at attention in a chair outside Chloe's room. The spit-and-polish kid was green and too eager, but he'd come through his training at the top of his class and didn't complain about grunt work.

"Kyle, any changes?"

"Nothing they've told me."

Thayne and Riley walked past him. They stood in the room. Chloe was breathing on her own now. Her dark-brown hair made her face appear even paler.

"She looks like she could just open her eyes and say something," Riley said in a low voice.

The swish of the door behind them caused Thayne to turn around. His sister walked in, every inch a doctor.

"I keep expecting her to wake up." Cheyenne tugged her stethoscope from around her neck. "I received word you were coming this way." She checked Chloe's vitals, and charted her progress. "Let's talk in the hall."

They followed Cheyenne, and she faced them. "I don't like to speak about patients' situations in the room. You never know what people can hear or understand."

"How is she?" Thayne asked.

"Except for not waking up, she's doing remarkably well. Her oxygen saturation levels are back to normal. She has a bruise on her head, but there's no skull fracture or intracranial pressure. There's no reason she shouldn't be awake, which means all we can do is wait."

"Damn," Riley muttered, rubbing the bridge of her nose. "Not what we were hoping."

"Any idea how much longer?" he asked. "Things have gotten more complicated on our end. We really need to talk to her."

Cheyenne chewed on her lower lip, a clear sign from the time they were kids that she didn't like the answer she'd give.

"At this point, your guess is as good as mine."

"Then we're down to picking Dad's memory from six or seven years ago." He kissed his sister's cheek. "Don't worry. I'll be gentle."

"I wish I could help, but I was in med school when the Jordans moved here, and they never visited me or Doc Mallard before I took over the clinic."

"That's okay. We're heading out to the ranch to see if Dad can fill in any holes. Want to join us? You could bring your husband. I haven't seen Brett for a while."

"Probably not a good idea."

Thayne raised a brow at the comment, but Cheyenne shook her head. "Don't worry about it. He's frustrated he's not recovering from the attempted poisoning as quickly as he'd like. I'll wear him down." She paused. "Eventually. I hope. Besides I'm going to read to Chloe tonight."

"Does that help?" Riley asked.

"There's some convincing evidence to indicate that activity and interaction with an unconscious patient can speed along the healing process. I'm game to try anything."

"What if I ask the family if they'll take turns reading?" Thayne asked. "I know they'd be willing."

"I like the idea. A lot." Cheyenne smiled, and the worry on her forehead smoothed some. "Sometimes the science of medicine has to take a back seat to the art along with a little bit of faith."

"Doc!" The attendant raced down the hall. "Dan Peterson is coming in! Unconscious and nonresponsive."

"What happened?" Cheyenne asked, running toward the emergency entrance.

"Found his truck off the side of the road west of town. EMT said the truck reeked of alcohol. Pills, too."

"What was he doing out toward the Jordans'?" Thayne raced up beside his sister. "Did he ever come to see you?"

She shook her head. "Dad couldn't convince him, but if he's drinking and blacking out, that might explain a lot."

Thayne glanced over at Riley. "Give me a minute, okay?"

"Of course. I'll be waiting."

Thayne rushed toward the ER. Sirens squealed as the ambulance pulled into the double doorway. They brought Dan in on a stretcher. His mouth was slack. The EMT carried a bottle of white pills.

"Oxycodone," he said. "Mixed with alcohol. No idea how much. The bottle spilled."

"Damn it," Cheyenne muttered. "Get him into exam room two and break out the Narcan. Let's see if we can save his life."

◆ ◆ ◆

A pink horizon glowed from the miles upon miles of Wyoming landscape. The deep ruts in the road put a strain on the SUV's shocks. The ride vibrated Riley's jaw as they approached the Blackwood family home.

"Dan almost didn't make it," Thayne said into his phone. "Cheyenne said if he's addicted to opioids, it could explain his confusion. She's keeping him in the hospital for observation. If he'll stay put. Tough old guy is already coming out of it and fighting to go home." He paused, listening, then said, "I know, Dad, but that's all we've got to go on. We're almost to the ranch. Talk to you soon."

He ended the call and glanced over at her. "Dad can't believe it. He said when Dan and Kat got married, they both went dry. He's going to spend some more time with Dan and try to convince him to see Cheyenne."

"People change," Riley said.

The tension between her and Thayne had dissipated, though she knew one wrong word would bring the situation front and center. The problem was that meeting him halfway was a big sacrifice. Singing River didn't have an FBI satellite office, though the nearest one was in Jackson Hole less than one hundred miles away. It would be a long commute, tough in the winter. Not to mention she'd have to resign from the newly formed Behavior Analysis Unit 6.

Or, she could try to find something else to do in Singing River. The consultant idea was a good one, but she'd need to find more work than this small town had to offer. Not exactly the obvious home base for someone who could voluntarily put themselves in the heads of depraved criminals. At least she could until the Jordan case stymied her.

"You've been quiet," Thayne said, pulling up in front of the house. "You okay to do this?"

"Of course." She grabbed her satchel. "I just wish Madison had agreed to come with us for dinner. She's been cooped up all day except for moving into her own room at the B and B."

"She could be gorging on those cinnamon rolls or Fannie's chicken and dumplings." Thayne parked the SUV in front of the house. "Give her some space. From what you said, sounds like your mom didn't leave her alone for a moment. She may just need some time."

"Mom tends to go overboard for sure. She always did with Madison. I just don't want to hover, either. She's so lost culturally. She's been through hell, but the world has moved on without her."

Thayne squeezed her hand. "Trust your gut with her the same way you do with our investigation and you'll be fine."

"Let's hope Carson can give us some answers." Riley shoved out of the SUV. Her present troubles were irrelevant. Chloe, on the other hand, needed an advocate.

They entered the kitchen just as Carson heaved a large pan of lasagna into the oven. "You're early," he said, following them into the living room. "Dinner won't be ready for an hour."

"That's okay. We have some business first."

Thayne's grandmother sat on a loveseat, flipping through her sketchbook. Riley hadn't seen her do that for several weeks. She strode over to Helen. "Were you drawing today?"

Helen looked up, her eyes clear and aware. "I can't seem to make the pencil do what I want, dear." She sighed and patted the seat beside her. "I see you brought your bag. Any sketches to show me?"

"Nothing particularly interesting." Riley wasn't about to show her the incomplete drawings of a house that had been burned to the ground. Normally, sketching provided insight. Not with this case. "Today was . . . frustrating."

"Try living with Swiss cheese for a brain." Helen chuckled. "It's not fun."

Riley stared in shock at Helen. Her days of self-awareness didn't come very often.

"Oh good grief, don't look at me like that. I know I can't think right most of the time." Her smile vanished.

Lincoln sat next to his wife. He lifted her hand to her lips. "Today's a good day," he said to her. "Let's be thankful."

She sank into him. "I don't want to be a burden to you or the rest of the family. Promise me you won't let that happen."

"You'll never be a burden, my love."

Riley's throat thickened at the love so transparent on Lincoln's face. His devotion truly humbled her. She chanced a glance at Thayne. He'd promised her a love like this, a love she'd never thought could be real.

Helen patted her husband's cheek. "Enough of these maudlin thoughts." She narrowed her gaze at Riley, then glanced across the room at Thayne. "Why are you two here? I'd expect Thayne to be wanting you all to himself. What's wrong?"

"A little girl's in the hospital, Gram." Thayne crossed the room and kissed her on the cheek. "We need Dad's help."

"Good boy. He's feeling a bit down in the mouth since he quit working." Thayne hovered over her, and she patted his arm. "Oh good grief, go do your job. I don't need anyone mollycoddling me but Lincoln."

"You heard the boss, Thayne. Get to work." Lincoln settled next to Helen, and she leaned her head against his shoulder, tucked her feet underneath her, and closed her eyes in contentment.

Riley couldn't remember seeing such utter joy on Helen's face, not to mention Lincoln's.

"Understood, Pops." He turned to his father. "Can we talk?"

Riley followed the two men into the kitchen. "She's having a great day."

Carson nodded and poured a cup of coffee before sitting at the table. "It's strange. Some days I'm not sure she recognizes any of us. She pretends, but I catch her looking at me or Pops with this blank stare that sends a chill right through me. She took a nap after lunch, woke up, and it was like a lightbulb turned on inside her head. For a couple of hours it's like I have my mother back."

Riley touched Carson's hand. "I'm happy for you."

"We don't know how many good days are left. Every moment she's here with us, we have to soak in."

Thayne placed a cup of coffee in front of Riley and sat at the table next to her. "Show him the photos."

She slid the newspaper photo across the table.

"The Jordans and their daughter." Carson frowned at them. "How's she doing?"

"She's not awake yet. That's part of our problem." She showed him the older photo. "Do you recognize them? They may have come to town about seven years ago. Maybe they stayed at the B and B, maybe rented a house."

Thayne leaned forward as if willing his father to provide some answers. Riley could only hope, but the way this case had gone, her optimism had cratered.

Carson studied the photo, and his brow furrowed. "Something familiar about them, but I don't think I've ever seen them walking around town . . ." He tapped his chin and snapped his fingers. "It's the same woman. What are you two up to? Testing me or something?"

Thayne shook his head. "I wish that were the case. Kim and Chloe Jordan had a prior identity. Whoever knew that identity may be who killed Kim and her husband."

Carson let out a low whistle. "I wish I could help."

"We do have something else," Thayne said. "The map."

Riley pulled out the sketch and slid it across to Carson. "We found this in the same location as the photos."

His mouth pursed in concentration, Carson squinted at the crude map. "Not very specific, is it?"

Pops walked in. "Helen wants a cup of hot cider," he said. "It's been a while since she didn't just take what I'm having." He passed by the table and paused. "That's funny. That looks just like a map of the east border."

Thayne's head snapped up. "What are you talking about?"

"You know the land the Rivertons claim we stole from them." He pointed to the square. "The old Riverton cabin sits between Singing River Creek and the Wind River Mountains. Old man Riverton peppered my butt with salt when I was a kid and sneaked out there. Nearly started a war. I'm surprised someone wasn't killed out there."

"Why in the hell would Kim Jordan have a map to a cabin on our ranch?" Thayne shook his head. "There's nothing particularly valuable on that land."

"That we know of," Carson said. "There has to be a reason the Blackwoods and Rivertons have been fighting over it for a hundred years. I never knew, though."

"My father never told me," Lincoln offered. "It's always just been." He heated up the apple cider in the microwave.

"None of this makes any sense," Riley said with a frown. Every time they discovered a new piece of information, it didn't fit.

"Just like it never made sense why Kim called the house before calling you. Did Gram ever tell you why, Pops?" Thayne asked his grandfather.

"Whatever memory she had of the phone call hasn't come back yet. Sorry." He took a sip of the drink and added another fifteen seconds on the microwave timer. "It may be lost."

"What about asking her now?" Riley said. "She seems so clear today."

"I'll give it a try, but don't get your hopes up." He paused. "I wish we could help more. I'll think on the stories my father told me about the feud, but it's been a long time." He disappeared out of the room with the cider.

So the Blackwoods had their own secret past. They *weren't* as perfect as she'd imagined. In many ways that gave Riley comfort. Oh, she knew the family had experienced their share of tragedy and heartache. Thayne had lost his mother; there was Helen's Alzheimer's and Cheyenne's kidnapping, not to mention Carson's cardiomyopathy. The Blackwood family had faced its fair share of challenges, but what had always struck Riley were the love and loyalty, despite tragedy.

"When's the last time you visited the cabin?" Riley asked Carson, her brow raised.

He shook his head in bemusement. "How'd you know I sneaked out there?"

"Just a hunch." She met his gaze. "What teenage boy wouldn't explore a forbidden stretch of land?"

"I admit I did, but I regret it." He let out a small sigh and glanced over at Thayne. "I'd overheard your grandparents talking about the feud and how the families still refused to communicate. Your grandmother thought the entire situation was ridiculous. Pops got mad because Gram had dated one of the Riverton sons when she was in high school. I think he was jealous."

Thayne let out a low whistle. "I had no idea. I always saw them together . . . I guess forever."

"Everyone has a past. I decided to explore, ignoring the sky. By the time I reached the land, snow was coming down. Hard. Your grandmother had seen me listening and took a chance. She found me and got me home before Pops realized I could've died out there. I've never seen her so angry. She never gave me up, though. I felt so bad I never went back. Truth is, it wasn't all that interesting. Nothing to see." He tapped the map. "Or so I thought."

A clatter sounded from the living room.

"I don't know. I don't know you, old man!" Helen's voice rose in panic-laced fear. "Why are you hounding me? Stay away or I'll tell my Lincoln."

Thayne shot to his feet and raced into the living room. Riley followed.

Pops held his hands up. "I won't touch you, Helen. It's okay. Calm down."

Her head whipped around, and her gaze landed on Thayne. She rushed over to him.

"Lincoln. What's going on? That old man wants to know my secrets. I can't talk about them. You know that. You promised you'd never ask, that you trusted me."

Thayne lifted his grandmother's chin. "Your secrets are safe. I promise."

She blinked and took a shuddering breath. "It's important."

Helen sagged against him, and Thayne hummed in her ear. Slowly her body relaxed and she swayed. Thayne's chin rested on her hair and he closed his eyes, but not before Riley witnessed the heartache. Day by day, Thayne's grandmother slipped away from her family.

With a long sigh, Lincoln made his way to the window, his body stiff with tension. He couldn't comfort his wife when she saw him not as her husband but as a stranger who terrified her. Riley couldn't imagine how he dealt with his wife's unpredictable behavior with such quiet dignity, but he did.

Whenever the family gathered around Helen, Riley felt as if she should disappear and leave them alone. With a last look, she vanished into the kitchen.

She'd learned over the last month that Helen's behavior could be stable for days, and then suddenly she'd shift, almost becoming another person. Even though Riley had researched dementia, the unpredictability still shocked her.

Thayne could visit tomorrow and she'd know that he was her grandson. She might even know why she'd given Riley's number to Kim. Then again, they might never know.

Riley picked through the map and photos. It was an obscure clue, but hardly worth a line in her notes. She couldn't remember a case that had provided her with less information. That awful sense of foreboding had risen inside her.

Unless Thayne's grandmother had another good day or Chloe woke up, Riley couldn't help but wonder if the Kim and Aaron Jordan murder case would ever be solved.

CHAPTER SEVEN

The lights outside Fannie's Bed and Breakfast glowed like a beacon in the chilly night. Thayne stood on the front porch and stared at Riley. Normally, he wouldn't have hesitated to follow her inside. The awkwardness between them didn't sit right.

Even Gram had noticed.

A curtain shifted, and Thayne caught the movement. Too many people wanted to know their business.

"I'd better get going." He dug his keys out of his pocket.

Riley stopped him with a touch of her hand. "Your grandmother surprised me today." Her gaze shimmered with sympathy. "She seemed so clear, and then so confused, within a matter of minutes."

Thayne took comfort in the warmth of her hand on his arm. Talking to his own family about Gram's condition could be difficult sometimes. They all took loyalty seriously. No one wanted to be hurtful, so sometimes they simply said nothing to each other.

What could they say? It's not like they could do anything except try to meet Gram in her world—wherever or whenever that happened to be.

He linked his fingers with hers and squeezed. "One thing about Alzheimer's—you can't predict much of anything. The only thing that's certain is she'll get worse."

"I wish . . ." Riley hesitated. "I wish I could help."

"You are. You treat her with dignity and you don't avoid her," Thayne said. "That's more than most."

"Do you want to come inside?" Riley's words were hesitant.

With a gentle touch, Thayne ran his thumb down her cheek. His gaze captured hers, and the vulnerability in her eyes made his heart skip a beat. He couldn't say no. Not tonight. "Sure."

He opened the front door for her, and she brushed past him. The living room was completely silent. Only the sound of the hall clock as it struck the half-hour mark escorted them up the stairs.

She slipped the key into her lock and pushed open the door. The first thing that hit him was the plethora of photographs attached to the longest wall of the bedroom. The ashen remains of the Jordan household. A sea of dark gray and white, a haunting reminder of what currently bonded Thayne and Riley together.

He'd read somewhere that danger and excitement triggered the same neurotransmitters as falling in love. Could their brains be fooling them? Was their love real—or an illusion?

To distract himself from a path he'd rather not follow, he studied the images on her murder board. "When you look at their home this way, it's . . ."

"Depressing and disturbing." Riley slipped off her coat and laid it on the bed. "It's too warm in here. Madison must've turned it up before she switched rooms. That girl always did sleep in a sauna." Riley adjusted the heater before crossing to the desk. She laid out her satchel and pulled out the prints of the photos she'd taken today, as well as those Quinn had provided. Along with the map.

Riley pinned up photo after photo. The panic room. Minute details of the horrifying charred remains on the bed. Traces of the quilt—the fire's point of origin. Images he wouldn't have noticed kept joining the overall picture of the destroyed house. Thayne ticked off a handful of identifiable items: the weapon, the lipstick tube, the lighter. Their placement alone had convinced her the Jordans were murdered.

Seeing the truth up on this wall rekindled the fury in his gut. What a horrible way to die. During one of his tours, he'd witnessed the murder of a civilian being set ablaze. There'd been nothing he could do, but the screams were unlike anything he'd ever heard. When his team had finally reached the outskirts of the village, the twisted agony had shown on the man's body.

The memory hit him like shrapnel between the eyes. He narrowed his gaze at the photo of the bodies more closely. "I should have noticed this before. The Jordans are lying prone, side by side. You mentioned that at the scene."

Riley backed away until she stood beside him. "It's as if they didn't react to the fire at all, even in sleep." She narrowed her gaze. "I can't imagine them not being dead before the fire was set."

Thayne paced to and fro in front of the growing collection of pictures. "Just one more inconsistency pointing to murder. You know, if you hadn't been there, it would've been labeled a tragic accident, case closed. We would've completely misread their deaths."

"Don't be so hard on yourselves. Most police departments would've reacted exactly the same way. This time the killer made a mistake," Riley said. "He wanted the murder to appear as if Aaron Jordan fell asleep smoking, the lamp fell over and ignited, and they couldn't get out." She pinned the map to the edge of the board. "How is Kim Jordan connected to the piece of property the Rivertons and Blackwoods have been feuding over, and how does Helen figure into the picture?"

A knock sounded at the door. Riley glanced through the peephole and opened it.

Madison walked in and smiled when she saw Thayne. She looked good, considering everything she'd been through.

He gave her a quick hug. “Welcome home.”

Madison patted his back and stepped away, eyeing him with a critical gaze. “You look like you could use some sleep. Riley’s sucked you into another one of her puzzles.” She glanced over at her sister. “I left my toothbrush in the bathroom,” she said, and disappeared through the door.

When Madison reentered the room, she shuddered at the photos on the wall. “I can’t sleep in a room with a crime scene staring at me. I don’t know how you do it, Thayne.”

“I can barely stay here since you cranked up the heat,” Riley groused. “You’ve turned my room into an oven.”

“I didn’t change the temperature,” Madison denied. “Maybe Fannie did.”

“If you say so,” Riley said with a frown. “Feeling any better?”

Her sister shrugged. “Rested, anyway. At least no one checked up on me every half hour while I slept.” She shifted. “I should get out of your hair, leave you to your . . . fun?”

Riley flushed and Thayne hid a grin. He really liked that Madison teased Riley. Truth was, he couldn’t stop himself from being in awe of Madison. Every one of the kidnapped children they’d recovered told the same story: Madison had protected them, had provided them with security and love in the midst of a prison.

He had to wonder . . . “Before you go, I have a favor to ask.” Thayne hesitated slightly. He didn’t want to impose, but he had a feeling Madison might be exactly what the doctor ordered. “Riley told you about Chloe?”

Madison nodded.

“She’s still not awake. Cheyenne hoped that reading to her or even someone speaking to her might help. I offered to round up some volunteers. Would you be interested?”

“I’d love to help.” She grinned and kissed him on the cheek. “You’re a good one, Thayne Blackwood. I’m glad you’re the one who fell in love with my sister.” She winked at Riley and disappeared out the door.

The click of the lock echoed through the silent room. Riley faced Thayne. "Everyone is so sure we belong together. Why aren't we?"

"If love were the only emotion we had to worry about, our choices would be easier." Slowly, searching Riley's every expression, he eased toward her until they were toe to toe. He breathed in, and the lavender scent of her shampoo filled his senses. His heart raced. "You being in Singing River is making a difference in this case. I hope you realize that."

"All I've done is create more questions than answers."

"But the answers you've found have focused our search. I couldn't do this without you. Hell"—he swept his hand down her hair until his palm settled on her shoulder—"I don't want to do this without you."

She smiled and cupped his face. "Thank you. I needed to hear that."

Ever so slowly he lowered his mouth to hers. Her lips had barely parted beneath his when he pulled away. If he didn't leave now, he never would. "Call if you need me."

He crossed the room to the door and opened it, hesitating in the threshold before turning toward the room. Riley was already focused, unblinking, on the wall of photos, muttering to herself, working through potential theories. He would like to stay, to hold her in his arms tonight, to help her, but she needed to work alone, in the quiet, away from any distractions, and she wouldn't forgive herself for not focusing every ounce of energy on finding the murderer.

Thayne shut the door and shrugged on his coat as he made his way to his car. He ignored a twinge of regret that he wasn't with Riley. When he got to his car, a light flickered off on the side of the B&B before brightening once more. He'd have to remind Fannie to change the exterior light bulbs the next time he saw her.

He let his gaze travel to the window in Riley's room. Her shadow paced back and forth, and he tamped down the sense of unease that threatened to suffocate him. He'd experienced the same feelings prior to a particularly risky mission.

The discomfort had to stem from Riley and their conviction that there was a killer roaming Singing River. If Thayne had learned one thing about human nature, it was that a killer would do almost anything not to get caught. Even if it meant killing again.

◆ ◆ ◆

The sheriff drove away. Finally.

For a moment he couldn't move, couldn't breathe. The scent of pine itched his nose. He'd almost sneezed. He would have given everything away.

Much too close.

He'd believed Singing River to be the perfect hunting ground. A new sheriff and deputy, a low crime rate. A sheriff's office with only five personnel.

Riley Lambert hadn't factored into his equation. She didn't belong here. When she'd flown to DC, he'd assumed she wouldn't be back.

He'd become impatient to kill the Jordans. A mistake he wouldn't make again.

He stuffed his rope, picklock kit, and ski mask into his black bag. His loose ends wouldn't cause any more trouble. One way or another.

◆ ◆ ◆

The midmorning sun bathed Riley's car in warmth despite the near-freezing temperatures. Madison sat in the passenger's seat, huddled in a bulky coat, woolen mittens, a scarf, and a hat. She looked ready for a blizzard. Riley smiled and took a long sip of coffee. After dropping her sister off at the hospital, she'd need to jump-start her brain before arriving at the sheriff's office.

Her smile slowly faded. She couldn't remember when a night had gone worse. She'd used every trick she knew to help her see past the obvious, but the truth was, there were no details to be uncovered. She could speculate and give Kim Jordan a dozen or more reasons for wanting to disappear—from financial troubles to an abusive marriage to witnessing or even committing a crime. Without more information, short of asking everyone in town to be fingerprinted, she was stuck.

The woman the FBI brought in to solve the unsolvable had only one idea left, though it felt more like assuaging her curiosity than a solid lead. Her gut just wouldn't let it go. She needed to search the no-man's-land between the Riverton and Blackwood properties.

"You look like hell," Madison said from the seat next to her.

"Gee, thanks, Maddy."

"I'm serious, Ri. Thayne didn't stay, and you didn't sleep all night. Is this what you do on every case? Is this how you found me? Because you can't keep it up. You'll burn out."

"A twelve-year-old girl is in trouble. How can I sleep when I know that?" She yawned. Clearly she needed more time to wake up. "Come on. I used to love to listen to you tell me stories. I bet Chloe will, too."

Riley pulled the SUV into the hospital parking lot. She took Madison on a quick tour of the small facility before leading her down the main corridor. Cheyenne stood just outside Chloe's door, peeking into the room with a gentle smile on her face.

Quietly they joined her. She placed a fingertip to her lips and eased open the door about halfway.

Helen sat in the chair next to Chloe and held her hand tightly. Lincoln hovered at her side. She wasn't holding a book in her hands but was speaking softly.

"The thawing lake was cold, and a flock of beautiful birds descended down to the lone bird. Drawing courage, the duckling swam out into the pond, uncertain if these majestic birds would reject him, but knowing the risk had to be worth it."

Cheyenne eased the door closed. The hospital was just starting to come to life. "I don't have much time, but Chloe's responding very well to Gram." Her eyes glistened with hope. "I remember snuggling up in bed with Gram and listening to her tell the story of 'The Ugly Duckling.' I could see the images in my mind. I didn't even know Hans Christian Andersen wrote it until I was in junior high. To me, it was always Gram's story."

Riley touched Cheyenne's hand. "I'm glad she's having a good day."

"Me too. She can't really learn new things these days, but something from the past—well, it's a window into the Gram I miss the most." She cleared her throat and looked past Riley. "I'm so glad to see you, Madison." Cheyenne gave her a huge hug. "You look well."

"I'm fine. I came to read to Chloe once your grandmother's finished."

Cheyenne focused exclusively on Madison as if Riley weren't even present.

"After you're finished here, would you like to have lunch with me?"

Oh good. Thayne must've spoken with his sister about Riley's concerns for Madison. Maybe she could wheedle out of Madison what was going on in her head these days.

Her sister smiled, brighter than she had since she'd been back. "I'd love to. Do you know what I've been craving? Blackberry pie."

"Great. The diner it is. I haven't been cooking much lately, anyway. Dessert first."

While Cheyenne and Madison set up a time, Riley nodded her acknowledgment to the deputy guarding the door and peered into Chloe's hospital room. The girl looked peaceful, and something else. Riley turned and clasped Cheyenne's arm. "Are Chloe's eyelids moving?"

"We think she's dreaming. It's our first really good sign since I pulled her off the ventilator. Gram is magic."

Gram's soft words drifted their way: "And they soared into the sky together. For the first time ever, he felt safe and loved." The story ended, and Helen glanced over at Lincoln. "Could I have some tea, my love? I'm not used to telling stories these days, and my throat's a bit dry."

Lincoln gave her a sweet kiss on her forehead and left to do her bidding. Helen shifted in her seat and whispered to Chloe, and began another tale. He paused in the hallway, a wide grin splitting his face. "Did you hear her? She remembered the entire story."

Cheyenne kissed her grandfather on the cheek. "A moment to cherish."

"Moments of clarity," he said and disappeared down the hall toward the small lunchroom.

Thayne used the phrase often. The Blackwoods lived for those moments of clarity. Riley hoped they continued for a long time.

When Helen's sweet-toned voice went quiet, Riley glanced through the doorway. Thayne's grandmother stood and bent over Chloe's bed. She whispered something into her ear and patted the girl's hand once more before walking toward the door.

"I'm finished," she said with a smile at Cheyenne, looking straight past Riley without a flash of recognition. "Where's Lincoln?"

"Getting you tea from the lunchroom," Cheyenne said. "Aren't you thirsty?"

Helen shrugged. "Not really. I need to go to my book club meeting. I'll find him." She wrinkled her forehead and looked first right and then left. "Which way?"

"Madison, you know where the lunchroom is. Could you keep Gram company to find Pops?" Cheyenne asked. "I need to check my patient."

"Of course," Madison said as Cheyenne disappeared into Chloe's room.

Riley's sister fell in step with Helen.

"Are you new to town, dear? You have a nice smile. I think I like you."

"I like you, too, ma'am." Madison linked arms with Helen and gave Riley a wink before they disappeared around the corner.

Cheyenne exited the hospital room with a frown. "Her vitals are excellent. If she's not awake by the end of the day, I'm calling in a consultant, maybe transfer her to a larger hospital."

The words quenched that flicker of hope within Riley that had risen with Chloe's improvement.

"Okay. I'm heading to the sheriff's office to meet Thayne. I want to go to the cabin your father told us about last night. It's a long shot, but maybe something will pan out."

"Good luck. I'll work with Madison."

"Thank you." Knowing Cheyenne would talk to Madison eased Riley's concern.

After hurrying out of the hospital, she drove to the sheriff's office. Once she entered the building, she greeted Alicia and strode over to Deputy Pendergrass's desk.

"Tell me you have a break in the Jordan case, even if it's a bread crumb."

The man scowled at her. "Good morning to you, too. I'll let you know." He shoved his chair back and stalked to the back room.

"Okay then." Riley sent Alicia a what-the-hell look.

"Don't mind Quinn. He's having a tough time right now. Personal issues."

"Aren't we all," Riley muttered before knocking on Thayne's door.

Though on the phone, he motioned her in and said to whomever he was talking to, "Stall for a couple of minutes. I'm on my way."

Thayne hung up and strapped on his gun. "We can't leave for the cabin just yet. That was a call from the bank. Dan Peterson is at it again. He's getting scammed."

◆ ◆ ◆

Thayne slammed out of his office door. "I'm heading to the bank; then Riley and I are working the Jordan case. I've got my phone if the rest of the town goes to hell, too."

At Alicia's wide-eyed stare, he winced. "Sorry. Call if you need me."

The sheriff's office went silent, but Thayne didn't have time for more than that. All he knew was that someone had encouraged Dan Peterson to withdraw all his money. And the man had agreed. He knew one thing for certain: Anyone who had the cojones to walk into a bank and empty out an old man's bank account was someone Thayne would engage up close and personal.

He passed his deputy's desk.

"You need backup, Sheriff?" Deputy Pendergrass asked, half standing as if he were ready to go.

"I've got Riley. I'll call you if I need you."

Pendergrass flopped unceremoniously into his chair. "Right. Take her." More and more the man was showing signs of discontent. Thayne had taken the job Pendergrass had thought was his, so it wasn't shocking, and now Riley was here. He felt for the guy. They needed to have a conversation, but now wasn't the time. He raced out of the building, Riley on his heels. He vaulted into his SUV, and she jumped in with him.

"Call my father. Tell him to meet us at the bank. I don't know what's going on, but if Dan Peterson gives me any trouble, maybe Dad can help."

Luckily the bank was only two blocks away. By the time Riley filled his father in, Thayne had reached the front of the bank. They walked inside.

He could feel the tension the moment he walked in. Thayne quickly scanned the room, identifying threats and exits. A young teller sat behind the counter, frozen. Yvonne from the Cuts, Curls, and Color Salon had plastered herself against the side wall, clutching a bank bag.

"It's my money and I'll do what I damned well please," Dan shouted, slapping his hand on the counter. He glared at the bank manager. "Give it to me now. All of it."

The con man standing next to Dan took a step back. "I'll wait outside, sir. Meet you there."

Before the guy could disappear, Thayne grabbed him by the scruff of the neck. "I don't think so." He pushed him toward the wall. "Hands on the wall, feet apart, and don't move. My FBI colleague has a weapon."

The guy swallowed. "FBI?"

"Shut up. I'm not talking to you," Thayne said. He faced Mr. Peterson. "What's the trouble, Dan?"

Mr. Peterson's face had turned tomato red. Sweat popped on his brow. "This idiot bank manager won't let me have my money so I can pay this young man for doing me a favor." He scowled at Thayne. "What are you doing? Causing trouble as usual. Don't think you can arrest this nice boy while I'm around." Dan took a step toward Thayne, and Riley stopped him. He craned his neck to see past her. "Why are you treating him like a criminal?" he yelled.

The shout echoed around the bank, and the stranger winced. "I don't want any trouble." He met Thayne's gaze. "I'll quietly leave. No harm, no foul. We can call it a misunderstanding."

"Identification," Thayne ordered. "Now."

The guy passed over his license, and Thayne zeroed in on the man's home base. "Out of state. Based outside of Boulder. Working for the natural gas company by chance?"

The man's eyes widened and he nodded.

Thayne tapped his radio. "Alicia, tell Quinn I need him at the bank. We've got a new overnight guest."

Dan grabbed Thayne's arm with both hands. "Oh no you don't. I've got to give that boy thirteen thousand dollars."

The words froze Thayne. "What'd he promise you, Mr. Peterson?"

"He's buying me a house so I can get away from my wife." Dan Peterson's eyes narrowed. "She tried to kill me. I told you, and you wouldn't listen. I gotta get away from here, and this young man said he'd help me. No one else will."

Dan crossed his arms and glared at Thayne. "I'm not moving until I get my money."

For the first time Thayne appreciated Dan's dogged stubbornness. Finally, Quinn rushed inside, hand hovering over his gun. "What's going on?"

"Everything's under control," Thayne said and nodded at their suspect. "Get this guy out of here. Read him his rights and book him on attempted fraud."

"You got it." Quinn shoved the guy through the door.

"I didn't do it. The old man offered me the money. I never asked for it."

Dan's expression sagged; his eyes darted around the room. He paced back and forth, his movements erratic. Thayne motioned everyone to stay back. He didn't want Dan to get hurt or hurt anyone else. The old man suddenly kicked a metal display over. The housing clattered as it hit the tiles, and pamphlets fluttered to the floor.

"You gone and done it this time," Dan yelled. "When you find my cold, dead body tomorrow, you'll be to blame." He returned to the teller window and pounded on the counter. "Close my account. I want my money."

Just as Dan shouted his instructions, Thayne's father walked through the door. "Dan? I hear you're making a bit of a ruckus. Look at poor Missy there behind the counter. She's plumb terrified."

At Thayne's father's words, Dan Peterson seemed to deflate. Thayne let out a long sigh and sidled over to Riley. "What do you think?" he asked, his voice soft.

"Hospital," Riley said. "Something's definitely wrong with him. He was normal when he helped us find Chloe. Maybe his wife is overdosing him."

"I agree." He cleared his throat. "Dad, could we invite Mr. Peterson to have a cup of coffee with Cheyenne? We were just headed that way."

"Good idea, son." His father smiled at Dan. "What do you say? My daughter might spring for a few chocolate chip cookies to go with that coffee."

Dan studied Carson for a few moments and frowned. "You made me go home to *that woman.* My daughter was furious. Maybe you're the one Kate's been seeing on the side."

Thayne's dad shook his head. "We've known each other all our lives, Dan. Do you really think I'd risk your friendship doing something like that?"

For a moment, Dan appeared confused; then he let out a long sigh. "Of course not. Kate . . . she hurt me, Carson." His eyes welled up. "No one's listening to me. Not about Kate, and not about those booze and pills belonging to someone else. I didn't know what else to do."

"Sounds like it's been a confusing couple of days. We're gonna talk this out. Let's go see Cheyenne." Carson led Dan outside and into his vehicle.

Thayne watched them leave before walking over to the bank manager.

A worried expression furrowed her brow. "Is Mr. Peterson going to be okay?"

"I don't know, but he has you to thank for protecting his money. You did the right thing calling me." He glanced over at the trembling teller and smiled at her. "Good job, Missy."

Her face reddened. "Thanks, Sheriff," she squeaked.

The manager gave him a quick hug. "Thank you. Let us know how he is."

Thayne tipped his hat and met Riley's gaze. They walked out together. He stroked his chin. "I hope Cheyenne can figure out what's happening to him."

Riley paused on their way to the car. "Before Mr. Peterson's incident, I was coming over to ask if you want to go to the cabin between the Blackwood and Riverton properties with me. Maybe I should just head out to the cabin. You can finish up here, and I'll report in later."

He held up his finger, motioning her to keep that thought while he placed a call.

"Quinn, we have a situation at the hospital. Dan Peterson had some sort of episode. He needs a medical workup. If he won't agree, we may need to get his family involved." Thayne filled him in on the details.

His deputy let out a low whistle. "What a mess."

"Yeah. I'm heading into the hills to check out a cabin connected to the Jordan murder. Contact me via radio if you need anything."

"You got it."

Thayne ignored Riley's pointed glare as they got into the car. While they headed toward the Blackwood Ranch, he glanced over at her. "You're quiet."

"I could've done this myself. I'm perfectly capable."

"I know that, Riley, but Dan's situation is medical. No one's hurt and we have Chloe to think about. We both know we're low on leads . . . unless you've done some of your profiler voodoo and solved the whole thing last night?"

"I wish. A handful of possible scenarios have played in my head, but none of them are solid enough to even begin putting the pieces together." She rubbed the bridge of her nose. "We've been investigating the Jordan case for about forty-eight hours. Two dead bodies, an unconscious twelve-year-old, and one very weak suspect—Chloe."

CHAPTER EIGHT

Though the afternoon sun glinted off the windshield, Riley knew if she rolled down the window, a blast of cold air would greet her. She flipped down the visor and squinted. The road was barely visible against the glare.

"Good thing there's not much traffic," she said.

The vehicle reached a fork in the road. Normally, they would've headed west toward the Blackwood Ranch. This time they took the eastern route.

"We're headed toward the Riverton place?" Riley asked, surprised.

"According to Dad, this will get us closer to a dirt road leading to the disputed land. I called Cheyenne's husband. Brett agreed to meet us to unlock the gate. Otherwise, we'd have to go on either horseback or ATVs."

Her entire body shivered at the thought. "The temperature is hovering around freezing. I prefer the SUV."

"My thoughts exactly."

"I've only spoken to Brett a couple of times, and the first time didn't go so well since he was a suspect in Cheyenne's kidnapping. As far as I can tell, he's like the invisible man. Do you see him often?"

"Nope. Cheyenne's closed-lipped. I don't even know if she's living out here. It's funny. They kept their relationship a secret for so long they can't break the pattern. If Gram were herself, she'd knock some sense into the two of them. If it goes on much longer, I'll have to do something. For now, we'll have to wait and see."

"A modern-day Romeo and Juliet." The cold battering the window chilled Riley's shoulder, and she shifted away from the door. "I guess they love each other enough to try and make it work."

She had said it without even thinking and shot Thayne a quick glance.

He flicked an unreadable expression her way. "I guess."

The highway veered to the right, and they sped along a metal fence. They'd reached Riverton Ranch, the largest in the county.

Tension rippled over Thayne's body. She couldn't tell whether it was from her question or because they were now on Riverton property. "Tell me more about this feud."

He sighed. "No one in our families talks about it, but the past impacts our lives anyway. The Blackwoods and the Rivertons never got along. Not in Pop's day, not in Dad's day. And not now."

"Except for Cheyenne."

"Except her, but then she always did bring home unwanted animals."

Was he really equating Cheyenne's husband to an unwanted animal? There was a story there, but all too soon they spotted a large black pickup parked on the side of the road. As they drew closer, she could just make out a dirt road leading off between two small hills.

Thayne pulled up to a gate and turned off the engine.

They both exited the vehicle and waited for Brett.

He slowly emerged from his truck. The last time she'd seen him, he'd barely been able to walk. He still used his cane, but his movements were fluid, even graceful. A skeletally thin man rounded the front and stood beside his boss.

Riley hadn't seen Brett's foreman for a while. His cancer had obviously progressed.

Brett reached out his hand to Thayne, then to Riley. "I was surprised to get your call."

"No more than I was to be making it." Thayne nodded toward the swath of land that ran the length between the ranches. "You ever step foot in the forbidden zone?"

"Have you?" Brett chuckled. "But to answer your question, nope. Dad whipped the living tar out of my brother when he explored it. I decided the punishment wasn't worth it. As far as I know, it's been abandoned for decades. I've seen the cabin at a distance while riding fence, but I'd imagined it's uninhabitable by now."

"Then why would Kim Jordan have a map?" Thayne asked.

"Show me the drawing?"

Riley pulled the copy from her bag and handed it to Cheyenne's husband.

He frowned as he studied the document. "I guess it could be my land."

"You mean *my* land," Thayne quickly corrected.

Brett ignored him as he twisted the map this way and that. "The focus is on the old cabin, but it also shows the Riverton Arroyo. It carries the water straight down the center of the land our great-grandparents fought over." Brett dug his cane into the mud at the side of the road. "Conditions aren't optimal for going out there."

"Are you trying to warn me off looking around out there? Makes me wonder if you're hiding something."

"Just offering a general warning to be careful. I imagine you'll see some remnants of last weekend's storm." He dug into his pocket for a key to the gate and passed it to Thayne. "You can give it to Cheyenne when you see her. I rarely use it."

"Thanks, Brett."

His brother-in-law stood there, silent, for a moment. "Maybe it's time we put this feud to bed once and for all. Everyone who cared is dead and gone, and I sure as hell have no interest in prolonging anything. Marriage is hard enough without a whole Hatfield and McCoy reboot."

Brett held out his hand.

Thayne took off his hat and stared at Brett. For a second, Riley thought he'd refuse. Instead he shook Brett's hand.

"I like the sound of that. I think I can convince Pops to let it go. I don't mind sharing the land. These days, fighting a century-old battle wouldn't even hit his radar. Every day he and Gram are fighting a war they won't win. There's not a lot of energy for anything else."

Brett frowned and glanced over at Shep, who appeared to sway just standing next to his boss. "I understand that."

Riley knew the bond between the pair was as strong as family, and it was hard to say which of the two men was luckier. Brett let go of Thayne's hand. "I hope you find what you're looking for." He stepped close and patted the older man's shoulder. "Let's go, Shep. We'll check the north pasture and then have a long, slow whiskey."

The ill man briefly nodded, doffed his hat, and shuffled back to the truck. Soon they disappeared down the road.

"I feel badly for him," Riley said. "He obviously cares about his foreman."

"When Brett's father disappeared and left him to run the ranch, Shep was there. Brett was just a kid then. Losing that old man will be tough. Shep was the glue that held that ranch together for a lot of years." Thayne looked up at the clouds forming above the mountains. "Isn't it ironic? Shep's body is eating itself alive while leaving his mind intact. Gram's body is strong, but her mind is disappearing piece by piece. Do you think one is worse than the other?"

"I don't know." Riley slipped her hand around his waist and hugged him.

He pulled her close. "I'd give anything to talk to Gram, to ask her questions that I never got around to asking when I was a kid."

"You can still ask her, can't you?" She looked up at him. "She still has good days."

Sadness transformed his face to reveal the heartache the family was going through. "I want to be confident the answers she gives me are based in truth and not something she's made up so the world she lives in now makes sense." He backed away and swiped his eyes. "This is ridiculous. She's still here."

"I'm so sorry, Thayne. I didn't recognize anything was wrong with her when I first met her a year ago."

"Most didn't then. Now, I think most people know." Thayne made a show of studying the key in his hand. "I see a flash of the Gram I knew most days, but I also see moments of this blank stare where she's standing in front of me, and I know she's gone." His jaw tightened. "I'd give anything to help her, but there's nothing to be done. Her medication makes it seem like she's doing better, but it's just masking the destruction going on inside her head."

"How long does she have?"

Thayne shrugged, but the pain he felt lingered in his eyes. "From what Cheyenne told us, when her medication stops working, she'll deteriorate very quickly. From there, it could last a couple of years. Could be five years, ten, maybe longer. By the time it's over, goodbye won't mean anything to her."

"A long, slow goodbye versus a short, excruciating journey." Riley didn't know which was worse. She rested her hand on his chest. "I hate that this is happening to Helen."

"Me too." He covered her hand with his and gave it a quick squeeze. "Sorry. I don't usually let it get to me." He let her go and walked over to the lock and chain. "Let's see if we can't figure out what's so special about this land, and why Kim Jordan would have a map."

He slipped the key inside and turned. The lock popped open. "That seemed too easy for a lock that Brett implied he never used."

Riley studied the metal. "It's a weatherproof lock. Not that old. He must've replaced it at some point."

They drove through the gate and stopped so Riley could jump out and relock the gate. Within a few hundred feet, the dirt road grew rough. Thayne hit one bump, and Riley jerked against her seat belt.

"This road could scramble my insides," she said. "This wouldn't be my favorite picnic location, that's for sure."

"But it might be a good place to hide something."

The SUV took a nosedive into a gully and splashed through some water. Thayne gunned the engine and they rumbled out, though their tires spun a bit before the front wheels gained traction.

When they reached the top of a rise, he stopped the SUV.

"Why'd we stop?" Riley asked.

Thayne grabbed his binoculars from the back seat. "It's a good vantage point for a look-see."

He and Riley exited, and while he surveyed the land surrounding them for anything suspicious, she gazed at the beauty in front of her. The Wind River Mountains loomed to the east, casting a shadow on the narrow valley. A deep intertwining series of trenches cut through the landscape. The dramatic scenery took her breath away. "Do you see anything?"

"A lot of arroyos," Thayne said. "The water runoff has cut deep into the earth. Those sides are steep and dangerous." He pointed at a fence following just beyond the dramatic landscape. "The Rivertons' fence keeps their livestock from getting stuck in a death trap. If a flash flood were to hit, anything inside the arroyos would get swept away by water moving as fast as nine or ten feet per second."

"No wonder the families tried to keep us away. It just doesn't explain why anyone would fight over a parcel of land that's basically useless."

He peered through the binoculars to the north. "I can't see the cabin, but it can't be too far."

"Can I have a look?" she asked. He handed her the binoculars, and the landscape rushed toward her. A few hundred feet ahead sat an oddly shaped pile of rocks. She returned Thayne's equipment to him and searched behind them for the map.

"Look directly ahead of us. There are two pyramids of stones," she said, indicating both mounds.

Thayne's forehead wrinkled. "I see them. There's a third farther up the hill."

"Markers?" Riley asked. "Maybe they're the triangles represented on the map." She pulled out the sheet of paper and pointed at the roughly drawn images and the cabin nearby.

"You're right," he said. "Let's get up to that cabin."

◆ ◆ ◆

The cabin was right where the map showed it would be. By the time they reached it, Thayne had more questions than answers. Two more pylons signaled the trail. The fifty-year-old cabin should have been dilapidated and unusable. Instead, repairs appeared to have taken place in the last five years or so.

As Riley took pictures of the outside, Thayne snapped on his gloves and stepped onto the porch.

"Someone's been using this place," he said. "These replacement planks on the porch can't be more than a few years old." He ran his gloved hand along the cabin's wall, surprised when his fingers edged a series of recent repairs. "Wood epoxy on the outside walls. This is *definitely* not an abandoned cabin."

"The Jordans built their home six years ago."

"It wouldn't be them. It doesn't make sense. Their house is in the middle of nowhere. It's not like they needed a remote getaway."

Riley put on her gloves as she joined Thayne on the porch. She snapped a few more photos before giving the front-door handle a good tug. "It's locked. If the Blackwoods and Rivertons don't visit this land, someone else has definitely been using it." She shook the door more violently. "For some reason, Kim had a map leading here. We need to get inside and search it."

Thayne scanned the front porch. No one who lived in Wyoming would leave a cabin like this locked without having a backup key. His gaze landed on a small iron pot full of decorative rocks. He picked up the pot and found a key hidden underneath. "Small-town living in the middle of nowhere. Can't afford to break down doors when you forget your key."

"If I did something that obvious in DC, I'd get cleaned out," she said as he picked up the key. She rubbed her hands together. The gloves they used so as not to leave prints were thin, and she looked up at the gathering clouds. The temperature had dropped drastically to just above freezing in the last few minutes, and the wind had picked up, whistling through the trees. Riley pushed away a lock of hair that blew across her face. "I just don't get why you'd need a key in the first place. It's not like this place has 'easy access' written all over it."

"I'm pulling Quinn up here to check for prints," he said with a frown. The look on his deputy's face this morning had made Thayne aware once again he needed to build a cohesive team here instead of going it solo. Well . . . as solo as Riley would allow.

He unlocked the door and pushed inside, Riley a step behind him. The interior was simple but functional. A queen-size bed, a wardrobe with drawers, and a small table filled one side of the room. A rudimentary kitchen lined the corner. Utilitarian, simple, a way station. Not what he'd expected, and he recognized the surprise on Riley's face as well.

"Nothing fancy." Thayne opened a door to their left. It led to a three-quarter bathroom. "It probably started out as an old hunting cabin."

Riley snapped several photos. "There's a year or two's worth of dust."

One by one he searched the cupboards. "Canned goods, powdered milk, basic staples. The expiration dates are still good. A well-stocked first aid cabinet. A few of these meds aren't over the counter." Someone had been using the cabin. Relatively often. But for what? A hideout? A lovers' retreat? Brett's name popped into his head, but his brother-in-law had handed over the key without blinking an eye, so he doubted he was using it.

A loud rumble sounded outside, followed by a crash and an electric crack. Riley jerked her head up. "That doesn't sound good."

It definitely didn't. The weather report that morning had mentioned a storm, but not in this area. Another loud boom reverberated through the air. Weather report or not, there was no mistaking the tenor of the thunder. A frisson of foreboding skittered across the base of his skull. He tugged back the window curtains and looked outside. The wind had grown stronger, bending the tall grass. Black, angry clouds hovered over the mountain peaks. "The storm's decided to come our way. It'll be raining soon. Let's search this place as quickly as possible. I don't want to get stuck up here."

Riley gave him a nod of understanding, but instead of tearing through the room, she squatted in the center. He recognized the process. She was taking in each and every detail. He fought against the urge to prod her along. Right now this place was their only lead, and they needed a break in the case.

"Perfectly neat," she muttered. "As if it's a guesthouse. Nothing out of place. Everything put away in its location."

"No weapons or ammunition, either." Thayne scratched his head. "That crosses out hunting."

Riley stood and opened the armoire. "Extra pillows and blankets." She slid open a drawer. "Towels and sheets. Nothing suspicious except neither family who claims ownership of the land and the cabin is using it. Why did Kim have the map?" She gripped her camera. "While you finish searching the last of the kitchen, I'll head outside to take a few more shots. Maybe Quinn will uncover some trace evidence he can process or that we can send to the state crime lab."

Thayne eased open the last kitchen drawer. "Riley. Check this out."

A stack of papers and several pencils lay in the drawer—but the paper wasn't blank. At least a dozen maps, identical to the one from Kim Jordan's box. With great care, Thayne removed several sheets and slipped them into an evidence bag. "Whoever drew these can provide information. If Quinn can pull prints—"

"We'll have an answer," Riley finished the sentence for him.

For the first time since he'd realized the Jordans had been murdered, Thayne could see a potential path for answers, even without Chloe's help.

Loud drops thwapped against the window. They'd run out of time. "Rain," he said, his voice urgent. "And it's coming down hard. We have to leave. I don't want to get stuck."

"Just a few pictures." Riley hurried out of the cabin and disappeared behind it so she could capture some images from the back. She stood beneath the roof's eave, lifted her camera, and snapped twenty or so shots but saw nothing unusual.

Lightning cracked across the sky and the clouds opened up. Sheets of rain poured down on top of them. "We've got to get out of here," Thayne shouted. "Those roads will turn to mud fast."

Riley nodded. "Done."

They raced to the vehicle, and by the time they were safely inside the SUV, Riley's hair and clothes had soaked through. She unzipped her coat and peeled it off. "That was fast."

Though he wore his hat, Thayne hadn't fared much better. He took it off and gave it a quick shake to dislodge any remaining water. "Weather can roll in quickly this time of year. It's probably snowing on the mountaintop."

Rain pounded the roof of the SUV. Thayne reversed and carefully turned around. He squinted through the layers of water, barely able to see the hood of the car. The windshield wipers squeaked back and forth at a dizzying pace but did little to improve visibility. The glass fogged up inside from the moisture evaporating from their doused clothing.

Thayne switched on the defogger and gripped the steering wheel tight. "We're probably okay until we hit those rugged sections of the dirt road. If the water's rushing through, we may end up back at the cabin to wait it out."

A frown tugged at Riley's mouth. He reached behind her and kneaded her neck. "Don't worry. I've driven in much worse."

Unfortunately, not on worse roads than what he feared lay waiting for them.

◆ ◆ ◆

The wind and rain buffeted the SUV. Riley gripped the console, her hands tight with tension as she dug into the leather until her fingers ached. The vehicle bounded over the rocks before sinking into the growing mud.

More than once the tires spun uselessly, vibrating the entire car before they caught and lurched the vehicle forward. She could hardly make out the terrain through the thunderstorm that hammered the area.

"Will we make it?" She'd faced her share of danger, but nothing matched Mother Nature when it came to her fury.

"The highway's farther than I'd like," he shouted. The storm nearly drowned out his voice.

The SUV slid to the left, and Thayne's knuckles whitened on the steering wheel as Riley let out a tight yelp. A four-wheel drive wasn't any good if none of the tires could grip the so-called road.

Her breathing rate had picked up. She wiped away the fog on the front window. The ground about ten feet in front of them seemed to move.

"What's that?" she shouted.

Before she could say more, the front of the vehicle plunged downward, and reddish-brown water splashed halfway up the SUV's doors. Thayne let out a loud curse. They'd driven straight into an arroyo, a conduit through which mud and water rushed down from the mountain. "Hang on."

He gunned the gas, but the SUV stuck to the spot. The longer they were stuck, the higher the muddy water rose, until it was almost up to the window.

The engine started to gurgle. Thayne pressed harder on the gas. With a quick yank of the steering wheel, the SUV shifted direction. The left side banged against something solid. The engine revved higher as Thayne urged the car forward. The right wheels spun, a high-pitched squeal that made Riley's stomach sink. A guttural sound clawed from deep within her. Suddenly the vehicle lurched forward. The left front wheel caught on solid ground and jerked upward.

Within moments, somehow—and Riley had no idea exactly how—they'd climbed out of the ditch. Thayne brought the SUV to a skidding halt. He let out a labored breath and patted the dashboard. "Way to go, girl. That was too close."

He met Riley's gaze, and she recognized the truth there. They'd almost been swept away. She hadn't allowed herself to think it was a possibility.

"How close?" she asked quietly.

"A few more inches of water, and . . ." He didn't finish his sentence. He didn't have to. "Let's get the hell out of here."

They bounced over the last several hundred yards where the land hadn't been carved up by the churning water.

When Thayne reached the gate, he let out a relieved sigh.

"Give me the key," Riley demanded. "I'll unlock it so you can drive through. It'll be faster."

He winced, but he handed it over. She got out and ducked over the lock. Rain slammed against her, and the sharp wind laced with freezing rain stung her face. Her fingers slipped against the lock, but after a few seconds, the key slid in and she twisted it. The lock popped open, and she yanked the gate open wide.

Thayne drove through, and she secured the chain before dashing back into the car.

Heat pelted her from the vents, and she basked in the warmth.

"It feels like the temperature's dropped another twenty degrees," she stuttered through chattering teeth.

Thayne pulled onto the paved road. No more bone-shattering dips, holes, grooves, or bumps. The road felt like they were sliding through warm butter.

"This is more like it." Riley sent him a sidelong glance. "Next time, can we check the weather before we visit that cabin?"

"I did. Weather here rarely cooperates. Tomorrow we could wake up to a sunny day and have a foot of snow on the ground by nightfall."

They'd traveled a few miles when Thayne's phone rang. He tapped the phone icon on his dash to pick up his father's call.

His dad didn't bother with a greeting. "Quinn told me you were headed out to investigate the cabin, but I had to tell you."

"Is Dan okay?" Thayne asked.

"Cheyenne's giving him an exam, but the truth is, I don't know." His father's voice cracked. "I'm sorry, son. I was wrong. I was so focused on the past I couldn't see beyond my preconceptions. When Dan removed his shirt . . ." He paused and lowered his voice for their ears alone. "There were more bruises up and down his back. Passing out in his truck doesn't explain it. I don't know what's going on, but something is very, very wrong."

Thayne whistled softly, and his father told him to hold on. Suddenly Cheyenne came on the phone. "Hey, are you still with Riley? I need her help."

Riley's body tensed. "I'm here. What's going on?"

"It's Dan Peterson. I have him in the exam room, and his wife and daughter are in my office. Someone's lying, and I can't tell who."

"How can I help?" Riley asked. "I'm not a doctor."

"No, but you read people better than anyone I know. Someone's lying about how Mr. Peterson ended up with several bruises on his back, legs, and chest. Until I know for sure, I'm not letting his family near him."

CHAPTER NINE

The sound of sirens pounded against Thayne's head, worsening his headache. He'd never imagined the emotional investment his father made on a day-to-day basis as sheriff. In a town of a thousand people, nothing was out of his jurisdiction. Thayne could tell his father blamed himself for not taking Dan seriously.

They'd have to figure it out.

Thayne sped into town past the dress shop, the diner, and the small antiques shop. From a glance, the town appeared sleepy and calm. He couldn't shake the truth that every answer he found—whether about Dan Peterson or that old cabin—would reveal a shadow lingering beneath the idyllic small town he called home.

Thayne studied Riley. Did she see it? Feel it? From the frown that hadn't left her face since the phone call, he had to wonder. That uneasy foreboding he experienced—usually before a cluster of a mission—settled in his gut.

She gripped the stack of maps, and he caught her chewing on her lip, deep in thought. He could practically see the wheels churning in her mind, but instead of the flash of insight brightening her eyes, they creased with worry. A long sigh escaped her.

"That good, huh?" he asked. He pulled the car to a stop as an elderly couple crossed the street. His flashing lights didn't seem to faze them. He drummed his fingers on the steering wheel to a beat that showed his impatience as they smiled and waved at him.

She picked at the soaked fabric of her pants. "Would you believe all I want is a shower, a change of clothes, and a cup of coffee?"

The couple finally gave them enough room to pass, and Thayne sped to the clinic. "Not hardly, though you've read my mind." His wet clothes clung to his skin, giving him that cloistered, trapped feeling. "What are you thinking?"

"About Dan? I have no idea what to think until I see them." She winced. "Is it bad of me to feel like his problems are interfering in the Jordan case?"

Thayne understood what she meant.

The sooner he dealt with Dan and his family, the sooner he and Riley could try to piece together the mystery of the Jordan murders.

He zipped into a parking place in front of Cheyenne's medical clinic. Several cars lined the street outside the now-closed office.

"I hate this place," he muttered.

She lifted a brow. "Scared of the doctor? She's your sister."

"Nothing good happens here. At least to me or mine. Broken bones, shots, life-changing diagnoses like cardiomyopathy and Alzheimer's." His parents had dragged him to the place whenever he'd been sick or needed a shot. The first time the word *dementia* had been uttered to his grandparents had been in one of the appointment rooms. Plus, Cheyenne had been kidnapped from and his grandmother attacked in the place just a month ago.

Nope, he hadn't grown fonder of the building. Thayne appreciated being able to check up on his sister every so often. He probably stopped by for coffee more often than he should've since she'd been abducted, but she put up with him.

"It's an old building," Riley said.

"The place has been an institution in Singing River for decades. Cheyenne took over for old Doc Mallard."

"Doctors keep permanent records," Riley mused.

"Doc's records go back generations." He shifted in his seat. "What are you thinking?"

"I don't know. That cabin's been there a long time. It had medical supplies, and didn't you say not all of them were over the counter? I just wonder if Doc knew anything. If he left any records. Or perhaps Cheyenne knows something."

"All we can do is ask." Thayne had just shut off the engine when, in his peripheral vision, he caught sight of Quinn racing over from the sheriff's office.

"We've got company." He exited the vehicle. Thayne met the deputy on the passenger side just as he opened the door for Riley. She slid out of the seat, clutching her evidence bag.

"You've got something for me?" his deputy asked, giving their drenched clothes a once-over. "Looks like the mountain wasn't happy to see you."

"Flash-flood unhappy. It's raining at the base of the mountains." Thayne tilted his head toward the gray streaks fading into the ground thirty miles away. "The storm's moving north. Tell Alicia to keep an ear out just in case the county roads become impassable."

"Will do."

"Hopefully these are a huge break." Riley retrieved the maps from her bag and handed them over to Quinn.

"These look like copies of the Kim Jordan map," he said.

"Numerous *handmade* copies," Riley said.

His eyes widened in surprise. "Someone's gone to a lot of trouble, but why keep maps in the place where it points to?"

Good question. "We need a name, Quinn, and we're counting on you. Maybe then we'll finally get some answers." Thayne shifted, trying to dislodge the clothes stuck to his body. "Run every test you can on the trace evidence. If you have to drive it up to the state capital and sit outside the lab to wait for the answer, do it. We need a lead."

"Whoever killed the Jordans has tried real hard to cover their tracks. I don't like sneaky people," Quinn muttered with a low curse. "I'll find something."

Thayne nodded in acknowledgment of the determination in his deputy's voice. "Contact me the moment you find anything, no matter how small." Thayne twisted some water from his shirt. "I have my phone."

Quinn nodded and rushed back to the sheriff's office.

"If there's anything there, Quinn will find it." Thayne turned to her. "Riley, are you sure you're okay evaluating Dan? It's not in your job description."

"He's a friend of your family. I want to help, but I don't know if I can. Contrary to what Cheyenne suggested, I'm no lie detector."

"You're the closest thing I've ever seen. Just do your thing and we'll find the truth."

Through the glass door of the clinic, Thayne could see Cheyenne's receptionist squirming behind her desk, an odd panicked expression on her face.

When he opened the door and followed Riley in, Violet jumped to her feet. "Thank goodness you're here. Dr. Blackwood-Riverton saw her last patient a few minutes ago, and the Peterson family's getting impatient. It's a mess."

Her gaze darted to the front door as if she couldn't wait to escape.

Thayne patted her hand. "Everything'll be fine. Before we head on back, could you bring us a couple of towels?"

"Of course." She didn't even have to ask what had happened to them. She'd lived in Singing River long enough to know the weather could be meaner than a bear. She brought them two towels from the supply room. "The doctor is down the hall on the left."

Thayne passed a towel to Riley, and they both mopped up what they could, but it didn't help much.

A door's loud slam ricocheted through the clinic.

"You can't keep us here any longer," an angry female voice shouted. "This is ridiculous. You saw the bruises. She's lying. *Of course* my stepmother is abusing him. If you won't help, I'm going to find the sheriff."

The receptionist winced. "She's been like that since she got here."

"Dan Peterson's daughter?" Thayne asked. This was one part of the job he still couldn't get used to. He hadn't realized until becoming sheriff that his father was part lawman, part psychologist, and part family therapist.

The young woman nodded. "Even Cheyenne hasn't been able to calm her down, and we call her the patient whisperer. She's like magic."

His sister had that effect on everyone she met. She could bring calm to the most chaotic situations. Thayne gave his hair one last good rub with the now-damp towel before handing it to Violet and then met Riley's gaze. "Here we go."

Riley passed her towel to the receptionist with a quick thank-you and followed as Thayne walked toward the noise. At the end of the hall, Cheyenne's office door stood wide open.

Thayne planted himself in the doorway. Two women—one petite with salt-and-pepper hair, the other tall and curvy—shouted over each other at Cheyenne. His sister stood behind her desk, trying to reason with them. She caught Thayne's movement, and her panicked expression screamed *help*. He'd never seen her lose control of a situation.

He let loose a sharp whistle, and the two women froze. Olivia Peterson's face was beet red, and her entire body vibrated with barely-held-in anger as she stared daggers at Dan's wife, who looked haggard, like she hadn't slept in days.

"What's going on here?" he asked in a soft, calm voice.

He'd discovered since returning home that his body language could calm the situation more quickly than his weapon. At least most of the time. He stood relaxed, conveying he had all the time in the world. "I appreciate how worried you are, but you need to knock it down a level or two, please, ladies. You sent young Violet scurrying into a corner. If this continues, I'll have to arrest the pair of you for disorderly conduct, and frankly, I don't want to do that."

Cheyenne didn't try to hide her relief at his entrance. *"Sheriff,"* she said, slowly and loudly emphasizing his title, "we have a situation."

"It's a hell of a lot more than that." Olivia faced him, her hands on her hips, unrepentant over her behavior. "About time you got here."

Ten years older than Thayne, she'd been one of his parents' favorite babysitters when he was a kid. She hadn't let him get away with anything—and he'd tried. It made encounters like this all the more awkward. Hard to garner respect when she'd ordered him to bed as a kid. He hadn't thought about her much in years. From what he recalled Gram telling him, Olivia had married one of the Riverton ranch hands and worked at the salon now. Two or three kids. Before the Alzheimer's, Gram had been the town's historian. She knew who married whom and what everyone did for a living. Gram was a true people person—something he had to work at, especially on days like this.

"What's the problem, Olivia?"

She flung her arms wide. "Dad's new wife is hurting him, and your saintly sister is stopping me from kicking her out of their house." She glared at Cheyenne. "Whose side are you on, anyway?"

"It's not true." Kate Peterson thrust her shoulders back, all five feet nothing and one hundred pounds of her. "I would never hurt him. I've told you a thousand times. He came in from working in the barn bruised and battered like that. He refused to tell me how. Then, when he put on his pajamas, he accused me of causing those bruises. I never touched him. I swear."

"You're lying." Olivia let out a scoffing laugh. "He told me you hurt him, and Dad would never make a thing like that up." She glared at her stepmother, then at Thayne. "I want her out of his house and out of his life. Today."

"It's actually *our* house." Kate raised her chin. "We bought it together after we married. I'm not leaving, and you can't force me." She turned to Thayne, her expression pleading. "This isn't my fault. Something's wrong with Dan. Why can't any of you see it?"

"Wouldn't you love us to believe that." Olivia shook her head. "He's fine. He's like he's always been. His story hasn't changed, and that's good enough for me. It wouldn't surprise me if you drugged him, too."

The color disappeared from Kate's face. "Why won't you listen to me? *He* has changed. I've been trying to tell you—"

"Because I know what you really want. What you've always wanted." Olivia lunged at Kate. "Over my dead body!"

Riley stepped between the women and held up her hands toward Olivia. "Calm down, ma'am," she said, her voice low and soft.

"Don't touch me," Olivia said, even though Riley hadn't even tried to do so. Olivia backed up and glowered at her. "You're that FBI agent, right? Why are you even here? This is our business, not yours."

Thayne could tell Riley had hoped to calm the woman down with her stance and tone, but clearly emotions were running too high. Still, he refused to let Olivia dismiss Riley's presence.

"She's part of this community as much as anyone," he snapped. "Agent Lambert's working with me on the sheriff's office investigations. She's the best there is."

Olivia's mouth screwed up in disdain. "She may have found your sister, but what's she going to do for my family?"

Thayne fought to keep his temper in check. She was worried about her father, and he could understand the fear that ran rampant behind her anger. "We've known each other for years, Olivia. Our fathers are friends. Let me do my job. I don't want your father hurt, either. Trust me."

His words seemed to deflate Olivia's anger. Cautiously, she nodded.

With the tension ratcheted down somewhat, Thayne focused on Riley. "Agent Lambert is going to interview you. She'll put all your concerns in writing, and then we'll make some decisions. Okay?"

"As long as Dad's safe. If he's not, I won't cooperate." Olivia crossed her arms, her entire posture challenging.

He met Riley's you've-got-to-be-kidding-me gaze. Well, he had his reasons. He needed to keep Olivia busy so he could get Dan's and Kate's sides of the story. The older woman had backed herself against the wall, clearly exhausted from the conflict.

He turned to Dan's wife. "Mrs. Peterson, please wait here in Cheyenne's office." He glanced over at Cheyenne. "I need to speak with Dan first."

Kate shuffled her feet, staring at them. "Sheriff, Dan doesn't remember things quite right. You can't believe everything he says."

Thayne quirked his brow. "I'll keep that in mind."

"Don't believe her," Olivia shouted as Riley led her to an exam room. "She wants his money. That's why she married him in the first place."

Cheyenne followed her brother out of her office, and he closed the door. "Riley, take Olivia's statement, then join me in the other exam room." He pinned Olivia with an intense stare. "We'll get to the bottom of this situation, but I expect everyone to remain calm."

Olivia sniffed at him and flounced into a chair before Riley closed the door. Thayne followed Cheyenne across the clinic into a small spill-over exam room where his dad and Dan waited. With a frown of concern lacing his features, Carson sat in a chair next to the exam table, where Dan Peterson perched, swinging his legs. Shirtless and shoeless, the old man sat with only his socks and underwear on, his too-big boxer shorts engulfing him. Thayne winced at the extent of the mottled blue-and-green bruises on Dan's chest.

His gaze traveled to the older man's legs. The discolorations on his shins obviously were older. He rounded the table. A large bruise on his lower back appeared to be recent.

Most people Thayne knew who were Dan's age would be laid up in bed with those kinds of injuries. Dan was a tough old geezer.

He squirmed on the table. "Well, everyone just come in and enjoy the show. Can I get dressed?" He glared at Cheyenne.

"Of course," she said and handed him his clothes. "Why don't you tell the sheriff what you told me."

The man slipped on his shirt and slowly buttoned it. "I said it a thousand times already—Kate's been hitting me. She drinks at night. She gets angry, and I end up bruised. End of story." He paused for a moment, then unfolded his pants. He slipped them on, leaving them unzipped before tugging on his worn boots. "Like I told the doc. I'm not going home. Ever."

"Does she hit you with her fists, Dan? Or did you get some of them when your truck went off the road?" Thayne asked. Mr. Peterson seemed sincere, but Thayne couldn't help but be skeptical as to how such a tiny thing as Kate could hurt a burly guy like Dan. She'd have to hit him with something hard. A pipe or a bat. It didn't make sense.

"Someone tried to kill me."

"Someone besides Kate?" Thayne pressed several more times to have Dan describe exactly what had happened. Finally, the old man threw up his hands. "Why does it matter *how* she hurt me? She just did." Dan glared at Thayne. "I'm not going home with her anymore, and that's final."

"Where do you want to stay?" Cheyenne asked in a soothing voice.

Dan paused for a moment. His brow furrowed before his face broke into a smile of relief. "Olivia will take me in. She's a good daughter."

Thayne couldn't deny she'd defended Dan with enthusiasm, but he wasn't so sure taking her father into her own home was quite what

Olivia had in mind. He glanced at his father. "Dad, can you wait with Mr. Peterson?"

His father nodded, his worried gaze landing on his friend.

Once the exam room door had closed, Thayne faced Cheyenne. "Well, sis? What's going on with him? Where'd the bruises come from? Did Kate really beat the hell out of him?"

Cheyenne motioned him back across the clinic and let out a slow sigh. "I know it's hard to believe, but he's adamant. And he hasn't changed his story."

"It would take a lot for someone her size and build to do that kind of damage." Thayne kneaded the back of his neck. "Is it even possible?"

"You've driven your body past the point you thought you could bear during your training. Human beings are capable of more—and worse—than we think sometimes."

"But Kate . . ." He stroked his chin and glanced at Cheyenne's closed office door, behind which Dan Peterson's wife waited for them. "Once she quit drinking, she became so passive."

"Dan claims she started drinking again. Of course, he also denies drinking or taking any medication, and Kate could be hiding the truth."

"If she'll let us, I'll search her house for proof." Thayne still didn't like the inconsistencies in Dan's story. "What about the severity of the injuries?"

"As we get older, our skin becomes thinner. It loses the protective fatty layer that helps cushion blood vessels from impact, but Kate's not very strong, so my professional opinion is that she couldn't do that amount of damage unless she used a weapon."

"He can't—or won't—tell us specifically how she hurt him. He evades any details."

Cheyenne's forehead furrowed in concentration. "I don't want to believe it happened, but I can't deny his symptoms. It's the most logical explanation."

"What else could be going on?"

Cheyenne flipped a sheet of paper in Dan's chart. "I ran some preliminary labs to see if there was a contributing cause to his bruising, but they came back normal. Kate claims Dan gets confused sometimes. Olivia denies there's anything wrong with her father, and I don't think he's lying. He believes Kate is hurting him."

At that moment Riley exited the room where she'd been interviewing Olivia. She joined them and let out a low whistle. "That is one ticked-off daughter."

"What's your takeaway?" Thayne asked.

"She believes her father's claims, but she also has a long-standing resentment toward Kate. She never wanted her father to remarry, and she thinks Kate married Dan to get his money. Evidently, he tucked away a nice amount from an auto-accident settlement twenty years ago, and it's been building interest since then." Riley handed over her notes to Thayne. "She encouraged her father to file a report. She won't back off until Kate is safely away from Dan."

"I can't force him to do anything. He can live where he wants to." Thayne rubbed his temple. "For now, I have to take Kate into custody for Dan's protection. Even if I have my doubts, his injuries are real."

"It's all you can do."

Thayne pushed open the door of the exam room. When he entered, Dan's daughter stood up, her stance still angry and defiant.

Thayne wasn't happy about any of this, but he had no choice. "We're arresting Kate."

"It's about time." Olivia gave a sharp nod. "I've been telling Dad for months he should report her. I'll make sure he calls an attorney so he can file for divorce." She clutched her purse. "I have to get back to work."

She scooted past him and strode down the hallway toward the exit.

"Hold on, Olivia." Thayne's voice yanked her to a halt. "What about your father?"

Her eyebrows shot up. "What about him? He'll be fine now that you're taking *her* to jail."

Thayne crossed his arms. "Dan doesn't feel safe. He wants to go home with *you*."

Utter shock froze Olivia's features. "That's impossible. I don't have room for him. He can be safe at his place now. She won't be there."

Thayne had figured she'd say as much. "You need to work that out with your father before you leave so we know where to drop him off," he advised.

Olivia glanced at her watch and groused. "I'm late for my next customer." She stalked across the clinic to where Dan waited. "Dad, Kate's going to jail. You can go home now. I'll stop by tomorrow after I take the kids to school."

Over her shoulder Thayne studied Dan's reaction.

His brow furrowed in confusion and he frowned. "I don't like it there. That's *her* house. Not mine. I want to come home with you. You're my daughter."

"We don't have room, Dad."

Her father bowed his head, his expression so downcast Thayne hated to witness it.

Olivia closed her eyes. "Fine. Go home and pack a bag. I'll figure out something." She kissed his cheek. "See you after work."

Olivia hurried out of the clinic without a backward glance. Dan sat in the room, fly still unzipped, and stared at his boots. "She's busy."

His expression growing more and more concerned by the second, Carson crossed over to Dan. "I'll take you home, old friend. Better zip up, though."

The older man flushed and turned his back to everyone. The sound of the zipper resonated in the room. "Kate usually cooks me an early dinner. It's about time to eat."

Thayne cleared his throat. "That won't happen tonight, Mr. Peterson. I'm taking your wife to the sheriff's office."

"Right, right. I know that." He glanced over at Carson. "How long will she be in jail? She doesn't like mean people. Most kind people don't."

What the hell? The man was sending his wife to jail, yet in the next breath he was calling her kind? How could a man vacillate so drastically between love and hate?

Riley touched Thayne's back. He glanced at her over his shoulder, her own discomfort written on her face.

"Did I just hear him right?"

Thayne gave a curt nod. "Yep, and unless Dan changes his story or we get new information, I have to lock Kate up. I don't have a choice."

◆ ◆ ◆

Table lamps and an overhead candelabra illuminated the living area of Fannie's B&B. Riley had showered and changed and silently climbed down the stairs. Normally, she would've relished booking anyone accused of abuse, but Kate's pathetic, hurt expression when Thayne had collected her prints and her photo just hadn't felt right.

Either Kate was lying or Dan was, and Riley believed both of them. Except their stories were mutually exclusive.

In DC, Adult Protective Services would have become involved before now, but Singing River wasn't large enough to support a local family-services organization. According to Thayne, a two-person office that serviced all of Sublette County, nearly five thousand square miles, was their only resource. He'd placed a call, but until the other group could step in, the sheriff's office had to do their best.

Small towns had their strengths—and their struggles, like everywhere else.

When she reached the base of the stairs, a chorus of laughter made her pause. The book club was in full swing. Riley could set her watch by the four ladies. Could she make it to the front door without the

Gumshoe Grannies seeing her? What a hilarious moniker Thayne had bestowed on his grandmother's book club when he was a teenager. He'd been a real rabble-rouser, as his father liked to say, and the family's stories about Thayne as a troublemaker never bored Riley. In fact, that adventurous boy had charmed her. Every so often she'd catch a glimpse of him when Thayne got a mischievous glint in his eye, and her heart would melt.

His childhood had been so unlike her own. Their families couldn't have been more polar opposites. Hers so dysfunctional and strained, while Thayne had experienced unconditional love from the day he'd been born. Riley, on the other hand . . . well, she tried not to dwell on unrealistic expectations.

Trouble was, she beat herself up more than anyone else, including her parents. She still couldn't quite comprehend why Thayne loved her. And yet he did.

She'd disappoint him. She knew that. Truth was, she already had. She'd given up when their love story had barely begun.

Riley gave herself a good shake and shoved the uncertainty and past aside. She'd think about the future later. Right now, the Jordan case waited.

Hovering partway down the stairs, she glanced at her watch. She and Thayne had a date to share a working dinner before reviewing the evidence for the umpteenth time.

While half of her couldn't wait to be alone with him, the other half dreaded it. Every moment with him tempted her more to stay in a place where she was afraid she'd lose herself, lose what made her the person she'd become.

In some ways she felt as if Singing River had already ripped away her edge. She normally pictured the crime the moment she walked the scene, but she'd foundered in understanding the motive of the Jordan murders, and she couldn't even help Thayne with Dan Peterson's odd case.

"You can't believe you could sneak out on us, Agent Lambert," Fannie's voice called across the room. "Haven't you learned anything in the last month?"

Riley's lips tightened in chagrin. She should've known. She faced the four silver-haired women sitting around a card table. In front of each of them rested a notebook, a blue pen, a pencil, a red pen, and a novel. Off to the side, a silver tray laden with desserts made Riley's mouth water. Not to mention the aroma of Fannie's coffee, which she'd take intravenously if she could.

She forced a smile and crossed the room. She still hadn't become used to everyone knowing or wanting to know not only her life's story but also her business. Especially when it came to her relationship with Thayne. "Ladies. How goes the book club? Did you catch the killer?"

Thayne's grandmother grinned at Riley. Helen Blackwood's eyes were bright this afternoon. She was having a good day. "We're starting from Agatha Christie's very first book, *The Mysterious Affair at Styles.* I've read it fifty times. At least."

Fannie's gentle gaze landed on Helen. Riley knew this same group of friends—Norma, the retired sheriff's dispatcher; Willow, who spent her retirement growing organic fruits and vegetables; and Fannie—met almost every week to read and discuss Agatha Christie novels. When Helen began showing signs of Alzheimer's, her best friends had been the first to spot it. Now they narrowed their choices to the stories Helen remembered best.

"I guess I should read one of her stories someday." Though Riley didn't know when she'd have the time.

All the women gasped, and the horrified expressions on their faces made Riley cringe.

"You've never read an Agatha Christie?" Helen squealed.

"You don't know about Poirot?" Norma fretted.

"Oh my dear." Fannie shook her head in befuddlement.

Willow didn't say a word, just opened and closed her mouth in shock.

Riley didn't have the heart to tell them she preferred scientific articles on criminal psychology, criminal archaeology, and forensics to fiction. Human beings' real actions shocked her a hell of a lot more than plot twists.

Fannie hurried across the living room and disappeared into her suite. Within moments she'd returned with a book and placed it in Riley's hands. "Here you are, dearie." She grinned. "You'll love it."

Riley smiled at the women and held the book close to her chest. "Thank you, ladies. I can't wait."

It was a lie, but she couldn't stamp out the eager expressions of hope on their faces. She waved and strode toward the escape of the front door.

"I need to tell you something, Riley." Helen's voice called out. "It's important."

She'd almost made it, but Riley couldn't ignore Thayne's grandmother. A month ago Helen's drawing had led to the discovery of a group of missing children and their abductor. She'd also solved the mystery of how Kim got Riley's number, so Riley returned to the living room and paused near Helen's chair. Willow plopped what appeared to be an oatmeal cookie on a plate and handed it to her.

"Don't eat it, Riley." Norma relieved Riley of the plate and returned the cookie to the large tray. "Try the petits fours. *I* made those. *Healthy dessert* is an oxymoron, no matter what Willow claims." She scowled at her friend.

Knowing she was trapped for now, Riley pulled up a chair and took the plate. "You wanted to tell me something, Helen?" she asked.

Thayne's grandmother frowned. "It's vital. You and Cheyenne need to help."

"Me and Cheyenne? Is this about Dan Peterson?"

Helen shook her head and her eyes clouded. "Not about poor Dan, though the man can't remember a thing anymore. He's almost as bad as I am." She pounded the side of her head with the heel of her hand. "Why can't I remember? You need to know."

Helen stood and paced, her movements growing more and more disjointed. She muttered to herself and wandered around the room, pausing here and there.

Riley got up and went to her. "Helen?" She gently touched her arm, but Helen jerked away.

"It'll come to you, Helen," Fannie said with a smile that didn't reach her eyes. "Shall we get back to our crime? When we left off, you were arguing wolfsbane is the best poison to use in a murder if you want to get away with it, as opposed to strychnine."

"Wolfsbane mimics a heart attack. Easy to keep it a secret. Strychnine is way too obvious." Helen sent Fannie a conspiratorial smile. "Don't you know the best way to keep a good secret is to be subtle and of course to never, ever tell anyone?"

That sounded heartfelt. Riley leaned forward, a chill skittering up her spine. "Do you have any secrets, Helen?"

"Definitely. I was telling that sweet girl in the hospital today about my best secret. She was very interested."

Riley froze. "Was Chloe awake, Helen?"

She blinked. "Who, dear?"

"Chloe. The girl in the hospital."

"Cheyenne works at her clinic, not the hospital, Riley. There is no Chloe. She doesn't exist. You should know that." Helen took a sip of coffee.

Riley leaned back in her chair. She met Fannie's gaze. The woman shrugged. Riley had learned one thing witnessing interactions with Helen: They had to live in Helen's world. They couldn't drag her back into theirs.

In fact, Thayne's grandmother created memories that fit reality when she couldn't remember. More than once she'd blurted out completely fabricated events that made sense to no one but her.

A blinding insight hit Riley. Dan Peterson.

She shoved back her chair and set her untouched desserts on the table. "Thanks for the talk. I need to speak to Thayne. Immediately." She kissed Helen on the cheek. "You may have saved an innocent woman."

"I have to save the innocent ones, Riley. That's my job."

◆ ◆ ◆

A blanket of stars pierced the black of the sky. He tapped his foot. Impatience poked at him with the persistence and irritation of a splinter. His eye twitched. He'd waited too long.

Finally the front door of the B&B opened. The FBI agent hurried down the stairs into the night. He tugged his coat around his body. The temperature had dropped another few degrees. The forecast would help his plan come together nicely, but the timing had to be perfect.

His dark clothes transforming him into a shadow in the moonlight, he eased along the side of the old Victorian building. With a credit card, he evaded the simple lock at the back door and walked inside.

The old women laughed and sipped tea. He had no care for them. This was all about setting things right. He wasn't heartless. They had a chance to survive, depending on several factors he hadn't bothered to compute. If not, they would simply be collateral damage.

He edged out of the kitchen, plastered against the wall to avoid any direct line of sight of the women enjoying their evening. Every step silent, he made his way up to the agent's room, avoiding the third and fifth stair. They squeaked.

Riley Lambert's room was, unfortunately, at the top landing. His greatest risk would be coming back down the stairs. He'd have to rely on his luck to hold.

"We need more hot water, Fannie," one of the women complained.

"I'll put the kettle on." A chair raked back.

Just as the woman appeared from around the corner, he slipped inside the room and eased the door closed. The lock snicked.

His heart raced and a wave of relief rushed into his brain. As much as the mistakes he'd made while killing the Jordans annoyed him, in some ways, he'd gained more satisfaction. Tying up loose ends without anyone being aware had challenged him in a way he hadn't anticipated.

He closed his eyes and breathed deeply, knowing he'd want to relive this feeling again and again.

The agent's room was cold, as it had been the last time he'd entered. He paused in front of the wall where she'd plastered photos from floor to ceiling. The Jordan house was prevalent, but she'd added pictures of a small cabin.

He chuckled. Whatever wild-goose chase they'd found themselves on, it had nothing to do with him. He walked over to the adjustable heating vent and carefully unscrewed the panel. He flicked the switch on so that the room heated, just as it had during his test.

With a flashlight in his mouth, he knelt beside the heater. Carefully, so as not to start the chemical reaction prematurely, he attached the twin vials securely to the mechanism. Smiling, he rocked back on his heels and surveyed his handiwork.

Those high school chemistry classes might not have been all that useful in his job, but they sure came in unexpectedly useful now. When Riley adjusted the temperature, the vials would break, and an odorless, colorless gas would be released.

Only one more task. He slipped a long tube from his bag and pumped caulk along the window's edge and the bottom of the door to make the room as close to airtight as possible.

When Special Agent Riley Lambert turned off the heat, she would fall asleep and never wake up.

One loose end down, two more to go.

CHAPTER TEN

The sheriff's office was eerily silent after dark. With a sigh, Thayne shut the steel door that led to the jail cells. The action buffered the sounds of Kate Peterson's quiet sobs. He doubted she'd touch the dinner he'd provided.

He rubbed the bridge of his nose. Today he hated his job. He found it difficult to align Dan's accusations with the woman he'd processed earlier. Even now she didn't show any signs of withdrawal. She showed no signs of long-term drinking or any other drug use. No marks on her arms, no broken capillaries on her face. Nothing made sense. Then again, neither did abuse in the first place.

Cheyenne had been waiting for him in his office, and when he joined her, she stood up. "This is insane. Is it really necessary to lock her up?"

He held his hand out to quiet her and closed the door. "The law's tied my hands. I can't ignore Dan's complaint, and I can't simply let her go. He's afraid of her." He sank into his chair behind his desk. "We're alone now. Come on, sis. Help me out here. What do you think?"

She sat, rubbed the center of her forehead, and let out a long sigh. "My first suspicion was that he suffers from undiagnosed leukemia or some other blood disease that would cause significant bruising with a light touch. Unfortunately for Kate, there's nothing abnormal but a high cholesterol level."

Thayne drummed his fingers on his desk. He'd have to bring up one of his suspicions. "Kate mentioned his behavior's been erratic. What about drug or alcohol abuse? We did find him passed out in his car, although he denied drinking or taking drugs even though the Narcan saved him. Tox screen is still out."

"There was no trace of those kinds of abuses when you brought him in."

"Then maybe it was a bad interaction to his medication? Or maybe a tumor or something."

"Possible. Poor circulation, maybe a stroke. Those *could* explain his behavior but not the bruises all over his body. There's no pattern—they aren't symmetrical." She shoved her hand into her coat pocket. "I need to do an exhaustive workup at a bigger hospital, but he refuses to be admitted. When Kate tried to talk to him, he was convinced she was trying to lock him up and take his money." Cheyenne lifted her gaze to his. "I'm stuck."

"Maybe we can convince Olivia."

"No good. I tried that before you arrived today. She denies he's acting strangely. She believes Kate is behind it all. What I'm seeing is that Dan has issues that need to be investigated at a bigger hospital, Kate's being blamed for the bruises that are appearing, and we can't move forward because our hands are tied. This totally sucks, Thayne."

The outer door to the police station flew open, causing the bell to clatter against the wood. Riley rushed in and made a beeline to Thayne's office. She paused on the threshold, and a spark of excitement highlighted her face. "Cheyenne, thank goodness you're here. I think I know what's wrong with Dan. What if he's in the first stages of dementia? What if he forgot how he got those bruises and is making it all up? He might not even realize it's not true."

Thayne's and Cheyenne's gazes snapped to meet. Strange he'd brought up a tumor but not dementia. Dementia made sense.

"What do you think?" he asked his sister. "Remember when Gram accused me or Dad or even Pops of hiding her money to control her?"

"If it's dementia, it's hard to nail down. Worse, there's no real cure."

Riley moved to the chair beside Cheyenne. His sister had leaned forward, conflict clear on her face. They both knew the implications. Riley was searching for a cause; she hadn't looked beyond the solution to see the wider impact. Thayne reached across his desk and put his hand over his sister's before looking at Riley. "What makes you think it was dementia?"

"The Gumshoe Grannies are having their meeting at the B and B," Riley said. "Your grandmother made a couple of comments that didn't quite follow. It reminded me of how you told me her brain would fill in the blank spots in her memory with anything that made sense even if it wasn't true. What if Dan fell in the barn, or tripped over something and he didn't remember getting hurt, so he replaced the facts with something that made sense to him?"

"God, I hope you're wrong," Cheyenne said.

Riley faced Thayne's sister and frowned. "You'd rather Kate be guilty?"

"Of course not," Cheyenne said softly. "But I'd take any one of a thousand reasons that's causing Dan's symptoms over Alzheimer's."

"I'm sorry." Riley averted her gaze. "I wasn't thinking . . ."

Thayne stood and skirted his desk to take Riley's hand in his. "It's okay. We both are too close to this."

Thayne let go of Riley's hand and returned to his seat. "Can you determine whether or not Dan has a memory issue, whatever the cause?"

"I need more time and more tests, and he's not likely to give either to me, but let's say it is dementia related. Our small town doesn't have the infrastructure to deal with the care he'll need, let alone his family."

Thayne drummed his fingers on his desk. "Can we at least figure out how Dan was hurt?"

Cheyenne's forehead wrinkled in concentration. "Sometimes Gram doesn't respond to questions, but out of the blue she'll just volunteer the information we asked for. She did that when Fannie asked for the cookie recipe. Gram couldn't remember for days, and then suddenly she just blurted it out. Fannie wrote it down, and they turned out perfect."

"It's a good idea, but Olivia's not going to help."

"Dad might," Cheyenne said. "Dan trusts him. He could very well open up. In the meantime, I'll get Dan on the social worker's calendar as quickly as I can."

"And until then?" Riley asked.

"I'll talk to the judge. See if he'll release Kate since Dan is staying with Olivia."

A phone call interrupted them. Riley pulled her phone from her pocket and glanced at the screen. Thayne waited to hear who it was, but she only flushed and muttered, "I need to take this. Excuse me."

She disappeared out the door and closed it behind her.

Thayne stared after her and could feel the frown that suddenly punctured his forehead. Cheyenne looked from the closed door to him. "What's going on with you two? Where's that lovey-dovey, share-every-moment couple from a few weeks ago?"

"It's fine. Just a few growing pains."

His sister crossed her arms, clearly not buying the denial. Thayne didn't blame her. He sputtered for a few seconds before admitting the reality. "Singing River isn't exactly an epicenter of career opportunities for Riley. We're figuring it out."

Cheyenne dropped her arms and leaned forward. "That's a tough one. She's good at what she does."

Thayne didn't need anyone else telling him that. "I know." He lifted his gaze to his sister's. "She loves me, sis. But I don't know if she'll stay."

"Love doesn't always solve all the problems, does it?" Cheyenne twisted her wedding ring around her finger.

"You and Brett?"

She shrugged. "Growing pains."

◆ ◆ ◆

The darkened corner of the sheriff's office hid Riley's shock. She stared across the room at Thayne and Cheyenne talking. Every few seconds, his gaze would veer toward her. He knew exactly where she sat. Sadness hid the usual glint in his eye.

"The higher-ups signed off on bringing you back, Riley." Tom Hickok's voice grew more urgent. "I need an answer."

A year ago, even six weeks ago, she would've given everything she owned to have this opportunity. Today, she had no idea how to respond.

"What if I need more time?" Riley asked.

"I don't know how much I can give you."

"I'm only as good as my last job. I get it." Riley frowned at the floor. She didn't like being pushed into a corner.

"You saved Sarah Ann Conway when no one else could. That counts for something, but the offer won't be out there forever, even after the Conway case."

Riley thrust her fingers through her hair. She'd lived and breathed the investigation for a week. She hadn't slept, had hardly eaten, and had lived off coffee.

Much like she was doing right now.

Thayne's office door opened. Cheyenne raised her hand in acknowledgment before leaving, while Thayne hovered in the doorway, not hiding his interest pointed in Riley's direction. She turned her back to him.

"I need more time," she finally repeated. But she couldn't deny the urge in her belly to say yes to the offer. She'd been trained as a behavior analyst.

"All right, but don't take too long."

Riley ended the call and forced herself to look at Thayne. His mouth was tight, but not in anger. She hated that he could see right through her.

He crossed the office. "Another case?"

So that's what he'd been thinking. She shook her head. "They need a decision on whether or not to return full-time. They want me."

Thayne hesitated for a moment before lifting his hand to her cheek. He stroked her skin gently and paused beneath her eyes. She knew she looked like hell. Dark circles, bloodshot. Her longest shut-eye had been on the plane from DC.

"Why wouldn't they?" He sighed in resignation.

She touched his hand. "I do love you," she whispered.

"I know."

The expression on his face nearly broke her heart. Part of her wished he'd yank her into his arms, kiss her, and refuse to let her go. Deep inside she also knew she'd resent him for it.

Why couldn't love solve all the world's problems the way it did in the movies?

Thayne slid his hands to her shoulders, then caressed her arms before linking his fingers with hers.

"I love you, too, but we both know the job is calling you back. That it means more than a paycheck. Singing River isn't for everyone. Sometimes I don't think it's for me, either." As if he couldn't resist, he pulled her against him and stroked her back. He kissed her hair. "I wish we could find a way to make it work."

She allowed her arms to encircle his waist. She rested her cheek on his chest, and gradually her breathing slowed, matching his. She didn't want to move. In his embrace she felt safe, secure, and wanted.

When she'd first come to Wyoming, she'd never experienced anything like the emotions overflowing within her when she held him close. They'd become almost normal. Almost, but not quite.

"How about we go to the B and B and have the homecoming we'd both planned on and a good night's sleep? If there's news, everyone knows where we can be reached."

"I'd like that."

She held his hand in the car the entire five minutes required to drive through Singing River from the sheriff's office to the B&B. For the first time since she'd returned, her entire being had found its center. She pushed aside the uncertainty of her future. She didn't want to think right now. She just wanted to be.

With Thayne.

He held out his hand for her key, and she bit back a smile. She appreciated his small gestures of old-fashioned etiquette. She recognized his grandfather and grandmother in those small actions. At least when he unlocked the door. He definitely didn't let her enter first.

SEAL training trumped etiquette every time. He preferred first entry. Just in case.

She placed her finger on her lips for silence. His brow quirked in question until the Gumshoe Grannies' laughter filtered through the B&B's living room. She eased the door closed and nodded toward the stairs. Maybe they could make it.

They hit the first step, and Riley breathed easier for the first time since they entered the room.

"Don't bother trying to sneak up, darlings," Fannie called out from behind the dividing wall. "I didn't mention when you tried to sneak around earlier, but you can't hide from that minuscule squeak at the base of the stairs. It's just the right frequency that my ears can still pick it up. My husband used to hate it. He couldn't pull off a surprise no matter how hard he tried, God rest his soul."

With a collective sigh, Thayne and Riley made their way to the game table, where all four women grinned.

"It's about time," Helen said with a wink. "You two need to do a little horizontal mambo and get back on the same page. Then I want to see a wedding. I don't know why you're avoiding the inevitable. Lincoln and I waited too long, and look at all the heartache that caused."

At Thayne's stunned expression, Riley bit the inside of her mouth. Helen's illness brought out some of the most interesting stories. Riley had the feeling Thayne's grandmother would have taken a few of those revelations to her grave if she'd been able.

"Gram, what happened to you and Pops?" Thayne leaned forward and placed his hand on hers.

"Another time," Helen muttered and patted him. "Some secrets should never be mentioned until the time is right."

Norma, Fannie, and Willow groaned.

"You should write mystery novels, Helen. You're too cryptic by half these days," Willow muttered. She tapped on a keyboard, her purple-streaked gray hair sticking up on end.

Riley had no idea whether Willow had created the style intentionally or from sheer frustration.

"Don't mind Willow," Norma said. "She's been buried in her computer, proving and disproving some of Helen's more off-the-wall comments lately."

"How's that going?" Thayne asked.

Riley recognized the concern. He and the whole Blackwood family were fighting to hold on to Helen for as long as they could. Everyone understood the war would be lost, but the struggle continued.

"Fifty-fifty," Willow said, her fingers flying across the keyboard. "Particularly if your grandmother is being more obscure than usual."

"You really should hire Willow as a consultant, Thayne." Norma flipped through a few pages at the end of the Agatha Christie novel. "She's our expert on hacking—" She slapped her hand over her mouth, but her eyes still twinkled as she spoke through her fingertips. "I mean searching databases."

Riley attracted Thayne's attention by pressing her hand to his back. She lowered her voice. "The photo of Kim and Chloe."

He gave her a quick nod and closed in on the ladies.

"Willow, could you do a search on the down low for us?"

The older woman stopped typing and looked up in surprise. "What do you have in mind?"

Riley opened her bag and pulled out the old photo. "Kristin and her daughter, Ashley. No last name. Known to all of us as Kim and Chloe Jordan. She hid in Singing River in plain sight for the last seven years, but we can't let anyone know we're looking. Chloe could still be at risk. Depending on what her past holds."

"That's all you have?" Willow clutched the photo in her hand. "Can you narrow it down to a region of the country at least?"

Thayne peered over the older woman's shoulder at the picture. "I'm sorry. We don't have any other leads. The Jordans didn't confide in anyone that Quinn's been able to identify. We're flying blind. Kristin obviously changed their hair color. Other than that, we've got nothing."

Thayne's grandmother cleared her throat. "May I see it, Willow?"

Willow handed Helen the photo. She clasped it and touched the edge. "Something . . ." Her voice faded and then a moment later her gaze cleared. "Of course. Poor dear." Helen stood and gripped Thayne's arm. "This is *my* secret, Lincoln. You have to stay out of it. You'll ruin everything." Helen pressed the photo to her blouse. "This is very, very bad." She paced back and forth, stopping next to Thayne occasionally. "No more questions, dear. Promise me, Lincoln."

Thayne winced, but Riley knew he'd play along. He took her hands in his. "I'm only trying to help."

"Sometimes help from law enforcement only causes more pain. Sometimes it takes just people helping each other to get justice." Helen slipped the photo into the pocket of her dress and patted it. "That's all I have to say about that."

When she crossed behind Willow, her friend nipped the photo and hid it from Helen's view. Riley leaned down. "Search for them. Cautiously."

"Helen seems to know something," Willow said. "Maybe Thayne can figure it out." She disappeared from the room.

Thayne spent the next fifteen minutes attempting to pull Helen into revealing information about the photo, but whatever had slipped into her mind was gone.

Riley wished she knew if Helen really did remember something or if she was mixing up this photo with another from days long gone.

There was no way to know.

A knock sounded at the door. Thayne answered, and his grandfather walked in. "Thanks for the text," Lincoln Blackwood said. He strode over to Helen, his movements slow and deliberate. "Hello, my love."

He took her hand in his and kissed her palm. She giggled. "Oh, go on with you, Lincoln. Not in front of our friends."

"I was thinking about taking a spin to the old swimming hole. Maybe dance under the moonlight. Care to join me?"

Helen bit her lip and stared down at the books on the table. "We're having a meeting."

"Oh no you don't," Fannie scolded. "You can't say no to a date with the biggest catch in Singing River. Wait here and I'll pack you a snack."

As Helen collected her things, Riley opened her bag and pulled out a second copy of the photo. She slipped it to Lincoln. "Helen seems to recognize this picture. Can you help us?"

"I'll try." Lincoln sighed. "I can't guarantee it, though."

Thayne touched his grandfather on the shoulder. "We know. Do your best."

Fannie reentered the room with a small basket. "Here you two go. Now be off with you."

Lincoln held out his elbow, and Helen slipped her arm into his. Her cheeks were flushed, and she looked up at Lincoln as if he were the only man in the world. "You make me feel safe," she said. "Even though I'm not as good as I used to be."

"You're just right for me."

Lincoln led her away. When the door closed behind the couple, Willow wiped her eyes. "My poor Helen. We lose a bit more every single day."

"It's not fair," Norma said. "Not fair at all."

Fannie plopped into her chair. "Well, we can't do anything about it, so we should make the best of it. Like Lincoln says, we've got to be thankful for what we still have."

"No matter how frustrating," Willow groused. "I saw that look in her eye. She knows something about this woman and her daughter. I'm sure of it."

"Then we've got to be her memory," Fannie said, pulling out her notebook. "Seven years ago. Does the time frame ring a bell?"

Norma squirmed in her chair. "Twenty years ago she started disappearing on those trips. Every so often she'd just take off. She stopped a few years ago, though."

Thayne stilled. "Where'd she go?"

"She wouldn't tell. Said it would be better for everyone if no one else knew. She didn't even tell Lincoln. Said he was a lawman first, and she refused to compromise him."

Riley shook her head. If Helen had kept that type of secret from her husband, she had to have been involved in something less than legal.

Before she could wrap her mind around the most obvious possibilities, Thayne's phone rang.

He glanced at the screen and frowned. "Blackwood?"

A loud voice sounded through the receiver. Riley didn't even have to strain to hear.

"I can't do it," Olivia said. "My father can't live with us. You have to find him a place to stay."

◆ ◆ ◆

Thayne closed the door to Riley's room, blocking out the continued chatter among his grandmother's three best friends. Finally. A little bit of silence.

What a day.

Riley threw her bag into the chair by the murder board and faced him. "It was kind of Fannie to agree to take in Dan temporarily."

"She'll watch out for him." Thayne flopped back on the bed. "At least until Cheyenne can convince Olivia that Dan should have the medical workup."

He rolled to his side and propped himself up on his elbow. "This isn't how I planned tonight."

Riley didn't answer. She froze, studying the small table near the room's window heating and cooling unit.

"What's wrong?" Thayne asked.

"The papers." Riley realigned a stack in the center of the table. "It's probably nothing. I guess I knocked them when I came back to change my clothes."

"Or Madison could have."

Riley rubbed her eyes. Thayne could see her shoulders slumping with fatigue. He patted the bed beside him. "How about we sleep? It's been a long day."

She smiled and joined him on the bed, snuggling into his arms. He wrapped her in his warmth and settled her back against his chest, spooning her close.

For a brief moment, the world felt right.

"Want me to close the heating vent?" he asked. "It's not an icebox in here like usual."

"Fannie keeps readjusting it. Just leave it. I'll crack the window later. Besides, I don't want to move." She pressed his arms against the front of her body. "I'm too comfortable like this."

He closed his eyes briefly, relishing the feel of her body close to his, but his mind wouldn't still. "You think Gram really knows about the Jordans?"

Riley's body tensed. She said nothing for a moment, but she didn't relax, either. There was his answer.

"I do, too," he said with a frown.

"What if your grandmother visited the cabin? What if that's why she was so angry when your father ended up on that land? What if her secret is out there?"

"And what's her tie to Chloe?" Thayne inhaled the scent of Riley's shampoo. "Damn this disease. I want Gram to talk to me. Tell me what she was doing that she couldn't tell Pops. She's the key to finding out about Chloe. I feel it in my gut."

She turned in his arms and faced him. She cupped his cheek and kissed him. "I'm sorry. I know it's hard, but maybe Lincoln can get some information out of her."

"I wish I could trust what she says, but we can't."

"One truth out of a string of lies could point us in the right direction. She's come through before."

Riley suddenly chuckled.

"What's so funny?"

"We've had two big cases in Singing River over the last month, and your grandmother has been eyebrow deep in both of them, and she could very well be the worst witness ever."

Thayne let out a bark of laughter. "It shouldn't be funny, but damned if it isn't."

She hugged him close. Every day he worked hard to focus on the present, to be thankful they still had Gram, that she still showed flashes of her former self. Even if every day fewer and fewer moments of clarity shone in her eyes.

He let his eyes close. Riley's breathing grew soft and steady, and his mind fogged in fatigue. Thayne's muscles relaxed. He'd let himself sleep for a while. Tomorrow, he'd hope they'd catch a break.

He focused on the hoot of the owl that planted itself near the window, and the trill of the crickets. Perhaps nature's melody would soothe his mind.

A sharp ring shattered the peace.

With a groan, he leaned back and plucked his phone from the bedside table. "Blackwood," he whispered.

"Sheriff. It's Quinn. I just received a phone call and follow-up email from a man who says he's looking for his daughter. The picture is an old photo of Chloe Jordan."

CHAPTER ELEVEN

This early in the morning, the hospital was mostly deserted. Riley stood outside the guarded room where Chloe still lay unconscious.

What a night. Morning had taken a long time coming. Her mind lingered through the wee hours on the girl in the hospital bed, wondering about the man who claimed to be her father. She eased open the door and peered inside. The closed window curtains kept the room dim, but a sly glint of sunlight hit the girl's blonde hair. Her eyelids moved slightly.

Was she dreaming? Or having a nightmare?

A few feet away, Thayne spoke into his phone, his Stetson obscuring his face but not his irritated tone. "I need your help, Willow. He says his name is Philip Andrews. Wife was Kristin. He says he's coming here. I need verification of his relationship to Chloe and a photo to confirm his identity, so get me whatever you can. He said he'd explain why Ashley—who we know as Chloe—was using an assumed name, but I want independent verification. I have my deputies requesting official information, but the guy said he used to be a mayor in Iowa, which means he had influence over the police. I have to be sure. For Chloe's sake."

Riley caught the determined expression on Thayne's face. Strangely enough, both of them were willing to go a little outside the lines on this one, because she wasn't going to argue that Willow might use less than legal means to find out the truth.

He disconnected the call and crumbled up the morning paper in his fists. "Somehow a reporter got hold of the picture of the Jordans at the market and ran with it." He scowled. "You'd think I could control information with only five people in the whole sheriff's office. When I find out—"

Riley took his hands. "If there's one thing I learned while working with local law enforcement, you can't control the narrative for long. Too many people go in and out of your office. It didn't necessarily come from your office. It's not hard to believe that the local paper would pressure people in town for a photo of the family."

"I don't like surprises, and speaking of one, Philip Andrews should be here sometime this afternoon." Thayne tucked his phone in his pocket. "Someone tipped him off by sending him the article which revealed that his daughter was here and his wife was dead." He frowned and joined her just outside Chloe's room. "I'm not letting him near Chloe until I'm sure she'll be safe."

A rustle sounded from behind the door, and Riley cracked it open a bit farther. Her gaze wandered the room and landed on Chloe. The girl's hand slid from her chest to her stomach.

"Chloe moved," Riley whispered. "Call Cheyenne. Let her know."

While Thayne dialed his sister, Riley walked inside and sat in a chair next to the bed. She scooted the chair closer, the scrape across the floor making her wince.

"Can you hear me, Chloe?" Riley placed her hand in the girl's and rubbed her arm with her other hand. She studied the girl's face.

Unlike the first time they'd visited, her features were no longer slack. She seemed to have a frown on her face. "Ashley? Can you wake up for me?"

The girl's hand spasmed. A tear slid down her cheek, but she didn't open her eyes.

"You're safe, Chloe. I promise. We won't let anyone hurt you."

Riley watched as the girl's body relaxed. She rose and met Thayne at the door.

"Cheyenne will be here soon. She has to drive from the Riverton Ranch."

"She stayed with her husband last night? Does that mean they're back together permanently?" Riley asked.

He shrugged. "I stay out of it for the most part. They'll figure it out." Thayne glanced at Chloe. "What do you think?"

"I believe she's awake," Riley whispered. "But for now she's pretending to be asleep."

"She can't keep that up forever."

Riley tugged him away from the hospital room door and out of Chloe's earshot. "I can think of several reasons. One, she set the fire, either accidentally or on purpose, and doesn't want to admit it. Two, she doesn't want to acknowledge that her parents are dead. Or maybe she's afraid because she knows who killed them."

Thayne let out a low whistle and rubbed the back of his neck. "And out of the blue, her supposed father comes to find her. Doesn't smell or feel right."

Riley pursed her lips. "Do you trust me?"

"Of course."

"Play along with me."

They entered Chloe's room, and Thayne arched his brow at Riley. She took a small breath. "If Andrews can prove Chloe is his daughter and he wants to see her or take her, there's not a lot we can do to stop him. Not unless Chloe can give us a reason why."

The small body in the bed stiffened. This time they both noted the reaction. They walked out of the room and met Cheyenne at the door.

"She can hear us," Thayne said to his sister.

Cheyenne narrowed her gaze at him. "What did you do?"

"It was me," Riley said softly and told Thayne's sister what she'd said. "We're out of time. Her father will be here soon, and we *have* to know the truth."

"You took a big risk thinking that she would recognize her name and her father's name." Cheyenne crossed her arms. "What if she doesn't know anything?"

"We needed answers," Thayne inserted. "She could still be in danger. For all I know, this man killed Aaron and Kim Jordan so he could get Chloe back."

Even though Thayne's words rang true, Riley closed her eyes to the worst possibility. "You really believe Chloe doesn't remember anything? She was at least five when they left Iowa."

Cheyenne faced them, hands on her hips. "I'm not a psychiatrist, but there are some studies that indicate after age seven, many earlier childhood memories vanish. It's a form of amnesia."

"Even if those events were traumatic?"

"If they want to forget them, yes, being unable to retrieve memories is a form of self-preservation. And if her mother tried to replace the old memories with new, I could easily see her not knowing." Cheyenne pulled her stethoscope from the pocket of her white coat and adjusted the diamond on her ring finger. A wedding ring Riley had only seen a few times. "I'll check on Chloe and be back when I know something."

She disappeared inside the room, and Riley let out a low curse. "What if I just messed—"

"You were trying to keep her safe." Thayne stroked her back. "Don't beat yourself up. The case is finally moving forward."

Riley leaned against the wall. The back of her neck pulsed. She glanced at Thayne. "Yeah, but this guy who claims to be Chloe's father sees her picture and sends an email? I don't like it . . . it's too—"

"Convenient?"

Riley pinched her nose. "Maybe I'm used to everything being hard. Maybe sometimes it just isn't as complicated as I think it could be."

Thayne sidled up to her. He caged her in his arms. "I trust your gut over anyone I've ever met." He kissed her lips. "What are you thinking?"

"The moment I saw the Jordans' home, something felt wrong. They were on the wrong sides of the bed. Their hands weren't clenched. I could even see their wedding rings . . ."

A faint memory of Aaron and Kim at the farmers' market tugged her brain. She followed the memory, seeing Kim's smile, Aaron hovering lovingly—or was it protectively?—behind his wife, the produce Kim carried. "Wait a minute. The rings." She opened the satchel she always carried and pulled out the newspaper photo. "There, on Kim's hand. It's a diamond wedding band. And her husband isn't wearing a ring at all."

"So?"

Riley's heart quickened. She grabbed the autopsy photos. "They're both wearing plain bands." Her mind whirled. She stuffed the photographs back into her bag and kissed him quickly. "I'm going back to my room. I need to check something out on my board." Inspiration lit within her. "I think we may be on the wrong track."

◆ ◆ ◆

Thayne doubted Riley heard his advice to be safe as she disappeared down the hallway. He recognized that look on her face, though. She loved her job. She was in her element, and he shouldn't want to take that from her. The door to Chloe's room opened, refocusing Thayne's attention as Cheyenne joined him outside the room.

"Where's Riley?" Cheyenne asked.

"She's chasing a lead. What happened? Was Riley right?" he asked his sister.

"I tried to get Chloe to open her eyes, and most patients do when I tickle their feet, but our girl is a hard nut to crack. She kept them closed, albeit a bit too tightly. I can't find anything wrong with her, and with her vitals looking good, I agree with Riley. Chloe's conscious."

Thayne paced back and forth. "You know what this means? She doesn't want to talk."

"Not to you or me. We're authority figures. Her parents lived as near off the grid as you can. Maybe they taught her not to trust anyone in a uniform." Cheyenne slipped her phone from her pocket. "Madison's been here every day, slowly building a quiet connection. She might be just the person to convince Chloe she can trust us." His sister kissed his cheek. "Leave all this to me and Madison. We'll get her to talk. You go do whatever it is you do when Riley's not by your side."

Did his sister know what she'd just said? He didn't know what he'd do when Riley wasn't here anymore. As he headed toward the hospital's entrance, he pushed the thought out of his mind. Once outside, he found his car gone. He didn't remember giving Riley the keys. He slapped his hat on his thigh, aggravated by his lack of attention. He'd have to call Quinn to bring him a vehicle.

At that moment a gray car sped into the parking lot and jerked to a stop in front of the hospital's entrance. "Your office told us you were here. We need your help."

Thayne bent and peered into Olivia's car. Dan blinked at Thayne from the passenger seat, looking half-asleep and disheveled but okay.

"Morning, Dan."

"If you say so," he groused. "The girl dragged me out of bed, didn't feed me, not even a coffee . . ." A deep frown settled over his face, and he turned away. "A man's not a man without coffee in the morning."

Thayne straightened and eyed Dan's daughter. "What's going on?"

"He can't stay with me. He's driving me crazy."

Thayne opened the door and motioned her out of the car. He had a feeling Dan didn't need to hear this. "Already? You've only had him for one night."

"And he's impossible! He's so stubborn. He wants me to cook like Kate cooks. He wants the schedule to be exactly like it is at home. He argues with everyone about everything. He even claims someone is trying to kill him. I can't take it, Sheriff. I really can't. I'll end up divorced if I let him stay. He refuses to go back to his house. Keeps repeating that it's Kate's house. I can't convince him otherwise."

Thayne tugged on his Stetson. "I talked to Fannie. She offered to take him in for a while if you're willing to pay. In the meantime, I'll call my dad and have him talk to Dan about moving back to his own house since Kate's still in custody."

Olivia grasped his arm. "Thank you."

"I can't promise Dan will agree, but for now, let's see if Fannie can't lure him with some cinnamon rolls and Southern charm."

The overwhelming expression of relief on Olivia's face gave Thayne an uneasy feeling in his gut. He wanted to observe Dan for a while. "Can I tag along?"

"Please."

Thayne slipped into the back seat of her SUV and buckled up while Olivia slid into the front seat. "Nippy morning for September, isn't it?"

"Could be worse," Dan growled. "When I was a boy, we'd have a foot of snow by now. Walked all the way to town from my folks' ranch. Till we lost it to that bastard Riverton."

"My pops nearly had to sell out," Thayne said.

Dan twisted as far as he could and met Thayne's gaze. "I remember. Carson wanted to beat up on Riverton, but your pops wouldn't let him. Said there were other ways to take care of a bully."

Now this was a story Thayne hadn't heard. "What did Pops do?" he asked, leaning forward.

Dan shrugged. "Not a clue, but whatever it was, Riverton didn't come after the little farmers again. Must've been some showdown." The man chuckled until the car pulled to a stop outside the B&B.

"We're here," Olivia said. "How about something to eat?"

Dan shoved open the SUV's door. "First order of the day is getting a farmer's full breakfast. I'm starving." He glanced at Thayne. "This daughter of mine and her husband eat rabbit food with a speck of meat—not enough to put a dent in a grown man's appetite."

He headed to the front door with the speed of a man half his age. Olivia sighed as Thayne grabbed a suitcase from the back seat. "He never used to be this—"

"Unpredictable?" Thayne finished for her.

Olivia nodded.

"Cheyenne wants to run a few tests, see if anything's wrong that could be causing these changes. I think it'd be a good idea."

"You know what I think? Kate spoiled him." Olivia's jaw tightened. "He just needs to get used to taking care of himself again. No more bossing around others to do his bidding. For pity's sake, the man cooked his own meals and did laundry fine enough after Mom died."

"That was a lot of years ago." Thayne opened the door to the B&B for Olivia.

"That's what I'm saying. He's been spoiled rotten."

Thayne sighed. There was no getting through to her. "Think about it. Please."

Olivia didn't answer. So much for the subtle approach.

When they walked in, Dan made a beeline for the breakfast room and the open morning buffet. Fannie hovered close by, her eyebrows raised as he plopped a mountain of eggs and bacon on his plate before sitting down.

"I put you right next to Riley." She smiled when Dan shoved the meat in his mouth. "You find yourself in trouble, that girl will get you out, Dan."

"She live here?" Dan asked. "I don't believe I know her."

Dan had seen Riley several times. Maybe he'd remember her when he saw her. Not everyone was good with names. "Is she here?" Thayne asked Fannie.

"I heard her run upstairs a while ago."

"Good. I'll go get her and you can meet her, Dan." Thayne squeezed the older man's shoulder before leaving the room.

He walked up the stairs and knocked on Riley's door.

No answer.

"Riley. It's Thayne." He raised his voice in case she was in the bathroom.

Total silence. Fannie had said she'd heard her, and his SUV was still on the street, so she had to be here. He pounded on the door. "Riley! Open up."

The hall dropped into an eerie quiet after the noise he was making. He backed away and glanced down the hall. Maybe she was with her sister.

He knocked on Madison's door until it opened. She stood in her robe and slippers. "What are you yelling about?" she snapped.

"Is Riley with you?"

"No, though I tried to get her to talk when she came upstairs this morning. She's at her murder board, as usual."

If she was in her room, why didn't she open the door? His gut twisted, and a feeling of foreboding settled over him. He went back to Riley's door, Madison in tow, and pummeled on it again. "Riley, open up, or I'm breaking down this door."

Heavy breathing preceded Fannie as she hurried up the stairs. "We can hear you all the way downstairs. What's wrong?"

"Riley's not answering. Are you sure she's here?"

Both of the women nodded, and Fannie produced a master key from her pocket and unlocked the door. She knocked. "Riley, honey? Is everything all right?"

She pushed, but the door wouldn't open. "It's stuck." Thayne pressed his shoulder to the door and heaved against the wood. Hard. With a sudden lurch, it cracked and gave way. He peeked around the older woman and saw Riley lying facedown in the middle of the room. "What the hell?"

He pushed past Fannie and dropped to his knees beside Riley. As the women cried out their alarm, he pulled Riley into his arms, and his breath caught in his throat. She was as still as death.

The alarm in the hall jumped to life. "Out. Everybody out. Now," he cried. He lifted Riley into his arms and hurried down the stairs and outside, where he laid her on the grass. Without missing a beat, he put his ear to Riley's chest and felt its shallow rise and fall. The morning dew seeped through his jeans to dampen his knees. Straightening, he swept her hair from her face and closed his eyes, his voice shaking from the fear icing his veins.

"Riley. Wake up. Please, darlin'. Wake up!"

◆ ◆ ◆

Riley's head pounded. Thayne shouted at her from somewhere far away, and she winced. The world dimmed to black, a strange cloying sensation settling heavily around her lungs. She couldn't breathe. Her mind buzzed before languishing to a soft, peaceful song.

The clanging of an alarm sounded nearby, wrenching her into a world of pain.

She ached everywhere. She just wanted it to end. Riley tried to open her eyes, but she failed. Her chest hurt; her stomach rolled with nausea.

She couldn't see, but she could hear.

"Riley!" her sister screamed. "Don't you do this to me. Not now."

Madison's sharp shouts tugged at Riley's mind, but she couldn't respond. Something was very, very wrong. Someone picked her up, jostling her. She groaned the moment her head moved. She wanted to scream, to tell them to put her down, until she recognized the strength of Thayne's arms carrying her down the stairs, into the cold. Thayne would take care of her. She was safe.

She couldn't fight anymore. She let the darkness steal her mind.

Urgent voices dragged her from peace and tranquility. Someone shoved a plastic mask over her face. She coughed, desperate to breathe easier, to take in large gulps of air. She shifted toward a familiar voice.

"Don't resist. Breathe in, Riley. Slow, deep breaths." Thayne's deep tones soothed her. She followed his instructions.

"Her color's coming back." Madison choked out the words.

What had happened? Her hands gripped the ground below her, sinking her fingers into the stiff grass.

With each breath of oxygen, her mind cleared a little more.

Riley blinked and opened her eyes. A spotlight shone over her. Blue and red lights spun in her peripheral vision. Thayne's fuzzy but worried face hovered above her. "Damn it, Riley. You scared me." He touched her cheek. "I thought I'd lost you."

His Adam's apple bobbed, and he rested his forehead against her hair.

"Keep breathing," Cheyenne encouraged. "We need to get all that carbon monoxide out of your system." Cheyenne sat just beyond Thayne and suddenly frowned. "Could someone please turn that siren off?"

"Wh . . . what happened?" Riley's throat was tight, and it sounded like she was speaking around a mouthful of gravel.

Thayne touched her lips. "Try not to talk. The carbon monoxide alarm sounded just after we opened the door to your room. The Riverton fire marshal is coming to check it out."

Thayne pulled away and Madison replaced him, bending over Riley. "You're not allowed to scare me like that, Ri-Ri," she whispered into her ear. "I can't take losing you."

Riley blinked up into the blue morning sky. Clouds drifted across the Wyoming landscape. "I'm not going anywhere," she said, even though the headache building behind her eyes pounded with the intensity of a gold miner. "Not yet, anyway."

Cheyenne checked the placement of the oxygen mask on Riley's face. "Get her to the hospital," she ordered. "And I want everyone who was in the B and B today to get their blood drawn."

Riley needed Thayne. Needed to feel safe, because she was sure she'd never come quite so close to dying. "Thayne," she called, though the weak voice didn't sound like her own. She searched for him, and when he came close, she gripped his hand tight. "Don't leave me."

"Not ever." The muscle in his jaw jumped, and he squeezed her hand before helping the paramedics load her onto a gurney.

They lifted her into the ambulance, and Thayne climbed in beside her.

"Did no one else pass out?" she asked after they secured her and closed the back doors.

"It was isolated to your room. Pendergrass is processing the area now, but I have my suspicions that your window and door were altered to make them airtight. If Olivia hadn't begged me to bring Dan to the B and B—"

He didn't finish the words, but she could see the agony in his eyes.

"Someone tried to kill me?" she asked, her throat still raspy.

Thayne raised her palm to his lips. "They very nearly succeeded."

◆ ◆ ◆

The ambulance sped away, and the remainder of the B&B's residents piled into their cars and headed toward the hospital.

From behind the tree at the side of the house, he slammed his fist into the wooden siding. The wood cracked beneath the force of his anger.

It had been a perfect plan.

It would've worked given a few more minutes, and then she would've been dead.

Ever since he'd set the trap, he'd been watching, and this morning he saw her circle the photograph she'd pinned to the wall, and he'd known in that instant she knew. She might not know the significance of what she was looking at, but she'd noticed something no other investigator had ever noticed.

Part of him admired her for that.

The smarter half of him feared her. No question—she had to die.

The sheriff had the luck of the Irish in him. What was it about this damned town that helped the less fortunate?

To finish the job, he'd have to outsmart all of them. He'd never failed before; he wasn't failing now.

One course of action was already underway. As for Special Agent Riley Lambert, he'd have to consider his options.

He needed to act quickly. He hung his head and rubbed the nape of his neck. He was tempted to be done with it all and burn down the whole damn town, but that would draw too much attention. Another accident was in order. One that would ensnare the sheriff as well. It would be challenging.

But he never refused a challenge.

CHAPTER TWELVE

The crime scene tape surrounded Fannie's B&B most of the day. The afternoon sun still hung high in the sky as Thayne helped Riley out of his SUV.

He didn't like her shaky legs or pale skin and kept his arm situated around her waist just in case. "You should've stayed in the hospital."

She walked away from his embrace. "I've just got a little headache, and my bloodwork is fine. I want to walk the room."

Thayne helped her climb up the porch steps, only to be confronted by two men they'd brought in from Casper. The men removed the hoods and masks of their white hazmat suits and nodded at Thayne, then turned their keen gazes on Riley.

"Are you the woman from room two?" one of them asked.

Riley nodded.

He smiled. "Nice wall."

She grimaced. "It's the job."

The investigator glanced at Thayne. "Can we have a word, Sheriff?"

"Go ahead," Thayne said through a clenched jaw. "She's FBI. She'll figure it out soon enough."

The man pulled out a plastic bag containing two broken vials. "The evidence will be held by the fire marshal because of your relationship with the intended victim, but we thought you'd want to see this."

"What are they?" Riley asked, squinting at the cracked glass.

The other man pointed at the vials. "They housed chemicals that were meant to kill you."

The investigator snorted. "Way to be subtle, Chris."

The guy shrugged. "She asked. Besides, *I* would want to know." He turned to Riley. "I hope you carry a gun. Or have eyes in the back of your head, because someone wants you dead. Bad."

Thayne could've strangled the guy. Riley's eyes widened at his words; then that determined, courageous, scare-the-hell-out-of-him look settled in her eyes. "How?"

His companion shoved Chris aside. "The room's window unit was rigged to generate high concentrations of carbon monoxide when you closed the vent. He added insulation to the window and a rubber seal to the door so the concentration would be high enough to kill, but it wouldn't cause harm to anyone else in the B and B. You were the target, ma'am. No question." He held up a small latch. "He also rigged a way to get into the window. I think he intended to come back and remove the vials so everyone would assume it was some kind of accident."

"Has Pendergrass checked out the room?" Thayne asked.

The man nodded. "No fingerprints or any trace evidence, from what he said. This guy is good."

Thayne stared at the house. Two of his deputies were removing the crime scene tape. "You're finished with the investigation already?"

The investigator nodded. "One room. No evidence. No motive." He looked at Riley. "Unless you know who would want you dead, ma'am."

"Here in Singing River?" She slowly shook her head. "I have no idea."

"Well, I'd think on it, because clearly someone's got it in for you."

Riley looked over at Thayne. "Only one case that I've caused trouble on, and that's the Jordan case. If I hadn't come along—"

"It would've been called an accident," she and Thayne said at the same time.

A sinister shiver settled at the base of Thayne's spine. "You must be closer to the truth than you think."

They made their way into the B&B. Fannie stood there, quietly staring around the room, her arms wrapped around her body. "I don't know if I'll ever be comfortable here again." Her eyes glistened. She hurried over to Riley and hugged her close. "I'm so sorry."

"You didn't do anything. It's me who should be sorry. I brought this to your home." Riley closed her eyes. "Maybe it's best I leave."

Fannie straightened her back. "You're doing no such thing. I'm changing the locks and getting an alarm system and placing smoke and carbon monoxide detectors in each room. I'm not letting a criminal drive me from my home."

"Good for you, Fannie." Thayne held out his hand to Riley. "Shall we look at your room?"

She took his. "If I've made our murderer uncomfortable, I'd like to figure out exactly why."

Once upstairs Thayne opened the door to her room, and Riley stepped inside. "What a mess," she muttered. They'd left her murder wall pretty much alone, though.

Thayne didn't like the quivering of her legs as she crossed the room. She swayed and clutched at the bedpost.

"That's it," Thayne said. "Tell me what you need and I'll throw a bag together. You're coming home with me for some real rest."

She sank onto the bed but couldn't stop staring at the photos. "I can't. I need to be here."

He sat next to her, rubbing her back and staring at her murder board. All he saw was a jumble of photos, each an entity unto itself. If there was a wider connection, he didn't see it.

"Look at that picture," she said. "The one of Aaron and Kim."

"The one you circled?" he asked.

Riley pushed herself to her feet. Thayne held her elbow to help her cross the room. She tugged off the grisly photo of the burned bodies and the picture of the Jordan family from the newspaper.

"Look at their rings." Riley pointed to the left finger of Aaron Jordan's remains, then the left of Kim's.

"Nothing special. Just plain gold wedding bands."

"Right? I came back to see this." She held up the photo from the newspaper. "Aaron isn't wearing a wedding ring, and Kim wore a ring with a small diamond. The rings don't match. The killer switched their rings."

"Why?"

"I don't know, but it suddenly feels really personal."

◆ ◆ ◆

The Blackwood Ranch was on lockdown. Thayne had finally convinced Riley to come home with him. He peered into his bedroom, watching her snuggled on the bed, finally passed out.

Madison tiptoed out of the room and hovered near the door. "I don't know how you got her here. There must be magic in your eyes," she whispered.

Thayne forced a smile at her. "Logic is more like it. Your sister is the toughest woman I've ever met, but I also know she hasn't been sleeping well. She never does on a case. She'll wake up too soon, unfortunately. And go right back at it."

Madison chewed on her lower lip, just like Riley. Madison was two years older than Riley, but because she'd been held prisoner for most of her life, she seemed younger. The reality of Riley's job upset her, and nothing but time would get her used to the idea. She glanced at her sister. "She's tough, but she shouldn't have to be. I'm her older sister.

That's supposed to be my job." She sent Thayne a sad smile. "I think I'll sit with her a little longer."

Thayne watched her disappear behind the door. He didn't blame her. He wanted nothing more than to pull Riley into his arms and lie with her today, tomorrow, forever.

But what he wanted wasn't in the plan.

He strode down the hall to the living room, where his brother Hudson stood looking out the front window, his rifle conveniently near his hand.

Thayne gave his brother a nod. "Anything?"

Hudson shook his head. "Quiet as a mouse. Gram and Pops are at the hospital taking turns watching the girl."

Thayne blinked in surprise.

"Don't worry," Hudson said. "Dad's with them, and your deputy's on duty." He kept his focus on the outside. "I wish Jackson weren't working those fires in California. We could use the hands."

"I don't even know who we're looking for," Thayne said. "I've been lucky so far. She could've died."

Hudson scanned the area one last time and crossed the room to his brother. "But she didn't. You've got to hang on to that."

"The man claiming to be Chloe's father should be at the office soon. If he doesn't have answers, we're back to square one."

"I'll watch over them. Quinn is here, and I've put the hands on alert. We'll be fine."

A high-pitched throat clearing sounded from the hallway. Madison stood there, her chin held high. "I know how to use a gun. Father may have kidnapped me, but he taught me to defend the other kids. It's time I started being Riley's big sister."

Hudson raked his gaze up and down Madison's body, his doubt clearly written on his face. "That nutjob who took you taught you how to shoot?"

"I know what you're thinking: Why didn't I turn it on him?" She shook her head. "I was young. Impressionable. And all too soon I was trapped into protecting the others from even worse than Father. Now I'm free and I won't allow someone to control Riley."

Thayne smiled at her. "Me neither. What's your pleasure?"

"Point nine millimeter. Preferably with a laser sight. Like Riley's."

Hudson's mouth twitched. "I got you covered." He disappeared into the study, where the guns were located.

Madison looked straight into Thayne's face. "Find out who did this to my sister. Or else I will."

Thayne didn't like the hard look that entered her eyes. He understood it, though. "Yes, ma'am." He grabbed his own weapon and his Stetson just as Hudson returned with a Glock. "Will this do?" he asked Madison.

She took it and the extra clip and nodded. "No one will get at my sister."

Hudson nodded at his brother. "What she said. Now go on."

"Okay then. I have a man to interview. I'll keep in touch. Tell Riley . . ." He paused. "Never mind. I'll be back before she wakes."

The knowledge that Riley was being watched over eased Thayne's mind. He jumped into his SUV and drove over the cattle guard and onto the highway leading away from the ranch.

This was their biggest lead. He might finally have the answers he needed, but his number one priority would be keeping Chloe and Riley safe.

The drive through the grassy hills didn't take long. Ironcloud gave him the latest rundown on Andrews. Wasn't much there, though. He turned onto Main Street, all the while wishing Riley were by his side. He'd have to trust his own instincts during the interview. It's not like he couldn't tell a liar when he heard one. For a decade his gut had kept him alive. But Riley . . . she was in a class he couldn't touch.

He pulled the SUV in front of his building and blinked once when he caught sight of Willow lying in wait next to her bicycle. There was only one reason she'd want to see him. She'd done her computer dirty work and found information on Mr. Andrews. Thayne got out of the car and approached her with a broad smile on his face. "This is a welcome surprise."

She didn't smile back. "I found something, and you're not going to like it."

His smile instantly vanished. "Figures. There's not much about today I do like."

"How's Riley?"

"She's a survivor. Always has been." Thayne glanced at the front door. "Want to go inside?"

Willow shook her head. "No." She passed a file over to him. "What did your deputies find out?"

"Their computer search didn't reveal much. Pretty nondescript childhood. Married Kristin, an only child, just out of high school. She gave birth to a daughter a few years later. Kristin's parents died in a car accident. Then seven years ago, she disappeared. Not as much coverage as I would've thought. He didn't run for reelection three years ago."

"Well, there's a lot you don't know," Willow said. "How about we start with a DUI arrest while he was mayor of Milford, Iowa, but it conveniently just went away."

"How does that happen?"

"The *mayor* controlled that town. He had such a tight lid on it you'd have thought he was part of the Mafia. He can't stop gossip, though. People have been whispering. Some believe he killed his wife."

She pointed out a couple of documents to Thayne. "Kristin accused him of abuse at least a half dozen times. Basically, she became his personal punching bag. Over the years with him, she had everything from concussions to a couple of broken ribs. Charges were always dropped.

From what I can tell, their sheriff didn't have the balls to confront the *good* mayor."

Thayne's stomach twisted as he skimmed the hospital's report. "What's this last entry?"

"When Ashley—I mean Chloe—was five, she went into a clinic for a broken arm. There were bruises, too. The doctor was concerned and voiced his worries to the mayor. After the next day, Kristin and Ashley Andrews were never heard from again."

It made him sick to think of the life Kim and Chloe had run from, only for Kim to end up dead.

Willow touched Thayne's arm and shook her head. "You can't give that sweet girl to him, Sheriff. Her mother risked everything to get her away from danger."

He covered her hand with his. "When I took this job, I did so with the promise to serve and protect. I'll fight to my dying breath to keep her out of his hands."

She finally smiled and sighed. "Thank you." She patted his arm. "You're just what this town needs. Being sheriff's about more than running a computer. Look what Kim was forced to do because the law didn't back her up. You know how to fight for justice, Thayne. And you don't give up. That's what a Blackwood sheriff has always been."

"Thanks." He cocked his head at Willow. "I know I shouldn't ask, but how'd you get Kristin's medical records?"

Willow just shrugged. "You're an upstanding lawman now. You don't really want to know, do you?"

He threw back his head and laughed. "Probably not."

His grandmother's friend gave him a quick hug, mounted her bike, and took off toward the B&B. He could just see the Gumshoe Grannies poring over the illicit files and making anonymous calls to Iowa's attorney general and demanding justice.

Thayne stuffed all the papers back into the file. He hated that he wasn't surprised. The official record of Philip Andrews showed nothing of what Willow had given him. Kristin Andrews hadn't had a choice but to run. She'd been brutalized and no one she'd known would help.

Somehow, someway, she'd made her way to Singing River. Where, after seven years of being safe from one hell, she'd been murdered. Life wasn't fair.

Perhaps law enforcement hadn't asked the right questions; perhaps Philip had convinced someone in the police department to lose a few pieces of evidence. However it happened, once this was over, Thayne planned on making a call to the Iowa attorney general himself.

Once he figured out how the hell a survivor like Kristin had wound up dead.

He tucked the file under his arm and entered the building.

Alicia's head popped up from behind the counter at the front of the office. "Is Riley okay?"

"She'll be fine. She's resting." He glanced over at a man sitting in the waiting area. His clothes were well tailored and he seemed relaxed. Oddly so. "Is that Mr. Andrews?"

"It is." Alicia leaned in close. "I think he's been drinking."

Not surprising. It fit his profile, as Riley would say. A gut full of alcohol had a way of turning a mild-mannered man into a raging bull. Thayne gave a quick nod and strode over. "I'm Thayne Blackwood, Singing River sheriff."

The man swayed to his feet. His talk, lanky form belied the monster that lived beneath his skin. He flushed and held out his hand. "Sorry. Not quite sure what's wrong with me," he slurred. "Philip Andrews. Where's my daughter?"

"Brew us up some coffee, Alicia." Thayne wasn't about to take this drunk to see Chloe. "Why don't you come into my office? Tell me exactly what's going on."

Andrews shook his head. "I need to see my daughter." He grabbed Thayne's arm. "It's really important."

Thayne removed the man's arm. "For right now, you need coffee. Do I make myself clear?"

"Coffee? Why?"

He pushed his visitor into his office. "You've been drinking, Mr. Andrews."

"I feel odd." Philip's words slurred, and he slumped into the chair.

"Booze'll do that to you," Thayne said. "How much have you had today?"

Philip's eyes widened. "I don't drink."

"Really? You want to blow into my Breathalyzer? Because your cologne has the aroma of high-quality vodka."

Philip stretched out his hand. It shook. "I don't understand. I don't drink. I just got my two-year chip." He dug into his pocket and pulled out a bronze medallion.

"Sir, no one's judging you. It happens. People fall off the wagon."

"I had a late lunch at the diner in town. Ended up talking to a guy. I had to work up the courage to come here . . . But I didn't have anything to drink."

Sure he didn't. Drunks lied all the time. Alicia tapped on the door with a pot of coffee and two mugs. Thayne rose and poured Philip a cup.

"I have to speak to my daughter," he choked. "I need to tell her . . . I'm sorry. For everything."

◆ ◆ ◆

Riley rolled over onto her side and peered at the afternoon light flowing into Thayne's childhood bedroom at Blackwood Ranch. The light illuminated the white curtains in a way that made them glow a pretty golden hue. Her head no longer had a marching-band drummer beating on it from the inside.

She pushed herself up. She couldn't remember ever sleeping so hard. Of course, she'd never almost been gassed to death, either.

With a bit of hesitation, she sat up, her movements slow and steady. Nausea gone. She was still tired, but most of her symptoms had dissipated since morning. She padded to the bathroom, threw some water on her face, and ran a brush through her hair.

She crossed the room and lifted the curtain to peer outside. Still a couple of hours of daylight left. She searched around Thayne's room, past a wall full of trophies scattered on his bookcase and his official military photo, but not much else. These were things a mother would keep.

Except Kim Jordan hadn't kept anything from her previous life but a small box of photos. And thank God she had. Riley's gaze landed on her computer bag, and she wondered if Tom had deleted her access to the database.

Riley hated inconsistencies, and the Jordans' wedding rings bothered her. She remembered a murder-suicide case where the dead couple's grown son had insisted the wedding rings found on his parents weren't their originals. They'd been switched. That was too much of a coincidence to ignore. She pulled out her computer, and with a quick press of the power button, the machine booted up. She logged in and smiled when the FBI search-screen window appeared.

It was like finding the entrance into a secret world.

From the FBI's databases, she'd reviewed as many files as possible, trying to find Madison.

She'd read every child-abduction case before and after Madison's kidnapping, but as the years had gone on, she'd focused on the cases that had unique identifiers. Research had made her a student of killers' signatures.

Someone out there liked collecting wedding rings.

She tapped in a few criteria in the FBI's Violent Criminal Apprehension Program search engine, and it spit out nearly a hundred cases. Too many to review in their entirety, but Riley had to start somewhere. She read through the first file. Burglary. No murder. Second file. Husband murdered. Wife left alive. No wedding rings found. The perpetrator was identified and confessed and recently died in jail. She went through the third file. Fourth file. Fifth file. The filter needed refinement.

After fine-tuning the search criteria for how the victims had died, Riley viewed a much shorter list. She clicked on a ten-year-old cold case with similarities to the Jordan case. Wedding rings missing, as evidenced by the tan lines on both the husband's and the wife's left hands. Bodies found in the living room, posed holding hands. The scene was clean of prints. Case still open, but stalled.

She clicked on several more files and found another case a year after the first one. Debate over whether it was a murder or a murder-suicide. Family and friends adamant neither would have harmed the other, but no clues pointed to a perpetrator. Bodies found in the living room. Holding hands. This time, the family claimed the wedding rings had been stolen and replaced. "This is more like it."

She skimmed a dozen more files, but nothing else fit. The ViCAP database was specifically for unsolved violent crimes. She sat back and thought through what she'd read. There was a precedent for unsolved cases where wedding rings were taken. The first one was clearly a double murder. The second leaned more toward murder-suicide, though the family didn't agree. Everything seemed to match up to a point.

Riley dug into her satchel and pulled out the photo of Aaron and Kim on their burned-out bed. She squinted at their hands. It was a mess of soot and ash, but . . . Were they touching? It looked like they were.

The hair on the back of Riley's neck stood on end. "You slippery son of a—" She picked up the phone and called Thayne's number. If she was right, this changed everything.

"Our perp is a serial killer."

CHAPTER THIRTEEN

Today couldn't end quickly enough for Thayne. He'd almost lost Riley, the Jordan case had knotted into a giant cluster, and his conflicting reactions to the latest visitor to Singing River didn't bode well. He closed the door to the drunk tank and let out a frustrated sigh.

"You should've let him sleep in his car or something," Alicia muttered with a frown.

"He's not getting behind the wheel of a car, and Fannie won't let him in her B and B. There's no other place to stay in town. I sure as hell don't want him near the hospital or Chloe."

His dispatcher packed up her purse. "You won't let him take that girl, will you?"

"I've ordered a paternity test, and I've let child services know he's a habitual abuser as well as an alcoholic. After that, it'll be in the hands of a judge."

He hated that he couldn't promise anything more. "I'm doing everything I can to keep Chloe safe, but if he's her father and if the courts say he can have her . . . there are some things even we can't control, no matter how hard we try." Maybe he'd suggest Cheyenne not tell anyone she believed Chloe was no longer unconscious. It could buy them some time.

Alicia gave his arm a quick pat and nodded. "I know you'll do your best. See you tomorrow."

She left the building, leaving only Thayne and his newest deputy, Kyle Baker, to man the sheriff's office. Thayne would be bunking down here tonight instead of heading back to the ranch. He wanted to be there when Philip Andrews woke up. Right now the man was so wasted Thayne had barely been able to get a straight answer out of him.

He probably should've arrested him instead of letting him sleep it off in the back room at the sheriff's office, but the guy hadn't technically broken any laws. That he knew of.

At least Kyle was keeping an eye on him.

The bell on the door jangled, and Thayne turned to face whatever crisis was about to hit next. Riley strode through the door, Hudson at her side.

Thayne groaned at the sight of her stubborn, beautiful face. "What the hell are you doing across town and out of bed? You should be resting."

"I feel fine." Riley lifted her chin and met his gaze.

"You're lying. You've got dark circles under your eyes, you're pale as a ghost, and your hands are trembling. In short, you look ready to pass out in front of me."

"I always look like this during a case." She shrugged and tapped him on the cheek. "Besides, how could I sleep knowing what kind of killer we're looking for?"

"And if you're right, the killer may have his sights set on you." She wasn't taking her brush with death seriously enough. Thayne glared at his brother. "Why did you let her leave?"

"Have you ever tried to stop either one of the Lambert sisters from doing anything?" Hudson crooked a brow.

Thayne couldn't deny they were the most stubborn, muleheaded women. "Point taken, but I'm not happy about it."

Riley ignored both of them and headed to the conference room, where she placed her laptop on the table and turned it on. "I have some news you're not going to believe. Andrews may be our murderer."

Thayne followed her inside. "What are you talking about?"

"You didn't check your email lately, did you?" She hit several keys and glanced at him over the keyboard. "Willow didn't get a response from you, so she called me instead."

He recognized that bright, eager expression in her eyes. Which meant he'd missed some important news. "I've been dealing with a very drunk Philip Andrews."

"Willow found some very interesting travel information on him." Riley pressed several buttons. "Last week he rented a car from his hometown of Milford, Iowa. He drove over two thousand miles—which happens to be close to the round-trip distance to Singing River—and returned the car two days later." She paused. "But that's not the most interesting part. Ask me when."

The back of Thayne's neck twisted with tension. "When?"

"He turned the car in the day after the Jordans were killed. It fits. Kim knew what he was, so he killed her."

"And he may want to kill Chloe."

Thayne's hand hovered over his weapon. He stared toward the back room where the man lay passed out.

"You're sure?" he asked. "No mistake. I didn't peg him for a killer."

"That's what makes them good at their job," Riley said. "They hide in plain sight." She motioned him around the desk. "I found two unsolved murder cases in which the wedding rings of the victims played a key role. Serial killers learn over time, and I think these were some of his first kills. Both have missing wedding rings, and both were found holding hands. One unusual characteristic is odd. Having two in two separate cases a year apart is unlikely. They're ten years old, but one has DNA. If we can find a match to him—"

"He's in the back room right now." Thayne unholstered his weapon. "His DNA is there."

Thayne strode toward the back room. Even as he closed in, he could smell the sour scent of alcohol and vomit. The air reeked. The odor obviously came from the wastebasket; the bed was rumpled, but it was empty.

"Baker?"

The kid peered at Thayne from the doorway.

"Where's Andrews?"

"The john. That dude is hurting. I had to help him in there."

Thayne knocked on the bathroom door. "Andrews?"

He didn't answer. Thayne jiggled the handle. Locked.

Maybe he was bent over the toilet, too nauseous to say anything. Thayne knocked harder, and still Andrews didn't answer. This was beginning to feel a bit too familiar. He pounded on the door and yelled with an authoritarian voice he'd learned in SEAL training. "Open up!"

When he still received no answer, Thayne kicked in the door. The tiny bathroom had one toilet; a sink; and a narrow, small window . . . which was unlocked and open. The man was so lean Thayne didn't doubt he could fit. "Damn it!" He rushed out of the bathroom and yelled at his deputy to follow. "Andrews is gone."

Baker stuttered and stumbled after Thayne. "How? I swear he was in no shape to go anywhere."

"He played you. He played all of us." Thayne lunged into the street, looking right and left as Baker headed to the back of the station.

Riley joined Thayne at the curb, her face clouded with worry.

"Andrews got away," he said.

"Chloe. She's either a loose end or his endgame."

Thane plucked his phone from his pocket, but before he could dial, the phone rang. It was Cheyenne. A cold shiver cupped his spine as he answered it. "Everything okay, sis?"

"No. Gram and Pops were watching Chloe. Pops went to the cafeteria for some coffee, and when he returned, they were both gone."

◆ ◆ ◆

Riley had never seen Thayne's face lose its color so quickly.

"What do you mean they're gone?" he said and started back to the station.

Riley's chest tightened and she grabbed Thayne's arm, throwing him a questioning look. He pressed the speakerphone icon, and Cheyenne's voice came through the line.

"I mean Gram and Chloe aren't here. I had everyone in the hospital search, thinking maybe Chloe had decided to get up and Gram went with her, but . . ." She started to cry. "They're gone, Thayne."

It seemed impossible. The one thing they had tried so hard to avoid had happened. They entered the station, and Thayne put his hand to his head. "This is my fault. I pulled Baker away from the hospital. Don't cry, sis."

At Hudson's startled expression, Riley told him what Cheyenne had said.

"They can't have gone far. Your grandmother doesn't drive anymore," Riley said.

Hudson let out a long sigh. "That's not quite accurate. We don't *let* her drive anymore, but she thinks she can. She asks Pops for the keys almost every day."

"Pops, do you have your car keys?" Cheyenne shouted. After a few moments, his sister let out a groan. "They're gone. He left them on the hospital tray. She must've taken them. Hold on." Shouts sounded through the phone, a rustling and finally a curse Thayne hadn't heard escape his sister's lips. Ever. A minute later Cheyenne picked up. "Pops's truck is gone."

Thayne grabbed the radio and put out a BOLO on his grandparents' truck. "It's an '89 dark-gray Ford F-150. Wyoming license plates."

He turned back to his sister's call. "I'm coming to the hospital."

Riley grabbed his arm, shaking her head.

Thayne paused. He was the sheriff. He'd screwed up. He needed to fix it.

"Don't," Cheyenne said. "There's no point. I can handle searching the hospital and my clinic. I've already got our security officer looking through the video footage. If he finds anything, I'll call. You do your thing, little brother."

Thayne let out a tortured groan, clearly fighting the need to go there. "Answer me this: Did you see a tall, thin man roaming the hospital this morning?"

"I'll ask around. It's quiet here. Any visitor would have been noticed."

"Okay. Keep in touch."

He hung up and raked his hand through his hair. Hudson smacked him on the back. "We'll find them." While Thayne coordinated the search for Philip Andrews and his grandmother and Chloe, Hudson waved Riley to him. "I just got off the phone with Madison."

She gave him a questioning look, and he lowered his voice so as not to draw Thayne's attention. "If Gram drove anywhere, I think it'd be home. I asked Madison to keep an eye out for them. I'm heading out toward the ranch to see if I can find them. That old truck is a bear and is always giving Pops trouble."

That made sense to Riley, *if* Gram and Chloe were the ones in control. If Philip Andrews had them . . .

They had to consider every contingency. There was another place Gram might go. "If you don't find her at the ranch, try the road out toward the disputed land between your property and the Rivertons'. I have a feeling your grandmother knows the area well."

Hudson gave her a questioning glance but then nodded toward his brother. "Keep an eye on him. He's got an overdeveloped sense of responsibility. He blames himself already."

"You can count on it."

Thayne ended his call. "Dad's coming out to head up the search from here."

She nodded. "Okay. What do we do then?"

He paced for a moment, then banged his fist against the wall. When he pulled away, he left a bloody knuckle imprint. He looked over his shoulder at her. "Best guess. Do you think Andrews could have taken Gram *and* Chloe?"

"If he was exaggerating his condition, it looks like it," she said gently. "He disappeared at the same time as Gram and Chloe." She stared out the window at the empty parking spaces.

"He drove here once. I'll bet he did again." He glanced at her. "Did Willow mention a current rental car agreement in the email?"

Riley shook her head.

"That's too bad. Sometimes skirting the rules is a lot faster." Thayne sat down at Quinn's desk, picked up the phone, and called the judge. Riley couldn't help but be impressed. She'd never seen a warrant issued so fast.

She grabbed her laptop from the conference room and did a quick search of the car rental companies available near Milford, Iowa. She passed two numbers off to Thayne, and she took the other two. He smiled. "I should be nervous you read my mind so easily."

Riley's calls were dead ends, but on Thayne's second call, he hit pay dirt. He grabbed a notepad. "Make, model, and license plate," he barked into the receiver.

He scratched the data on the notepad and broadcast the information over the speaker while Riley called Hudson and gave him the description.

Thayne blocked off the back room. "I'll have Quinn get DNA samples from the vomit. Maybe we can find proof linking him to the other deaths." He threw his notepad on the desk and rubbed his hands across his face. "Of course, it won't help until we find them."

She crossed the room to him and held his hand in hers. She didn't want to say anything, but she had to. She kept her gaze averted from his.

"If he killed his wife, a woman he once loved, it won't take much for him to kill his own child. If he's taken Gram and Chloe and he's also our serial killer, having loose ends would drive him crazy. According to the files I found, each of the previous crime scenes were meticulously cleaned. There wasn't a speck of evidence left behind. That's a level of dedication few people can achieve."

"Where would he take them?"

Whenever a case became overwhelming, she always went back to the behavior, to the psychology. People didn't change. Not usually. She drew him to his feet and into the conference room. "There are too many mountains, too many places to hide. Let's figure this out."

She sat down, but he resisted her. He paced back and forth before glancing at his watch. "Dad should be here by now."

"Thayne. Tell me about Philip. What kind of man do you think he is?"

Thayne took a couple of deep breaths and sat next to Riley. He met her gaze. "A contradiction. He smelled of alcohol, was drunk, but had a two-year AA coin. He said he met up with someone at the diner but hadn't taken a sip of liquor. He looked . . . guilty. When I finally got him into my office, he claimed he needed to apologize to his daughter."

Riley drummed her fingers on the counter. "Was he telling you the truth?"

"Hell if I know. With what you found, added to what Willow told us and his sudden escape, and Chloe's disappearance, it looks like he's guilty."

Riley's head ached. "Let's look at it from another angle. He's a father who says he wants what? Redemption? Would he kidnap his daughter to do it?"

"Does he even view it as a kidnapping? He's her dad."

"That might make sense," she said and turned when the front door opened and Carson Blackwood entered the building. Dan Peterson followed closely behind him.

Carson nodded to her, but his focus landed on his son. "I'm watching Dan while Fannie and the girls put their heads together to find Gram and Chloe. They promised to keep you informed if anyone shows up. You go find your grandmother, Thayne. She . . ." His voice broke.

Riley went to him and gave him a hug. "It's going to be okay."

Thayne grabbed his rifle and hat. "Alicia's on her way in to man the radio." He motioned Riley over and placed his hand on her back when she drew near. "Riley and I won't come back until we find them."

◆ ◆ ◆

Thayne met his father's gaze and gave him a sharp nod before heading to the door. Search and rescue was a part of every rural sheriff's job, but for it to be Gram and Chloe in the hands of a potential serial killer made Thayne's blood run cold. "Let him be an overzealous dad," he whispered.

Just before he closed the door, he looked back at his father using colored pins to mark the spot where Gram and Chloe had disappeared, as well as potential search sites, on the county map mounted to the far wall.

He jumped in the SUV as several groups of townspeople on foot headed toward the sheriff's office. News traveled fast in a small town.

Hopefully this wouldn't end up being a multiday search. If it did, he feared they wouldn't find Gram and Chloe alive.

Riley's brow furrowed. "The search parties could get hurt if Andrews is involved."

"Dad knows that. He'll keep the search focused as if Gram and Chloe left the hospital voluntarily. We know Gram was involved with Kim. Maybe she's trying to help in her confused mind. You and I will focus on the Andrews theories." Thayne drummed his fingers on the steering wheel. "You're a newcomer," he said. "Where would you hide?"

"Mountains. I'd find a dirt road that didn't look like it was used much, and I'd disappear. The Wyoming landscape makes a car visible for miles."

"I agree. Let's head toward Fremont Lake. It's at the base of the Wind River Mountains, and there are a lot of trails from there. Pops's truck is a four-wheel drive. On a good day, the vehicle can get pretty far into those hills without too much trouble."

The car went silent. They didn't talk about what they might find. They both knew the truth. Most abductions didn't end well.

They wound their way into the foothills and up by the huge lake. Few people ventured up there this time of year. A smattering of snow frosted the mountaintops. The surface of the lake mirrored the jagged peaks. "No sign of his truck." Thayne pulled over and checked his phone. "No news, either."

"If I were looking for a place to hide, I'd be nervous," Riley said. "I'd take the first off-road I could."

"We could try the dirt trail on the far side of the Riverton property," Thayne muttered. "It's deserted, but the truck could definitely drive it."

He maneuvered over a cattle guard and headed down the mountains, cutting through a piece of land that would take them along a curved road and spit them out on the other side of town.

When they cleared the lake, Thayne's phone rang. He hit the speaker button. "Blackwood."

"Sheriff," Pendergrass said, his voice tight. "We just got a report of that rental vehicle. It went through the crash barrier on Highway 17 heading toward the Jordan place. It's over the edge about thirty feet. Looks bad."

Riley grabbed Thayne's hand and squeezed.

"I'm sending the rescue team from Pinedale," the deputy continued. "They'll be there soon."

"How many victims?" Thayne could barely form the words.

"They don't know. They can't get to the car without assistance."

"I'm fifteen minutes away." Thayne skidded to a halt and turned the car around. His hands gripped the steering wheel hard. "Damn, I wish Jackson were here. He's an expert in climbing these mountains."

"But you have equipment in the back. I've seen it," Riley said.

"I can rappel, but I only have basic first aid knowledge." He flicked on the lights and pressed the accelerator. "It's got to be Andrews, right? What if he took Gram and Chloe in Pops's truck and then switched cars? Or maybe Gram and Chloe aren't even with him."

She hated to see him torture himself. "We can hope they're safe. And that I'm wrong about Philip Andrews."

Thayne pushed the car even faster. "You being wrong doesn't happen very often."

She rubbed the back of her neck. "Nothing about this case feels right, Thayne. I'm in uncharted territory. I don't have enough information to do my job. If it makes you feel better, Andrews's behavior is erratic. Messy, even. That doesn't match my theory of a meticulous goal-oriented killer."

Too quickly they eased into the mountains. Deputy Ironcloud's four-wheel drive was parked ahead. Thayne stopped the car and jumped out, not waiting for Riley. "What have we got?" he asked Ironcloud.

Ironcloud stood near the edge of the road, measuring the break in the barrier. He looked up when Thayne joined him. "No movement."

Thayne peered over the side of the small cliff. An SUV was upside down, front grille facing toward them, steam spewing from the engine. He couldn't see any motion, but the side window was painted with a stripe of blood.

"I'm going down," Thayne said. If anyone was going to pull out a member of his family, it would be him. "You'll spot me?"

His deputy didn't look happy about the idea, but he nodded.

Thayne raced to his SUV to grab his climbing rope, harness, and a figure eight. While Ironcloud anchored the rope, Thayne slipped into the harness and clipped a carabiner to it. He looped his rope over and through the figure eight's metal rings before locking it in place.

After a quick double-check, Thayne slowly eased over the short cliff's edge, braking with his right hand. He kept his feet perpendicular to the cliff for stability and walked his way down slowly, carefully.

The smell of burning rubber wafted up to him as he rappelled down the side of the mountain, and it didn't take long to reach the vehicle.

He wiped a spray of dirt from the window and saw the crumpled body and sightless gaze of Philip Andrews.

"It's Andrews. He's dead."

Bracing himself, Thayne maneuvered so he could get a good look in the back seat.

Empty. Thank God.

"Gram and Chloe aren't here," he called up.

On the floor was an envelope. Thayne wrenched the door open and reached in to grab it. At this point any information might help them.

He tied a Klemheist hitch and created a sling to work his way back up. Not exactly elegant, but he made it to the top. He heaved himself over the edge, and Ironcloud steadied him.

Riley stood to the side, and he shook his head.

"Philip had no chance. But I found this." He handed Riley the envelope. "Maybe it'll help."

"Any idea of the cause?" Ironcloud asked.

"Nothing obvious except a possible DUI. I'm not sure we'll know until we get the car up here. Normally, I'd say it looks like an accident. Going too fast maybe?"

"No skid marks, but you said he'd been drinking."

Thayne unhooked the rope and stepped out of the harness. "He never copped to it, but his behavior said otherwise."

"*Another* accident?" Riley asked quietly and pursed her lips.

He recognized the skepticism in her voice—and on her face.

He met her gaze. "Sometimes accidents just happen. Not every out-of-the-ordinary incident is a serial murderer on the loose." Thayne grabbed his gear and stuffed it into a duffel. "Right now, we've got a higher priority than dealing with a dead body. To find Chloe and Gram. If they're not with Andrews, they have to be somewhere."

Thayne called the station and walked away from Riley. He activated his radio. "Alicia, take the BOLO off the rental car. We found it, but we didn't find Gram or Chloe. Tell Pendergrass to work with search and rescue on identifying the cause of the crash. Have some of the volunteers search the area between the hospital and the location where we found the car, just in case Gram and Chloe were in the car at some point. Got it?"

"Yes, sir."

He ended the transmission and went to the back of the SUV. Ironcloud joined him. "Do you think he has them hidden somewhere?" his deputy asked.

Thayne tossed his bag in the back of the vehicle. "Until we find them, I'm covering all the possibilities."

He didn't want to think about the implications of Gram and Chloe still being missing. Until he had proof they were in that car, he wouldn't even think about what that serial killer could have done to them.

"When the guys from Pinewood get here, ask them to search for any evidence that Gram and Chloe were in that vehicle. I didn't see a thing, but we can't be certain."

Ironcloud nodded and put his hand on Thayne's shoulder. "Everyone's looking. We'll find them."

"I know." Thayne closed the back end and got behind the wheel.

Riley slipped in beside him. "I was wrong," she said softly.

Thayne shifted in his seat. "About what?"

"Listen to this. It's dated two years ago." Riley removed a sheet of paper from the envelope.

> Dear Kristin—
>
> You may never read this. I haven't been able to find you, but I've tried. I'm going to stop searching now. I've realized that you lived in fear every day of our married life. I've been sober for a few months now. I live one day at a time.
>
> I created a new life out of the ashes of ours. I hope you've done the same.
>
> I want to apologize to both of you. I was a mean drunk and I took it out on you. I hurt you. Badly. I'm so very sorry.
>
> I don't expect you to forgive me—How could you?—but I wanted to thank you, Kristin. Thank you for protecting our daughter from her own father. I'm sick when I realize what I did to our little girl. I hope, wherever you are, that you have found a good life. Maybe, somehow, someway, I'll be able to tell you I'm sorry in person.
>
> Sincerely,
>
> Philip

"He wasn't obsessed with them?"

Riley shook her head. "I think he told you the truth. He saw that photo and he wanted to apologize to his daughter. Especially when he learned Kristin was dead."

Thayne stilled. "You do realize what you're saying?"

Riley returned the letter to the envelope and slipped it into her satchel. Her expression sent a long chill that settled behind his neck.

"Philip Andrews had nothing to do with what happened to the Jordans." Riley pulled the autopsy photos of the Jordans out. "We're back to square one, but my theory about a serial killer is still viable. Look at all the accidents that have been happening. The Jordans' fire. Me. Now Philip Andrews. We're all connected in some way. I just have to figure out how."

CHAPTER FOURTEEN

The mountains to Riley's left loomed above them, their jagged peaks dangerous and foreboding as the darkening sky closed in on the night. She clutched her satchel. She'd been wrong. Again.

"What if Chloe and your grandmother left on their own like Cheyenne first believed?" She glanced over at Thayne. "Maybe Chloe's father had nothing to do with it."

"A coincidence?" Thayne clutched the steering wheel with a white-knuckle grip. "I don't believe in them. Neither do you."

"Perhaps not, but assuming his arrival here isn't a coincidence, that means someone else is involved and we need another theory." Riley head throbbed. Her mind struggled with the inconsistencies. "Whoever killed the Jordans wanted it to look like an accident."

"The other wedding ring murders didn't," Thayne challenged. And he was right.

"The ones I found in the ViCAP database didn't, but like I said, they could've been early in the killer's development. It doesn't mean there aren't others out there, but they'll be much harder to track down. If the police believe they were accidents, or even a murder-suicide . . .

or if they identified another perpetrator, they won't be in any database. They'll simply be closed cases."

"Come on, Riley. You're reaching. Trying to find something that isn't there."

"I may be reaching, but it fits. Whoever set the fire was very good at what he did." She stared out the window, searching the shifting patterns of shadows against the mountains. The darkness danced, coalesced, then parted once more. Patterns had to fit. "You know, if I wanted to make someone look guilty, I'd create information for the investigators that would provide means, motive, and opportunity."

Thayne drummed his fingers on the dash. "How do we prove that?"

"What if the travel records were tampered with?"

Thayne let out a low whistle. "That takes some heavy-duty computer skills."

"But it can be done. No system is foolproof." Riley raised her eyebrow. "Look at what Willow, a retired schoolteacher and self-taught computer hacker, did."

Thayne turned right and headed toward his family's ranch. "Keep an eye out for Gram. I'll call Willow. Maybe she can tell us if last week's rental car records from Philip Andrews could have been altered in some way."

Riley squinted through the dimming light. "The temperature drops below freezing at night."

"I know." Thayne hit a number on his phone. "We have to find Gram soon." He hit the speakerphone button and the rings echoed through the car.

"Thayne." Worry laced Willow's voice. "Did you find her?"

"No, ma'am. We're still looking. I'm here with Riley."

"Hello, Agent Lambert." Willow let out a long sigh. "Helen's never gotten lost before, but I suppose it was only a matter of time."

Riley couldn't argue. Getting lost in a familiar setting was a common symptom of the illness. That being said, not every Alzheimer's patient lost their way home. It all depended on what part of the brain was affected the most.

"I was informed that Brett Riverton volunteered his plane to search," Thayne said. "They were up for hours, but it's too dark to fly now. We're searching the road leading out to the ranch. Hopefully we'll catch a glimpse of Pops's truck."

"The ladies and I think you should try the old swimming hole," Willow said. "That's her favorite place on the entire property."

Thayne nodded. "I should've thought of that. Thanks."

"Fannie, Norma, and I are going back out to search. I came home to take my medication before we hit the road."

Riley couldn't help but be blown away by the generosity of the Singing River community. She'd never lived in a place where friends and family dropped everything to help.

"We appreciate any assistance you can give," Thayne said, "but that's not why I called."

"What do you need?"

"The rental car records for Philip Andrews. Could the information have been planted?"

The speakerphone went silent. "You've got to be kidding."

"He's not, ma'am," Riley chimed in. "Andrews's trip here doesn't make sense with what we've learned about him."

Willow grumbled, and the sound of papers rustling crackled through the phone. The chime of a computer being booted up followed. "Give me a bit of time, and I'll call you back." Her voice trailed off, and the call ended without so much as a goodbye.

"I guess we'll find out." Thayne slowed the SUV to a crawl. A dirt road veered off to the right. "I wonder . . ."

"What?"

"This road used to lead to the old corral. Hudson built barracks there for the summer hands, but they're empty now. Hudson didn't mention searching there."

"It's worth a try." Riley hesitated to bring up another wrinkle, but she had to. "Everyone's searching for your grandparents' car, but your grandmother and Chloe may not be together."

"You're a hotbed of sunshine and hope, aren't you?" Thayne scowled. One more piece of bad news just might break him.

The comment caused Riley to wince.

He took her hand in his. "Sorry. I know you're right, but there's nothing we can do but keep searching."

"It's getting dark soon. I pray both of them are smart enough to find shelter where they'll stay warm tonight."

"From your lips to God's ears, as Gram would say."

The vehicle wound its way along the dirt road. The once-green grass bent in response to the September wind. Thayne couldn't stop his heart from pounding. Nights were cold. Gram had become frailer over the last six months, her disease taking its toll on her body as well as her mind. He didn't know if she could survive the night. As more land became visible with no sign of the truck, his hope dimmed. Finally, the SUV rose over a small hill, and a hundred feet below, a long building sat deserted. Riley couldn't see the main house, but a glimpse of something behind the building reflected the remaining bit of sun.

"What's over there?" Riley pointed.

Thayne jerked the steering wheel. He'd recognize that faded black anywhere. "Pops's truck." He couldn't believe they'd found it, and they pulled to the back of the building.

More hopeful than he'd been all day, he jumped to the ground. Riley followed. He peered into the vehicle, but no one was there.

"Let's try the building." Thayne jiggled the doorknob. "Gram. It's me."

No sound came from inside. Riley walked in behind Thayne. He tried the light switch, but it didn't work. Night was falling fast, and the interior was dim with many dark recesses.

She couldn't see anything. She grabbed her phone and turned on the flashlight mode. The thin beam bounced around, highlighting boxes, an old desk, and a rickety chair. There were bunks in the far corner and odd bits and pieces of someone's life, stuffed in the long shed for safekeeping and then eventually forgotten. An old rocking horse. A box filled with pots and pans. Riley and Thayne maneuvered between more boxes and old furniture, and she spotted dozens of places to hide.

Riley tugged on Thayne's hand, and he bent close so she could whisper. "Act like your granddad. She might respond to that."

Thayne straightened and let his voice drop to his grandfather's level. "Helen. It's Lincoln. It's time to go home."

The light landed on one of the bunk beds in the far corner. A plastic grocery bag rested on the mattress. She let the light fall, and from beneath the bed, a tuft of blonde hair peeked out.

"Chloe? Is that you?"

◆ ◆ ◆

The last sliver of sunlight gave way to night. Normally, he loved the night. The cover provided invisibility from a multitude of sins. This time, however, his less-than-perfect execution simply made the darkness a merciless audience of laughter.

The girl had vanished, so his plan to kill her and her father was no longer viable.

Agent Lambert had survived, and he'd been unable to retrieve the vials before the investigator had discovered them. They knew he existed. She was even looking into areas of his past that she shouldn't know about.

He'd studied, he'd researched. He'd learned. He was supposed to be the best. He may not always have been, but he'd found his truth. Proving lies, proving deceit. Punishing the deceivers.

At least until he'd come to this cursed town.

Where had it all gone wrong? His sharp thumbnail dug into the fourth finger of his left hand, rubbing over and over and over again until the old scar bled.

It was all Agent Lambert's fault. She'd ruined everything.

She doesn't know everything. She'd fallen for his ploy. For a while, anyway. The voice inside his head echoed the truth. *Get rid of her, and life will be perfect again.*

"Get rid of her. We have to."

He yanked his car into gear but didn't turn on his headlights. He knew exactly where to go to find out where she was. And when he did . . . everything would fall into place. Life would be perfect. He'd find peace. One more time.

◆ ◆ ◆

The final wash of light ducked below the horizon. The dim bunkhouse fell into complete darkness. Thayne's light illuminated the area in a sea of fluorescent white. With each slow step, the sound of his boot heel scraped against the wooden floor. He strode to the end of the hallway and squatted down next to the bed where the little girl hid. "Chloe. You remember me? It's Sheriff Blackwood. I bought some of your mama's blackberry jam at the fair last year."

He could see her head shake.

"Chloe, come on out. You don't have anything to be afraid of."

"You want to send me back." Her voice trembled, and the scratchy tone reminded Thayne of a lifelong smoker, or his football coach after the state championship game. "Mama said we could never go back. Mrs. B promised I wouldn't have to."

"Are you talking about Helen Blackwood?" Riley asked.

The girl's face peeked out from beneath the bed. "She told us to call her Mrs. B when I was little. No names."

Thayne lowered to the floor and sat cross-legged. He motioned to Riley to search the room. Just in case.

"How about you come out from under the bed and we can talk? Otherwise I'll have to scoot under there, and I'm afraid I'll dent my hat."

Chloe glared at him. "You promise not to take me back to the hospital?"

"I promise."

Hesitant as a wild animal, Chloe Jordan unfolded her coltish frame and scooted out from under the bed. "I'm trusting you even though Mama said never to trust the law." Chloe studied her fingers. "Mama and Daddy are dead."

"I know, honey. I'm sorry." Thayne leaned in closer. "Where's Mrs. B?"

She shrugged and made a motion of locking her lips as if she'd promised not to speak.

She knew something. "Look, Chloe." Thayne tried to keep calm. "Mrs. B isn't well. She's sick. She can't remember things that well anymore. I'm worried about her. She's my grandmother."

Chloe averted her gaze. "I know something's wrong with her. Mama knew it, too."

Thayne shifted back on his heels. "Are you telling me my grandmother has been visiting you?"

"She brings me a birthday present every year. She and Mama have long talks after I go to bed."

Riley sat beside them. "You sometimes listen, though, don't you, Chloe? I know I did when I was about your age."

Chloe wrinkled her forehead. "Who are you?"

"My name's Riley Lambert."

The girl's eyes widened. "You were supposed to help us. Mama was scared. Mrs. B told her to call you. That you'd help and wouldn't tell."

Chloe glared at Riley. "She said you'd left Singing River and wouldn't answer the phone."

Riley's face fell. "I'm so sorry, Chloe. I was . . . out of town on business. I was too late to help your mother. But I can help you, if you can tell us why your mother called me."

Chloe folded her arms across her chest. "I'll only talk to Mrs. B. I can't trust anyone else."

Thayne placed his hand on the girl's foot. "That's what I was trying to explain. My gram is missing. We can't find her."

The fear on Chloe's face was real. "She said she was going home."

Thayne shot a glance at Riley. "She didn't make it."

Once she realized Gram was in danger, Chloe stood up and followed them outside. She pointed toward a footpath. "Mrs. B walked down that one."

"That's the way to the ranch. I don't get it."

As Riley wrapped her arm around Chloe's shoulders and whispered for her not to worry, Thayne dialed Hudson's number.

"Have you found Gram?" Hudson snapped before Thayne said a word.

"No, but we found Chloe at the bunkhouse. She's been camped out there."

His brother threw out a flurry of curses. "What about Gram? Chloe didn't find that place on her own."

"She claims Gram started walking *home*."

"Here?" The sound of Hudson hurrying through the house, opening doors, and flicking on lights was distinct. "She's not here."

"Did you search every room?" Thayne asked, seeing Riley hug Chloe and give the worried girl a quick kiss on the top of her head. "Maybe Pops knows of some place she went when she was upset."

"I'll ask him."

"We're taking the south footpath to the house. That's the one Chloe said Gram took. Be there soon."

Thayne ended the call. He went to the SUV and pulled out a flashlight and held it out to Chloe. "We're going to walk to the house the way Gram went. I know it's difficult to understand, but Gram isn't doing well."

Chloe took the flashlight and flicked it on. "Mama said Mrs. B's brain is sick."

"Yeah, it doesn't remember very well and she gets scared when she's alone. It's dark and she might not know how to get home if she strays from the path. We need to find her."

He showed her how to sweep the beam from side to side. He held up his phone, and its flashlight feature pierced the darkness in front of them. "Keep a lookout for Gram in the grass. She could've fallen."

They started forward, walking slowly, Chloe a few steps ahead of him and Riley. Each took turns calling Gram's name, then waiting to hear a reply. Chloe's expression grew more and more concerned.

"She cares about your grandmother," Riley offered in hushed tones.

"I can tell. Gram has that effect on people."

The trek back to the ranch's driveway felt ten times longer than normal. They spotted the house through the trees, and it looked like every light had been turned on. The home glowed like a little pearl of radiance at the bottom of a dark sea. Surely if they could see the house, Gram had. They quickened their steps, and Thayne drew close to Riley. "Once we find Gram, we've got to pry the truth out of Chloe."

"She's been through so much. I wish Helen could answer our questions," Riley said.

"So do I." He raised his voice so Chloe could hear. "This is where Gram lives."

When they rushed up the front porch steps, Hudson threw open the door. "Thank God you're here. I was just about to call you. We found her. She was stumbling around near the back shed totally disoriented."

Thayne rushed inside after his brother, Riley and Chloe close on his heels. "Is she okay?"

Hudson led them past the living area. "She won't stop crying, and she doesn't recognize Pops."

"Where is she?" Thayne asked.

Hudson led them toward a long hall. Their old bedroom was in the original part of the house. "Pops thought it'd feel more familiar. Maybe calm her."

"Makes sense."

Carson hovered in the doorway near Madison, who looked on with tears in her eyes. Hudson nudged them clear to make room for Thayne and entered the small room that had been converted years ago into a guest room. The regular-size bed and small dresser appeared crammed into the room, which might have been large in the 1950s but now seemed too small to even turn around in.

Pops sat on the edge of the bed, looking down at his wife. She lay huddled on the quilt, clutching a pillow in her arms. Her sobs were real.

"Don't cry, Helen, my love. Please."

"Go away, you old letch. I want my Lincoln."

Thayne's heart broke at the words. Both for Gram and for Pops. He'd had to face her rejection too many times over the last year. His sad eyes lifted to Thayne's and he nodded, giving Thayne permission to take over.

Careful not to startle her, Thayne crouched next to the bed, hating that he had to pretend to be his grandfather but thankful that he could. Her sobs made his soul weep, and he slowly reached out his hand to gently stroke her hair. "I'm here, sweetheart."

She wiped her eyes and blinked at him. A smile tilted the corners of her mouth up. "Lincoln. Something awful's happened." She grabbed his hand and squeezed with a strength he didn't know she had.

"What's wrong? I can help."

She shook her head violently. "I can't tell you. I promised myself I'd never involve you. If anyone ever found out, you could lose everything you care about."

"I care most about you, Helen. You know that."

She patted Thayne's face. "And I care most about you." She sat up in the bed and rubbed her eyes. "I don't know how, but they've been found. I have to help them, but I can't remember . . ." She bit down on her lip. "I can't remember who to call. What am I supposed to do?"

Rocking back and forth in despair, Gram glanced up. Her gaze landed on Chloe. "Oh, my dear girl, what are you doing here? Where's your mother? She has to get help. We have to ask . . . Riley." Helen's gaze snapped to Riley, who was holding Chloe's hand. "You're not FBI anymore, right? But you know people. You can help them get away. I don't know how he found out. How does he know? Everyone's in danger."

Gram leaned forward and put her head in her hands. "It's a secret. It has to be a secret forever. Can't tell anyone. Not Lincoln, not Carson, not Thayne."

Thayne couldn't take her rambling any longer. The line between fantasy and reality was getting more blurred day by day. He grabbed his grandmother in his arms and began to hum her favorite song, then quietly sing.

"Could I have this dance . . ."

This time, though, the waltz didn't calm her. It worked a different kind of magic.

"Thayne, let me go. You're holding me too tight."

He released her and backed away. "Gram? Are you okay?" He held his breath, scared it was too good to be true.

Helen glared at the entire room. "What are you all standing around for?" Her gaze traveled across the tiny room until it landed on Pops. "I told you we should've just bulldozed this section of the old place. It's colder than a cow's hindquarter in a snowstorm in here. Take me back to our room, Lincoln. I need a cuddle."

Thayne should have been smiling, but Gram's quick transformation left him speechless. He bowed his head and rubbed the back of his neck.

Riley entered the room and slipped her arms around him from behind. "What just happened?" he asked her, his voice low.

"Are you okay?" She hugged him tight.

He covered her arm around his waist with his. "Stunned, but grateful. She's back to being herself. For the moment."

Thayne glanced at Chloe, whose disturbed gaze followed his grandparents down the hall. "Gram may be on a temporary new normal, but how do we connect with Chloe, get her to communicate with us?" he asked Riley.

"She's got to start trusting someone. I think Cheyenne was onto something when she asked my sister to sit with her."

Thayne turned in Riley's arms. "Chloe's about the age of your sister when she was abducted."

"They have a lot in common," Riley agreed. "And she became a mother to all the kids that man kidnapped. She has experience dealing with teenagers with posttraumatic stress."

He turned to see Hudson speaking in low tones to Madison, who was still wiping tears from her eyes. "She seems . . . fragile."

Riley gazed lovingly at her sister and smiled. "She has a big heart. That doesn't mean she's fragile."

Women were complex, and Thayne was just starting to understand that concept. "So you think she'll agree to speak with her?"

Riley hugged him tight. "I don't believe there's any doubt about it."

CHAPTER FIFTEEN

The house grew silent as Pops escorted Gram down the hall. Riley's gaze followed with concern. It seemed to her as if Helen Blackwood was snapping back and forth between the present and the past more and more often. The family had called off the search and let the town know Helen was safe.

Now they all moved to the living room, and Riley plopped onto the couch next to her sister as Thayne and Hudson took the chairs opposite them. Madison picked up Riley's hand and laced their fingers together. "It's all just so horrible," she whispered. "I feel so badly for them. I don't know how to help."

"It's called sundowning," Thayne said to Riley, Madison, and Chloe. "The evening is tough for Alzheimer's patients. I haven't seen any good explanation, but it's common. Gram gets anxious and more confused. The quieter, the better."

As Thayne talked, Chloe roamed the room, growing closer and closer to the front door. Subtlety wasn't one of Chloe's skills. Riley caught Madison's eye and nodded toward the girl.

Her sister mouthed, "I got this," got up, and crossed the room to Chloe, who went immediately still with a very guilty look on her face.

"Hi. I'm Madison." She stuck out her hand. "I sat with you sometimes when you were at the hospital."

Chloe screwed up her face. "Why?"

"Everyone deserves a friend." Madison grinned at Chloe. "Do you like ice cream?"

Chloe glanced between Riley and her sister, looking for something to be wrong. How strange had her life been that she expected the worst out of every situation? "It's okay, Chloe. Madison is a good person. I'm pretty sure you're going to like her. I know I do."

With skepticism pursing her lips still, Chloe nodded. "Chocolate. No vanilla. I mean, what's the point if it's just vanilla?"

Madison didn't hesitate but grabbed Chloe's hand. "You'd be surprised what you can do with good ol' vanilla. Come on. That big cowboy over there makes really good hot fudge sundaes. I've talked him into making one already today, and I think it's time for another."

With a quick wink at Riley, Madison led Chloe to the Blackwoods' kitchen. Hudson trailed in their wake.

Riley couldn't stop smiling. Hudson followed after Madison a little like a loyal hound. She met Thayne's gaze. "Interesting development between my sister and your brother."

"He talks about her a lot." Thayne frowned after them. "Hudson doesn't date much. I don't know why exactly, but he seems to like her enough to actually pursue a relationship."

She glanced toward the kitchen and lowered her voice. "Don't take this wrong, but I don't know if she's ready. She doesn't talk about men." Riley folded her hands in her lap and then immediately unfolded them. "She's different, Thayne . . . and you know what I mean by that. Tell him if he's not really interested to walk away. Otherwise, if he is, he needs to go slow—as in a-sloth-that's-not-in-a-hurry slow."

"Got it." Thayne craned his neck, trying to see into the kitchen, but the angle wasn't quite right. He leaned forward and cocked his head, trying to hear what they were saying. A frown dug across his forehead.

"What do you think's going on? Should we join them?"

"Not yet," she whispered, slightly amused by his impatience. "Give Madison time. If Chloe can connect with her, we'll have a better chance at getting information."

Thayne sat back. "I won't dispute that. Nothing is on the back burner with this one. I feel like—"

His phone rang, and he glanced at the screen. "It's Willow."

He got up and moved to sit beside Riley. He answered the phone. "Hey, Willow, did you find anything?"

"He's good, whoever he is," Willow said, her voice clear and somewhat in awe. "He's created a back door in the car rental database. He added a record for Philip Andrews."

"How can you be sure?" Riley asked.

"Because the date that record was added wasn't until you started investigating the Jordan deaths as a murder."

◆ ◆ ◆

"Hold on, Willow." Thayne rose, grabbed their jackets, and motioned Riley to follow. He didn't want to alarm Chloe if she heard him say anything about her parents.

He and Riley ended up on the front porch surrounded by a chorus of chirping crickets. They slipped into their coats. The crisp night air captured the light of the moon as it rose high above the mountain peaks. The setting was beautiful and peaceful, and completely at odds with the Jordan case.

"So Riley's right," he said. "These are no accidents happening. Our guy is manipulating our lives. Like the pro that he is. Can you identify him, Willow?"

"There's no trail that I can see from here. Maybe if I had access to the original server . . . but for that I'd need either inside contacts or it'd have to be official."

"Let me see what I can do," Thayne said and hung up. He turned to Riley, who stared at the bright moon hanging above them. "What do you think? Would your boss help us?"

She winced. "We don't have enough for a warrant. At least not that Tom would feel comfortable presenting to a judge." She switched her gaze to his and held out her hand. He clasped her fingers and let her drag him back inside the house. "It's time to ask Chloe what she knows."

They headed toward the kitchen, but when they got close, soft sobs stopped them from entering. The high-pitched voice shook with vulnerability.

Thayne hated the helplessness that had settled over him the moment he'd realized Chloe had saved herself even as the Jordans had been murdered.

"I should've died with them."

No twelve-year-old should feel that way, though Thayne had met too many who did on his tours overseas.

"No, Chloe," Madison immediately said. "Don't say that. Your mother and father wanted you to live."

Thayne and Riley hovered just outside the kitchen with a narrow view of the room.

Chloe wiped her eyes. "I know. Daddy yelled out our *big trouble* word 'cause someone bad was in the house. I snuck into the panic room while the man was yelling at my dad." She toyed with the spoon and stared out the window into the night.

"I stayed a long time. Then the fire and smoke started coming in through the ceiling, so I closed the steel door." Silent tears escaped from her eyes and rolled down her cheeks. "I couldn't breathe and it got so hot."

Brave kid. She deserved to have it easy, and he couldn't promise her that. Not in the investigation, not with her biological father.

"Did you see the man who visited your house?" Hudson asked.

Chloe shook her head. "No, but I heard him. He was really angry. He called my mom some really bad names. Told my dad he shouldn't have married her. I don't remember falling asleep, or anything else . . . not until I woke up in the hospital. I heard people talking outside my room and I knew the fire got Mom and Dad. I knew my real father wanted to take me away. I couldn't let that happen. Mom didn't know, but I remember how he used to hurt her. He's the reason we came here."

She still didn't know her real father was dead, and that the danger from the man who'd hurt her and her mother was gone. Thayne would have to tell her, but he wasn't quite sure how. She'd been through so much.

Chloe's spoon clattered in her bowl as she swiped through the hot fudge. She tipped her face toward Madison and confessed, "I knew you were there in the hospital. I pretended to be asleep while you read to me."

Madison bopped Chloe's nose. "You fooled me."

A smile pulled at her lips. "Mrs. B knew. She told me to keep pretending until it was safe. So I did." Chloe slid her finger through the remainder of the hot fudge and licked it clean. "That's when Mrs. B helped me escape. Just like before."

Thayne nodded for Riley to follow as he stepped into the kitchen. "How's the ice cream?"

Riley went to her sister and stole a spoonful before grinning at Chloe. "What's going on in here?"

Their appearance startled the girl, and she immediately pressed her lips together. The wall was back up.

Madison held her hand. "You can trust my sister. I promise."

"What about him?" Chloe pointed at Thayne. "Mama told me we can't trust anyone with a badge. They have rules that can hurt you."

Thayne winced at the truth. It would've been difficult to keep Philip away from Chloe if he were still alive.

"I'll leave if you feel that way, but I only want you to be safe." He crouched down and met her eye to eye. "You remember when I told you your father couldn't get you? That's because he died in a car accident."

Chloe blinked. "Did you kill him?"

"No. It was an accident."

"Mama would've been happy. He was mean to her." She laced her fingers with Madison's. "I really don't have anyone now, do I?"

Madison squeezed her hand. "You have all of us, honey. I promise."

The words made Thayne pause in worry. That was a big promise, but then again Madison knew exactly how Chloe felt.

Riley sat down across from Chloe. "Can I get some ice cream like my friend's here?" she asked, her voice innocent and pointed.

"Of course." Hudson got another bowl and began building another sundae.

"When Maddy and I were little girls, we'd have ice cream together sometimes," Riley said. "We played together a lot and told each other everything."

Chloe leveled an annoyed look Riley's way. "You're not even slightly subtle. What do you want to know?"

Riley straightened and met Chloe's gaze, unblinking and unflinching. "Okay, Miss Smarty-pants. The man who was in your house killed your parents and tried to kill you. I want to stop him, but I need your help. I don't know who he is. Did you hear them talking to each other? Did he say anything unusual?"

Chloe swallowed deeply. "Madison told me you never give up. Is that true?"

"I'm sort of stubborn like that. I won't stop looking for him."

"Cool." Chloe swallowed. "He told my dad my mother had lied. That she wasn't a very good wife, but I knew they were lies. He said he knew everything about us. Even about who we really were. That's when they started yelling. There was the sound of a crash, and Dad shouted out the word."

Thayne glared out the window. So the perp had been watching them, looking into their lives. "And you never noticed anyone hanging around your place who shouldn't have been there?"

He looked back at Chloe, who shook her head.

Thayne focused on Riley's intense gaze. He tried to see her thoughts. He'd learned a lot from her, and he had his own experiences with his SEAL team. So if Chloe didn't see a drifter hanging around, then this appeared to be a pointed attack. But why? Riley believed the perp to be a serial killer. Serial killers had signatures. There was usually commonality in victims, so the killer would have to have a reason for picking the Jordans. But why? Because they were survivalists? They lived alone? It could be anything.

Riley drummed her fingers on the countertop, then glanced at Thayne with a small smile. She'd co-opted one of his moves. Another reason they belonged together? "When you were in the panic room, before you closed the door, did you peek out at all?"

"I wasn't supposed to."

"That's not what I asked you," Riley countered.

"It's okay, Chloe." Madison rubbed the girl's back. "Tell Riley what you remember."

"I didn't look. I was supposed to close the door right away, but I was hoping they'd find a way to get away from him, and I didn't want them locked out. My dad suddenly stopped talking, and my mom shouted for me, but she didn't say the safe word, so I didn't answer." She bowed her head. "Maybe I should have."

"You did the right thing, Chloe." Madison gave her a quick hug. "None of this is your fault."

"Is that everything?" Thayne asked. It was hardly front-page material. "Can you think of anything else? Did you hear anything odd or smell anything weird?"

Chloe chewed on her lip. "Well, I do remember that his feet pounded when he walked, like his boots were too heavy. When he first came in, my dad shouted at him to get out so he wouldn't get oil all over Mom's clean floor." She paused, and a line burrowed into her forehead. "I j-just can't remember anything else." She gazed up. "Does that help?"

Riley gave Chloe's shoulder a gentle pat. "That was perfect."

Thayne's mind whirled with possibilities. "Thank you."

Thayne's phone rang again, and he rose. "Excuse me." He put the cell to his ear and left the room, and within seconds Riley followed him.

"Blackwood."

He pressed the speakerphone button. "Quinn, you've got both me and Riley."

"We finally got Andrews's rental car and his body up," the Singing River's forensics lead said. "The remains are headed to DCI to be autopsied, but I can tell you right now this wasn't an accident."

Another murder made to look like an accident. "How do you know?"

"The guy was dead before he crashed his car. Someone bashed in the back of his skull."

Granted, whoever did it had tried hard to make it seem like it happened during the crash. "How can you be sure it didn't happen during the accident?"

"Not enough blood. His injuries would have caused massive bleeding if he'd have still been alive."

◆ ◆ ◆

Staying at the Blackwell Ranch had a comforting effect on Riley. It was a real home, with a warm, big family and a sense of security. She knew Madison, who was used to an active household, loved it, and secretly she did, too.

It was late and Cheyenne had just left after checking in on Chloe, and though twelve, the girl asked Madison to sit with her until she fell asleep. The entire house had grown quiet in the way that instilled a sense of peace. It made Riley believe that all was right and always would be. She tiptoed down the hall to Madison's room and opened the door. Peeking inside, she saw Chloe asleep in one of the twin beds and Madison sitting on the floor between the beds with her hand clasped firmly in Chloe's.

Riley motioned her sister out. Madison gave her a quick nod and eased her hand from Chloe's before quietly leaving the bedroom and closing the door.

"Poor thing. She reminds me of . . ." Madison's voice caught in her throat. "Heather. Except her hair color, of course."

"I'm sorry." Riley winced. Heather had been one of the children brought into the compound where Madison and more than a dozen other children had been held captive. The girl had been punished so severely she hadn't survived, despite Madison's doing everything she could to help her.

Maddy wrapped her arms around Riley. The two of them walked into the living room, where Thayne and Hudson were, and the two men looked up.

"You okay, Madison?" Hudson asked.

She nodded and then slowly shook her head, contradicting herself. "At least Chloe's asleep."

"I made some of my special hot chocolate, if you want some," he offered.

"Thanks. That sounds delicious."

Riley agreed. The pair settled on the sofa, and Hudson was gone and back before they knew it. All it took was one sip for her to know what made the hot chocolate unique. The man had a heavy hand with the whiskey. Before she could warn her sister, Madison tipped up her mug and took a deep sip. Her eyes widened, and she promptly coughed until her eyes watered. Gasping, she managed to say, "Oh my."

Riley laughed and Hudson looked confused until Madison put him out of his misery. "I never learned to drink." She placed the still-full mug on the coffee table. "I don't wish to be rude, but it tastes like medicine."

Thayne frowned at his own mug. "That's Pops's smoothest whiskey. He'll be heartbroken you don't approve."

Madison winced and picked up her mug again. "Maybe it'll grow on me."

Shaking her head, Riley took the mug away from her sister. "If something has to grow on you, I'm not sure you should put it in your mouth. Take brussels sprouts, for example."

"Excellent point," Thayne agreed. "Though Gram's got a recipe that actually convinced me they weren't boiled socks in disguise."

"What did Cheyenne say about Chloe?" Riley asked and tucked her feet underneath herself.

Madison stretched before placing her head on her sister's shoulder. "That she's healed nicely. She probably could've been released from the hospital yesterday."

"That's good." Gram hadn't done any damage by helping the girl escape.

Madison bit her lip. "What's going to happen to her now?"

"She's staying here," Hudson said. "So we can keep an eye on her."

"She is?" Thayne asked. "Who decided this?"

"*I* did. She needs to be around people she trusts."

"We'll have to get Child Protective Services involved at some point," Thayne said with a grimace. "But for now, I have no problem placing her in protective custody. I'm assigning Deputy Ironcloud to primary guard duty here. He'll switch up when he needs a break."

"She can't go anywhere alone," Riley said firmly. "None of you should."

"Which means you, too," Thayne said.

Riley agreed. "What about Madison?"

"I can't leave Chloe." The desperation in her voice sounded loud and clear.

Hudson came out with a fresh cup of normal hot chocolate for Madison and a coffee for himself.

"What about us?" Thayne scowled at his brother, showing his empty mug.

"You're not a guest. Get it yourself." Hudson passed the cup over to Madison, his expression growing gentle.

He took a seat. "We have the house set up with pretty good surveillance to keep an eye on Gram, thanks to Brett's brother. I usually don't turn on the door tones unless it's night, but I can make them active. That way no one can come in a door or window without us knowing about it."

Riley hadn't realized they'd outfitted the house so well. Staying here would work until they could identify the killer. And she had an idea for that.

Thayne rose, picking up Riley's recently drained mug. "Now's the time I wish I had my teammates at the ready to watch our six, but it'll have to do." He paused and sent his brother a disgruntled look. "Since Hudson bites as a host, what would you like, Riley? Hot chocolate, a beer, or coffee?"

She glanced at Hudson. His entire focus was on Madison. "I'll go with you."

She followed Thayne into the kitchen.

"What's your pleasure?" he asked.

"Nothing. I'm not thirsty." She bit her lip. "I've been thinking about what Chloe said. Oil on his boots. A roughneck would be a great job for a serial killer. Oil workers travel from job to job, blend in with a bunch of other strangers, and can pretty much leave anytime they want without attracting notice."

Thayne pulled a beer from the refrigerator. "Okay. What are you suggesting?"

"The special agent for the FBI in me would suggest requesting information from coroners and police departments in areas where there are a lot of temporary oil jobs." Riley sent him a wry look. "It could take a while."

Thayne stroked his chin. "Are you suggesting I find someone who can work around the delay?"

She shrugged. "If Willow were interested, she could start with the surrounding states. Look for explained deaths that mention missing wedding rings or unusual circumstances. Maybe family members who are convinced there was foul play involved but the cops didn't buy the story."

"It's a long shot." Thayne took a long sip. "But we're down to long shots unless he comes after you or Chloe."

Hudson came out onto the porch looking disgusted. He handed his brother a beer and said, "I messed up."

Thayne shot a quick glance at Riley, then took the bottle. "In what way?"

The light from the house highlighted Hudson's misery as he turned to Riley. "You'd best go see your sister."

Her sister? A twinge of panic caught in her throat. She raced inside, hearing Thayne ask, "Damn it, Hudson. What did you do?"

Madison sat in the corner of the sofa, curled into herself, her head bowed to her chest. As gently as possible, Riley sat next to her and rubbed her back. "What's wrong?"

"It's my fault," came the soft admission that had Riley leaning closer. "I asked him to kiss me. And I kissed him back, but I shouldn't have. It was wrong." She twisted her fingers in her lap. "I'm broken, Riley. He deserves someone who . . . someone who can be his partner, not a needy head case."

"Is that what he said?" Riley glanced at the men drinking just outside. She'd murder Hudson for being so callous.

"No. He said he'd wait for me. As long as it takes."

Riley let her hand drop. "I have firsthand knowledge of the Blackwood persistence. If he says he'll wait, he will."

"That doesn't mean it's right." Madison wiped a tear from her cheek. She looked wounded, but she lifted her chin. "I have to fix myself first, and that's not going to be easy. Tell him he's better off with someone else." She stood, her face pinched from holding back another rush of tears. "He'll only find loneliness waiting for me."

Before Riley could say anything, Madison escaped to her bedroom.

The front door opened, and Thayne entered and locked it. She looked behind him, but Hudson wasn't there. "Where's your brother?"

"He's bunking down at the stables. Don't be mad at him, Riley. He said she asked."

"I know. I'm not mad." She glanced down the hall after her sister. "I just don't understand. Loving someone shouldn't be this hard. It should come naturally. Easily. But we make it difficult because we're stubborn and selfish and—" She rose from the couch and stepped close to him. She was no longer talking about Hudson and Madison. This hit too close to home. Without asking, she wrapped her arms around him and sighed. "I'm tired of making it hard."

She placed her cheek on his chest, and Thayne tilted her chin up. "We're eyebrow deep in a complicated case again, Riley. The excitement of the hunt is a real thing."

She didn't want him to be reasonable. She wanted his passion. She wanted to feel loved. Cherished. Her voice grew thick with emotion. "I want you, Thayne. Not because of all this, but despite all this."

He sighed. "We've been down this road before."

"I know." She leaned into him and breathed in his unique scent. His muscles bunched under her fingers as they played over his back.

"What happens when we solve the case? Do you fly back to DC to get your intellectual fix, then come home to Wyoming and use my body for a release?"

She leaned back and met his gaze. He wasn't teasing. He was serious. She should have felt insulted, but if he truly believed that about her . . . "How can you say that? You mean more to me than that."

"God, I hope so, but we're heading into a pattern here, and I'm not sure I like it."

He led her to the couch, put his beer bottle on the table, and pulled her down astride him on his lap. She could feel his desire pressing against her, exactly as he intended. It had been too long since they'd been together.

She wrapped her arms around his neck and looked down at him. His expression remained serious, even as his body seduced her with each small movement.

With a sigh, Riley stared into his gaze. "I've lost my way, but with you I feel home."

"I know. I feel the same." He circled his hands around her waist. "I feel lost, too. Half the time, I can't believe I'm sheriff of this town. And the truth is, I shouldn't be. What business do I have running an investigation on a murder case? Just because I'm prior military and made it through SEAL training doesn't mean I'm qualified to be a law enforcement officer. Even if I did complete the training at DCI."

"Do you want to go back to DC with me?" she asked. "It would solve all our problems."

"You know I can't. My family needs me here. And I need *you*."

She groaned, thrilled to hear him say that but horrified by it just the same. "I love you, Thayne. I want more than anything to be with you, but what's happening in Singing River right now is unusual. My job is important to me, and this place can't supply a never-ending stream of deviants for me to analyze and arrest. As sick as that sounds, that's my job, and I'm damn good at it."

He wrapped his arms around her, and Riley rested her chin on top of his head, his hair tickling her skin. She pressed closer. His hands slipped from her waist to knead her hips. His heartbeat thudded against her, racing in reaction to their close proximity. She'd kept control of her emotions, suppressing her needs since before she'd left for DC. Why were they torturing themselves? She didn't want to hold back any longer.

She missed him. She wanted him. More than ever. She moved his hand to her breast and ran her lips down his neck. It was all about him. It was all about her. Simple.

Why couldn't life be simple?

She cupped his cheeks and captured his mouth for a long, slow, deep kiss. Heaven waited in his kisses. She pulled away and sighed. "We'll figure something out. Right?"

"Yes," he growled as he pulled her close. "I'll think of a way we can be together." His lips slid over her skin to her collarbone.

"It's late."

"It's not that late," he corrected, his hot breath tickling her skin. "For now, everyone is safe. I want to make love to you, Riley."

"Yes," she sighed and threw her head back as he gently raked his teeth along the sweet spot near her shoulder. "All night long."

CHAPTER SIXTEEN

The beer stayed on the coffee table. Thayne rose from the couch, and Riley wrapped her legs around his waist, clinging to him as if she'd never let go, and his arms refused to let her leave. Her lips were soft and familiar and so very missed. They locked onto his as he made his way down the hall to his childhood room.

He shifted Riley, groping for the handle so he could open the door. With a quick twist, the door sprang open and they stumbled inside. He kicked it closed and shuffled to the bed as one button fell open on his shirt and then two. She had nimble fingers.

She slid down his body, exploring every inch of him, touching him in places that made him harden with need. While he could still think, he removed his weapon and placed it beside hers on the bedside table.

"I won't give you up without a fight," he said softly. "Remember that."

She pulled his head down, and her mouth opened in welcome under his. They hadn't kissed this way—as two lovers—in far too long.

Thinking could be highly overrated. Tonight, Thayne would forget the problems. He would only feel.

He slipped his hands beneath her shirt and caressed her, pulling her close, pressing her up against him, leg to leg, hip to hip. She belonged in his arms. She always had. She always would. She was soft where it mattered and strong where it counted. She made him weak at the same time she strengthened him. They made a good team. And not only in the bedroom.

His heart thudded with urgency. He couldn't wait. It had been too long. With ease he pulled her shirt off, threw it on the ground, and followed with his own. Neither of them was in any mood for slow and sweet. He could tell by the clutch of her hands on his back that she needed strong and fast.

He shoved her pants off and soon they were both nude. He clasped her close and, unwilling to lose the contact of skin to skin, walked her backward to the bed. She tumbled onto the soft mattress, pulling him on top of her. She cradled him against her hips, hugging him close, entwining her legs with his.

"Now," she muttered against his lips. Her hands roamed up and down his back to his hips. She demanded everything from him. "I want you now."

He could never deny her. He shifted away and rolled on a condom before hesitating for one moment. He looked into her passion-filled eyes. He could never give her up. His gaze held her captive and he thrust inside her, taking her with all the pent-up needs he'd coiled away in his heart. In this there were no doubts, no hesitation. They belonged together.

She wrapped her arms and legs around him, matching him thrust for thrust, engulfing him in sensuality and desire. His heart soared. She surrounded him, seduced him, held him tight.

He was home. They were one. His breathing erratic, Thayne rode wave after wave of pleasure in tandem with Riley. A crest washed over them. His body shuddered in completion, and Riley sighed with satisfaction beneath him.

He could hardly breathe. His heart nearly burst, and her arms held him tight, refusing to let him go.

Why argue? He sagged against her, never more content.

She was his home. She always would be. No matter what life threw at them, no matter where they lived. Riley was his person. He had no doubts when they lay side by side.

He pushed the damp hair back from her face and kissed her lips. "This feels right. *We* feel right. Can you not see that?"

She burrowed her face in his neck. "I do."

He slid to her side and tugged her against him, throwing his leg over her hips, trapping her as if she'd fly away if he wasn't careful. He couldn't stop touching her. His thumb stroked her face. "I don't like the distance between us."

Her gaze shifted from his. "This is hardly keeping our distance."

"I'm not talking about sex, Riley. I'm talking about you closing me out. You stopped talking to me the moment Madison left for your parents' house. You slammed shut a door, and I didn't push." He lifted her chin. "I'm through backing off. I'm fighting for all of you. Not just this." He slid his hand down the side of her body, pausing at her hip.

Riley stilled, her breath caught in her lungs. When she finally exhaled, she placed her hand on his and squeezed. "I was born to solve the unsolvable. To help those who others have given up on. For years searching for Madison completed me. I couldn't let anyone else in. I got used to being alone, being self-sufficient, being isolated." She placed her hand near his heart. "Then you came into my life. Piece by piece I opened myself up to you in ways I'd never imagined. I organized my life around those Friday-night phone calls. I have no doubt you are the one person in the world who sees through the walls I've built, but every instinct in me is fighting against giving in completely. And I don't know why. I hate it about myself. I love you. I thought those three words solved everything. I need you in my life, Thayne. You're my center. Sometimes I think you're the only thing that keeps me from tumbling down a dark hole of chaos, but I'm afraid. Deep in my soul, I know I'll let you down. I'll ruin this for us. I don't know how to give you what you need. What if I never do?"

His thumb caressed her lower lip. He could feel his heart cracking in two. "I can't be only your touchstone, Riley. There has to be more to our relationship." He rolled away from her, unable to look at his heart's desire any longer. "Do you know what I feel when I say I love you?"

She bit down on her lip and shook her head.

"When you smile—I mean really smile—a light shines from your eyes. Your joy lightens my heart. When you struggle, when that darkness of uncertainty smothers you, I hurt with you, and I want nothing more than to ease your mind. I want to ease your burdens, I want to prop you up when you no longer have the energy to go on. I don't need someone who is perfect, someone who has no troubles, who is always certain. I need someone to share a life with. Someone willing to prop me up when I'm not strong, someone to love me when I have doubts. Someone to stand with me against the world."

Thayne could barely make out the sob catching in Riley's throat.

She shivered against him. "I never knew that kind of love existed."

She acted like she couldn't reach out and grab what he was offering. All she had to do was hold out her hand and take a risk. He'd catch her when she fell.

She lay huddled in his arms, and he could almost feel her fear. Something snapped inside him. He sat up, throwing off the hands that begged him to stay, and pulled on his jeans. Sitting on the edge of the bed, he leaned his elbows on his knees. "I want you to really consider something, Riley." He looked over his shoulder at her. "What will your life be like without us? Personally, I don't like the view very much."

"Do you want the truth?" Riley sighed and sat up, pulling the sheet with her. "I don't trust happy. I've found it with you—some of the happiest moments of my life—but I've seen the other side. I don't know if I can believe in forever."

Did she really think that? He twisted and faced her. "If I knew you were all in, Riley, whatever you do, you couldn't drive me away."

"You can't know that."

He picked up her hand and kissed her palm. He stared into her eyes, seeing the fear that clouded them. "And that's the problem. I actually do know that."

◆ ◆ ◆

The early-morning sun pierced through the slats of Thayne's bedroom window blinds. She'd tried to stay above the emotions whipping through her last night, but they'd pressed down on her until she'd asked him to leave. He had, though she knew he hadn't gone far. She'd hugged her pillow, breathing in his scent, and fought back the tears that threatened to drown her. The bed was cold without him, but she couldn't ask him back. She couldn't give him hope. How could he be so sure about everything? Truthfully, his confidence scared the hell out of her.

She slipped into clean clothes and ran a brush through her hair. No new threats had appeared, though she doubted the killer had given up. She reached for her red notebook, which highlighted the criminal's profile she'd been building, and read through what she'd already written. *Obsessive personality.* She circled it. *A man who didn't take to losing.* Though she believed he'd carried out his objective to kill the Jordans, he'd made mistakes, and that wouldn't sit well with him. He could be anywhere, planning his next move or carrying it out. He didn't show a preference for the cover of darkness. If she was right, he'd killed Philip Andrews—maybe as a scapegoat. He'd tried to kill her in broad daylight. He was trying to fix his errors. More than that, though, it meant he had a job that gave him free rein to come and go.

A bell tone pierced through the house, interrupting her thoughts and alerting everyone inside that the front door had opened.

Without hesitation she tossed the red book on the bed, grabbed her gun, and raced to the front room.

Hudson stood frozen just outside the door, his hand on the knob, geared up for the day with a cowboy hat pushed back and work gloves on. Pops sagged against the wall near the kitchen, holding his chest, his old shotgun pointed at the floor.

"Boy," he growled, "you trying to give me a heart attack?" He shook his head and went back into the kitchen.

A sheepish expression crossed Hudson's face, and he called after Pops, "Sorry. Chores."

Riley let out a sigh of relief. She locked her gun and tucked it near the small of her back. Madison and Chloe slowly stumbled from the hallway, both half-dressed and half-asleep.

"Is everything okay?" Madison asked.

Hudson avoided Madison. "Before anyone leaves the house, let either me, Pops, or Thayne know. If the tone goes off, one of us needs to be aware who it is."

"Can I use the study, Hudson?" Riley asked.

"Sure," he said with a shrug. "Have at it."

He turned around and strode out the door.

"How about some breakfast?" Madison asked Chloe a bit too cheerfully. The girl nodded and Madison laughed. "This isn't a free meal. You'll have to help me cook. Between you and me, we can make a spread to feed everyone."

Riley strode over to her sister. "I have work. Please take Hudson's warning seriously. You'll watch out for each other? And if you need anything—"

"We know. You'll be in the office, digging up dirt on very bad people." She grabbed Chloe's hand. "Did I ever tell you my sister's supercool?" They both joined Pops in the kitchen.

"Madison knows you well," Thayne whispered from behind her.

She jumped and smacked him on the chest. "Don't sneak up on me."

"At least I have your back," he said, his voice not angry, not curt, and not hurt.

In fact, it sounded like they hadn't even had a deep, emotional conversation last night.

Riley faced him. His hair was wet from a recent shower, his clothes sharply pressed. "Are you going somewhere?"

"Can't a man look pretty?"

She let out an unexpected laugh. He was in a strange mood.

"Quinn's researching jurisdictions where a lot of roughnecks reside," he said. "As soon as we have the list, I'll pass it on to Willow so she can do a little digging. In the meantime, we sit tight."

Thayne's phone jingled in his pocket. "Hopefully it's Quinn." He glanced at the screen. "It's my dad." He answered and pressed the speakerphone on. "What's wrong? Is Fannie okay?"

Riley leaned in to listen until Thayne punched the speakerphone off.

"She's fine. It's Dan, son. He passed out. Cheyenne came over and realized he didn't take his medication. He hasn't been taking it since he stopped living with Kate. He didn't even bring it with him."

Thayne pinched the bridge of his nose. "Didn't Olivia know he took medication?"

"That girl's got her own life to live. She doesn't have a clue what's going on with her father. Hold on a minute." The phone went silent for a few seconds. "Sorry. I needed to walk into the other room. He's definitely got dementia, son. I don't know what kind. Could be it's his meds or cardiovascular system, but he can't be left alone. He can't take care of himself. I tried to tell Olivia . . ."

"She's in denial."

Carson sighed. "Yeah. She doesn't want to talk about it."

"What about the bruises?"

"Well, he's pretty unstable. Since yesterday, he's got a knot on his head and a big old bump on his upper arm. He doesn't know what happened. He started accusing Fannie of manhandling him."

"If Cheyenne could make a diagnosis, we could probably make the accusations against Kate go away."

"Olivia doesn't want more tests."

Since watching his granddad and father when he was a child, Thayne knew small-town lawmen didn't just arrest unruly citizens; they were the glue that held people's lives together, poking their noses into all sorts of personal business. "Does anyone have a power of attorney?"

"Kate would if she hadn't been accused of abuse, and we can't get the mental confusion diagnosed without getting him in to see a doctor. It's a vicious circle." Thayne's father didn't speak for a few moments. "We're lucky our family is on the same page in dealing with your grandmother. This isn't going to end well for Dan. I can feel it."

"See if you can't convince Dan to let Cheyenne run a couple more tests. You may have to lie to him—say it's a yearly exam. Anything to get him to see Cheyenne."

"It feels sneaky."

"Maybe he's just got hardening of the arteries or something. If they can treat him, maybe he'll be back to normal. They'll thank you for it later."

"I'll do my best, but I'm not a miracle worker." His father sighed and then hung up.

"Dan's not that much older than my father," Thayne said to Riley. "I hope it's something they can treat. There's nothing good about having dementia."

"You do a lot for these people."

"Not nearly as much as I'd like; otherwise Kate wouldn't be in jail and Dan would be getting treatment and a serial killer wouldn't be terrorizing you and Chloe." Thayne rubbed the nape of his neck. "How about we call Quinn and see if he's made any headway?"

Riley followed him into the office. A monitor with split images from around the house rested on one side of his desk. They showed

Chloe and Madison in the kitchen having fun as they made an extra-large mess.

Riley shook her head. Her sister was becoming quite the instigator. "Hope you're hungry."

"Not particularly."

Thayne was looking at the monitor that showed Lincoln and Helen. They sat in the sunroom, Pops reading the paper and holding Gram's hand. Neither spoke. Gram leaned into Pops, and a smile lit his face. Riley couldn't stop her own grin. "Your grandparents are having a good morning."

"Let's hope it stays that way." Thayne cleared off an area. "You can set up your laptop here. I'll call Quinn."

Thayne tapped in the number.

After a few rings the deputy answered. "Pendergrass."

"That good of a morning, huh?" Thayne asked.

"Oh yeah. It started with the DNA coming back on those maps." Quinn let out an aggravated shout. "And now I just spilled my drink. Damn it."

"Trouble comes in threes, buddy. Did you get a hit on the DNA?" Thayne asked.

"And then some. Female with a partial match to one of the members of the sheriff's office."

"You're kidding? Who?"

"*You.* And unless you've got a kid running around that I don't know about, it has to be your grandmother. She either created the maps or at least significantly handled them."

◆ ◆ ◆

Thayne glanced at the monitor, wishing he were surprised by the news. Gram sat calmly with Pops, a perfect picture of a content, ordinary grandmother. It seemed odd she'd be involved with whatever was going on at the cabin, but Gram was obviously strongly connected to the Jordans. Exactly *how* Thayne might not ever know, but somehow she'd helped them when they needed help the most.

"Thanks. And what about the other task, Quinn?"

"How many of our colleagues are you trying to piss off?" Several papers rustled. "After a half dozen or so hang-ups and hearty chuckles, I talked to two possibilities. Both small-town police. One in Williston, North Dakota, and the other in Wamsutter, Wyoming."

"They had crimes that fit the pattern?" Thayne pulled out his notebook and jotted down the names.

"The police chief in Williston said he closed a murder-suicide case under pressure from the mayor about four years ago. It shocked the entire town. Until that weekend, everyone believed the victims were the perfect couple. In love, happy family, all that. Always holding hands. When the wife's sister came in to settle the estate, she couldn't find the wedding rings. The couple were wearing fake gold bands when they died, which didn't make sense to anyone. There were some big withdrawals in their account. The family didn't push, and the case was closed."

"What would you have done?" Thayne asked.

Quinn clicked his tongue. "Searched for an unknown drug problem, maybe prescriptions. That's usually what eats up money."

"How about Wamsutter?"

"The Sweetwater County Sheriff's Department handled a case last year. This one may sound familiar. Carbon monoxide poisoning of a married couple. Well thought of in town. Apparently upstanding citizens. Everyone called them the perfect couple. Ruled accidental death. The report carried a footnote mentioning wedding rings missing from the home. The bodies had fake plain gold wedding rings on, and they were holding hands when they were found."

"Another perfect couple die holding hands. Two more missing wedding rings. *And* carbon monoxide poisoning." Thayne met Riley's pensive gaze. "You've got to be kidding."

"Have we got a serial killer in Singing River, Sheriff?" Quinn asked.

"Keep it quiet for now." Thayne scribbled a few notes. "I need a list of employees working for the oil companies near those towns during the time in question. Plus a current list for the company working outside of Pinedale."

Quinn let out a low whistle. "That won't be easy."

"You run into any hassle, let me know. I have . . . another option."

"I don't want to know, do I?" Quinn said.

"Definitely not."

Thayne ended the call.

Riley paced back and forth. "Don't wait. Call Willow. No company that retains a lawyer is going to give you that information. I've got a bad feeling we're running out of time."

While he spoke with Willow, Riley made some notes in her red book. She tilted the pages so he could read several words. *Perfect. Happy. Love. Accident. Murder-Suicide.*

Thayne nodded. "That's great, Willow. Thanks." He ended the call and slipped his phone into his pocket. "She'll get back to us. Hopefully it won't take too long."

Riley tapped her pen on her notebook. "I believe the first two murders I uncovered through the FBI files were his training ground. Since then he's been a ghost." She paced back and forth and reviewed the photos. "He wants to be invisible. Chloe was a witness and pushed him out of his game plan. He'd normally have been gone by now, but the more we've investigated, the more dangerous he's become. I made him panic. Leaving the vials in the wall unit in my room shouldn't have happened. And then there's Andrews. If the sheriff's office hadn't found his car, we might not have known he was killed. It looked like an accident. I have to wonder, because I don't believe in coincidences."

Thayne stared out the office window. "If he's as obsessive as you think he is, what'll be his next move?"

Riley stroked the image of the burned bodies. "If we don't find him first, I have a strong suspicion he'll find us."

◆ ◆ ◆

The Blackwood Ranch was an easy enough target. The house, not so much. He'd been unable to hack into the camera system. Whoever had designed it knew their way around zeros and ones better than he did. So he'd have to provide another opportunity.

Luckily, the cold weather had culled the number of ranch hands. He studied the back of the house from their prime vantage point behind a small rise. Out of sight, but oh so close.

A deputy with a watchful eye patrolled. If the timing worked, by the time everyone realized what had happened, the operation would be over and done.

Not one of his targets had left the house all day. The old woman was soft in the head. She was their focus. He could use that to his advantage. She made a beeline for the sunroom whenever she could, and the whole family catered to her.

They believed they were safe inside, but surprise was a formidable tool.

He lay belly down just below the crest, near the SUV he'd stolen. He'd divested it of its GPS so no one could track him. He was ready.

He adjusted the fingers of his gloves and glanced over at his companion. Like the idiot he was, the man didn't wear gloves, said they sissified real men. He was proud of his calluses. It worked out quite well, actually. His prints would be visible—and traceable. Exactly the plan.

It hadn't taken much to encourage the guy to go after the sheriff. Feed his ego after that night in jail.

"Just so we're clear, are you prepared to do whatever it takes? It might not be pretty. We'll have some collateral damage."

The man pumped his fist. "Thayne Blackwood has a stick up his ass. Nobody puts me in jail and walks away without feeling my wrath. He's gonna pay for what he done. I don't care what I have to do."

"Excellent."

He handed over a rifle, making sure the man held it firmly enough to leave fingerprints. "Keep it with you."

The man took the weapon, sighting it toward their targets before nodding. "Ready."

"We'll be showing this entire town Thayne Blackwood should never have been made sheriff. All your troubles will go away when he's discredited."

The idiot man grinned with lethal satisfaction.

Truthfully, some gene pools should never be allowed to continue. And for the man helping him . . . he wouldn't get the chance.

Through the tall grass, they belly-crawled back to the SUV and slipped inside. He slammed the door and grabbed the cell phone tucked in the console between the seats.

"Here she is." He held a phone in his hand and punched in the number of the cell he'd used as the detonator. He covered his face with a ski mask. "You ready?"

"I was born ready." The cliché tripped off the man's tongue, and he grinned as if he were clever.

The sooner this was over, the sooner he could leave the guy's dumb ass behind. "Put on your ski mask."

He nodded and slipped it on.

"You know what to do?" he asked, and again the man nodded.

He glanced at his watch. The deputy would be circling the barn in seconds.

"Three. Two. One."

He gunned the SUV and swerved across the grassy lands to the northeast side of the house. He skidded to a halt just feet from the back door and just out of view of the corner of the sunroom.

Without speaking, they exited their vehicle and stood at the ready at the back door. Crowbar in one hand, he nodded and pressed the screen of his cell phone.

A loud explosion rocked the Blackwood Ranch. The old woman screamed. Her husband let loose a curse and told her to stay put. Farther inside, surprised shouts erupted from all around the house.

This was it.

CHAPTER SEVENTEEN

Thayne raced through the study door, Riley at his heels. "What the hell was that?"

He shoved open the front door, and the alarm's tone sounded.

Riley gasped at the sight. One end of the barn had erupted into a hellfire storm. Flames licked up the side.

"Hudson!" Thayne shouted. Everything inside screamed at him to run.

Riley grabbed his shirt. "Diversion," she shouted and pulled her weapon from its holster.

He knew she was right.

Crouched next to the open door, she aimed it outside and swept the area in sight. "Clear for now."

Pops exited the sunroom and shoved past Thayne. "You save your brother and the horses. I'll take care of Helen and the others."

Thayne followed his grandfather into the study. Pops had already unlocked the gun case. He grabbed his old police rifle and shoved in a clip.

Thayne seized his father's favorite, and they headed back out the door.

"The fire's blocked the barn door. The hands can't get in," Riley shouted.

Thayne looked on in horror as two hands fought with the water hose. The spray barely made a dent. The flames crawled up the barn's wall. "Where's Ironcloud?" he asked.

Riley shook her head. "I don't know."

"Go!" Pops shouted. "I'll lock us in, get us into the utility room. Center location."

Thayne nodded. He and Riley rushed into the chaos, crouched as best they could to make for a smaller target. Truth was, they were sitting ducks. A sniper could pick them off easily. Black smoke billowed into the air, the wind sweeping the dark soot toward them. Horses whinnied in terror just behind a thick wooden wall.

If Hudson was still alive, he wouldn't be for long.

Thayne headed for one of the windows. Heat blasted at them from just feet away. He braced his shoulder and shoved it through the glass.

Smoke engulfed him, and he squinted through the black. He lifted his shirt over his mouth to use as a mask.

"Hudson!" The fire roared in his ears. Flames licked at his skin. He stumbled another few feet forward and slammed to his knees. His eyes watered and his lungs heaved. A large shape huddled on the ground beneath a large beam.

Please be alive.

Thayne crawled to the body. "Hudson."

Fire leaped down the wood toward his brother.

"Get some water in here. Hurry!" he shouted.

Thayne braced his legs and edged the wood off his brother's back just as water from the hoses washed over them both.

He crouched down. Hudson wasn't moving.

Thayne looked over his shoulder. Riley. Thank God. "We've got to get him out."

◆ ◆ ◆

The shouts from outside the house caused him to smile. He stood in the sunroom, a good five feet between him and his companion. The old woman sat wide-eyed on the sofa, clutching an artist's sketchpad.

The girl, Chloe, sat huddled next to the woman, frozen in fright.

The woman he knew to be Riley Lambert's sister stood in the center, not moving.

The old sheriff faced him, aiming a rifle in his direction. The black ski masks hid their faces. No one would be able to tell them apart. He aimed at the girl.

"Who are you willing to let die, old man?" he said. "Because if you shoot me, he'll shoot the girl before I hit the ground. Could you live with yourself, knowing you were responsible for her death?"

He nodded to his right. The man tightened his aim.

The old sheriff glanced over his shoulder.

"They won't get here in time. I made sure of that."

The old man had no choice. They all knew the truth. His grandson wouldn't have had a choice, either. Outgunned and outnumbered, with innocents in the line of fire. They couldn't make the sacrifice.

"Don't hurt them," ex-sheriff Lincoln Blackwood said and lowered his weapon.

"Of course not," he said with a smile and pointed at Madison. "You, come here."

She straightened her back and walked over, her gaze full of hatred. He didn't like her.

He handed her a zip tie. "Restrain him. You so much as twitch the wrong way, I kill him in front of you." He paused. "Or maybe I'll have my assistant here shoot the girl."

She glared at him but took the tie. In his head he counted down the time. They were running out.

Once the old man was subdued, they took care of tying up the old woman and the Jordan girl. He crossed the room and tilted his head at Madison, taking a tie from his pocket and binding her wrists. "You're not in my plans." He held the rifle barrel beneath her chin. "I could just kill you. Less mess."

He leaned forward.

She clenched her fists. He leaned closer, his mouth brushing the curve of her ear. She shivered at his touch, and he couldn't help but smile. He reached for his holster and tugged out his pistol.

"The only reason you're not dead is to deliver a message. Tell your sister and her lover that they'll never catch me. They'll never win. I'll always be one step ahead of them. And that will never change."

◆ ◆ ◆

The smoke burned Riley's eyes. She tugged off her jacket to protect her hand and swiped along the window's edges to clear the glass.

Smoke filled the barn. Thayne shoved his hand into his pocket and handed her his keys. "Drive the SUV into the side of the barn," he shouted. "I'll get Hudson, but we have to open the stalls and get the horses out."

"I could hit the horses," she said.

"Drive into the barn about five feet from the far end of the building. Empty stalls there."

Riley gripped the keys and rushed across the dirt. She jerked open the door and jumped into his car before strapping herself in. She pressed on the accelerator and headed for the target. She braced herself and gunned it.

Her eyes snapped shut just as she hit. The airbag exploded into her face, and for a moment she couldn't breathe. She sat there stunned, then blinked. The airbag deflated, and she peered into the hole she'd created. She yanked the vehicle into reverse and a gaping hole remained, wooden planks hanging along the jagged edge.

She slammed on the brakes. The fire had moved quickly even in those few seconds. She raced back to the window. He'd removed the beam from his brother's body, but Hudson's eyes hadn't opened. Thayne's back muscles strained as he pulled his brother through the gap she'd created.

"Open the stalls," he yelled over his shoulder.

At that moment, Deputy Ironcloud stumbled from behind the barn. His hand was pressed to his head. Blood seeped from a wound. He blinked. "Horses," he muttered.

Riley nodded and raced into the burning barn. The roar of the fire drowned out most sounds. She headed toward the stall closest to the fire and flicked the latch up. She opened the gate. Ironcloud did the same.

She opened the second stall, then the third. Some horses rushed out in a panic, but a few refused to leave their stalls. The mare closest to the blaze whinnied in fear.

Thayne rushed in. He grabbed a rag that hung on the wall and covered the horse's eyes before leading the terrified animal out.

Riley took his lead. She might not be the best with horses, but they were running out of time. Within a few minutes, the last horse was running free.

Her lungs burned and her legs felt like she'd run through a swamp. She could barely lift them. She lurched from the hole in the barn and made her way over to Hudson's still form. Sucking in air, she knelt down and placed her ear against his mouth. He was breathing, but he didn't move.

Thayne shouted orders at his men as they pointed hoses at the flames. The faint sound of sirens rose above the howl of the fire. They weren't going to save the barn. She glanced at Hudson. Nothing she could do for him. She ran toward one of the hoses. The ranch hand looked ready to pass out, his face blackened with soot. She grabbed hold, and he gave her a tired nod of thanks.

Riley had no idea how long they kept at it before the fire engine finally screeched toward them. Four men launched themselves at the burning building. Ironcloud dragged a hose to the far end and doused the winter-dry grass to keep the fire from spreading.

While several arcs of water hit the flames, a truck barreled toward them. Cheyenne jumped out, her medical bag in hand. Her gaze widened when she saw her brother on the ground.

She rushed over to him. Thayne and Riley met her there.

"What happened?" she asked, quickly examining him. "How long has he been out?"

Riley tried to speak, but her throat closed off. "A big piece of wood fell on him. He was unconscious when we got to him."

Cheyenne pulled out her stethoscope and examined her brother.

Her husband, Brett, limped over, leaning on his cane. "I could call for more hands," he said with a narrowed gaze.

"However many you can spare," Thayne said. "We've got to corral the horses and make sure the house isn't in danger." He looped his thumb through his belt. "This was a deliberate attack. Tell your men they should come armed and cautious. If you still want to help."

Brett ignored Thayne's comment and simply pasted his phone to his ear. He obviously wasn't about to back down.

Thayne reached out to pat his brother-in-law on the shoulder. "Thanks."

"You'd do the same for me."

Riley knew the truth of Brett's statement. It's one thing she'd noticed about the people in this very sparsely populated state: They came to help whether you asked or not.

Thayne moved to stand next to Cheyenne. "How's Hudson?"

Cheyenne pulled back one of her patient's eyelids and flicked a light across his pupil. Once, then twice.

"Stop that." Hudson slammed his eyes closed, gripped her hand, and turned his head away.

He groaned and struggled to sit up, but Cheyenne pushed him back down.

"Take it easy," she said, her face streaked with relief.

"What happened?" He ignored his sister and rose before holding his head with both hands.

"Take it easy," she said. "You almost got blown up." She glanced up at Thayne and blinked away the moisture in her eyes. "He's got too hard of a head not to be fine."

"Damn, Hudson." He clapped his brother's shoulder.

Hudson stared at the barn in shock. "Everyone make it out?" he whispered.

"Hands and the horses. We got them all."

"Who did this?" Hudson said.

"We don't know." Thayne stood and glanced over at Brett. "Keep an eye on them. We need to check the house. Can you handle this?"

Brett scowled at him, and Riley had seen the look before. Brett's physical condition had improved since he'd almost died from being poisoned a month ago. He had made a remarkable recovery, but still wasn't 100 percent.

"I can still give you a run shooting a target," he said. "I'll take care of it."

Riley rose to her feet and shoved her hand through her hair. Thayne gave his brother-in-law one last nod.

The stench of soaked wood and ash filtered through the air. "That was close," Thayne said. "If the fire had reached the grass, the house would have burned to the ground. Do you think that was the plan?"

The hairs on the back of Riley's neck stood on end. "Doesn't feel right. He burned down the Jordan home to make it look like an accident. No one could mistake this fire for an accident."

They climbed up the steps to the house. The front door was still locked. Thayne turned the key and pushed through the door. The tone sounded, and Riley relaxed just a bit.

"Pops, we're coming in," Thayne called out. When no one answered, he shouted again.

"Maybe they can't hear you in the utility room," Riley said.

She picked up her pace anyway. That sinking sensation in her gut made her entire body tense.

They crossed the living area and veered toward the centrally located utility room. Thayne pushed inside.

"Empty," he said.

They sprinted toward the sunroom. Thayne paused in the kitchen.

"Door's been pried open," he said. "Damn it."

Riley could barely keep up.

"Pops! Gram!"

"Madison! Chloe!" Riley shouted at the top of her lungs.

Thayne hit the sunroom. Riley gasped. Madison lay on the floor, her hands zip-tied in front of her.

She groaned and tried to sit up.

Riley knelt beside her sister, helping her. Thayne pulled out his Buck knife and sliced the plastic bindings.

"What happened?" Riley asked. "Where is everybody?"

"Two men dressed in black. Ski masks. They took them all away." Madison pressed the heel of her hand against her head and lifted her tortured gaze to them. "I'm so sorry. I couldn't stop them."

CHAPTER EIGHTEEN

Thayne knelt next to the tire tracks at the back of the house and studied them.

Hudson stood beside him, along with Madison. The scent of smoke cloaked him, and Thayne knew he reeked of the same scent. Hudson had refused to rest, of course. Not that Thayne would've done any differently.

Madison showed the same grit as her sister. A knot bulged on her head, which Thayne didn't envy. She pressed an ice pack to it, but that was the only weakness she'd allow to show.

"Please." Thayne rose. "Go on inside. You both look like you're about to fall over."

Hudson ignored his brother's order. He studied the ground, keeping away from the footprints and scrapes in the dirt just outside the door.

"Pops and Gram walked side by side," he said. "They dragged Chloe to here." He pointed out a set of skid marks that suddenly vanished. "Someone picked her up. Probably to stuff her into their car."

A small smile tugged at the corner of Thayne's lips. "Almost as good as Jackson."

"Wish he was here." Hudson frowned. "We could use him."

"She fought them all the way," Madison whispered, her gaze glued to the etchings in the earth. "She's one tough kid."

"That's right, she is." Hudson faced Madison. "We're going to find her." He turned to Thayne. "Right?"

Damn his brother. Thayne couldn't promise anything. He didn't know where to start looking, and he wasn't about to lie. Not even to Madison's hopeful face.

A thunder of hooves galloped toward them, saving him from responding.

Ironcloud rode in and dismounted in a fluid motion as if his head wound had never happened. "They drove north until they hit the highway. Once they made pavement, I couldn't track them. From the turn, it looks like they headed away from town."

"They could be anywhere within a hundred-mile radius by now," Thayne muttered, rubbing the nape of his neck, where the tension had settled into a series of knots. "We don't have the make or model of the car. Our only description of the perps is black ski masks."

He hated the direction his mind headed, but he couldn't see the situation ending well. For Chloe or for his family.

Riley pressed her body close to his side and stroked his arm. "Don't go there," she said softly, her warm breath bathing his ear.

"Too easy to do." Thayne's shoulders tightened. A familiar, dark foreboding settled deep inside, that metallic, sour taste in his mouth when a mission just felt wrong. He'd survived them all, but they'd never ended well. Damn it to hell. "I'm used to causing the surprise ambush. I don't like being on the receiving end."

He bit out the words. Riley pressed closer and gripped his upper arm. "This wasn't your fault."

He studied the broken doorjamb. "We made it easy, though. A big house. Too many entrances." He jerked away from her, and the frustration boiled in his gut. He forced it down when all he wanted to do was slug the side of the house with his fist. "We *knew* they were coming here."

"We knew that they might." She folded her fingers through his and squeezed. "Until now, I never considered this a two-man operation. It's a complete shift in his MO. He's been subtle up until now."

"A pipe bomb isn't subtle. It's a message."

"Exactly. Up until now, his attacks have been anonymous, hidden. Labeled an accident. This is different. They left an obvious message."

Thayne rubbed his temple. "I can almost understand Chloe, but why take Pops and Gram? They'll only slow him down." He tried to take comfort in Riley's touch, but how could he? The three most vulnerable people he should have been able to protect were in the hands of two men who'd killed at least two and, according to Riley, probably many, many more.

"Enough dwelling. We need action." Thayne faced Ironcloud. "We need search teams, as many as we can get."

"Already in the works." Brett Riverton stood just to the other side of the destroyed door, holding Cheyenne's hand with one hand and leaning on his cane with the other.

"I'll head to the sheriff's office and help coordinate there," Ironcloud said, holding the reins with an easy grip. "We'll find them."

He flicked the reins and guided his horse away. Thayne hoped his deputy was right.

Brett tucked Cheyenne's hand in his arm. "I've placed all my hands on alert. When they're needed, they'll be there. The plane is gassed and ready to search. Mac's standing by to fly a search grid as long as it's daylight."

"Thanks, Brett." Thayne kneaded the tightening muscles at the back of his neck.

"You and Riley rescued Cheyenne last month." He squeezed his wife's hand. "I owe you more than I can ever repay."

They disappeared into the house, leaving Thayne and Riley alone. He stepped away from her and picked at the splintered wood. "Pops will protect them as long as he can. He's tough as nails, but he can't win a battle with a bullet. And if they threaten Gram . . . he'd give his life for her. Without hesitation. Chloe, too."

"I know."

Thayne made a fist; his knuckles whitened. "I should never have left them alone."

"Hudson was in danger. Your grandfather is still a good shot. There were two of them."

"If one of us had stayed with them—"

She tugged him away from the door and pulled him close. She grabbed both of his hands and stared up into his face. "If one of us had stayed, maybe Hudson wouldn't have made it. Maybe we'd both be dead. If someone's determined, they'll eventually succeed. You know that."

"I should've been able to *do* something."

Riley gripped him even tighter. "I've spent every day since Madison was kidnapped living with that thought. I was in the room. I should've screamed. I should've fought him. I could've done *something*. It ate at my soul. It still eats at me." She leaned into him. "Even after we found Madison, I can't shake that little voice. The 'should haves' drove me back to DC. Almost convinced me not to come back to Singing River. And you."

He focused on her face, but she averted her gaze. He wasn't surprised. He'd known in his heart, in his soul. "I know. I was surprised you came back. I still don't know if you'll stay."

She shook her head slightly, and Thayne tried to avoid the hurt welling up inside him. He'd wanted a denial. Riley had given him nothing.

A hawk sailed overhead, swooping toward the ground, then soaring back into the blue sky. He flew, claws empty, and glided, searching for prey.

"Do you know what changed my mind?" Riley's voice was quiet, soft.

Thayne had heard enough. He simply shrugged.

"*You* did. This case has been a nightmare from the beginning. Even when you doubted, you listened. You trusted that I could help. You believed in me."

"I still do. I'm the one who failed. My grandparents and a twelve-year-old girl are out there somewhere." He threw his arm toward the far horizon. "They may be dead, and my decisions made them vulnerable. There's no way around the truth. I did this."

"We still have a chance, Thayne. This isn't over. These guys are determined to prove they're one step ahead. They want us to realize they're smarter and better than we are. If this was about the Jordans, they'd have simply killed Chloe. They took your grandparents, your family. This is personal. They're not done yet. Which means we have a chance."

Thayne lifted his gaze to hers. "You believe that?"

He focused on her eyes, searching them for the truth. She stared, unblinking. "I have to believe."

◆ ◆ ◆

The SUV bounced along a dirt road. They'd been driving forever. Chloe squinted toward the seat in front of her. Gram was sobbing, leaning against Pops. Chloe liked calling them that. She'd never had grandparents, at least not that she remembered.

"Everything will be fine, Helen," Pops said, whispering to her. He kissed her forehead.

Poor Gram. She really couldn't remember anything. Chloe wished she weren't ill. She'd always liked Gram. She'd brought Chloe these amazing cookies that her mom hadn't ever figured out how to bake.

Her mom. Her dad. Her eyes burned. She hadn't been able to cry since it happened. She'd been afraid. Afraid her biological father would find her and take her away. Afraid the police or a judge would force her to go with her father.

Maybe she should've just died with her family. It would have been easier. Gram and Pops wouldn't have been taken by these creeps.

The more Chloe thought about what the men driving had done, the more the anger within built until she wanted to scream.

She had to *do* something. Madison had told her there were always options when bad stuff happened. Madison thought about life a lot like Chloe's mom had, actually. They had both survived.

The front of the car tilted down, and a huge bump threw Chloe into the air. She slammed down onto the floorboard, jarring her shoulder. She couldn't stop the grunt from escaping.

Gram stopped crying and looked behind her. Her eyes widened when she met Chloe's gaze. "You have to let that poor girl go," she said. "Hey, there up front. I'm speaking to you."

"Shh, Helen," Pops pleaded, his voice low and urgent.

The man with the ski mask turned around. "Shut up or I'll finish you off now. Is that what you want? To die."

Gram's mouth opened in shock.

"Helen, you need to be quiet. Please." Pops scooted closer. "For me."

"Okay, but he's not very nice," Gram huffed, but she didn't say anything more. "He doesn't get any cookies when I make them."

Chloe almost laughed out loud. Gram was too funny. She shifted her body to peek out the back. She couldn't see much, just a lot of wilderness and a dirt road behind them.

"How far?" one of the men asked.

"RV is coming up," the obvious leader muttered. "Just near the creek."

"How'd you find this place? It's in the middle of nowhere."

"I've been exploring Singing River for months."

"Why? There's nothing in this town but a bunch of ranches and that bar. And even that place is lame."

"I found a few people of interest," the leader said. "The Jordans were a very interesting couple. Not at all what they seemed."

"You're talking loony again, boss."

"Shut up. I don't need you that bad."

Chloe swallowed and her head sagged. She pulled at the plastic on her wrists. They were all going to die.

Pops glanced over the back seat. Chloe met his gaze. He nodded at the floor, toward the back. "Metal. Hands," he mouthed.

She followed his line of sight. Sure enough, poking from the side of the worn carpet was some sort of metal latch.

The SUV hit a large bump, and she scooted toward the metal. "Rub," he mouthed.

"What are you doing, old man?" A click sounded from the front seat. "Face forward or I blow you away in front of your crazy wife."

"She's not crazy," he growled. "Show some respect."

"Just as crazy as that old man I overdosed. A waste of time. His brain is half gone. He won't remember seeing me at the Jordans' anyway. He's a witness and doesn't even know it."

The men in the front seat laughed. Pops didn't turn around again, but Chloe knew what he was trying to say to her. She pulled her wrists as far apart as she could and began to rub the zip tie against the metal latch. She didn't know if it would work, but she had to try.

Her mom would never have given up. Neither would she.

◆ ◆ ◆

The midafternoon sun streamed through the window shield. Riley flipped the visor down and slipped on her sunglasses. The days were getting shorter, but they still had plenty of daylight.

Thayne drove only a few miles per hour, his door propped open as he followed the SUV's tracks. He stopped just shy of the highway and turned off the ignition.

"I'm walking it," he said.

She nodded and followed. It was hard to watch when she couldn't help. So unlike the last time he'd asked for her assistance. It may have taken a while to find his sister, but they'd had so much more to go on.

He paused and knelt, fingering the tire mark. "Ironcloud was right. It looks as if they turned away from town."

"But . . . ?"

"They backed up here. I think they turned around and headed east, toward the Wind River Mountains." He glanced over at her. "You were right. They're staying nearby."

He grasped his phone and tapped a number.

"You find them?" his father barked through the speakerphone. "Tell me they're okay."

"Sorry, Dad. I wish I had better news, but we think they're headed toward the mountains. See if Brett can't have Mac fly a grid over the foothills. Maybe he'll see something out of place."

Thayne leaned back against the hood and peered along the majestic mountain range. Riley had never seen anything like the landscape out here. She'd fallen in love with Wyoming, with the Blackwoods, at the same time she'd resisted staying. Both stark and beautiful at the same time. Isolated and calming.

Unforgiving.

"How about the dogs?" Carson asked.

"Search and rescue's bringing them in, but they won't arrive until dark. It'll be tough going."

"We can't wait until tomorrow," Thayne's father said. "We need to find them today."

"I know. We will."

Riley recognized the determination in Thayne's eyes. She had no doubts he'd do whatever it took to bring them home safely.

"Oh, and Willow called. She couldn't get through to you. Call her. She said she has new information."

Thayne ended the call and immediately tapped in Willow's number. Riley hoped the woman could provide them a break. Maybe figure out where to look.

The phone rang once, twice, and a third time.

"Thayne?" Willow's breathless voice carried through the speakerphone. "Did you find them?"

"No."

A sailor's curse exploded through the line. "Pardon me, but I'd like to get hold of this guy by his bits and pieces and make him sing until he leads us to them. Then I'd use my knife and—"

"Remind me never to upset you, Willow." Thayne's gaze twinkled with a flicker of humor. "What have you got?"

"A name."

The brief amusement melted from Thayne's expression and Riley's breath caught.

"Do you know a man named Earnhardt? Was in your jail a few nights ago."

"You've got to be kidding." Thayne shook his head. "I wouldn't have pegged him for the brains to do any of this. He's an obnoxious drunk."

"Well, I pulled employee records from each of the crimes you gave me, including the Jordans. Guess who was working an oil job within a hundred miles of all of them?"

"Earnhardt." Thayne met Riley's gaze.

What was she supposed to say? They had one name, but not a location.

"Willow, it's Riley. Does he show any credit card charges in Singing River? Maybe a cabin in the mountains, something like that."

"Give me a moment, hon." Keys tapped through the phone. "Just a pretty hefty bill at Clive's from a couple nights ago. Otherwise, just standard gas and grocery charges in Pinedale."

Nothing about this case was easy.

"Thanks, Willow, but there were two of them. Can you run the list again? See if you can't find someone else. I suppose Earnhardt could use locals to help him, but I want to be sure."

"It'll take some time. Anything else?"

"Can you compile a record of employment over the last decade? If we have all the locations where he worked, it may help us identify any other victims."

"You got it." Willow paused. "Thayne. Find them, will you? They deserve more time with each other. They've earned it."

Her voice was hesitant, small.

"Everyone's out in force. We'll find them," Thayne said with a frown.

Riley recognized the doubts reemerging. A chilly breeze from the east brushed through her jacket, and she shivered.

"Guess we head to the mountains." Thayne slid into the front seat.

With a quick snap of her seat belt, Riley buckled up. "You can't give up."

"I'm not, but if we're going to save them, someone's going to have to help, because I have a feeling we can't do it on our own."

CHAPTER NINETEEN

Trees lined the car on both sides of the road. Chloe had given up trying to remember which way they'd turned a long time ago. She had no idea how much time they'd spent driving. It felt like forever, but she needed more.

Please don't stop. Please keep going.

She hoped someone heard her prayer. She rubbed the plastic of the zip tie against the metal. Even though the edge wasn't very sharp, she'd worked through a bit of the heavy plastic. Every so often she pulled her arms apart as far as they'd go. Ridges dug into her wrists. Drops of blood trickled to the carpet, staining it.

They'd notice the moment they pulled her out of the van. Chloe pressed harder and harder.

She bit down so tight her jaws ached. The tie gave way just a tad. Back and forth, back and forth. She shifted onto her knees and pressed all her weight down. The skin on her wrists burned. She wanted to cry out. Instead, she allowed herself a small whimper.

Pops glanced over his shoulder. His eyes widened when he saw her wrists, but they also gleamed with approval.

"Keep going," he mouthed. "You can do it."

He turned around before their kidnappers noticed. Chloe shivered. He couldn't do anything from his seat. Their escape was all on her.

She had to focus. She had to break free.

Her mind pushed aside the pain and the hurt. Back and forth, back and forth. The friction burned. Again, she pressed her hands apart as hard as she could, but the plastic still wouldn't give.

Tears rolled down her cheeks. She wanted to curl up and sleep. She didn't want to hurt anymore. Shaking, she bent her elbows. Her hands throbbed; a circle of red ensnared her wrists.

"RV's right up there," the leader said. "Final resting place."

He chuckled at the words, but Chloe didn't get what was funny. And she definitely didn't want to rest.

The vehicle rumbled to a stop.

Was this it? Were they going to die here?

She rubbed even harder.

"Earnhardt, get out. We've got preparations to make."

A door opened.

"Lock it up," the leader said.

They slammed the door shut.

"Chloe?" Pops asked under his breath.

"Yes." Her voice was a whimper.

"Are they off?" he asked.

"N . . . no." She choked back a sob. She sucked in a breath and grunted, pressing the worst side one last time.

The zip tie gave way, and she hit her head against the side window.

"I . . . I did it."

"Stay down," Pops whispered.

"Lincoln, I don't want to go camping. It's too cold."

"I know, dear." Pops's voice was choked. "Chloe . . . we've got one shot at this. They're heading into the RV. I have a knife in my pocket.

You need to grab it and cut Helen's ties and then mine. We're making a run for it."

"O . . . okay. Is he looking?"

"Now," Pops ordered.

Chloe launched herself toward the seat. She dived over the side. Pops leaned to his left, and Chloe dug into his loose front pocket. She tugged out the knife.

"Helen first," he said softly.

She plunged into the back seat and hid on the floor.

"Hurry!" Pops said. "Oh God. Just cut."

Chloe pressed the knife against the plastic. It didn't slice through immediately, but within a half dozen strokes, the tie split. She turned to Pops.

"Head down!" he ordered.

A gunshot, loud and terrifying.

"Hand me the knife," Pops said, his voice gruff. She gazed up at him. His face was pale, but he had that look of her mom when she knew she had to do something important.

"You're going to open that door, and you and Gram are going to go through the trees just a few feet away. There's a large rock maybe ten feet away. Head for it. Get behind it as fast as you can. You won't have much time. Hold tight. Don't stop. There's a river not far. Follow it and it'll lead you to a road. They're looking for you. They'll find you soon."

Chloe could barely feel her body. "What about—"

"Don't worry about me. I'll catch up," he choked. He sliced through the zip tie. "And, Chloe, don't look back. Don't look back for anything."

Pops stared straight ahead. "Helen, I love you. I've always loved you. I always will."

"Of course you do, dear. I love you, too."

Tears streamed down Chloe's cheeks. She grabbed Helen's hand and put her other hand on the door.

"Okay, Chloe. Go!" Pops shouted and thrust open the door. A man grunted.

Chloe shoved her side wide. She grabbed Gram's hand tight and tugged. "Come on!" she shouted.

"What the hell?" their kidnapper shouted.

A loud thud sounded. Chloe didn't look back. "Come on," she said and practically pulled Gram through toward the trees. Her legs pumped.

"Run to the rock," she said.

"But Lincoln . . . ," Gram whimpered.

"He made me promise," Chloe choked. "Please, Gram. We have to go fast."

"Well, why didn't you say so?" Suddenly Gram straightened, and together they raced through the trees, toward the big rock.

"Old man, you've ruined everything," the kidnapper shouted.

A dull clunk echoed behind them just as they reached the rock.

Chloe dragged Gram behind it. She could barely make out the river through the dense trees, but she did see more rocks.

"You son of a bitch!" the kidnapper shouted.

Chloe looked back. She gasped. The one called Earnhardt lay still on the ground, all dressed in black, his eyes staring unblinkingly at the sky.

Pops stood facing the other man, his hands in the air. Chloe froze.

"Run!" Pops yelled. He launched himself at their kidnapper.

The gun exploded, echoing through the mountains. Chloe gripped Gram's hand. "We've got to run. We have to find the sheriff."

"Lincoln's the sheriff," Gram gasped. "So is Carson. So is Thayne. All my boys are the sheriff."

"We've got to find them. We've got to get away and hide."

Chloe chanced a glance back. Pops lay on the ground. The man stood over him with a weapon.

"Duck," she said to Gram.

They plopped down behind a rock. Chloe's heart pounded. "No—*Pops*." She blinked away the tears.

"You can't get away," the kidnapper shouted. "I'll find you. And you'll pay for this!"

Chloe panted and scanned the terrain around them. They had to stay low and out of sight. "We'll have to go that way, Gram," she said quietly. "We can't let the bad guy catch us."

"I know about bad guys." Gram blinked and looked around. She grinned. "I know where we are, dear. I know where we can hide. No one will find us there."

Hope leaped inside Chloe. "Really?"

"Oh yes, dear. That's my job. To help people in trouble. Like you and your dear mama." She narrowed her gaze. "The bad one is after us? Do you have a gun?"

Chloe shook her head. "But he does."

"It's okay. If we can make it to the cabin, I've got a gun. He won't get you." Gram took her hand. "Stay down. Follow me. I'll take care of us. Lincoln will be angry, of course. He doesn't know about the cabin. But we'll see him at home."

Gram was confused, but Chloe didn't say anything about Pops. No way could he have lived after being shot like that. Madison said sometimes Gram knew things. Chloe would just have to pray that now was one of those times.

"I'm gonna find you, girl." A gunshot sounded through the woods. "And you won't like it when I do."

◆ ◆ ◆

A pickup honked at Thayne as they sped past each other on the highway leading out of town. A group of ranch hands from the Riverton place were joining the search. His brother-in-law had done better than his word.

Too bad it appeared as if Gram, Pops, and Chloe had disappeared.

Thayne swerved his vehicle into the municipal airport. He could see Mac waiting near the hangar.

He glanced at Riley. "Last time I was out here, I was dropping you off." He didn't add that he'd wondered if it would be for good. They both knew.

But she'd come back. For now.

"How sure are you the tire tracks headed toward the mountains?" Riley asked.

"Sixty–forty. I'm reading a lot into the angle on the tires."

"I think he wants to be hidden," Riley said. "There aren't that many trees until you get to the foothills and up closer to the lake."

"Let's do this," Thayne said and exited the vehicle. He walked over to Mac and shook his hand.

"Wished you'd hired me for a ski trip or something instead of finding people who should be home safe and sound," Mac said.

"Us too." Riley shook Mac's hand. "How have you been?"

"Can't complain. Who's riding shotgun?" he asked.

"Thayne," Riley said. "He knows the terrain much better than I do. He's used to looking for the unusual."

"Got it."

Riley climbed into the small aircraft and settled behind the copilot's seat. Thayne took his place, strapped in, and grabbed the headphones.

Mac finished up his checklist and walked the aircraft, and soon the engine purred.

"Singing River Ground, Warrior three two nine five Xray ready to taxi, east departure." Mac's voice droned through the communication system.

"Warrior three two nine five Xray, Singing River Ground, wind is two one zero and one zero, altimeter three zero one four, taxi to runway two zero."

"Taxi to two zero, nine five Xray."

The propeller spun in front of them, and the plane headed forward, gaining speed until they lifted off and soared into the sky.

Within minutes Mac had negotiated past the airport and taken a northern trajectory. The Wind River Mountains loomed at their right.

"I'll fly a standard search grid pattern," Mac said. "You see anything, we'll take another pass."

"How long can we stay up?" Riley asked.

"I have enough fuel to last us a few hours, at least until dark, but I hope we're not up there that long. I hope we find them before then."

"Me too," Thayne said.

"What were they wearing?" Mac asked.

"Chloe had on a bright-yellow jacket. Gram wore purple. She always wears purple these days. She can't seem to get out of the rut."

"I'm glad Chloe likes bright colors," Mac said. "It'll make her easier to spot."

They searched grid after grid. Most of the movement was from other search vehicles. Thayne shifted in his seat. "Let's try a little farther from the mountains."

"You thinking they could be on the Riverton Ranch?" Mac asked in surprise.

Thayne rubbed at the knot on his shoulder. "It's a big property. Easy enough to hide on this time of year."

"You ain't kidding."

The farther off the highways they flew, the fewer signs. Thayne scanned the tree line, searching for anything odd.

"Any luck, Riley?" he asked, trying not to let his frustration filter through the tone of his voice.

"Just the arroyo where we almost drowned," Riley commented.

He glanced below. The floodwaters had carved out slides of earth, leaving behind a strange alien landscape.

Mac chuckled. "I bet your grandfather wasn't happy when you mentioned being on the disputed land. Whew. My dad once told me the Rivertons and Blackwoods might very well go to an all-out war on that piece of property."

"It's terrible grazing," Thayne said. "And it's dangerous."

"But it's got water and all the snowmelt during the spring. During a drought, that water could save the day."

"Do you know what the fight was over?" Thayne asked.

"My father told me it was personal, which in my day meant a woman, but I wouldn't know. Your grandmother did date a Riverton for a while, from my recollection, but the feud goes back another generation."

"See anything?" Thayne asked Riley.

"Nothing."

A curse escaped Thayne. "Let's try west and then north."

The aircraft tilted. Thayne gave one last look below.

"Where are you, Pops? Gram? Why can't we find you?"

◆ ◆ ◆

The plane veered away from Chloe. Her entire body sagged, and she leaned back against a rock. "They didn't see us."

Gram stuffed the stick she'd found on their trek into the dirt. "Can't see a lot from that high up. Not with all these trees."

Chloe knelt down and scooped up some water from the brook and scrubbed her face. "We can't stop," she gasped.

They trudged along the side of the creek, weaving in and out of the trees and the water.

"I haven't heard him for a while," Chloe whispered. "Do you think he's still back there?"

"Of course. Men like him don't give up. We have to disappear." Gram stopped at a large mountain of boulders blocking their path. "Cross the stream," she said.

Chloe shivered. "We'll be out in the open."

"Turn that coat inside out, dear, so he won't see you so easily. We'll be fine until we get to where we're going."

She should've thought of the yellow being a beacon for the man chasing them. Chloe's mind couldn't get past Pops falling to the ground. Maybe he was okay. Maybe Gram was right and he'd show up at the Blackwood Ranch.

It could happen.

Chloe zipped up the coat and pulled it over her head before slipping it back on. The inside was gray. At least it wasn't like a big sun shining directions.

A loud curse echoed from somewhere behind them.

Gram crouched down, as if by instinct. "Come on, dear heart."

Chloe held Gram's hand, and they picked their way into the fast-moving stream. The water pushed against Chloe's legs and buffeted her. She had to let go of Gram and steady herself on a rock. Half–bent over, half-falling, she finally solidified her feet beneath her.

"That was close," she said.

Gram teetered next to her. Her lips had turned an almost blue tinge. She clutched at her walking stick and pitched forward. Frantically she struggled to right herself. Chloe grabbed for her jacket, but Gram fell on her side. Her feet upended, and the water carried her downstream.

Chloe scrambled to the other side of the creek, chasing Gram. The old woman's arms and legs flailed. She reached for a rock, but it slipped out of her hands.

Everything inside Chloe wanted to scream and shout, but she couldn't. Not with the kidnapper still behind them. She wished the sheriff were here, or Pops, but mostly she wished her dad were here to take care of her. He'd never let anything happen to her.

The stream widened. The water slowed. Gram floated toward a large boulder in the center of a deep section. She hugged the rock and winced.

"Are you okay?" Chloe said, desperate to keep her voice low.

Gram nodded and took a deep breath. She shoved herself away from the boulder, toward Chloe. The water pulled her under, but somehow Gram lifted her hand and launched herself toward the side. She grabbed a large root with her hands and held on tight.

Chloe flattened her body on the edge and reached out to Gram. Mud slid down from beneath her chest.

Gram's frightened gaze captured Chloe's. She launched herself toward Chloe, and as if someone were watching over them, they linked hands. Chloe pulled back as hard as she could, and somehow Gram pushed up over the edge.

Chloe fell back on the grass and sucked in deep, long breaths. Gram groaned and lay beside her.

"That would've been fun if I were sixty years younger," Gram said, wiping her face with a muddy hand.

Chloe reached over. "You scared me."

"I'm sorry. I didn't mean to."

"You can't hide forever," a voice shouted out.

Chloe ducked down. "Is he closer?"

"Farther away. That little adventure put some distance between us, but we're more out in the open now. We need to get back on the other side of the stream, under the cover of those trees."

Gram slowly got to her feet, but when she stepped on her left foot, she winced and fell to the ground.

"That's not good," she said. She looked at Chloe. "I need a walking stick, one that reaches my shoulders. And make it strong."

Chloe searched, but she didn't see anything. "I'll be right back," she whispered. "Stay down."

There had to be something she could use. Crouching, Chloe scampered toward the edge of the stream. A tree had fallen across the water, its long limbs still attached. That wouldn't work, and she didn't have a saw.

A limb stuck up from behind the large tree trunk. She scrambled over to it and pulled. It was close to her height and bigger than a baseball bat around. She pried it loose and headed back to Gram.

When she reached the side of the stream, Chloe froze. Gram lay in the grass, eyes closed, skin pale.

She knelt down and clutched Gram's hand to hers. "No, don't leave me. Please don't. Everyone's left."

Gram's lashes fluttered, and she gave Chloe a weak smile. "Just resting my eyes, Cheyenne, my love."

"I'm Chloe, Gram. Not Cheyenne." Chloe's heart seized. She'd seen Gram get people confused. She squeezed her hand tight. "We have to find the cabin. Please."

Gram sat up and looked around. It was as if she'd woken up from a dream or something. "How'd we get way out here?" She frowned at Chloe. "You're not supposed to be here. This is a secret. Not even my Lincoln knows."

A gunshot exploded, echoing through the woods. "He's found us."

Gram's narrowed gaze studied the tree line. "No one there but that big buck."

"What are you talking about? I don't see a deer—"

At that moment the trees rustled clear across the stream. A huge animal straightened, his majestic horns broad and tall. The deer looked at Chloe and darted into the trees.

Gram was back. For how long, Chloe didn't know. With a shiver, she handed Gram the walking stick. "Can you make it?"

Gram heaved herself up and tested the weight of her foot on the ground. "For a while. We need to get to the cabin." She pointed a finger downstream. "Not much farther that way."

Another shot exploded. Louder than the first.

"We'd better hurry," Gram said. "Before he finds us and finishes the job he started."

◆ ◆ ◆

The plane dipped below a cloud. Milky soup surrounded Riley. She couldn't make out the nose of the plane, much less anything below them. Suddenly, the Piper cleared the white soup. Trees loomed above and Riley gasped.

"Look. See the white? At ten o'clock."

"An RV," Thayne said with a frown. "Take us closer, Mac."

Riley squinted at the motor home, parked half under the tree line. She lifted her binoculars to her eyes and scanned the vehicle.

"I can't make out the license plate," she muttered. "But there's an SUV parked down there, too."

"I see it." Mac adjusted his head.

"I've got a body down there." Thayne let out a shout. "Black clothes. Looks like black covering his face."

Riley leaned forward, trying to adjust the binoculars. A shoe came into view, but it wasn't black. Oh no.

"Pops is down there. Not moving." Thayne went quiet.

"There's a field not too far," Mac said, his voice sober. "I'll set you down."

"Radio the airport. Tell them to send everyone they've got to these coordinates. Including an ambulance."

Riley swept the area. "Where are Helen and Chloe?"

"Good question." Thayne's voice didn't show signs of strain. In fact, the emotionless tone made Riley shudder. He'd turned off his emotions, just as he did when he was preparing for a mission.

She understood. She wanted to touch him, to remind him that she wasn't going anywhere, but she knew it would distract him, so she kept her hands wrapped around her binoculars, searching for Helen and Chloe, and the second man.

Mac landed the plane in a field more than a quarter mile from the site of the RV. Thayne didn't even wait until the propeller stopped before he jumped out. He sprinted toward the RV. Riley chased after him.

She was out of breath when they reached a grove of trees. Thayne held his pistol at the ready, and Riley did the same.

Slowly they sneaked closer. Thayne held up his hand. Riley froze. Water from the nearby stream bubbled in the distance. The high-pitched chirp of birds filtered through the trees, and a grove of aspen quaked nearby. Other than that, there weren't any sounds.

Thayne slipped through the trees and eased into place just outside the door to the RV. Riley planted herself on the other side of the door.

He signaled her. She placed her hand carefully on the door and pressed into the cheap aluminum handle. The button gave, and she nodded at him.

Three. Two. One.

She yanked open the door, and Thayne burst through the entrance. Within seconds he reappeared. "All clear."

He frowned and hurried to Pops. "He's been shot." He knelt down and felt the older man's neck. Riley held her breath.

Thayne sagged and bowed his head. "He's alive. The tough old guy."

"Thank God." Riley checked the kidnapper's pulse. "This one's dead." She ripped off the ski mask.

Thayne glanced over. "Earnhardt." He went back to working on his grandfather. "Willow got her man."

"Who could the other kidnapper be?"

"I don't know," Thayne said, looking over his shoulder. "Hopefully I can stabilize Pops and he can tell us which way they went. Otherwise, we've got a lot of forest to search."

After cutting the material away from Pop's wound, Thayne tried to peel back the part of his shirt stuck to the bullet hole. With a wince, he gave a tug.

Pops let out a low groan.

"I need bandages," Thayne said.

Riley disappeared into the RV and opened one drawer after another until she found the dish towels. She raced out to Thayne.

Mac crouched beside him. "You scared the hell out of your grandson, Lincoln."

"Helen? Chloe?" Lincoln's words were slurred and barely audible.

"Which way, Pops?"

"South. Told them to run and hide. He went after them. Tried to stop him."

"I can see that."

Thayne stood and stared down at Mac. "You got a weapon?" he asked.

Mac patted his side. "You bet."

"You okay to watch him until the ambulance arrives?"

"You go find your grandmother and that sweet girl," Mac said.

A shot echoed through the woods south of them. Riley's gaze flew to Thayne's.

Thayne leaned down and gripped his grandfather's hand. "We'll find them, Pops. I promise."

CHAPTER TWENTY

The thick trees would've provided some cover. Chloe and Gram hadn't tried to conceal their footprints. Neither had the man chasing them.

Thayne pushed himself hard. He could hear Riley's footsteps behind him. They raced down the hill, and when they reached the river, the trail vanished.

"Good job, Gram," Thayne said.

"Or Chloe."

Thayne stared at the ground. "Good point." They stayed close to the trees to keep out of sight.

"They must be terrified."

Thayne increased his walking pace. He couldn't run; he had to be smart. Gram and Chloe were up ahead, but so was a murderer. He glanced behind him. "Do you think this guy and Earnhardt were partners in the wedding ring murders, too?"

Riley picked up the pace. "The MO is so specific I didn't expect two perps. Something feels off."

"The guy we're chasing killed Earnhardt. That makes him the alpha in my book." Thayne jumped over a fallen tree just as Riley climbed up and over it.

"I'll agree with you there." Riley sucked in a deep breath. "It makes me wonder about Earnhardt's role."

"There's only one way to find out." Thayne increased his pace. "You good to speed up?"

"For now." Riley matched his steps. "They're headed toward the cabin, aren't they?" she said. "We're on the back end of the disputed land."

Thayne gave her a sharp nod. "We know the maps were Gram's. She obviously visited the area often enough. It's in her long-term memory. She'll take Chloe there."

"They'll be cornered."

"Or he'll find them sooner."

They trudged along the side of the creek. The water continued to rise. Soon the terrain grew rocky.

"We have to cross," Thayne said, sucking in a few deep breaths. "You making it okay?"

"No choice . . . but to keep . . . after them," Riley panted, bent over at the knees.

Thayne knelt near the water and studied the ground. "We're on the right track. Gram and Chloe were here. I don't see the guy's boot prints. They lost him. For a while, anyway."

"He could've stayed up in the trees," Riley said. "He doesn't know where they're headed."

"Which gives us the advantage. Let's move."

Thayne pushed hard, weaving over the rocks, crossing the stream whenever the going got too tough.

When he spied the roof of the cabin, he stopped and crouched down. Riley hunkered beside him. His heart raced and he pulled out his pistol. "Should've brought my rifle," he muttered.

He scanned the wet earth near the stream. Two sets of footprints, one very asymmetrical, headed toward the rustic hunter's retreat. "Gram's using a walking stick. Looks like she hurt herself. Chloe's prints seem sluggish but normal."

Riley unholstered her weapon. "Do you see *him*?"

"No sign here, but let's approach slow and easy."

One hundred yards, two hundred yards. The landscape opened up. Fewer and fewer boulders and trees could shelter their movements.

Thayne squinted twenty feet away toward some tall grass. He crawled closer. A large boot print was visible deep in the waterlogged earth.

"He's close," Thayne whispered.

"Come out, come out, wherever you are," a voice called out. "No one's going to save you."

"Like hell we won't," Thayne whispered under his breath.

"Come and get us." Gram's voice was cold and angry, carrying over the trees. "Where's my Lincoln?"

"Dead and gone. Like you'll be soon enough."

A high-pitched scream pierced the air.

Thayne and Riley took off running. If only they weren't too late.

◆ ◆ ◆

Chloe had dreamed of this cabin every night. She'd been here before with her mother. Mrs. B had saved them both. The cabin made Chloe feel safe. The man pointing a rifle at Gram didn't terrify her, though. She recognized his voice.

"You killed my parents," Chloe spat out. "You're a monster."

The weird thing was, he didn't look evil. He looked so *normal.*

The man wasn't anything extraordinary. He sort of blended into life. Except his eyes. They were cold and dark, and they sent a shiver through Chloe.

"If I'd known you were there, Chloe, everything would have worked out exactly like I planned." He shifted his aim just a bit. "Put the gun down, you old bat, or I shoot her. I can do it, too."

Gram wavered, uncertainty clouding her gaze. The tip of her gun dipped.

"That's it. Just a little lower," he coaxed. "It'll all be over soon."

Chloe eyed movement off to her left. She fought not to look. Out of the corner of her eye, she caught sight of the sheriff. She didn't know much about guns, but she knew a rifle was for long distance, a pistol was for short. The sheriff was too far away to help.

"Why did you kill them?" she asked quickly. "They never did anything to you. They never did anything to anyone."

"They lied," he spat. "They were living a lie. Did you even know?"

"Of course Chloe knew," Gram said. "Her daddy hurt them, hit them. They had to escape, but he was a powerful man in his small town. The cops wouldn't help her—no one would. So she found another way. I helped her just like I helped a lot of families escape."

"This is your fault!" He shifted the gun to Gram.

Gram stood straight and faced the murderer, her chin held high. She was so brave. "Young man, I didn't make you chase us or hurt Chloe's parents."

"They pretended to love each other. It wasn't true. Love's never true."

"Well, that's just baloney," Gram said. "Love is real. My Lincoln loves me just the way I am, even though I'm not as good as I was before. He's mine." She raised her gun. "I won't let you hurt him anymore."

Chloe shut her eyes. She hoped Gram forgot Pops was dead. She hoped he stayed alive in her mind forever.

"If you don't drop that gun, I'll kill Chloe," he spat. "This is over."

"I couldn't have said it better, Decker."

The sheriff's words made Chloe's heart hope for the first time in a very, very long time. She'd never trusted law enforcement. Her mother had drilled that into her, but Chloe was so glad to see the sheriff right now. Thayne was less than fifty yards away. Riley stood next to him. Both aimed their weapons at Decker's back.

"I must admit I didn't expect to find you here," the sheriff continued, moving a step forward with each word. "I figured you'd be drinking it up in Pinedale with your roughneck buddies."

Chloe's eyes widened as Thayne and Riley continued to walk forward. Closer and closer. Were they close enough?

"You have two guns aimed at you," Thayne said, his voice soft but deadly. "If you shoot either one of them, if you so much as make a movement without lowering the gun, you die. Unless you take your finger off the trigger nice and slow and lower it to the ground."

"I killed your grandfather. You won't let me live."

"I'm not you," the sheriff said. "But just so you're aware of another failure, Pops is alive."

Chloe's knees shook. Gram's eyes widened with a memory. "You shot my Lincoln."

Her finger pulsed against the trigger. Chloe held her breath.

"Gram, it's okay. I got this." Thayne's voice soothed her.

She shook her head. "He hurt my family."

Decker stiffened; then a small smile crossed his lips, giving Chloe the shivers. "Sheriff. I'm surprised you found us, but the truth is you've made it easy. I'm assuming your lover is there, too."

"Fiancée," Riley said. "I suggest you lower the rifle. Sheriff Blackwood doesn't miss. And neither do I."

Decker turned his head and looked at Thayne and Riley. "You love each other?"

"Of course," Thayne said.

The man smiled, his eyes cold and black and dead inside. "Haven't you learned anything? Love isn't real or true. All they do is pretend they care. First your mother and father lie, until they can't anymore and they abandon you. Then you think you find *the* one. Until she leaves you, steals your home, steals your family, finds someone else."

Riley shifted her position. "They abandoned you," she said in a soft voice, still moving closer to him.

Chloe held her breath. What was she trying to do? *Just shoot him.*

"They ignored me like I never existed." Decker chuckled. "I was a fool. I still believed in love, so I began searching across the country. The ones who prided themselves on love were the worst. They lied. They don't know what love is. I do."

His gaze fell to Thayne. "You love the FBI agent, don't you?"

Thayne nodded. "I do."

"I'll save you the trouble, then." He whirled around, sweeping the barrel toward Riley.

Chloe gasped and flattened to the ground.

Two guns went off at the same time, the loud blast causing Chloe's ears to ring. She squeezed her eyes tight.

Silence rang through the woods. With a deep breath, Chloe raised her head. She blinked once, then twice.

It was over.

◆ ◆ ◆

A whiff of wet dirt and grass invaded Riley's nose. Her body lay prone on the ground.

Thayne raced over and knelt beside her. "Did he hit you?" He turned her over and checked each inch of her before pulling her into his arms.

She could feel his heartbeat racing.

"I'm okay." She wrapped her arms around him and held him close, basking in the warmth of his heat.

She didn't bother checking the body. Decker was dead. Thayne had placed the head shot where few could. They were outside optimal range for a pistol.

Her fingertips gripped his flannel shirt, and she clutched the soft fabric. "It's over," she whispered. "We make one hell of a team, you and I. I especially like that you're an ace shot."

Thayne stroked her hair. "I get to thank you again for saving my family from despair."

Riley shook her head and pulled back so she could meet his gaze. "No, this time I get to thank you." She smiled at him. "You don't give up, do you? Not ever. No matter what." She couldn't stop the awe from lacing her voice. Somehow, somewhere, her heart filled with joy and the unbound thrill of being close to him.

"It's one of my more annoying traits," Thayne said. His brow quirked. "What's wrong? You're giving me an odd look."

"Just thinking I wouldn't mind waking up next to you for a long, long time."

Thayne's face stilled. "Are you serious?"

"I—" Riley's gaze drifted to the cabin.

Helen still stood in the door, holding her weapon.

"Thayne." She tugged at him. "Your grandmother."

He glanced over and, in an instant, crossed the distance between them. He placed his hand on the weapon. "Let me have it, Gram. Please."

She didn't move for a moment and didn't move before swiping her gray hair from her face. "Where's Lincoln?"

Riley's throat tightened at the lost look on Helen's face.

Thayne's loving gaze warmed her heart as he cupped his grandmother's cheek. "Pops is fine. He's probably at the hospital by now. Cheyenne will take good care of him."

"Cheyenne. Oh yes. She's a doctor now, isn't she?"

His grandmother turned from Thayne and strode into the cabin. Thayne placed his arm around Chloe's shoulder. "You okay?"

She nodded. "Gram saved me. She knew about the cabin. She knew how to hide from him."

"Really?" Thayne couldn't hide his surprise.

"She was the Gram I remember. At least part of today."

"That's a gift, Chloe. She'd want you to always remember her like that." Thayne followed his grandmother into the house.

Riley reholstered her weapon and walked over to Chloe. She glanced at the girl's wrists. "Zip tie?"

Chloe looked down. "I forgot about that. I used some metal in the back of the car to break it."

"That was smart. You're very brave."

"Pops told me." Chloe leaned in to Riley. "You're sure he's okay? You didn't say that just for Gram?"

"As far as I know."

"He was so brave." Chloe swallowed and blinked back tears. "He went after that man instead of running away, just to give us time to escape. He's a hero."

"The Blackwoods are heroes, all right." Riley hugged Chloe to her and glanced into the room, where Thayne held on to his grandmother. "They'll do anything for the people they love."

"Like my mom and dad," Chloe said. She walked into the log building. Two planks had been pried from the floor.

"Gram hid the gun down there."

Riley had to hand it to Helen. The woman was resourceful.

Chloe reached into the hole and pulled out a box. "Is it okay if I show them, Gram?"

A blank look had taken over Helen's expression. "What are you talking about, Cheyenne? That's not mine."

"Show us," Thayne said. "I don't think she'd mind." He hummed in his grandmother's ear, and she sank against him, closing her eyes, swaying to the music of *their* song.

Chloe lifted the lid of the box and pulled out a drawing. "I made this for Gram when I was little. When we came here for the very first time."

"May I?" Riley asked.

With a nod, Chloe gave her the picture, obviously drawn by a small child. Harsh lines of black scrawled all over the page. The world was dark and scary, but in the center, a figure with brown-and-white hair was bathed in yellow like the sun. Almost as if the woman had a halo around her. She stood next to a red-haired woman and a red-haired child. Both were smiling.

"Your mother and you and Gram?" Riley asked.

"Yes. There are a lot more drawings inside."

Riley sat cross-legged on the ground and pulled out paper after paper. "Are they yours?"

Chloe shook her head. "No. I guess there were other kids who stayed here, too."

The emotions in the drawings punched Riley in the gut. So much hurt. And so much hope. And in almost every one, a figure representing Helen Blackwood stood guard, like a protective angel.

When she reached the bottom of the box, she pulled out an envelope with Cheyenne's name scrawled across the front.

Riley lifted it up for Thayne to see. "That's Gram's handwriting," he said.

Outside several shouts sounded through the woods.

Riley rose and headed to the front door. "We're here. They're okay!"

Ironcloud showed up first, riding a horse. He dismounted. "The others are on their way." He glanced down at the dead body. "Isn't that the oil foreman?"

She nodded. "Thayne's grandmother needs help."

Ironcloud passed her and disappeared inside the cabin. Within minutes, Thayne carried his grandmother out of the cabin, and Ironcloud followed with the gun. Chloe tagged along behind them, the metal box clutched in her arms.

"Quinn and a few other searchers are on their way on ATVs," Ironcloud said.

"I think Gram would prefer the horse." Thayne set Helen on the ground next to the animal. Her eyes lit up, and she patted his nose.

"You want to go for a ride?" he asked.

She nodded. He lifted her into the saddle and mounted the horse behind her. He looked down at Riley. "See you back at the ranch?" he said, the meaning clear in his eyes.

Riley could feel the adrenaline seeping out of her body, weakening her body and limbs, but in its place, a satisfied warmth spread from the inside out.

"I'll be there. For good."

The corners around his eyes crinkled. "Come on, Gram. Let's go home."

◆ ◆ ◆

Seventy-two hours later, the Blackwood kitchen overflowed with more people since . . . Thayne couldn't remember when. Luckily the brunt of the damage had been to the back of the house and the sunroom, so the family had decided to host a huge potluck for all the volunteers from the search to celebrate an ending they'd all survived.

Thayne surveyed the slew of family and friends. He couldn't believe it was over.

Madison and Hudson stood side by side, looking like two rejects from a prizefight, dishing out food and shooting each other glances that should've lit the kitchen on fire.

More than one person winced when they faced them, then scowled at Hudson before Madison set them straight.

Chloe stood next to them, unwilling to leave their sides. Seemed like she'd glommed on to Madison, and Hudson by extension.

Maybe they could heal each other.

He carried two plates through to the sunroom. Gram sat in her chair, flipping through her sketchbook, pointing out every picture of Thayne she'd ever drawn.

He'd never live the bare-baby-butt drawing down. It was actually worse than a photo as far as he was concerned.

Cheyenne and Brett met him at the door.

"When can Pops come home?" Thayne asked.

"If he does well tonight, I'll release him tomorrow. Dad and Dan are sitting with him right now."

"How about Dan?" Part of Thayne didn't want to know the answer, but "denial never saved a body from pain." Another of Gram's sayings that Thayne found all too true.

Cheyenne grimaced in sympathy. "Dad has documented quite a few examples that point to some form of dementia over the last couple of days."

Thayne frowned. "Alzheimer's like Gram?"

"I won't know until we run some tests. Dad convinced Dan to let me figure out what was wrong with him. Maybe Dan will be luckier than Gram."

Thayne could only hope so. He glanced over at his grandmother. He hated losing more of Gram every day, but this week she'd come through like a champ. She'd saved Chloe; she'd stood down a serial killer. He would be thankful for today and deal with the worst . . . when the worst came.

He caught Riley's gaze and made his way to her. Slowly he bent his head to hers, and she reached up for a long, lingering kiss. He ignored the laughter and shouts around them. He didn't care. She gripped his arms, and he finally took one last kiss from her and lifted his head.

"Did you plan on putting on a show?" she asked.

"Just reminded us both we're here to stay."

"I'm not changing my mind." Riley picked up her cell. "I received a call from the FBI. They searched Decker's RV and want me to consult with them."

Thayne raised his brow.

"I informed them that I'd decided to do a little consulting. I have some paperwork hoops to navigate, but—"

"A consultant can live anywhere." Thayne pulled her up into his arms. "We have our life. Together. I love you, Riley Lambert."

She hugged him back before tugging at his shirt. "You need to let Cheyenne see the letter. There's no point in waiting. Everything's out in the open now." She sent a pointed look at the letter on the coffee table.

"You're right." Thayne grabbed his sister's hand. "I have something to show you."

He handed Cheyenne the letter. She looked down at it and blinked. "Gram's handwriting."

"It has to be at least four years old. That's her normal writing."

Cheyenne's hand shook. Brett stood and crossed over to her. "Are you okay?"

She nodded. "From Gram."

She slit open the envelope and pulled out a page.

> My dearest Cheyenne—
> I hope I remember to give you this before it's too late. I'm going to put a note to myself in the back of my sketchbook. You're just starting your residency, but I pray you come home to Singing River. We need a good doctor, and Doc Mallard is creeping up on eighty.
>
> I've had some bad days in my life. When your grandfather went missing in the war, when we lost your sweet mother, and others I probably won't ever mention, but yesterday I learned I have Alzheimer's disease. Lincoln and I cried long and hard, but I think

I knew. You may not know this, but a couple of my great-aunts were "soft in the head" as it was known back then.

I'm so sorry for what you and the family will go through. I don't want to be a burden, and I've told Lincoln that, but knowing my stubborn husband, he won't stick me on top of a hill and let me die with dignity in the old ways of my grandmother's people. There's nothing I can do to stop this. I know that. I'll take the medication and try to stay healthy as long as I can, but I can tell things are starting to disappear from me.

Sometimes my head feels like a television that's got static. Then it will come back and I see the world again. Please tell everyone that I'm sorry for whatever I say or do that hurts them. I love you all with every ounce of my being.

I could have written this letter to all of you. It's your choice who you want to share it with. I never told Lincoln or Carson or Thayne because they are in law enforcement, and I never wanted them to be dragged into my business.

The truth began when I was a girl. One of my good friends used to come to school with bruises on the backs of her legs. She tried to hide them. She made me promise not to tell anyone. I didn't listen. I told my mother and father. Things were different back then. A week later, she didn't come to school. After another week, we learned she'd died. Fell off the top of the barn, or so we were told. I blamed myself for years, so when another friend married a man who drank way too much, I decided to do it differently. I helped her run.

A few years later I made contact with some friends at church. There's an organization that moves battered women and children across the country, to a new life. It's not the ideal solution, but sometimes laws protect perpetrators more than victims.

I pray that I tell you this story before I forget, but I can't risk it. I won't be able to help them anymore, Cheyenne. If you're so inclined, I'm hoping you'll take on this mission for me. You've always had a soft heart. If you choose not to, I'll understand. Just contact the women at the bottom of this note, and they'll take your name off their list.

I love you, my beautiful angel.

Your loving Gram

Cheyenne didn't hide the tears rolling down her cheeks. She walked over to her grandmother and sat beside her, laying her head on her shoulder. "I love you, Gram," she whispered softly.

Gram patted her head. "Of course you do. Now, don't look so sad. Today is a good day. We're having a party. Would you like some ice cream? We can have your favorite. With sprinkles."

"I'd like that."

Thayne let out a long, slow breath. "So that was Gram's secret. Do you really think Pops didn't know?"

Riley shrugged. "You could ask."

"Or you could let it go," Brett said. "Some things aren't meant to be told."

Thayne stroked his chin. "Take it from me, Brett. Secrets will bring down more than they'll protect."

The doorbell rang. Thayne excused himself, still lost in thought. Quinn stood outside in gloves, holding a leather case.

"What's going on?"

"We were processing the RV. I thought Riley would want to see this."

"Come on in," Thayne said and led him into the sunroom.

Quinn walked over to Riley. "Could we talk out of the way?"

"Sure."

Thayne led them to Hudson's study and closed the door. "What have you got?"

Quinn set down the case and flipped open the latch. Inside, side by side, were pairs of what appeared to be wedding rings.

Riley's slipped on a pair of gloves. Her finger hovered over an engagement ring with a small diamond. "This is Kim Jordan's ring," she said softly.

Thayne's gut turned at the implication. "Six, eight, ten pairs. Only two slots empty."

"That's not even the beginning."

He lifted the velvet shelf. Beneath was a second set, this one completely filled. And finally a third shelf.

"Oh my dear God," Riley uttered.

"It gets worse," Quinn said with a frown. "There's nothing but the rings. No names, no towns, no addresses. We may never be able to find out who belongs to these wedding rings. There are people who don't know this psycho killed their families."

Riley stood silent. "I guess we start with couples who died who were in love and happy."

"Definitely not a happily-ever-after kind of ending, though."

Quinn shut the case. "I have to return this to the FBI. They're going to try to follow up. Crosses state lines and all of that."

"Thanks, Quinn. Good work."

He nodded. "You too." He stuck out his hand. "I wasn't convinced you'd be a good sheriff, but you've changed my mind."

He exited the room, and Thayne looked over at Riley.

"Your gut did that," he said softly. "How many more would he have killed if you hadn't recognized the flaw in his plan?"

She closed her eyes and shivered. "I could use a hug."

He strode toward her and wrapped her in his arms. She laid her head on his chest. "We can find the families," she said softly. "You and me."

With a small smile, he pulled back from her. "You want to work together?"

"Why not? What if *we* open a consulting company, not just me? Singing River Security. We could take cases all over the country. We could help whoever we wanted. We could be based in Wyoming. The best of both worlds."

"Riley, I have a job."

"Do you love it?" She bit her lip.

Thayne lifted his gaze and met hers. "I love helping the people in my town. I love being available as much as I can for Pops and Gram and Dad. I don't love being sheriff." Thayne glanced at Quinn. "You think a new sheriff who's been wanting the job for a decade would hire a part-time deputy who used to order him around?"

"I think he'd jump at the chance. You do good work."

"Then I think we just might have a deal." Thayne pressed her close against him. "How did you get to be so brilliant?" He kissed her lips. "Does this mean we get to live happily ever after?"

Riley tilted her head. "Of course."

"It's about time," Hudson and Madison shouted in exasperation.

Brett, Cheyenne, and Chloe laughed and looked on.

Gram limped forward and handed Thayne her engagement ring. "Now you can make it official."

Riley held out her hand, and Thayne slipped the ring on her finger.

Gram grinned. "So when's the wedding?"

EPILOGUE

The full moon brightened the road in front of Riley on the outskirts of Singing River. Two headlights blinked, and she signaled back. She transferred a duffel full of clothes and several boxes of food and supplies into the back of Cheyenne's SUV.

Pops had been upset when he'd first learned of Helen's secret life, but he'd kissed her forehead softly when she'd cried in his arms. She'd only been trying to protect him. Some anger wasn't worth holding on to. Tonight, Helen Blackwood's legacy would continue.

Riley knocked softly on the window. Cheyenne rolled it down.

"That's everything," Riley whispered. "Did it go well?"

Cheyenne smiled. "Yeah. We're headed up to the cabin."

Riley peered into the back seat. A woman hunkered down, the left side of her face mottled with bruises. A small girl nestled at her side. Too thin, too solemn, and a cast on her right arm. "Welcome to Singing River," Riley said with a smile. "You're safe here."

◆ ◆ ◆

The Wind River Mountains loomed tall in the sky to the east. Riley slipped out of the Jeep and joined Thayne at the edge of the creek. "It's a beautiful spot, and far enough away from the cabin to be protected."

Thayne glanced in the direction of the hideaway. "Did everything go as planned last night?"

Riley gave a slight nod and followed his line of sight: the cabin where they'd discovered his grandmother's secret life, the cabin where a feud had begun generations ago. Both legacies had found new life. One continued on; the other transformed.

"We're doing the right thing," Thayne said. "Gram would be proud if she understood."

Riley slipped her hand into his. "I've been thinking," she said softly.

Thayne's back stiffened. "Should I be nervous?"

"No. I think maybe I'm the one who should be. I want to take your name when we get married."

Thayne froze. "What about your career and your reputation?"

"We're starting a new venture together. I like the idea of Mr. and Mrs. Blackwood against the world."

Thayne cupped her cheeks and pressed his lips against hers. "Do you know how much I love you?"

"As much as I love you."

An SUV rumbled up the dirt road. Cheyenne and Brett exited their vehicle, both grinning at them.

"You two need us to leave you alone for a while?" Brett leaned lightly on his cane.

"I'll try to maintain my self-control." Thayne smiled. "You bring it?" he asked.

Brett handed over the document. Thayne pulled out the papers Pops had given him along with the new deed.

"Signed, sealed, and delivered," Thayne said. "All we need is your signature."

Brett nodded. "I guess the feud is officially over."

"And the Blackwood-Riverton Alzheimer's Care Facility has a home." Cheyenne smiled at her husband. "We're not Romeo and Juliet anymore."

"I don't plan on dying for a long time." Brett handed the deed back to Thayne and shook his hand. "How about coming over for dinner tonight?" he asked.

Thayne glanced over at Riley. "How about we take a rain check?"

"Gotcha, brother. So how's the newly minted deputy?" Brett asked.

"Singing River Security already has a case. We're tracking down the families of Decker's victims." He wrapped his arm around Riley. "It's what we were meant to do."

"And Quinn?"

"He's in the sheriff's job exactly like he should be. He's even asked Dad to do a bit of consulting."

Cheyenne frowned at Thayne.

"Don't worry. Dad's going to spend most of his time coordinating the building of the facility. It'll keep him busy but without all the physical stress."

"Good job, brother dear." She kissed Thayne on the cheek, and she and Brett headed back to their car before driving away.

After they'd disappeared down the road, Riley leaned into Thayne. "How about Christmas?" she whispered.

He hugged her close. "Are you sure?"

"A Christmas wedding would be a memory never forgotten," she said.

Thayne held her tight and they looked across the landscape. "Gram might not remember, but her legacy will run through this valley and this town for generations."

"A legacy of love, of compassion, of protection. She'll be pleased."

AFTERWORD

The Singing River series of novels (*Forgotten Secrets* and *Forgotten Legacy*) grew in part from witnessing my mother's battle with Alzheimer's disease. We have learned to cherish and embrace the small moments of joy even as we navigate through the tears. If we have learned one truth, it is to be thankful for what we still have and not to wish for what used to be.

When I wrote the first book, my mom still occasionally spoke my name and kissed me on the cheek as I helped put her to bed. That is no longer the case; however, she still holds my hand. For that small joy I am blessed.

My mother's journey has been a long one, and my family would not have survived without our faith, friends, and the support of the Alzheimer's Association (http://www.alz.org, Alzheimer's Association, PO Box 96011, Washington, DC 20090-6011). The local chapter of this organization has provided us with knowledge, support, and understanding, and I cannot express my gratitude enough to everyone who has touched our lives.

I am donating 10 percent of the royalties I receive from all the Singing River novels to the Alzheimer's Association in honor of my mother, my father, and all those who support them as they travel this difficult road. The Alzheimer's Association's vision is a world without Alzheimer's, and I pray for that day.

To that end, I have created the #1MemoryChallenge, an awareness and fund-raising campaign. This effort encourages the sharing of special memories before they are lost as well as support of the Alzheimer's Association and its good work. You can find out more about my personal story and the #1MemoryChallenge at http://act.alz.org/goto/1MemoryChallenge or at http://www.facebook.com/1MemoryChallenge.

If you have a friend or loved one who is facing Alzheimer's disease or another form of dementia, it can feel like a lonely battle. Please consider contacting the Alzheimer's Association (or a similar organization) for assistance, and please support the association through your time or donations.

You are not alone.

ACKNOWLEDGMENTS

This story has been a labor of love, and those who know me well recognize the joy and the challenges in bringing this book to life. To you all: I thank you.

Anh Schluep—your patience as I fought through this book was more than I could have expected. I will be forever grateful to you for helping me bring this second visit to Singing River to life.

Jill Marsal, literary agent extraordinaire—your understanding, faith, and support never cease to amaze me. I couldn't travel this road without you.

Charlotte Herscher, editor—your supreme patience, kindness, and insight made this book what it is today, and I will be forever grateful.

Sherri Buerkle—your talent, honesty, and astuteness humble me. Thank you for going above and beyond with this book. The words within are sprinkled with your magic touch. I am blessed to call you my fellow author and dear friend.

To Bobbie Archuleta, our caregiver and lifeline. Mom's smile when you enter the room is enough to lighten my heart. You, Zoë, and

Azri'el have gifted our lives with light and joy during this long, dark journey. You are a blessing to all of us and will always be a part of this family.

And, as always, to Mom and Dad. They live the words *in sickness and in health* every day of their lives. They are the definition of true love, loyalty, and devotion, and I am honored and blessed to call them my parents.

AUTHOR'S NOTE

Thank you for reading *Forgotten Legacy*, the second book in the Singing River series of novels. I hope you enjoyed it! If you liked the characters, *Forgotten Secrets*, the first book, is also available.

If you're interested in my other novels, the Montgomery Justice series is available:

In Her Sights
Behind the Lies
Game of Fear

If you would like to know when my next book is available or want special information and a chance at giveaways, you can sign up for my newsletter at http://www.RobinPerini.com.

You can connect with me online at the following:

Website (www.robinperini.com)
Goodreads (www.goodreads.com/RobinPerini)
Facebook (www.facebook.com/RobinPeriniAuthor)

If you enjoyed reading this story, I would appreciate it if you would help others enjoy this book, too.

Lend it. Please share it with a friend.

Recommend it. Please help other readers find this book by recommending it to friends, readers' groups, and discussion boards.

Review it. Please tell other readers why you liked this book by reviewing it.

Authors are nothing without readers. I thank you all for taking this journey with me.

BOOK CLUB QUESTIONS

1. Riley Lambert is an FBI special agent who is on leave from one of the FBI's behavioral analysis units. She believes she must choose between her career and a life with Thayne. What do you think she should have done? Did she have other options?

2. What do you think the greatest strengths and greatest weaknesses of the following characters are?

   a. Riley Lambert
   b. Thayne Blackwood
   c. Madison Lambert
   d. Chloe Jordan
   e. Helen Blackwood

3. Alzheimer's disease is one of the top ten causes of death in the United States. In *Forgotten Legacy*, the hero's grandmother lives with the disease, and another character may be facing the disease.

a. Do you know anyone who lives with this illness?
b. What insights did you gain about the disease from how the author portrayed Gram in the story or how Dan's family was portrayed?

4. Chloe Jordan and her mother ran away from an abusive situation to disappear in Singing River, Wyoming. What other options could Kim Jordan have had? Did she do the right thing?

5. Which scene in the book did you find:

a. the most suspenseful?
b. the most unexpected?
c. the most emotional?
d. the most memorable?

READ ON FOR A PREVIEW OF

IN HER SIGHTS,

BOOK ONE OF ROBIN PERINI'S

THE MONTGOMERY JUSTICE

NOVELS,

AVAILABLE NOW.

PROLOGUE

Seventeen Years Ago

She hurt too much to cry.

At the slam of the screen door, Jane burrowed her head under her lanky arms. Her ten-year-old body shrank beneath the lopsided kitchen table, its cheap pine scarred and rotten with age. Her heart pounded as she swallowed down the sobs. Quiet. She must be quiet. Mama said so.

Slowly she closed her eyes and let her mind drift to another place, the safe place she visited when things got too bad. Her body floated on the cool water in her dreams. Protected, safe.

For a fleeting moment, the pain went away.

Please, don't let him come back.

As if in answer to her prayer, the heavy footsteps didn't cross the scuffed linoleum toward her. Instead, they lumbered down the front porch. A loud tumble followed by a sharp curse echoed through the rickety shack she and her mother called home.

When the diesel engine cranked to life, Jane gulped back the relief. He'd left. For now.

"Mama?" She barely recognized the muffled whisper through her bruised and swollen lips. With a groan she tried to sit up, but the second she raised her head, sharp pain scissored through her arms and legs. She fell back with a whimper and fought to stop a scream from escaping her. Mama would cry, and he'd hurt them enough tonight.

"I'm sorry . . . I tried to stop him, Mama. I tried to do my job."

The wind beat against the gray wood walls, and she could almost feel the house sway around her. She waited for the soft shuffle of her mother's footsteps to pad down the hallway. Tonight would be better than most. The whiskey bottles were empty. *He* was gone.

She shoved her hair out of her face and blinked against the darkening of the room. The aches had settled to a dull throb. Gingerly, Jane straightened and rose, her eyes squinting as she eased down the hallway. "Mama?"

One step, then another, then another.

Her feet slipped on something wet and cold and dark. She stumbled forward. Her mother lay at a strange angle on the floor, her blonde hair plastered against her head, stained red with blood.

"Mama!" Jane fell to her knees. "Mama?"

She barely recognized her mother's face, one eye nearly swollen closed, her cheek multicolored black and purple.

Her mother's eyelids flickered. "Jane?"

Jane tugged at her nightgown, using the thin cotton to wipe away the blood oozing from her mother's injuries, but they kept bleeding. "What can I do, Mama? What?"

A gurgling sound echoed from her mother's chest. "Too late."

"No!"

"Shh." Her mother's voice was a bare whisper, and Jane leaned forward, her ear right next to her mother's lips. "It's okay. Better this way." She tugged in another shallow breath. "Leave. Do what we planned. Change who you are."

Jane fell against her mother's breast, the red blood soaking the polyester that her mother had pretended was silk. "I can't."

"You will." The words were so quiet. Her mother raised a hand and gripped Jane's chin. "Don't be like me. Be strong, like the jasmine growing in the windowsill. Never count on anyone."

A gasp for air shook her mother's broken body. The deathly cold fingers tightened, hurting Jane's bruised jaw. "Never let them inside . . . your heart."

Her mother shuddered. Her hand dropped, and the wheezing from her chest went silent.

Her eyes stayed open.

Trembling, Jane hauled her mother's hand back to her chin.

"Mama, please. Wake up," she whispered.

But tug after tug wouldn't wake her. And Jane knew.

She scooted away, huddling in the corner of her mother's bedroom, splinters digging into her heels until the final rays of sun sliced through the window's blinds. "I'm sorry, Mama. I tried to protect you. I tried. But he was too strong."

She buried her face in her arms. She didn't move. Didn't weep. A chill wrapped around her heart.

She hurt too much to cry.

CHAPTER ONE

Present Day

The trigger felt right.

The sight was zeroed in, the balance perfect. The Remington 700/40 fit her body and her mind like an old friend she could trust, and Jasmine "Jazz" Parker didn't trust easily. But she and this rifle were connected in a way a lover, friend, or family could never be. The Remington would never let her down.

The only hitch—she didn't have an ideal shot at the kidnapper. Not yet, anyway.

Sweat beaded her brow in the Colorado midmorning sun. Without taking her gaze from her target, she wiped away the perspiration. Every second counted, and she had to stay ready. Negotiations had fallen apart hours ago, and the ending seemed inevitable. To save the governor's daughter, Jazz would excise the five-year-old girl's captor.

Jazz shifted, relieving the pressure against her knees, the stiffness in her hips, but the rifle remained steady. She centered her sight on the small break in the window.

Having focused through the high-powered Leupold scope for hours, she waited for an opportunity for the scumbag's blond head to move into range. They all made a mistake sooner or later. His face or the back of his head, she didn't care, but she needed a clear shot through to the medulla oblongata. The kill had to be clean; the man had to crumple with no time to think and no reflex to pull the trigger.

"Blue Four, have you acquired the target?"

The question came through her earpiece loud and clear, but she spoke quietly into the microphone. "Negative."

"Blue Two, what is target's position?"

"Zone Two, pacing. He's carrying the girl, a gun at her head, a bowie on the southeast corner table. He's nervous, unpredictable."

Jazz could trust Gabe Montgomery's assessment of the situation. He, unlike his brother, Luke, she could count on. And what was Luke doing in her head anyway? Now was *not* the time to be thinking about the one guy she should never have let near her.

"Blue Two to Blue Leader." Gabe's voice filtered through the communications system. "He's on the move again. Going toward Zone One. I repeat. He's headed to Zone One."

Jazz's body froze in readiness. He was coming her way. If Blue Leader ordered the guys to rush the house, she had to be on her game. She *would* protect them. She wouldn't fail.

The blinds fluttered. Jazz forced her breathing into a comfortable, familiar pattern. "Blue Leader, this is Blue Four. I see movement."

A blond head peered out, face straight on front, the area between nose and teeth in clear view.

"Target acquired. It's a good shot."

"Can you see the girl?"

"He's got a gun to her head."

Only a second passed before the expected order came through.

"Take the shot, Blue Four."

"Ten four, Blue Leader."

Slowly, deliberately, Jazz exhaled and, between heartbeats, squeezed the trigger.

ABOUT THE AUTHOR

Photo © 2013 Kyle Zimmerman

Robin Perini, the *Publishers Weekly* and internationally bestselling author of *Forgotten Secrets*, is devoted to giving her readers fast-paced, high-stakes adventures with a love story sure to melt their hearts. A RITA Award finalist and winner of the prestigious Romance Writers of America Golden Heart Award in 2011, she is also a nationally acclaimed writing instructor. By day, she's an analyst for an advanced technology corporation, but in honor of her mother, Robin has become a passionate advocate for those who battle Alzheimer's disease. She loves to hear from readers. Visit her website at www.robinperini.com.